GRIDIRON GREATS

GRIDIRON GREATS
A Century of Polish
Americans in College Football

Ben Chestochowski

HIPPOCRENE BOOKS
New York

Copyright© 1997 Ben Chestochowski.

For information, address:
HIPPOCRENE BOOKS, INC.
171 Madison Avenue
New York, NY 10016

Library of Congress Cataloging-in-Publication Data
Chestochowski, Ben.
    Gridiron greats : a century of Polish Americans in college football /
Ben Chestochowski.
        p.   cm.
    Includes bibliographical references and index.
    ISBN 0-7818-0449-3
    1. Polish American footballl players—Biography. 2. Polish American
football players—Rating of. 3. College sports—United States—History.
I. Title.
GV939.A1C47 1996   96-29442
796.332'63'0922—dc20   CIP

Printed in the United States of America.

DEDICATION

*To my parents, John and Mary Czestochowski, my in-laws,
Stanislaus and Emilia Wojtaszek, and all other Polish immigrants
who had the desire and courage to seek a new life for themselves and
their children in America. We thank you and our children thank you.*

TABLE OF CONTENTS

FOREWORD

*By Pat Harmon, Historian, National Football Foundation
and College Football Hall of Fame*

College football recently celebrated its 125th season. In that time span there have been, it is estimated, 425,000 games, 2.8 million players, and 1.4 billion spectators.

Polish American players have been a brilliant and enduring part of that picture. Ben Chestochowski has researched the history of these fine athletes and citizens. In this book he presents a record of their achievements as both players and coaches.

He used the archives of the College Football Hall of Fame for some of his research. He also contacted schools and family records.

The result is awesome. This is a book that will prove valuable to any student of ethnic history or sports history. Or, for that matter, any student of history.

PREFACE

In the absence of any comprehensive publications about Polish Americans in college football, I felt this book was needed to honor the American football players of Polish heritage, and to commemorate their 100 plus years of participation on the college gridirons.

My fascination with college football and the Polish American players began as a teenager listening to the radio announcers describe the Saturday afternoon action on the football field including the activities of players like Danowski and Wojciechowicz. These and other Polish Americans were and still are my heroes. Being a former college newspaper sports editor at Clemson University, I have a great deal of respect for the college scholar-athletes who play football or any other sport for their alma mater regardless of their ancestry. I have heroes among the Italian Americans, German Americans, African Americans and other ethnic groups, but being the son of Polish immigrant parents, there is a bond with the Polish Americans about whom I feel more qualified to write.

The question of who can be called a Polish American was resolved for me by the directors of the National Polish American Sports Hall of Fame. They ruled that only the father or mother of an athlete must be Polish to be considered of Polish American extraction. I have tried to adhere to this ruling.

Information obtained from various sources through years of research enabled me to prepare individual sports biographies concerning the outstanding Polish Americans who played college football through 1993, and include some promising players of the future. These biographies are the main feature of the book and are written about the following:

1. Recipients of the Heisman Memorial Trophy and other major college football awards (only one player is chosen each year to receive one or more of these awards)
2. Members of the College Football Hall of Fame (roughly one in 5,000 players is inducted into the Hall)
3. Members of the National Polish-American Sports Hall of Fame
4. Members of Division I-A All-America teams (around one in 1,000 players is selected to an All-America team)
5. Academic All-Americans and winners of other Academic Awards
6. First team All-Americans below Division I-A
7. Honorable Mention All-Americans
8. School, conference and national record holders and award winners
9. Players who excelled in college football but were not All-Americans (The All-Stars)
10. College football coaches
11. Members of family groups such as the Modzelewskis, Tomczaks and Kulakowskis
12. Promising players of the future

The bios vary in length depending upon the amount of pertinent data found about each player.

We could not discover any reference to All-Time Polish American college football teams. The temptation to select the "Dream Teams" was too hard to resist. Information used to pick the first, second and third All-Time Polish American team members was based on highly respected sources. Only players who were chosen to an All-American team by any of the major selectors such as American Football Coaches Association, Football Writers Association of America, Associated Press, Walter Camp Foundation, and others, were eligible. First team All-Americans below Division I-A chosen by the American Football Coaches Association and Associated Press were also qualified. Although being named Honorable Mention All-American is a distinct honor, those who did not make an All-American team were ineligible. In addition, the accomplishments of former college players in professional football were not considered.

The honors and awards bestowed upon the college football

players by persons qualified to judge their talents as they performed on the gridiron during the past 100 years formed the basis for our selections. Those who received the highest and most awards were picked to the All-Time teams.

Players chosen to the All-Time first, second and third offensive and defensive teams are another feature of the book. Their biographies are covered in the first three chapters, and are listed in the same order as their names appear in the team lineups.

Biographies of other players who were not selected to "Dream Teams" are covered in later chapters under their appropriate headings such as Academic Award winners, Honorable Mention All-Americans, Football Coaches, etc. These are arranged in alphabetical order in each chapter.

It was impossible to include all of the Polish Americans who played college football. We apologize to those who were omitted and ask them to accept this publication as a tribute to all Americans of Polish descent for their contribution to college football.

It is not the intent of this book to suggest superiority over college football players of any other ethnic groups. Its objective is to honor the Polish Americans who played college football over the past 100 years.

ACKNOWLEDGMENTS

It would have been impossible to write this book without the encouragement and help received from Pat Harmon, curator and historian of the National Football Foundation's College Football Hall of Fame in Kings Island, Ohio. The great wealth of information revealed to me by Pat about specific college football players would have required many additional years of research to accumulate. During my numerous, lengthy visits to the Hall of Fame, Harmon was always available to answer any questions or direct me to the proper source of information. He opened his files, invited me to investigate his collection of books and football media guides and treated me like a friend and a member of the staff.

I wish to acknowledge the support given by Joe Owens, the National Football Foundation's Midwestern Regional Coordinator, and Rick Walls, Hall of Fame staffer. Examples of their help include Owens confirming Emil Sitko's Polish ancestry by checking with his friend and colleague, Bob Elkins, in Fort Wayne, Indiana. He went out of his way to introduce me to Ron Jaworski during a college football awards ceremony at the Hall of Fame, and called my attention to anything that would aid my research. As for Rick Walls, he was always there when I needed a helping hand. My sincere appreciation to Pat, Joe and Rick.

Articles written by Tom Tarapacki, Sports Editor of the Polish-American Journal, were helpful in identifying college football players of Polish heritage such as Ted Kwalick, Greg Skrepenak, Greg Landry and others. Information about these and many other Polish American college football players was also useful.

The National Polish-American Sports Hall of Fame in Hamtramck, and Orchard Lake Michigan was a good source of data concerning American athletes of Polish ancestry who were honored for their contributions to the particular sport in which they participated. I wish to thank Buck Jerzy, former Chairman of the NPASHFM, who opened this door for me.

The Indiana Football Hall of Fame in Richmond, Indiana provided me with facts about college football players and coaches from the state of Indiana. A special thanks to Joyce Crull, Secretary of the Hall of Fame.

Reprints obtained from Paul Montells of the Associated Press about All-Americans from 1918 through 1990 were useful and greatly appreciated.

I am also very grateful to the Sports Information Directors and their staffs at the following colleges and universities for sending the information requested: Adrian College, Air Force Academy, Alfred University, Amherst College, University of Arkansas, Army (U.S. Military Academy), Boise State University, Boston College, Boston University, Bowling Green State University, Brigham Young University, University of Buffalo, University of California, Carnegie Mellon University, University of Central Florida, Central Michigan University, Clarion University of Pennsylvania, Clemson University, Colgate University, University of Colorado, University of Connecticut, Cornell University, Dartmouth College, University of Delaware, University of Detroit, Duke University, East Stroudsburg University, Edinboro University of Pennsylvania, University of Florida, Florida State University, Fordham University, University of Georgia, Hamline University, Harvard University, University of the Holy Cross, University of Houston, University of Illinois, University of Indiana, University of Iowa, Ithaca College, University of Kentucky, Lafayette College, Lehigh University, Louisiana State University, University of Maryland, University of Massachusetts (Amherst and Lowell), University of Miami, University of Michigan, Michigan State University, University of Minnesota, University of Missouri, University of Montana, Montclair State College, Muhlenberg College, Navy (U.S. Naval Academy), University of Nebraska, New Mexico State University, Northern Arizona University, University of North Dakota, Northern Illinois University, Northern Michigan University, Northwestern University, North-

ACKNOWLEDGMENTS

western State University, University of Notre Dame, Ohio State University, University of Oregon, University of the Pacific, University of Pennsylvania, Pennsylvania State University, University of Pittsburgh, Princeton University, Purdue University, University of Richmond, College of St. Francis, Salisbury State University, University of the South (Sewanee), Southern Methodist University, University of Syracuse, University of Tampa, Temple University, University of Tennessee, Texas A&M University, University of Toledo, University of Tulsa, UCLA (University of California-Los Angeles), Villanova University, University of Virginia, Wake Forest University, University of Washington, Washington University (MO), Washington State University, Western Michigan University, University of West Virginia, University of Wisconsin, University of Wyoming, Xavier University and Youngstown State University.

I am also deeply grateful to John and Nancy Wojak for their invaluable editing contributions.

It would have been very difficult to take the time required to research and compile the information needed for this book without my wonderful wife's encouragement, cooperation, and patience. In addition, her timely suggestions and editorial comments were extremely helpful in preparing the manuscript. Genia, *dziekuje serdecznie.*

INTRODUCTION

American collegiate football was born when Princeton University played Rutgers University on November 6, 1869. The game was a blend of soccer and rugby and not football as we know it today. But it was the start of a colorful, exciting athletic activity that swept the nation in changing form over the years to become the extremely popular sport being played on college gridirons.

The appearance of Polish Americans on the college football fields was slow in developing. No evidence was found of their participation in football in the 1870s and 1880s. Information in school sports was not well organized in the early days, and it is possible there were some Americans of Polish heritage playing college football during those years.

About 2.5 million immigrants came to the United States from Poland between the 1870s and the first World War (1914). The sons of these immigrants adjusted to the new way of life and became interested in American sports activities such as football, baseball and basketball. Those who excelled in high school football went to colleges and universities all over the country from industrial cities, steel mill towns, coal mining areas, farms and other regions to earn a higher education and play football.

The earliest record found of a Polish American to letter in college football was Stanley Tomoszewski, Boston College Class of 1893.

We celebrate the 100th anniversary of Polish Americans in college football in 1993 by honoring the memory of these gridiron greats who contributed so much to the advancement of the popular American sport.

19

CHAPTER I

ALL-TIME POLISH AMERICAN—FIRST TEAM

OFFENSE

Position	Name	School	Ht.	Wt.	Year
End	Ted Kwalick	Penn. State	6-4	230	1968
End	William Swiacki	Columbia	6-2	198	1947
Tackle	Zygmunt Czarobski	Notre Dame	6-2	250	1947
Tackle	Jim Dombrowski	Virginia	6-5	295	1985
Guard	Edward Molinski	Tennessee	5-10	190	1939
Guard	Mark Stepnoski	Pittsburgh	6-3	265	1988
Center	Alex Wojciechowicz	Fordham	6-0	196	1937
Q.Back	Johnny Lujack	Notre Dame	6-0	180	1946
R.Back	James Grabowski	Illinois	6-2	211	1965
R.Back	Emil Sitko	Notre Dame	5-8	180	1949
R.Back	William Osmanski	Holy Cross	6-1	205	1938
P.Kicker	Chester Marcol	Hillsdale Coll.	5-10	170	1971

DEFENSE

Position	Name	School	Ht.	Wt.	Year
End	Leon Hart	Notre Dame	6-5	260	1949
End	Walter Patulski	Notre Dame	6-6	260	1971
Tackle	Dick Modzelewski	Maryland	6-0	235	1952
Tackle	Lou Michaels	Kentucky	6-2	235	1957
N.Guard	Harvey Jablonsky	Army	6-0	190	1933
L.Backer	Chester Gladchuk	Boston Coll.	6-4	245	1940
L.Backer	Jack Ham	Penn. State	6-3	212	1970
L.Backer	Casimir Myslinski	Army	5-11	186	1944
D.Back	Victor Janowicz	Ohio State	5-9	189	1950
D.Back	Arthur Murakowski	Northwestern	6-0	195	1948
D.Back	Walter Kowalczyk	Michigan State	6-0	205	1957
Punter	Chester Marcol	Hillsdale Coll.	5-10	170	1971

Ted Kwalick—Pennsylvania State—Off. End—1968

A native of McKees Rocks, Pennsylvania, Thaddeus "Ted" Kwalick came to Pennsylvania State University and became part of a new chapter in football history of the Nittany Lions. Kwalick and Joe Paterno, perhaps the greatest college football coach in the modern age, began their first year together at Penn State. Ted joined the varsity at a time when the tight end position was being developed in college football. The tight end position required a man with the versatility of a blocker and receiver. Kwalick had the size for a blocker; height 6 feet 4 inches, weight 230 pounds, and he was a skilled receiver. The 1966 season was an uneventful one for Paterno's Penn State team and it ended with a 5-5-0 record. In 1967, Kwalick was solidly entrenched in the starting tight end position and began to show signs of greatness. He caught 33 passes for 563 yards and four touchdowns, including nine receptions for 89 yards against Miami (Fla.). Penn State

22

finished the regular season with a 8-2-1 mark, were 10th in the nation, and selected to play Florida State in the Gator Bowl. Kwalick started the bowl game at wing back and caught a 12 yard touchdown pass which tied Florida State 17-17. His contributions during the 1967 season were recognized, and he was selected All-America by the American Football Coaches Association. In 1968, Kwalick continued to star at tight end by catching 31 passes for 403 yards and two touchdowns. He was not only a good receiver but also a well-rounded player. During the 1968 game with Army, he showed that aptitude. A wild second half was settled when the Cadets tried an onside kick. Kwalick scooped up the crazily bouncing ball and dashed 53 yards for the touchdown that clinched the bitterly contested victory, 28-24. Penn State finished with a terrific unbeaten, untied 11-0-0 record, were ranked second in the country and played Kansas in the Orange Bowl. Ted caught six passes for 74 yards and led Penn State to a 15-14 victory over Kansas. This time, Kwalick was named unanimous All-America thus becoming Penn State's first two time All-American. He was also a canddate for the Heisman Trophy and finished fourth in the voting. Ted's career receiving totals of 86 catches for 1,343 yards (average of 15.6 yards per catch), and ten touchdowns remain Penn State records for a tight end. He also rushed for 115 yards with 19 carries, returned seven punts for 34 yards and three kick-offs for 58 yards. In all, he scored 12 touchdowns and eight extra points for a career total of 80 points. The greatest tribute to Ted was paid by Joe Paterno who said "He's what God had in mind when He made a football player." Kwalick was chosen to play in the College All-Star, Coaches All-America and Senior Bowl games following his senior year. He is considered the best tight end ever to play at Penn State. Ted was San Francisco's number one draft choice in 1969 and went on to enjoy a successful National Football League career with San Francisco (1969-1974) and Oakland (1975-1978). Kwalick organized his own sportswear company, Tight End Sportswear, Inc. in Los Gatos, California. He was inducted into the National Football Foundation's College Football Hall of Fame in 1989.

William Swiacki—Columbia—Off. End—1947

William Swiacki came to the College of the Holy Cross from Southbridge, Massachusetts and played only one season in 1942 before entering the service during World War II. After his discharge, he resumed his college education but this time enrolled at Columbia University in New York City. Columbia had a winning season under coach Lou Little in 1946 and Swiacki, playing end at 6-2, 198 pounds, contributed greatly to that success. However, it was the 1947 season that gave Swiacki the opportunity to make a name for himself. Although Bill was an outstanding end, he would have remained relatively unknown nationally were it not for one game which gave him nationwide exposure. That game was the 1947 classic against the Cadets of Army who brought an incredible 32 game winning streak to Columbia's Baker Field. Swiacki ran the Cadets ragged by catching nine passes that afternoon, one for a touchdown with a diving finger-tip clutch in the end zone to make it 20-14 with Army still leading. Late in the fourth quarter, Columbia had the ball on the Army 27 yard line when quarterback Gene Rossides dropped back to pass. He threw the ball hard and low causing Swiacki to fling his out-stretched body and arms toward the ball. It looked like an incomplete pass when suddenly the crowd erupted into wild cheers as Swiacki's fingers grabbed the ball just above the turf at the Army three yard line. Red Blaik, the Army coach, tried to finesse the officials by claiming that Swiacki trapped the ball on the grass, but the officials stood by their decision. (Photographs taken of Swiacki making the historic catch clearly show that he had possession of the ball before hitting the ground, proving beyond any doubt that the officials made the right call.) Lou Kusserow scored two plays later and Venton Jablonski kicked the extra point that spelled a 21-20 victory for Columbia, and the end of the Army winning streak in a game called the "upset of the decade." Swiacki made the impossible catch and was named consensus All-America and the Heisman Trophy nominee in 1947. Swiacki's catches in this game were voted the most decisive and spectacular of the 1947 football season. Bill was selected to the East-West Shrine and Blue-Gray teams in 1948. He went on to play professional football for five years with the New York Giants and Detroit Lions. Swiacki was the Giant offensive coach in 1954 and taught Vince Lombardi (then assistant Giant coach) important lessons about the passing game. He also coached in the Canadian football league, and then entered the real estate business in Brookfield, Massachusetts. Swiacki was inducted into the National Football Foundation's College Football Hall of Fame in 1976.

William Swiacki, Jr. attended Amherst College where he was a starting tight end in football and also an excellent baseball and basketball player. After graduating from Amherst College in 1978, Bill played professional baseball with Los Angeles and Oakland until 1982. He was a good enough football player, however, to be a ninth round draft choice of the New York Giants in 1978. Swiacki, Jr. is a business executive in Philadelphia.

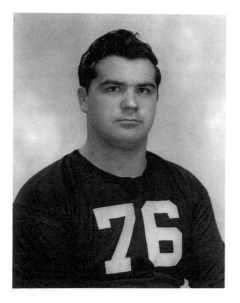

Zygmunt Czarobski—Notre Dame—Off. Tackle—1947

A native of Chicago, Illinois, Ziggie Czarobski attended Mt. Carmel High School where he was the starting left tackle on the football team for three years. He was an All-Catholic selection for all three years, and chosen All-City and All-State as a senior.

Czarobski enrolled at the University of Notre Dame and played football under the legendary coach, Frank Leahy. Ziggie was not only the orator and jokester who kept the team relaxed, but also a bit of trouble for the coach. Leahy lived and breathed football, whereas Czarobski, although a talented player, thought of football as only a game. The popular extrovert also had a tendency to gain weight causing Leahy to caution him about staying in shape. Despite their differences, both men gained a great deal from their association. Leahy enjoyed three national championships with Czarobski starring at tackle, and Ziggie earned All-America honors with Leahy coaching. A back-up right tackle in 1942, Czarobski was the starting tackle on the 1943 squad. Notre Dame ended the 1943 campaign with a good 9-1-0 record plus the national championship. After military service in the Marines, Ziggie returned to Notre Dame. He played on offense and defense, and contributed greatly to make the Irish virtually unstoppable. Besides opening holes in opponent lines for the Notre Dame runners, he was equally as adept in plugging any openings on defense. He was a complete player. Notre Dame finished the '46 season with an excellent 8-0-1 record and the national championship. Ziggie followed with an outstanding outing in 1947. He proved to be not only an excellent physical tackle, but also an extremely clever one. Other teams were outplayed and beaten badly as Notre Dame completed a perfect unbeaten, untied season with a 9-0-0 record and the national championship. The 1947 team is considered by many to have been the greatest ever. During Czarobski's varsity seasons, Notre Dame had a record of 33-3-1. He was selected All-America in 1947, and chosen to play in the College All-Star and East-West Shrine games. Elected captain of the East squad, Ziggie led the team to a 40-9 victory over the West. He played two years of professional football in Chicago before going into public service in the State of Illinois. He devoted a great deal of his time to charity. His pet was the Maryville Academy, a residential home and school sponsored by the Archdiocese of Chicago for dependent children. Czarobski was the founder and organizer of "Operation Chuckwagon," which became the single largest fund raiser in Illinois and grossed $2.2 million in 1993. Ziggie also took it upon himself to organize reunions of the Notre Dame football players from the Leahy years. In 1984, Czarobski, dying of colon cancer, was present at the gathering honoring him as the Notre Dame Monogram Club Man of the Year, and in his incomparable style, entertained the crowd. He died a month later and was buried on a hill overlooking the Maryville Academy. The "Ziggie Reunions" continue in honor of one of the most lovable and popular football players to attend Notre Dame. He was inducted into the National Football Foundation's College Football Hall of Fame in 1977, and the National Polish-American Sports Hall of Fame in 1980.

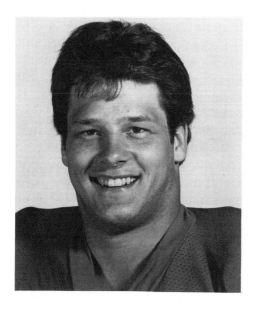

Jim Dombrowski—Virginia—Off. Tackle—1985

Coaches dream about athletes on scholarships who strive to achieve excellence not only in the sports activity they selected but also in the classroom. Dombrowski was this type of a scholar-athlete. Head football coach, George Welsh, knew that his dream had indeed come true when Dombrowski came to the University of Virginia from Williamsville, New York where he was a star athlete and an honor student at South High School. Following a good freshman season, Dombrowski nailed down the first string varsity offensive tackle position and was the starting tackle for three years. At 6-5, 295 pounds, Jim was instrumental in helping Virginia to start making their upward movement in the Atlantic Coast Conference standings. In 1984, the Cavaliers finished the season with a record of 8-2-2, were ranked 20th in the country, and defeated Purdue in the Peach Bowl, 27-24. Dombrowski had a spectacular college football career at Virginia, and the long list of his awards and honors attest to the greatness he achieved. Jim was chosen the Atlantic Coast Conference Player of the Week after the Virginia-North Carolina game in 1985. He was selected by the Atlantic Coast Sportswriters Association to the All-Atlantic Coast Conference, first team, for three consecutive years and was the leading vote getter on the team the last two years. The Associated Press chose him first team All-Conference for two consecutive years. Dombrowski was nominated for the Vince Lombardi College Lineman of the Year award in 1985, being one of just two offensive linemen nominated for this honor. He received the coveted NCAA Today's Top Six Award in 1985. The award is presented annually to six senior student-athletes from various colleges and universities and is based on athletic ability, academic achievement, leadership characteristics and involvement in campus activities. He was given the Toyota Leadership Award for his contributions to the University of Virginia football program, academic accomplishments and citizenship. The Norfolk and Portsmouth Sports Clubs named Dombrowski the Outstanding Athlete in Virginia in 1985, and *USA Today* honored him as the Collegiate Athlete of the Year in the state of Virginia for 1985. He was selected to the Atlantic Coast Conference All-Academic football teams in 1984 and 1985. The head football coaches in the Conference voted Jim the recipient of the Jacobs Blocking Trophy as the best blocker in the Atlantic Coast Conference for those years. Dombrowski was chosen first team All-America in 1984 and first team unanimous All-America in 1985. Jim's uniform No. 73 was officially retired by the University of Virginia, becoming only the fifth football player to receive this honor in Cavalier history. He was picked to play in the Hula Bowl and Senior Bowl All-Star games. Jim holds a degree in Biology and played his final year of collegiate football as a graduate student. Dombrowski plans to pursue a medical career as an orthopedic surgeon after retiring from professional football. He was the New

Orleans Saints' number one draft choice and the first offensive lineman selected in 1986. He has been with the Saints nine years as of 1995, and has developed into an outstanding starting offensive guard.

Edward Molinski—Tennessee—Off. Guard—1940

A Scranton, Pennsylvania native, Edward Molinski played football at Washington High School in Massilon, Ohio where he earned All-State honors under the coaching of the legendary Paul Brown. Molinski enrolled at the University of Tennessee in 1937, and played varsity football from 1938 to 1940 under another famous coach, General Robert Neyland. In 1938, Tennessee finished the regular season with a 10-0-0 record and beat Oklahoma, 17-0, in the Orange Bowl to remain undefeated and untied and ranked second in the country. Molinski showed good promise during the '38 campaign and was selected to the All-Southeastern Conference team. He really established himself as an outstanding football lineman at the guard position in 1939. He was chosen first team All-Southeastern Conference and earned consensus All-America honors. Ed anchored the Vols line that did not yield a single point in regular season play. Tennessee once again finished their regular season with a 10-0-0 record, but lost to the University of Southern California in the Rose Bowl. Their record was good enough to be ranked second in the nation. The Volunteers' 1940 season came to a successful conclusion with a repeat undefeated, untied ten game winning streak which earned them fourth place in the national rankings. Ed was again selected to the All-Southeastern Conference team and named All-America guard. Molinski and his team-mate, Bob Suffridge, were considered to be two of the most formidable guards on one team in college football history. They were a great combination because they both could run and lead the blocking for the tail backs. During Molinski's three year varsity football career, the University of Tennessee compiled an exceptional 31-2-0 record. Ed was a scholar-athlete who worked hard at everything he did. He was always one of the first on the practice field and usually the last to leave. In addition, Ed was an outstanding boxer. He captained the Tennessee boxing team and won the State Golden Gloves heavyweight championship. Despite the time consuming athletic activities, Ed pursued his educational goal and graduated with a Bachelor of Science degree. He went further and completed his graduate studies leading to a Master of Science degree. Molinski served as an officer in the Marines during World War II. After the war, Ed worked as an assistant football coach at Mississippi State and Memphis State Universities while attending the University of Tennessee Medical School. After getting his M.D. degree, Doctor Molinski was team physician at Memphis State University before going into private practice. After a successful career as a physician in Memphis, Tennessee, Molinski died on June 26, 1986 at age 68. Ed was elected to the University of Tennessee Athletic Hall of Fame and inducted into the National Football Foundation's College Football Hall of Fame in 1990. The late Dr. Molinski was honored as a College Football Hall of Fame inductee by the National Football Foundation at halftime of Tennessee's football game with Notre Dame at Neyland Stadium in 1990. Ed was also a member of a Polish American All-American college football team.

Mark Stepnoski—Pittsburgh—Off. Guard—1988

Stepnoski attended Cathedral Prep High School in Erie, Pennsylvania where he was a star football player and member of the National Honor Society. In 1984, he was named a high school football All-America by *USA Today* and *Parade Magazine*. Stepnoski chose the University of Pittsburgh to study and play football and became a starting guard for the Panther team in the third game of his freshman year in 1985. The 1986 season, under head football coach Mike Gottfried, was rather uneventful, ending with a 5-5-1 record which could not be rated good for Pitt. Mark proved to everyone that he was an outstanding scholar and athlete by being named first team Academic All-America, third team All-America and first team Sophomore All-America (*Football News*). The Panthers went 8-3-0 in 1987 and played Texas in the Bluebonnet Bowl only to lose and finish with an 8-4-0 mark. Stepnoski's contribution to Pittsburgh's performance received national attention and he was named All-America again. The Panthers had another winning season in 1988 and Mark was selected for many honors and awards in addition to being chosen first team consensus All-America. At 6-3, 265 pounds, he was also co-captain of the 1988 Pitt squad. Mark was given the Blue-Gold Award which is presented to the graduating athlete with the best combination of academic and athletic achievements, leadership qualities and citizenship. He was the recipient of the NCAA Top Six Award which is given annually to six senior student athletes from various colleges and universities based on academics, character, leadership and achievement. Stepnoski was a National Football Foundation and Hall of Fame Scholar-Athlete Award winner. Qualifications for the award are outstanding academic application and performance, exemplary school leadership and citizenship, and superior football performance. The NFF's National Scholar Athletes are truly representative of our nation's best and brightest. He was also the NCAA Post-Graduate Scholarship winner in 1988. To qualify, student athletes must maintain a 3.000 grade point average (on a 4.000 basis) during their collegiate careers and perform with distinction in varsity football. Mark was also selected first team Academic All-America for the second time. Stepnoski was a Walter Camp Award winner and one of three finalists for the Outland Trophy which is presented to the outstanding lineman in college football. He was also a Vince Lombardi Award semi-finalist for the outstanding college lineman of the year. Mark was chosen to play in the East-West Shrine game at the conclusion of his senior year. He was the Dallas Cowboys' third-round draft choice in 1989 and became the first rookie to start at center for Dallas since 1979. He has become one of the premier centers in professional football. It took just four seasons in the NFL for Stepnoski to earn the Pro Bowl recognition that came in 1992. Mark was also named to the Associated Press All-Pro Team and received All-NFC honors from UPI and *Football News*. Stepnoski was selected Pro Bowl center for the National Football Conference in 1993 and 1994. He became the starting center for the Houston Oilers in 1995. Mark has a degree in communications from the University of Pittsburgh.

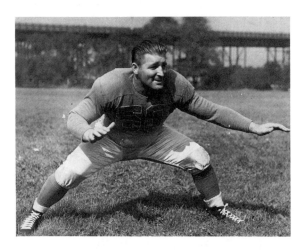

Alex Wojciechowicz—Fordham—Center—1937

The heart of Fordham University's immortal "Seven Blocks of Granite," Alex Wojciechowicz, was one of the finest centers ever to play in college football. He was the perfect example of football basics, blocking and tackling, and had a fierce pride in the way he played football, in his name and in his nationality. It all began for Alex at South River High School in South River, New Jersey where he was chosen All-State in football and baseball. He was also an excellent basketball player and a track and field performer. Notre Dame, Cornell and Duke were among the many universities attempting to recruit Alex, but he chose Fordham on the advice of his high school coach. Wojciechowicz played center and linebacker on the Rams unbeaten freshman squad in 1934. Head football coach, the legendary Jim Crowley, was happy to have Alex on the 1935 squad which finished the year with a 6-1-2 mark, losing only to Purdue and tying Pittsburgh and St. Mary (California). The most significant game was the 0-0 tie with Pitt. Fordham was a 17 point underdog, but the tough defense led by Wojciechowicz held the Panthers to just 76 total offensive yards while not letting them cross midfield. Throughout 1936, Alex led Fordham's offensive and defensive lines which finished the season with a 5-1-2 record, and allowed only 33 points. They tied Pitt again and their only loss was to New York University. This game cost the Rams an unbeaten season and a trip to the Rose Bowl. In 1937, the Rams, led by Wojciechowicz, performed like a well-oiled machine and finished with a 7-0-1 record—marred only by a tie. This came against Pitt in a game where neither team could score. Alex was brilliant throughout the game, and stopped the Pitt star, Marshal Goldberg, on the Ram three yard line for no gain on fourth down. He also got his revenge against N.Y.U. and won the Madow Trophy (awarded annually to the outstanding player in the Fordham-N.Y.U. game). The 1937 Ram squad had Alex at center, Harry Jacunski at end, William Krywicki at quarterback, and Joe Granski and Joe Woitkowski at halfbacks. They finished the season ranked third nationally. Wojciechowicz was as adept on defense by stopping plays as on offense by opening huge holes for the ball-carriers. He was a devastating charger and his range was so great that coach Jim Crowley often switched to a six-man line so that his best linebacker might roam loose on defense. He was well known for his characteristic wide stance in the center of the Ram offensive line, crouching menacingly over the ball with rolled up sleeves. That was the Wojciechowicz trademark which terrorized the opposing defensive linemen. Wojciechowicz was Fordham's first consensus All-America selection for two consecutive years, 1936 and 1937. He was a Heisman Trophy candidate in 1936 and runner-up in 1937. Alex played on the East-West Shrine team in 1938. The Detroit Lions made him their number one draft choice in 1938. He played for 13 years in the National Football League for the Detroit Lions and Philadelphia Eagles from 1938 to 1950. He was named to the All-Pro team twice, and helped Philadelphia to two NFL championships. He retired from the pros after the 1950 season and entered the real estate business. In 1968, he helped to establish the National Football League Alumni Association which helps needy former NFL players. Because of his contribution to the association, Alex was inducted into the Order of the Leather Helmet in 1982. (Only Bronko Nagurski and Red Grange were former players so honored). He made numerous Halls of Fame including the National Football Foundation's College Football Hall of Fame in 1955 and the Professional Football Hall of Fame in 1968. In 1970, he was inducted as a charter member into Fordham's Sports Hall of Fame and named to the New Jersey Sportswriters Hall of Fame. He received additional honors by being elected to the elite National Polish American Sports Hall of Fame in 1975, being the first football player to be chosen. Alex had a successful real estate career and retired in 1981 to his ocean side home on the New Jersey coast. Alexander Wojciechowicz, the consummate college football center, linebacker, and member of Fordham University's famed "Seven Blocks of Granite," died on July 13, 1992 in South River, N.J. at age 76.

Johnny Lujack—Notre Dame—Quarterback—1947

Johnny Lujack (Luczak) is rated as the finest T-formation quarterback of all time by many grid experts. He began his football playing days in Connellsville, Pennsylvania under the tutelage of his three older brothers who were good athletes. As a skinny 130 pounder, the 13 year old Lujack got his first taste of football at Cameron Junior High School. He made the varsity team at Connellsville High School in 1939 and was named All-State in football, baseball and track. In his best game, he returned two successive punts 70 yards for touchdowns. John led his school in scoring as a basketball guard, became an honor student and was elected senior class president. He was considered a professional baseball prospect as a shortstop but refused an offer from the Pittsburgh Pirates to attend Notre Dame. He was recruited by over 50 colleges and offered an appointment to West Point, but chose Notre Dame. Lujack became the Notre Dame quarterback as a sophomore in the seventh game of the 1943 season after Angelo Bertelli joined the Marines. In his first start against Army, Johnny threw two touchdown passes, ran for another and intercepted a pass in a dramatic 26-0 upset victory. He was commissioned an Ensign in the U.S. Navy in 1944 and received his honorable discharge in June 1946. Lujack returned to Notre Dame and guided the Fighting Irish to a new pinnacle of football glory the next two years. Frank Leahy, the Notre Dame head coach, referred to John as the "coach on the field" who provided leadership, poise and daring. Through his signal calling, Lujack kept the defense in a state of confusion and his teammates on their toes. He knew the job of every man on every play. John guided Notre Dame to a 8-0-1 season and the national championship in 1946. He preserved a scoreless tie between second ranked Notre Dame and top ranked Army by making a touchdown saving tackle of Doc Blanchard from his defensive position. John was the only one between Blanchard and a sure winning touchdown but stopped Doc with an ankle tackle on the Irish 37 yard line. In 1947, Notre Dame went undefeated for the second year in a row under the leadership of Lujack. During Johnny's three varsity years (1943, 1946 and 1947), Notre Dame finished with a 26-1-1 record and won three national championships. Lujack's career total passing yards were 2,094 (.514 percent) for 18 touchdowns, rushing yards of 438 and six touchdowns, giving him a total of 2,532 yards and 24 touchdowns. He intercepted seven passes for 106 yards and punted 62 times for a 36.2 yard average. Lujack was named unanimous All-America in 1946 and 1947, was Heisman Memorial Trophy runner-up (third) in 1946, and Heisman Trophy winner in 1947. He won the Walter Camp Memorial Trophy as the College Back of the Year, and was named Associated Press Athlete of the Year in 1947. John was also named to the American Board of Football's 25-year Anniversary team, and chosen the best college quarterback of the quarter century by All-America Review in 1949. Lujack is considered by many to have been the greatest quarterback in Notre Dame football history. He went on to play pro football for four years with the Chicago Bears and proved to be an all-round performer. He led the Bears in scoring each year, tied a record with eight interceptions as a rookie, threw for a record 468 yards in one game and played in the NFL Pro Bowl his last two seasons. After retiring from pro ball, John was a Notre Dame backfield coach for two years. He went into sports broadcasting and now ows a successful auto dealership in Davenport, Iowa. Lujack was elected to the National Football Foundation's College Football

Hall of Fame in 1960, and inducted into the National Polish-American Sports Hall of Fame in 1978.

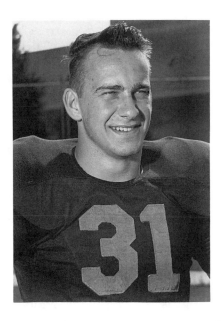

James Grabowski—Illinois—Running Back—1965

Coaches dream about having excellent scholar athletes on their teams. The dream became a reality to head football coach Pete Elliot when James Grabowski enrolled at the University of Illinois in 1962. Grabowski came from the northwest side of Chicago where he played football at Taft High School. Jim was only 16 years of age when he started his senior season, but was selected Chicago's Prep Player of the Year in 1961. Many colleges and universities were actively recruiting Jim, but he chose the University of Illinois. In the fall of 1962, Grabowski proved as a freshman that he was the best fullback among the recruits and was listed as a starting back on the varsity squad. After overcoming early-season injuries and nervousness, Jim had a good freshman year. In 1963, Grabowski earned second team All-Big Ten Conference honors as a running back. Illinois finished with a record of 8-1-1, third rank in the country and beat Washington in the Rose Bowl, 17-7. Jim rushed for 125 yards on 22 carries and was named the Most Valuable Player in the Rose Bowl game. Illinois finished the 1964 campaign with a 6-3-0 mark and were ranked 16th in the nation. Grabowski had one of the most phenomenal days of his college career that season against Wisconsin when he ran for 239 yards in 33 carries. He picked up 1,004 yards as a junior during the '64 campaign. Jim was selected first team All-Big Ten Conference running back, and named first team All-America. He was also chosen first team Academic All-American for that year. Illinois had another winning year in 1965, and Grabowski, after setting the Illinois record for yards rushing in a season with 1,258, took almost all the top honors that were available to him. He was elected the team captain and named the Most Valuable Player for the season. Jim was the 1965 Silver Football Award winner as the Big Ten Conference's Most Valuable Player, and naturally repeated with first team All-Big Ten honors. Grabowski was selected a unanimous first team All-America, and, as in 1964, was named first team Academic All-America. He was chosen Co-Player of the Year by *Sporting News*, and placed third on the ballots for the Heisman Trophy. In addition, Jim was given the Walter Camp Memorial Award as the Outstanding Back in college football for the year. Before he ended his varsity career in 1966, Grabowski wiped out all of Red Grange's rushing records with 2,753 yards. He was one of the most productive runners in Illinois football history. Jim broke all Illinois and Big Ten Conference records during his varsity years. In 1966, Grabowski was awarded the Illinois Conference Medal of Honor for excellence in scholarship and athletics. A butcher's son from Chicago had come a long way on the road to success. Jim played with the College All-Star team in 1966. He was the number one draft pick in 1966 by the Green Bay Packers and played with them for five years under coach Vince Lombardi. He had a modest rookie season with the Packers, then got off to a great start in 1967. Jim was Green Bays' leading rusher halfway through the season. In the game against Baltimore, Grabowski got hit hard and his right knee snapped. He underwent surgery, but was never the same football player again. Jim continued playing with the Packers through 1970, and then finished his football career after a year with the Chicago Bears. As a Business Administration major, he became associated with a merchandising company in Chicago after retiring from pro ball. Grabowski was inducted into the National Polish-American Sports Hall of Fame in 1993. He was also chosen to the GTE Academic All-America Hall of Fame. Jim was selected among nominees by the College Sports Information Directors of America from past Academic All-Americans. As of 1993, there were only 22 former NCAA college football players in the elite Academic Hall of Fame. In 1995, Grabowski was inducted into the National Football Foundation's College Football Hall of Fame.

Emil Sitko—Notre Dame—Running Back—1949

Son of Polish immigrant parents, Emil Sitko played varsity football, basketball and ran track at Central High School in Fort Wayne, Indiana. He was recruited by Notre Dame head football coach, Frank Leahy, after coming out of the service in World War II. Leahy met with the Sitko family in Fort Wayne hoping to interest Emil in enrolling at Notre Dame and ask the family out for dinner. However, Emil's father had spent all day preparing the traditional Polish hearty delicacy called Bigos (Hunter's Stew), and like a good host, insisted that Leahy dine with them. Leahy dined on Bigos, Emil decided to enroll at Notre Dame, and the rest is football history. Sitko, at 5 feet 8 inches and 180 pounds, started at right halfback as a Notre Dame freshman and remained a starter for the balance of his college football career. He played with such immortals as John Lujack, Leon Hart and Ziggie Czarobski. Emil was a tough, well-built player who was an exceptionally fast starter. He would quickly break through the line for five to ten yard gains, but once past the secondary, there was no stopping him. Against Illinois, the strongest Big Ten Conference team in 1946, he demonstrated his remarkable running ability by dashing off tackle, breaking into the clear and going for a spectacular 83 yard touchdown run. He was equally impressive by running for two touchdowns against Iowa. Sitko and the Fighting Irish had an outstanding season. The team finished with an 8-0-1 mark and the national championship. Sitko had an excellent outing during the 1947 campaign and helped Notre Dame to an undefeated, untied 9-0-0 record and the national championship again. The 1948 season had Sitko, Tripucka and Swistowicz leading Notre Dame to another undefeated 9-0-1 year, but the championship went to Michigan and the Fighting Irish were ranked second in the country. Sitko was selected consensus first team All-America and was a Heisman Trophy candidate. During the 1949 campaign, Sitko not only led the team in rushing yardage but also became the leader in kick-off returns, averaging 22 yards per carry. Notre Dame enjoyed another undefeated, untied season with a 10-0-0 mark and were named national champions. Emil was selected unanimous first team All-America halfback, and was eighth in the voting for the Heisman Trophy. (Leon Hart won the Heisman Trophy that year). During Sitko's four year college football career, Notre Dame did not lose a game and recorded a magnificent 36-0-2 mark. He led the team in rushing each year. Emil finished his career with 2,226 yards on 362 carries for a 6.1 yard average and 25 touchdowns. He really earned his nickname of "Six Yard Sitko." Emil was the Los Angeles Rams' first round draft selection but played for San Francisco in 1950. He was a halfback for the Chicago Cardinals in 1951 and 1952. After retiring from pro ball, Emil returned to Fort Wayne and ran a successful auto sales business. He died in 1973, at age 50, after a heart attack. Sitko was inducted into the National Football Foundation's College Football Hall of Fame in

1984. He was also chosen a member of the Indiana (State) Football Hall of Fame.

Steve Sitko, who was Notre Dame's All-American starting quarterback during the national championship 1938 and 1939 seasons, was Emil Sitko's first cousin.

William Osmanski—Holy Cross—Running Back—1938

William Osmanski came to the College of the Holy Cross as an All-State fullback from Providence, Rhode Island to help head football coach, Dr. Edward Anderson, establish a virtual dynasty during his three year varsity career. Osmanski showed his running skills early by scoring a touchdown on his first carry for the Crusaders against Yale and returning an 80-yard pass interception in the next game. From then on, there was no stopping Bill on his road to a successful career at Holy Cross. He provided the backfield leadership for the greatest teams in Crusader football history. Bill utilized his quick starting speed and terrific power to lead one of the best offensive threats in Eastern college football during the late 1930s. Osmanski was very impressive as a freshman and Coach Anderson was looking forward to Bill playing on the varsity. He was described as one of the hardest hitting backs in Holy Cross history. During the 1936 campaign, Osmanski's 76-yard pass interception return sparked Holy Cross to a 7-0 win over Dartmouth. Bill made the All-East team as a sophomore and was named All-America. Holy Cross finished with a 7-2-1 season. Osmanski was greatly responsible for the successful Crusader 8-0-2 campaign in 1937 and their number 14 national ranking. Bill repeated as an All-East back and was named to several All-America teams. In 1938, Coach Anderson and team captain Bill Osmanski carried the Crusaders to another excellent 8-1-0 season and a national ranking of ninth. Osmanski finished his spectacular Holy Cross career by leading the Crusaders to a 29-7 win over Boston College, and he scored a touchdown on his last college carry. For his performance during the '38 season, Bill was selected first team All-America. During his three varsity years, the Crusaders compiled an excellent 23-3-3 record. Their three losses came to a total of only five points. Osmanski was as punishing on defense as he was on offense. Coach Anderson compared him to the immortal Hall of Famer, Tom Harmon. Bill was chosen to play on the East-West Shrine and College All-Star teams in 1939. He was Chicago Bears' first round draft choice, and became the National Football League's first ever All-League performer as a rookie. While studying dentistry at Northwestern University and playing for the Bears, he accumulated five World Championship rings and was a Pro Bowl team selection twice. Following service in the Navy during World War II, he returned to Chicago to play two more years with the Bears. Bill retired in 1946 to become the Bears' backfield coach, and was the head football coach at Holy Cross in 1948 and 1949. After receiving his Dental degree, Doctor Osmanski settled down to a practice in Evanston, Illinois. He is a member of the Holy Cross Varsity Club Hall of Fame, and was inducted into the National Football Foundation's College Football Hall of Fame in 1973. The only football number ever retired by Holy Cross was No. 25, worn by Bullet Bill Osmanski, called "The Greatest Crusader of Them All." In 1977, Osmanski was elected to the National Polish American Sports Hall of Fame.

Joseph Osmanski, Class of 1941, was also a fullback for Holy Cross in 1939, 1940 and 1941, and then played for the Chicago Bears from 1946 through 1950. He attended Law School at DePaul University and after graduating, became an attorney for the Cook County Circuit Court. He spent more than 30 years as a supervisor for the court until his retirement in 1993. He died at age 75 in October 1993.

Leon Hart—Notre Dame—Defensive End—1949

Leon Hart attended Turtle Creek High School, Turtle Creek, Pennsylvania, a small steel mill town, and became the most sought after athlete in the Pittsburgh area. The honor student won ten letters in football (captain), basketball, baseball (captain), and track and field before graduating high school in 1946. By his senior year, he had grown to 6 feet, 5 inches and 225 pounds, and Notre Dame and their head football coach, Frank Leahy, were very fortunate and happy to have him. Hart had fulfilled his boyhood dream by enrolling at Notre Dame. The Fighting Irish did not lose a game during Hart's four years, compiling a fantastic 36-0-2 record, achieving a 21 game winning streak, and capturing three national championships in 1946, 1947 and 1949. As a 17-year old freshman, Hart alternated at defensive and offensive end with a veteran player and earned his first of four varsity letters as a member of the 1946 national championship team. He scored a touchdown against Southern California on a 22-yard pass and set up a touchdown against Iowa with a one-handed grab of a long Johnny Lujack pass. The following season (1947), he caught touchdown passes to help Notre Dame beat Pittsburgh, Navy and Northwestern, and on defense, recovered two Navy fumbles for additional touchdowns. Hart frequently played fullback in short yardage situations and became an extra back on end-around plays. He also proved to be an outstanding defensive rusher and was named to his first All-America team as a sophomore. During the 1948 campaign, he scored on pass receptions against Southern California, Pittsburgh, Michigan State and Washington. Against Southern Cal, Hart caught a pass and ran 35 yards for a touchdown even though he was hit six times by potential tacklers. Leon was rewarded for his efforts by being selected first team consensus All-America. He had his best year as a senior when he led Notre Dame to nine victories in their first nine games. Hart caught 19 passes for 257 yards and five touchdowns, rushed 18 times for 73 yards (4.1 yards average) and one touchdown, and recovered three fumbles. He led a tough Notre Dame defense with bruising hits on Southern Methodist passers to grab a 27-20 victory for an undefeated season and a third national title. He made 49 career pass receptions for 742 yards and 13 touchdowns, and made two touchdowns on runs from scrimmage. Hart was a devastating blocker and an outstanding defender. He co-captained the 1949 Notre Dame squad, called the signals on defense, and was named unanimous first team All-America. All honors were bestowed upon him as he won the 1949 Heisman Memorial Trophy as the nation's outstanding college football player and became only the second lineman to receive this prestigous award. Hart was also selected for the Maxwell Award (nation's outstanding college football player), Knute Rockne Trophy as the college lineman of the year, named United Press Lineman of the Year and Player of the Year, and Associated Press Athlete of the Year. He was the Senior Class President before graduating with a B.S. degree in Mechanical Engineering with a B average. Leon played on the East All-Star and the College All-Star teams helping both to victories. He starred at end for eight years with the Detroit Lions, played on three NFL championship teams and one Western Conference title. Hart retired from pro football at the young age of 29 and went into private business. He lives in Birmingham, Michigan, a Detroit suburb, and is a very successful business man. He was inducted into the National Football Foundation's

College Football Hall of Fame in 1973, and the National Polish-American Sports Hall of Fame in 1988.

Walter Patulski—Notre Dame—Defensive End—1971

A high school All-American at Christian Brothers Academy, Walter Patulski came to the University of Notre Dame from Liverpool, New York. Patulski had an excellent freshman year and established himself early in his college career by winning the Hering Award as the Outstanding Defensive Freshman. He took over the starting defensive left end position at the beginning of his sophomore year and did not relinquish it during the three year varsity career. In 1969, Notre Dame had a good winning season with a record of 8-2-1 under head coach Ara Parseghian, were ranked fifth in the nation, but lost to the No. 1 team, Texas, in the Cotton Bowl. Patulski was named to the *Football News* sophomore All-American team after his first varsity campaign. Walt missed the 1970 spring drills due to corrective shoulder surgery, but was ready to go when the fall season started. He made 58 tackles during the 1970 season, threw opponents for losses 17 times for a total of 112 yards, broke up one pass and recovered two fumbles. Notre Dame finished the year with a 10-1-0 mark, were ranked second in the country and beat Texas in the Cotton Bowl. In the voting to select the Outstanding Defensive Player of the bowl game, Patulski came in third. He received honorable mention on UPI's All-America selection, but was named All-America by several other selectors. During the 1971 spring's Blue-Gold game, Walt made 16 tackles, broke up one pass and recovered two fumbles. As a senior in 1971, he was elected co-captain of the Notre Dame squad and was one of the most popular men on campus. At 6 feet, 6 inches and 260 pounds, Patulski played on the defensive line that averaged 260 pounds. Notre Dame finished the year with a 8-2-0 record, and were ranked 13th in the nation. Patulski made 74 tackles, threw opponents for losses of 129 yards on 17 occasions, broke up six passes, recovered one fumble and returned a punt for 12 yards. During his college career, Walt made 186 tackles, 40 for minus 241 yards, broke up 10 passes and recovered five fumbles Patulski was one of the very best defensive ends, an instant starter. He had excellent size, good speed, mobility, lateral quickness and strength. Walt had started every Notre Dame game at defensive end for his last three seasons, and won the Hering Award again as the Outstanding Defensive Lineman. Patulski was selected unanimous first team All-America, and received the coveted Vince Lombardi Award honoring the Outstanding Lineman of the Year for 1971. He was also a Heisman Trophy candidate that year. Walt was selected to the College All-Star team and played with Steve Okoniewski, the University of Montana All-America guard. He was the Buffalo Bills No. 1 draft choice in 1972 and played pro ball for five years. He graduated from Notre Dame's College of Arts and Letters and planned a career in law. Patulski was inducted into the Syracuse, New York area Sports Hall of Fame in 1991.

Dick Modzelewski—Maryland—Def. Tackle—1952

Dick Modzelewski, son of Polish immigrant parents, was a native of West Natrona, Pennsylvania, a small coal mining town, where he was an outstanding high school football player. Dick was all set to enroll at the University of Cincinnati to play football under the coaching of Sid Gillman, but was persuaded to follow his older brother, Ed, to the University of Maryland. He had a good freshman year at Maryland, and was the starting defensive tackle as a sophomore during the 1950 season. Guided by head football coach Jim Tatum, Maryland finished the year with a good 7-2-1 record. Their biggest win was over the favored reigning national champion, Michigan State. The Terrapins, with excellent contributions by Dick at tackle and Ed at fullback, defeated Michigan State, 34-7, and established themselves as a national power. The Modzelewski brothers were members of the unbeaten, untied 1951 Maryland team which beat Tennessee in the Sugar Bowl, 28-13, to finish with a 10-0-0 record. In the Sugar Bowl, the Terps separate offensive and defensive units dominated Tennessee and the Maryland fans happily chanted "we are number one." Ironically, the Terps were edged out by Michigan State and Tennessee and were named number three even though they beat No. 1 Tennessee in the Sugar Bowl. Modzelewski was selected All-Southern Conference tackle and chosen All-America at the end of the season. Dick was one of the bigger collegiate linemen in the early 1950s at 6-0, 235 pounds. In 1952, Maryland went 7-2-0 and were ranked 13th nationally. Dick continued to star at the tackle position and was known to talk to himself in Polish when things weren't going well for the team. He was selected All-Southern Conference again and chosen consensus first team All-America. Dick became Maryland's first winner of major national honors when he was awarded the Outland Trophy (best collegiate lineman of the year), and the Knute Rockne Memorial Trophy (best college lineman of the year). Modzelewski played three varsity years as defensive tackle for Maryland on the great teams which finished with a total record of 24-4-1. Through a 22 game unbeaten streak, the defense, led by Dick, allowed only 147 points, with only four teams scoring more than one touchdown and six being shut out. Dick was selected to the College All-Star team in 1953 and was a second round NFL draft pick. He played with the Washington Redskins in 1953 and 1954, the Pittsburgh Steelers in 1955, and then starred the next eight seasons (1956-1963) for the New York Giants. During his 14 year pro career, he appeared in eight NFL championship games, was on two championship teams, and played in 180 consecutive games. After retiring from active playing, he was a defensive line coach and co-ordinator for the Cleveland Browns. He returned to the Giants as defensive co-ordinator and then was a line coach for the Cincinnati Bengals and the Detroit Lions. Modzelewski was inducted into the Professional Football Hall of Fame in 1985, and into the National Polish-American Sports Hall of Fame in 1986. He was elected to the National Football Foundation's College Football Hall of Fame and the University of Marylan Hall of Fame in 1993. Dick retired from pro ball and lives in New Bern, North Carolina.

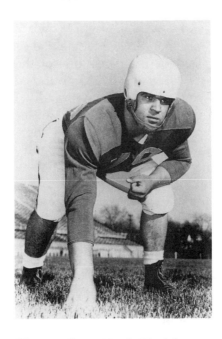

Lou Michaels—Kentucky—Def. Tackle—1957

A native of Swoyerville, Pennsylvania, Lou Michaels (Majka) came to the University of Kentucky with the unusual distinction of winning All-State high school honors in two different states-Pennsylvania and Virginia. The latter honor came as a result of his transfer to Staunton Military Academy in Virginia for his final prep year. Kentucky head football coach, Blanton Collier, almost lost Michaels to Washington and Lee University, the alma mater of Lou's older brother, Walt. When Walt learned that Washington and Lee was de-emphasizing its athletic program and that Collier was leaving the Cleveland Browns for the head coaching job at Kentucky, he decided to steer his kid-brother to the Blue Grass school. After a sensational high school career, Michaels was widely sought by many colleges and universities. Lou caught everyone's attention as a freshman at Kentucky in 1954 with his sparkling performances, offensively and defensively at left tackle, and handled the point-after-touchdown kicking chores. He showed unmistakable signs of greatness as a sophomore, improving with each game and gaining a spot on the All-Southeastern Conference team as well as honorable mention on many

All-America selections. Michaels' skills caught the attention of pro scouts and made them drool over the interior lineman who was only a sophomore. This was a good indication of bigger and better things to come. As a junior, Lou displayed his all-around talent in the Georgia Tech game with stellar offensive and defensive line plays and a fantastic kicking performance. If ever an All-America was made in one game, Michaels accomplished the feat with a great day against Georgia Tech on opening day of the 1956 campaign before millions of television viewers looking at the "Game of the Week" in Lexington, Kentucky. He made a fantastic pressure kick with a 61-yard punt on the fly out of Kentucky's end zone. Lou finished with 13 tackles in the game, eight un-assisted. The Georgia Tech coach commented that Lou ruined every play that came near him. That's the way it went all season. He was selected consensus first team All-America, Southeastern Conference Lineman of the Year, and first team All-Southeastern Conference. He also received the fourth highest number of votes for the Knute Rockne Memorial Trophy (nation's best lineman). During his senior year, Michaels left no doubt that he was an outstanding lineman and a great kicking and punting specialist. It was hard to decide what Lou did best, but the pro scouts agreed that he was most spectacular on defense. He was a repeat consensus All-America in 1957, got the Knute Rockne Memorial Trophy, was a Heisman Trophy runner up, made first team All-Southeastern Conference and was chosen the SEC Lineman of the Year. He was selected to play in the Hula Bowl game. Lou was the Los Angeles Rams first round draft choice in 1958 and played pro ball for 13 years. He retired in 1971 as the fourth leading scorer with 977 points on field goals and PATS. He was selected to the Helms Hall of Fame and chosen to the Quarter Century All-SEC team (1950-1974). Lou was elected to the National Football Foundation's College Football Hall of Fame in 1992, and inducted into the National Polish-American Sports Hall of Fame in 1994.

Harvey Jablonsky—Washington (Mo.) & Army—N.Guard—1933

Harvey Jablonsky was one of only a few men in college football who played six years of varsity ball. He was captain his senior year at two schools, Washington University in St. Louis, Missouri and Army. It began at Washington University in 1927. Jablonsky quickly distinguished himself as a tough, intelligent, aggresive middle linebacker who was depended upon for his brilliant performances through his senior year in 1929. His talent and skills were recognized and rewarded when he was named to the All-Missouri Valley Conference teams in 1928 and 1929. He captained the Battling Bears' squad in 1929 and was named All-America for that year. Under the collegiate rules of the time, he was eligible for three more years of varsity football. Jablonsky received an appointment to the United States Military Academy at West Point, New York in 1930 and began his second college football career. He played guard at Army under the legendary head football coach, Earl "Red" Blaik. Blaik was quick to recognize Jablonsky's playing abilities and leadership qualities and said that Harvey was "a fierce, inspirational leader on the team." In 1931, Army lost only to Harvard and beat Navy to finish a successful season. They had a winning year again in 1932 and repeated by beating Navy, 20-0. The 1933 team, which Jablonsky captained, was one of their most outstanding, with only 26 points scored against them the entire season, whereas they rolled up 227 points for a final record of 9-1-0. (Notre Dame beat them by one point, 13-12.) Seven of their opponents were held scoreless, largely due to Harvey's aggressiveness and leadership. They also defeated Navy again by a score of 12-7. Jablonsky was chosen for All-East honors in 1933 and was named on several All-America teams. Army knew better than to lose a prize like Jablonsky, so he remained at West Point as an assistant coach for nine years until World War II in 1942. Colonel Jablonsky commanded the 515th Parachute Infantry Regiment which was part of the 13th Airborne Division when it saw action in France during the war. In 1946, he returned to West Point as an assistant coach under "Red" Blaik. Jablonsky later rose to the rank of major general and commanded the 1st Airborne Division. He retired from the Army in 1968 as a highly decorated major general, having spent thirty-four years in the service. He joined the Northrop Company in Los Angeles, California after retiring. For his contribution to college football, both as a coach and a two-time All-America player, Jablonsky was elected to the National Football Foundation's College Football Hall of Fame in 1978.

Chester Gladchuk—Boston College—Linebacker—1940

A native of Bridgeport, Connecticut, Chester Gladchuk was a four-sport letterman at Warren Harding High School in football, basketball, baseball and track. He enrolled at Boston College in 1937 and played offensive center and defensive linebacker in 1938, 1939 and 1940. Chester won the starting position in 1938 as a sophomore playing under head coach Gil Dobie, and remained a starter under the legendary coach Frank Leahy in 1939 and 1940. At 6-4, 245 pounds, Gladchuk was also a three year starter at center on the basketball team. In 1938, the Eagles finished with a good 6-1-2 record, and Chester's offensive and defensive performances earned him the starting position. Under new head coach Frank Leahy, Boston College had an excellent 9-2-0 campaign in 1939 and played Clemson in the Cotton Bowl. Although the Eagles lost 6-3, Gladchuk contributed greatly to the defense which held Clemson's much heralded offensive attack, led by Hall of Famer Banks McFadden to a single touchdown, blocked the PAT and forced 11 punts for a Cotton Bowl record. The 1940 Boston College team had five Polish Americans on the starting eleven with Gladchuk at center, Joe Zabilski at guard, Henry Woronicz at end, and Frank Maznicki and Henry Toczylowski in the backfield. Toczylowski was captain of the squad. They finished the season with an undefeated, untied 11-0-0 record, and were, without doubt, the Eagles' all-time best team. Boston College even upset Bob Neyland's powerhouse University of Tennessee team in the Sugar Bowl, 19-13. Gladchuk was selected first team All-America by Associated Press and other selectors at the end of the year. Chester proved that he was one of the best centers and linebackers developed in the Northeast. He was the first Boston College player to be selected in the first round of the NFL draft in 1941. He played with the New York Giants in 1941, and then had a four year tour of duty as an officer in the U.S. Navy. Gladchuk returned to play with the Giants in 1946 and 1947. He was selected as All-Pro Center with the Giants. In 1948, Chester became the head football coach at Bridgeport University and in 1949 coached the Montreal Alouettes. He was assistant coach at the University of Massachusetts in 1952, and later became assistant to the Athletic Director. He was active in civic service as a recreation commissioner and a little league manager. Chester Gladchuk died in 1967. He was inducted into the Boston College Varsity Club Hall of Fame in 1970, and into the National Football Foundation's College Football Hall of Fame in 1975. His son, Chester Gladchuk, Jr., became the Athletic Director at Boston College in 1991.

Jack Ham—Pennsylvania State—Linebacker—1970

Jack Ham attended Bishop McCort High School in Johnstown, Pennsylvania where he participated in football and track. After graduating in 1966, he was one of the most lightly recruited players to enter Pennsylvania State University having received the last football scholarship available that year. Coach Joe Paterno summed it up by saying, "Jack Ham's career is a monument to the work ethic. He was not a highly recruited athlete, but his exceptional intelligence and capacity for hard work made him an extraordinary football player. I don't think that any of us knew then what an enormous talent we were getting. Jack Ham will always be the consummate Penn State." Ham majored in real estate and insurance at Penn State and started three years as linebacker on the football team. The Nittany Lions, under third year coach Paterno had a brilliant, undefeated, untied regular season record of 10-0-0 in 1968 and defeated Kansas in the Orange Bowl for their 11th win. They were ranked second nationally. Jack was beginning to show that his speed, quickness and ability to anticipate plays made him an extremely effective defensive player against the running as well as passing attacks. Ham blocked three punts in 1968, setting a school record that was finally tied in 1989. He continued to work hard, learn and improve and was one of the main reasons why Penn State went on to another unbeaten and untied season in 1969. They finished with an 11-0-0 record having beaten Missouri in the Orange Bowl, and were ranked second in the nation. In his senior year, 1970, Ham was the defensive team captain, had 91 tackles, four interceptions, and was named consensus All-America. He finished his college career with 251 tackles, 143 unassisted. The Pittsburgh Steelers chose Jack in the second round of the 1971 draft. Ham was the only linebacker named to the Pro Bowl eight straight seasons. He was named the NFL Defensive Player of the Year in 1975 and the only unanimous defensive choice for the NFL's Team of the Decade. He played 12 years with the Steelers and contributed to four Super Bowl wins. Ham is credited with setting the standard for modern day linebackers. Ham retired after the 1982 season and was named to the Professional Football Hall of Fame. He was elected to the National Polish-American Sports Hall of Fame in 1987, and the National Football Foundation's College Football Hall of Fame in 1990. Ham is the only Nittany Lion selected for membership in both the College and Professional Football Halls of Fame. He was presented with the Distinguished Alumni Award by Pennsylvania State University. A successful business man, Jack lives in Sewickley, Pennsylvania.

Casimir Myslinski—Army—Linebacker—1943

Casimir Myslinski went through an accelerated three-year high school curriculum at Steubenville, Ohio and received an appointment to the United States Military Academy at West Point. He entered the Academy in September 1941 as part of the last pre-World War II class. Because of the war, Myslinski again undertook an accelerated academic program, and graduated in three years with a Bachelor of Science degree in Engineering and a commission as a 2nd Lieutenant in the U.S. Army. While at the Academy, Myslinski also earned his pilot wings and distinguished himself on the football field as an outstanding lineman at center. Army had a winning season in 1942, but it was in 1943

54

that head football coach "Red" Blaik gave the college sports world the first indication of great things to come for the Cadets. They ended 1943 with a 7-2-1 season and were ranked 11th in the nation. Myslinski was chosen captain of the 1943 squad and was voted the Most Valuable Player of the Year. Henry Mazur at back and Joe Stanowicz at guard played on the same team with Casimir. Both Mazur and Stanowicz were named All-America. Myslinski was selected unanimous All-America center and received additional honors by getting the Knute Rockne Memorial Award as the nation's outstanding lineman. Following graduation from the U.S. Military Academy in 1944, he entered the U.S. Army Air Force. After the war, he was "drafted" by the 3rd Air Force football team—a service team that played an excellent brand of football—and played for one year. Again Myslinski distinguished himself by being named to the All-Air Force team as center. In 1952, Casimir returned to West Point as Deputy Head of the Department of Physical Education, and made time to receive a Master's degree in Education from the Teacher's College at Columbia University. In 1956, Myslinski became Head of the Department of Physical Education at the U.S. Air Force Academy in Colorado. He also became an assistant football coach of the Air Force team in 1957. He remained at the Air Force Academy until 1968 when he became the Director of Athletics at the University of Pittsburgh. When appointed, Myslinski promised to bring the Pittsburgh athletic teams to "the heights they deserve," and thoroughly rebuilt the Pitt Athletic Department. Under his leadership, the Pitt athletic program achieved national distinction while establishing an equally strong reputation for high academic standards. During his 14 year tenure, the Panther's inter-collegiate athletic teams established an enviable record of achieving 13 consecutive overall winning seasons. The football and basketball programs grew to new heights of glory. One of his top achievements was uniting several financial contributing bodies into one, starting the now thriving Pitt Golden Panthers Boosters Club in 1971. The Golden Panthers raised over $800,000 to help support the athletic program in 1986, the year that Myslinski retired. He is a candidate for election to the National Football Foundation's College Football Hall of Fame and should be elected shortly. He also deserves membership in the National Polish-

American Sports Hall of Fame. Myslinski was ill with Parkinson's disease and died in 1993.

Victor Janowicz—Ohio State—Def. Back—1951

One of the most versatile players in Ohio State University football history was Victor Janowicz. One of nine children of Polish born Felix and Veronica Janowicz, Victor was an outstanding athlete at Elyria High School, Elyria, Ohio. He distinguished himself early in competition in track, basketball, football and baseball at Elyria High. A star halfback, he led Elyria to an undefeated football season in 1947, made the All-Ohio football team twice and was also named All-Ohio in baseball and basketball. He aspired to a pro baseball career as a teen-ager, but decided to play football at Ohio State after being recruited by over 60 colleges and universities. The five foot, eight inch, 185 pound Janowicz had plenty of power, speed and agility when he entered Ohio State in 1948. As a sophomore in 1949, he started occasionally as a left halfback and fullback in the single-wing formation, but an injury in mid-season limited his play. Ohio State, under head coach Wes Fesler, finished the season with a 7-1-2 record including a 17-14 Rose Bowl win over California. The next year proved to be a fantastic football season for Janowicz as Coach Fesler gave him many distinct responsibilities. He ran, passed as a quarterback and halfback, called offensive signals, punted, kicked extra points, and keyed the defense as a safety. His greatest game was played against Iowa, as he ran for two touchdowns, passed for four touchdowns, kicked ten extra points and recovered two fumbles. He led the Big Ten Conference in total offense for the season, and was named consensus first team All-America. Janowicz also won the Heisman Memorial Trophy in 1950 as the best college football player in the country. He was only the second junior at the time to receive this coveted award. In 1951, Victor had the misfortune of playing under a new head coach, Woody Hayes, who converted the Buckeye offense from a single-wing to a split T formation. The single-wing was made for Vic's versatile skills, the split T was not. Hayes used Janowicz "only when the going got tough." This change nullified Janowicz as either All-America or a Heisman repeater. Years later, Hayes admitted that changing from a single-wing and not utilizing Janowicz's ability was one of the worst mistakes of his coaching career. Vic was chosen to the College All-Star team after graduating from Ohio State. He entered the military service and then pursued a pro baseball career. He played for the Pittsburgh Pirates for two years as a catcher and third baseman. In 1955, Vic starred in the National Football League for the Washington Redskins. A near-fatal automobile accident ended his athletic career in 1956 and paralyzed the left side of his body. Through physical therapy, Janowicz was able to overcome the paralysis and worked as a broadcaster, public relations director and as a sales executive. In 1976, he was elected to the National Football Foundation's College Football Hall of Fame. The next year, Vic was enshrined with a charter group of outstanding athletes in the Ohio State University Sports Hall of Fame. Janowicz was inducted into the prestigous National Polish-American Sports Hall of Fame in 1987. He worked for the Ohio state auditor, and died of prostrate cancer on February 27, 1996.

Arthur Murakowski—Northwestern—Defensive Back—1948

An All-State fullback at Washington High School in East Chicago, Indiana, Arthur Murakowski was a member of the 1942 mythical state championship prep football team. He joined the Navy in 1943 and played on the Great Lakes Naval Training Base football team which upset Notre Dame that year, 19-18. Art also served as a fireman aboard a destroyer minesweeper in the Pacific. After 32 months, he was discharged from the service and enrolled at Northwestern University. Murakowski went on to become an outstanding football player for the Wildcats and established several school records which are still good today. He was a three year member of the varsity squad and played as fullback on offense and right halfback on defense. In 1947, Northwestern was the only team that was able to score more than one touchdown against Notre Dame, and Murakowski was selected as the Wildcats' Most Valuable Player. In 1948, Northwestern had a 7-2-0 record under head coach Bob Voigts and was ranked seventh in the nation. They climaxed this successful season by going to the Rose Bowl and beating fourth ranked California, 20-14. Murakowski set up Northwestern's second touchdown in the bowl game with a tremendous exhibition of sheer strength as he carried four California players almost 10 yards on his back to the one yard line. He scored on the next play. Art felt that the Rose Bowl game was his greatest sports thrill. He also felt that his 91 yard touchdown sprint against Notre Dame in 1947 was another great experience. He intercepted a Tripucka pass and went all the way for the score. Murakowski is still considered to be one of the finest backs (offensive and defensive) in Northwestern football history. He led the Wildcat ball carriers for three straight years. During the 1948 campaign, Art carried the ball 119 times for 922 yards, a 5.2 yard average. He also tied for the team scoring honors. His open field tackles in the Ohio State and Wisconsin games prevented almost sure touchdowns and allowed the Wildcats to win both games. Murakowski doubled his value by playing on defense as well as on offense. He was voted the team's Most Valuable Player again at the close of the 1948 year, and won the Chicago Tribune's Silver

Football as the Western Conference (now the Big Ten) Most Valuable Player that year. Art was also selected consensus All-America in 1948. He was selected to play in the College All-Star and the East-West Shrine games. After graduating from Northwestern, Art was the Detroit Lions third-round draft choice and played pro football for the Lions and the Chicago Cardinals. He retired from pro ball and settled in Hammond, Indiana to become active in politics. Murakowski worked for the Lake County (Northern Indiana) government for 31 years. He was an Indiana state representative for eight years from 1965 through 1972. He was also a football official for 20 years. Art was inducted into the Northwestern University Athletic Hall of Fame in May 1985, and died shortly after in September at age 60. He was also a member of the Indiana (State) Football Hall of Fame.

Bill Murakowski was an outstanding fullback at Purdue University, elected team captain in 1955 and chosen first team All-Big Ten Conference.

Walter Kowalczyk—Michigan State—Def. Back—1957

A fantastic high school athlete, Walter Kowalczyk came to Michigan State University in 1954 from Westfield, Massachusetts where he attended Westfield High School. He earned four letters in football and baseball, three in basketball and two in track. Walter was co-captain of the football team in his senior year and was chosen All-State in both his junior and senior years. In baseball, he won All-State twice. He won the state 100-yard dash championship for two years, won the 220-yard once and was runner-up on another occasion. His high school career was climaxed by being named the Outstanding Athlete in New England. Once at Michigan State, Kowalczyk soon lived up to his fabulous high school record. Even as a freshman, the coaches predicted he would be a regular when the Spartans opened the 1955 season. And so it was—he was a starting halfback in his sophomore year and held that position for the rest of his college career. He started slowly, but once he learned how to use his speed and power to full effectiveness, Walt became one of the most powerful runners in college football. In the Wisconsin game, he rambled for 172 yards and two touchdowns in ten carries. As a stocky 6 foot, 205 pounder with the speed of a sprinter, Kowalczyk generated a lot of momentum that was hard to stop. Walt finished the 1955 season as the top rusher on the team with 584 yards on 82 attempts for a 7.1 average, and was selected to the All-Big Ten Conference team. Michigan State ended the regular '55 campaign with a 8-1-0 record under coach Duffy Daugherty, then beat UCLA in the Rose Bowl, 17-14, and were ranked second nationally. Kowalczyk rushed for 88 yards, completed a 25 yard pass and was voted the Rose Bowl's Most Valuable Player. The Spartan starting line-up for the Bowl game had Joe Badaczewski at center, Dave Kaiser (Kajzerkowski) at end and Kowalczyk at halfback. Walt's eagerly awaited junior season proved to be a disappointment when he suffered a crippling ankle and foot sprain in the early fall scrimmage. He saw limited action, but never fully recovered from the injury until after the season was over. The 1957 season was his finest as he showed his old speed, power, finesse and newly acquired ability to run over the opposition. Against Michigan, Kowalczyk ran amuck as the Spartans beat the Wolverines, 35-6, for their worst loss in 22 years. Michigan State finished with a 8-1-0 record and were ranked third nationally. Walt was named consensus All-America, first team All-Big Ten Conference and was the Heisman Trophy runner-up (third) in 1957. His net rushing average for three years was 5.6 yards, he scored 102 points and gained 1,257 yards on the ground and 187 in the air. He was selected to play in the College All-Star, Senior Bowl, and East-West Shrine games. In the All-Star game, Walt started at fullback with teammate Jim Ninowski at quarterback and Lou Michaels at tackle. They beat the Detroit Lions, 35-19. Kowalczyk was the first round draft choice of the Philadelphia Eagles in 1958 and played professional football through 1961. Being a physical education major, Walt became active in coaching and teaching after retiring from pro ball. He was chosen as an alternate member of the All-Time Michigan State University football team.

Chester Marcol—Hillsdale College—K/P—1971

Chester (Czeslaw) Marcol was born in Opole, Poland in 1949 and came to the United States with his family in 1964 at age 15. He enrolled at Hillsdale College, Hillsdale, Michigan in 1968 and went on to establish numerous school and conference records as a football placekicker and punter. He was an outstanding soccer goalie since his boyhood, and kicking and punting came naturally to him. He was a four year letter winner from 1968 through 1971, and a three year All-American in 1969, 1970 and 1971. Hillsdale finished with a winning 6-3-0 record in 1968 and Marcol was their leading scorer with 20 points after touchdowns and six field goals for a total of 38 points. The Chargers had a 9-2-0 season in 1969 with Chester's stellar performances in kicking and punting. He set two Hillsdale College records by kicking 43 conversions and the longest field goal of 62 yards against Fairmont State. Marcol was selected NAIA (National Association of Intercollegiate Athletics) Division I All-America kicker at the end of the 1969 campaign. Hillsdale finished 9-2-0 again after the 1970 season and Chester had another excellent outing. He kicked the most consecutive conversions of 104 for new and still existing Hillsdale College and Conference records. His longest punt was 75 yards against Findlay College. Once again he was selected first team All-America kicker at season's end. In 1971, Marcol was the Chargers scoring leader with 55 points (28 PATS and nine FGs). His punting improved to give him a career average school record of 43.2 yards per punt. He also established a Hillsdale College career 48 conversion record of 132 from 1968 through 1971 and kicked eight field goals of 50 yards or more. For the third time, Marcol was selected first team All-America place kicker. He was chosen on the second round of the NFL draft by the Green Bay Packers in 1972. As a professional, Chester kicked four field goals against the Detroit Lions and was the NFL field goal leader with 33 during the 1972 season. He was also the professional scoring leader with 128 points and became the first football player ever to lead the NFL in scoring on place kicking alone. Marcol was selected All-National Football Conference and named Rookie-of-the-Year for 1972. He scored 82 points in 1973 and was selected to the Pro Bowl. In 1974, he led the NFL in scoring again, and repeated as a Pro Bowl selection in 1975. Marcol had a brilliant pro ball career with the Green Bay Packers through 1979 and retired from professional football after playing with the Houston Oilers in 1980. Chester returned to Hillsdale College and received his degree in Health, Science and Physical Education. He was inducted into the Green Bay Packers Hall of Fame in 1987, and now lives with his family in northern Michigan. Marcol is a candidate for election to the National Polish-American Sports Hall of Fame.

CHAPTER II

ALL-TIME POLISH AMERICAN— SECOND TEAM

OFFENSE

Position	Name	School	Year
End	Johnny Wysocki	Villanova	1938
End	Casimir Banaszek	Northwestern	1966
Tackle	Gregory Kolenda	Arkansas	1979
Tackle	Greg Skrepenak	Michigan	1991
Guard	Steve Okoniewski	Montana	1971
Guard	Steve Wisniewski	Pennsylvania State	1988
Center	Thomas Brzoza	Pittsburgh	1977
Q.Back	Steve Bartkowski	California	1974
R.Back	Eugene Filipski	Villanova	1953
R.Back	Steve Juzwik	Notre Dame	1941
R.Back	Ed Modzelewski	Maryland	1951
P.Kicker	Chris Gardocki	Clemson	1991

DEFENSE

Position	Name	School	Year
End	Robert Brudzinski	Ohio State	1976
End	Marvin Matuszak	Tulsa	1952
Tackle	Raymond Frankowski	Washington	1941
Tackle	Johnny Guzik	Pittsburgh	1958
N.Guard	Frank Piekarski	Pennsylvania	1904
L.Backer	Stas Maliszewski	Princeton	1965
L.Backer	Bill Romanowski	Boston College	1987
L.Backer	Frank Rydzewski	Notre Dame	1917
D.Back	Edward Danowski	Fordham	1933
D.Back	Frank Dancewicz	Notre Dame	1945
D.Back	Walter Matuszczak	Cornell	1940
Punter	Chris Gardocki	Clemson	1991

Johnny Wysocki—Villanova—Off. End—1938

One of the most outstanding football players in the history of Villanova University athletics, Johnny Wysocki starred as a varsity offensive and defensive end in 1936, 1937 and 1938. He played the key role on a team whose three year record was a remarkable 23-2-3 under head coach Maurice "Clipper" Smith. In 1936, Villanova finished the regular season with a 7-2-0 mark and then played Auburn in the Bacardi Bowl. This was the Wildcats' first football bowl appearance, and it was also the first bowl game played outside of the United States. It was played in Havana as the climactic event of Cuba's National Sports Festival. The game developed into a defensive battle with Auburn scoring one touchdown in the first half to take the lead. Late in the fourth quarter, Wysocki blocked Auburn's quick kick attempt, recovered the ball and scored for Villanova. The contest ended in a 7-7 tie, and for Cuba it was the beginning and an end of a football classic. In 1937, with Wysocki leading the Villanova defensive line, the Wildcats held every opponent scoreless except for seven points tallied by Marquette. Always the center of action, Wysocki blocked punts, recovered fumbles, blocked for runners, caught passes, and in 1937 was Villanova's leading scorer with 40 points. The Wildcats ended the season with a 8-0-1 mark, marred only by a scoreless tie with Auburn. Villanova was ranked sixth nationally and Wysocki was honored by being selected first team All-America end. The 1938 season ended with a 8-0-1 record again, the tie being a 6-6 deadlock against South Carolina. Wysocki's brilliant offensive and defensive talents were recognized and he was again chosen first team All-America. He has the distinct honor of being the only Villanova University football player ever to earn All-America selection in consecutive years, 1937 and 1938. Johnny played with Walter Nowak as the other end during the '38 campaign. During his college football career, Wysocki scored three touchdowns on blocked kicks. He ended his football playing days by starring in the College All-Star and the East-West Shrine games. Wysocki was selected to the "Wildcat 100" in 1993 as a tribute to the 100 most important football players and coaches in the Wildcat Century.

Casimir Banaszek—Northwestern—Off. End—1966

Casimir Banaszek was a three year football letterman at Northwestern University in 1964, 1965 and 1966. He proved to be an excellent offensive end during a period which can be considered to have been the Wildcat's lean years. Michigan dominated the Big Ten Conference in 1964, Michigan State took over for 1965 and 1966, and Northwestern was relegated to the underdog role for the three seasons. In 1964, Banaszek was the Wildcats' receiving annual champion with 27 catches and a total of 316 yards for an average of 11.7 yards per reception. He was the champion again in 1965 with 30 catches for a total of 332 yards, an average of 11.0 yards per catch. Casimir was a smart player, blessed with good hands, and a dependable receiver who knew what to do with the ball once he caught it. Banaszek was considered to be a hard-nosed competitor known for his excellent, aggresive blocking. From 1964 through 1966, he made 88 receptions for a total of 920 yards and caught for two touchdowns. His career average was 10.5 yards per reception. He is among the All-Time Leaders in career catches per game and in total career catches at Northwestern. For his outstanding performances as a Wildcat offensive end, Casimir was selected to the All-Big Ten Conference teams in 1965 and 1966. He was also selected All-America in 1965, and was an All-America choice again in 1966. Banaszek was a very versatile athlete who played as linebacker on defense and was a good punter during the 1966 campaign. He played in the North-South All-Star game in 1966 and in the College All-Star game in 1967. Casimir was the San Francisco 49ers' first round NFL draft choice in 1967 and had a fantastic professional football career. He played with San Francisco for eleven years and retired from pro ball after the 1977 season. In 1991, Banaszek was a manufacturers representative at GNA Electronics in Mountain View, California.

Gregory Kolenda—Arkansas—Off. Tackle—1979

Kolenda came to the University of Arkansas from Kansas City, Kansas in 1976 with blue-chip high school credentials earning All-America, All-State, All-County and All-Metro football honors as a prep senior. He played on the state championship team as a sophomore, and in the Kansas high school all-star game as a senior. Gregory also lettered in track and wrestling. Kolenda began to shine early under head coach Lou Holtz at Arkansas, and won his first varsity letter as a back-up center as a freshman. In 1977, his offensive line play at tackle contributed greatly to the Razorbacks' extremely successful season as they finished with an 11-1-0 mark, beating the Big Eight Conference champion, Oklahoma, in the Orange Bowl by a score of 31-6. They were ranked number three in the nation. In 1978, Kolenda continued to excel in every game he started and began to take over as the offensive line leader. Arkansas completed another successful season with a 9-2-1 mark, was ranked 11th in the country, and tied UCLA 10-10 in the Fiesta Bowl. His outstanding performances were recognized and Kolenda was a unanimous selection to the All-Southwest Conference team and was further honored by being chosen All-America. The 1979 campaign was another winning one for the Razorbacks as they finished with a 10-2-0 record, were co-champions of the Southwest Conference, and ranked number eight nationally. By this time, there was no doubt that Kolenda was one of the best offensive linemen in America. At 6-1, 258 pounds, Greg was the strongest player on the team and usually played his best in big games. He was a dominating blocker who started every game during the 1978 and 1979 seasons. Kolenda was a unanimous All-Southwest Conference selection at right tackle, and a unanimous choice All-America offensive tackle at the conclusion of the 1979 year. He was chosen to play in the Hula and Senior Bowls in 1980. Greg was selected to the University of Arkansas Decade Team for the 1970 through 1979 seasons as an offensive tackle.

Greg Skrepenak—Michigan—Off. Tackle—1991

An outstanding athlete at G.A.R. Memorial High School in Wilkes Barre, Pennsylvania, Greg Skrepenak won four varsity letters in football, basketball and baseball. He began starring on the high school varsity football squad at age 13. Greg was everyone's first team All-America selection and the Player-of-the-Year for Pennsylvania. He was also the finalist for the Columbus

Touchdown Club Player-of-the-Year award. Skrepenak was an All-America selection in basketball, and was named the league's Most Valuable Player. He was also an all-league player in baseball. On top of that, Greg was an honor student and a member of the National Honor Society. In his first year of action at Michigan in 1988, Skrepenak took over the strong tackle position and earned honorable mention All-Big Ten Conference honors. He started all 12 games and was named Offensive Hustler for the Northwestern game. In 1989, Greg started again at strong tackle in all 12 games and received Offensive Hustler of the Week honors. He was a second team AP and UPI All-Big Ten Conference honoree. Skrepenak kept improving with each year, and in 1990 he was named Co-Most Valuable Player of the Gator Bowl with his teammates on the offensive line, and named Offensive Champ for the UCLA game. He was selected first team All-Big Ten Conference by coaches and the media. He was also chosen first team All-America. Greg was one of the nation's outstanding linemen during the 1991 season. He was everyone's choice first team All-Big Ten Conference selection and named unanimous All-America offensive tackle. He was also a candidate for the Outland Trophy and the Vince Lombardi Award. Skrepenak was the biggest player to ever put on a University of Michigan uniform at 6-8, 322 pounds. He was the Los Angeles Raiders second round draft choice in 1992, and one of only three rookies to make the roster of the Raiders. Greg was a starting guard in 1995.

Steve Okoniewski—Montana—Off. Guard—1971

A native of South Kitsap, Washington, Steve Okoniewski came to the University of Montana in 1968 and developed into one of the greatest players in Grizzlies football history. At 6-5, 260 pounds, Okoniewski was an intelligent player who had great speed, quickness, and tremendous instincts—the perfect qualifications for an offensive lineman. He played both guard and tackle positions with equal ability. Okoniewski's honors attest to the greatness he achieved on the Montana gridiron. He was selected as the University of Montana Most Valuable Player in 1971 and was elected co-captain of the football team that year. Steve was All-Big Sky Conference first team selection in 1970 and repeated in 1971. Associated Press chose Okoniewski All-American offensive guard for 1970 and 1971, and he was also chosen first team All-America by the American Football Coaches Association in 1971. He received the Weskamp Award in 1971 for being Montana's Outstanding Offensive Lineman, and the Grizzly Cup award in 1972 which is presented annually to the University of Montana Top Student Athlete in recognition of excellent athletic and academic achievements. Steve was chosen to the College All-Star team in 1972 and played guard on the starting offensive line. Walt Patulski of Notre Dame was on the same team as defensive end. Okoniewski also played in the Senior Bowl and was selected the Most Valuable Player in the game. In addition, Steve played in the Coaches All-America game in 1972. He was Atlanta Falcon's second round NFL draft choice and had an outstanding eight year professional football career. After retiring from pro ball, Steve became a school teacher, and as of 1994, he was the Principal of Luxemburg-Casco High School in Luxemburg, Wisconsin. Okoniewski was selected to the Big-Sky Conference 25-year Silver Anniversary football team in 1989, and is a member of the University of Montana Football Hall of Fame.

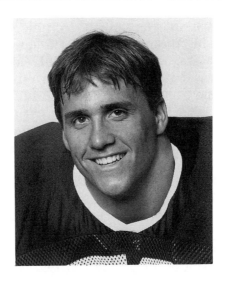

Steve Wisniewski—Pennsylvania State—Off. Guard—1988

Steve Wisniewski was born in Rutland, Vermont, but hails from Houston, Texas where he was a two-way lineman, guard on offense and tackle on defense at Westfield High School. Steve was an All-District and All-Greater Houston selection. He played in the 1985 Texas All-Star game for the victorious North team. In 1985, Wisniewski at 6-4, 260 pounds was a backup offensive guard as a freshman at Penn State and was the only freshman lineman to record any significant playing time. The Nittany Lions, under head coach Joe Paterno, had a 11-1-0 record, were ranked third nationally, but lost to Oklahoma in the Orange Bowl. A substitute at the start of the 1986 season, Wisniewski became a starter and played in nine games and the Fiesta Bowl. Penn State was ranked No. 1 with a 12-0-0 record and beat Miami in the Fiesta Bowl. A starting guard in 1987, Steve logged more time than any other player, participating in 789 offensive plays. Wisniewski was particularly impressive in the final regular season game against Notre Dame. Penn State had another winning record but lost to Clemson in the Citrus Bowl. Steve was a three year Nittany Lions' offensive starter from 1986 through 1988. He was selected All-America offensive guard in 1987 and repeated as a first team All-America in 1988. Wisniewski is only the third

Penn State offensive lineman to win two-time All-America honors. He was also the co-captain of the 1988 squad. He capped his senior year by playing in the East-West Hula Bowl and the Japan Bowl college football all-star games. Steve graduated as a marketing major in the College of Business Administration. He was selected by the Dallas Cowboys as their first round pick in the 1989 NFL draft, but was immediately traded to the Los Angeles Raiders. Wisniewski has proven to be an outstanding pro offensive guard and was selected to the first team NFL All-Pro squad in only his second year with the Raiders. He is considered to be the best pure blocker by the Raiders and is one of the most powerful guards in pro football. He made the All-Rookie team in 1989 and was the youngest man on the Raider roster at age 22. He was chosen first team AFC Pro Bowl guard in 1991. Steve was named Pro Bowl starter for the AFC in 1992, 1993 and 1994. He was selected to the Raiders All-Time Team as an offensive guard in 1995.

His older brother, Leo, was a tackle at Penn State in 1981 and a pro with the Balimore Colts.

Thomas Brzoza—Pittsburgh—Center—1977

A native of New Castle, Pennsylvania, Thomas Brzoza came to the University of Pittsburgh in 1974 to play under the legendary head coach Johnny Majors. Brzoza became a starter on the varsity football team in the fourth game of his freshman year and held a starting position for the rest of his career at Pittsburgh. He began as an offensive guard in 1974 when the Panthers finished the season with a 7-4-0 mark. Brzoza remained an offensive guard through the 1975 campaign which saw Pitt end with a 8-4-0 record and a 15th ranking nationally. The 1976 season proved to be an excellent one for Brzoza and Pittsburgh. Tom's fantastic offensive line plays were evident when he made the move from guard to center and he was rewarded by being selected an All-America center. The Panthers finished with an undefeated, untied record of 11-0-0 and were unanimous national champions. Brzoza was selected as an Outstanding Player on the 1976 Panther championship squad. Pittsburgh also defeated Georgia in the Sugar

Bowl, 27-3, to preserve their perfect record. At 6-3, 240 pounds, Tom was a good player with great speed and quickness and he provided the spark for the offensive line. Brzoza was one of the team captains during the 1977 campaign. The Panthers finished with a 9-2-1 record including a Gator Bowl victory over Clemson. They were ranked eighth in the country and Brzoza was selected consensus first team All-America center. He was chosen to play on the Japan Bowl and the Hula Bowl All-Star teams in 1978. Tom was an early round NFL draft choice of the Pittsburgh Steelers in 1978.

Steve Bartkowski—California—Quarterback—1974

Born in Des Moines, Iowa, Steve Bartkowski attended high school in Santa Clara, California where he won four letters each in football, baseball and basketball. Steve passed for 3,105 yards and 36 touchdowns in his junior and senior years at Buchser High, captained the football team in his senior year and was chosen first team All-Northern California. He was deluged with over 100 football scholarship offers from colleges and universities. In addition, the Kansas City Royals chose Steve in their 1971 baseball draft and pressured him to pursue a baseball career rather than play college football. Bartkowski decided to enroll at the University of California where his scholarship would allow him to play both football and baseball. Steve had an excellent football season as a freshman quarterback and broke virtually all frosh football passing and scoring records. As a sophomore, he was California's starter initially and passed for 260 yards in his debut against Colorado. He ended the 1972 campaign with 944 passing yards and four touchdowns after splitting the quarter backing with another player. The Golden Bears finished with a dismal 3-8-0 record. Also as a sophomore, Bartkowski set the University of California season and career records for home runs, batted .344 in Pac-8 play, and earned All-Conference, All-District 8 and second team All-America honors in baseball. Steve decided to concentrate on college football as a junior in 1973. He became a more accurate passer, but shared the quarterback duties again and finished with a disappointing 910 yards and eight touchdowns. The team ended with a losing 4-7-0 record, but Steve resolved to win the starting quarterback position for the 1974 season. He passed up baseball that spring to give football his best effort. He became the starting quarterback to begin the 1974 campaign and no one could challenge him for that position. After leading California to a victory over Washington State, Steve was named College Football Offensive Player of the Week. He led the Golden Bears to their best winning season in years with a 7-3-0 mark. Steve had four 300 yard passing games during the campaign and set several California and Pac-8 records. He became the Major College Champion in Passing for 1974, leading the nation with 182 completions for a total of 2,580 yards and 12 touchdowns. He was selected consensus first team All-America, the college quarterback of 1974. Bartkowski was also named first team All-Pacific 8 Conference, University of California's Most Valuable Player and a Heisman Trophy candidate. He played on the College Football All-Star team in 1975 as the starting quarterback and was a first round NFL draft choice of the Atlanta Falcons. Steve had a fantastic professional football career with the Falcons and set club records with 23,468 passing yards and 154 touchdowns. He led Atlanta to the NFC Western Division crown in 1980, passed for a club record of 3,830 yards in 1981 and took the league passing title in 1983 with 3,167 yards. In 1984, Steve was rated the third most accurate in league history. After 11 years of pro ball, Steve became a successful business man. In 1993, Bartkowski was inducted into the National Polish-American Sports Hall of Fame.

Eugene Filipski—Villanova—Running Back—1953

Eugene Filipski played two years of varsity football in 1952 and 1953 as a half-back at Villanova University after playing two years and lettering one year at Army. The Wildcat records he set still stand as a tribute to his fantastic running ability on the gridiron. Filipski had four 100 yard or better rushing performances with 191 yards against Detroit in 1952, 170 yards against Fordham in 1953, 117 yards against Boston College in 1952 and 112 yards against Kentucky in 1952. Gene was the Villanova rushing leader in 1952 with 889 yards and seven touchdowns and in 1953 with 705 yards and six touchdowns. His career best rushing total yards of 1,594 is still one of the best top totals achieved at Villanova. He was the Wildcats' scoring leader with 42 points in 1953. The records for individual highest rushing yards per game of 98.8 per season (1952), and 83.9 for career (1952 and 1953) established by Filipski are still the best at Villanova. In 1952, the Wildcats compiled an excellent 7-1-1 record under head coach Arthur Raimo, losing only to Tulsa and tieing the Parris Island Marines. They beat Kentucky, Clemson, Detroit, Wake Forest, Boston College, Xavier and Boston University. Filipski was honored for his terrific performances game after game by being selected consensus first team All-America for the 1952 season. Villanova had a losing 4-6-0 season in 1953, which could explain why Filipski was named only as an honorable mention All-America. His game performances were still outstanding as attested by his being the Wildcat scoring leader for the year. Despite playing only two years, Filipski ranks sixth overall in career rushing yards gained by a Wildcat back. He was chosen to play in the College All-Star and the East-West Shrine games. The Cleveland Browns picked Gene as their draft choice in 1953, but he had to fulfill his military obligations by a tour of duty in the service. After his discharge, Filipski played pro football with the New York Giants in 1956 and 1957, and the Hamilton (Canadian) Tiger-Cats from 1958 through 1961. Filipski was selected to the "Wildcat 100" in 1993 which consists of the 100 most important football players and coaches in the Wildcat Century. Gene was in the outdooor advertising business in Calgary, Alberta (Canada) in 1993.

Steve Juzwik—Notre Dame—Halfback—1941

One of the most versatile football players to perform at the University of Notre Dame, Steve Juzwik began his college career as a reserve right halfback on the 1939 squad which was coached by Elmer Layden. (Layden was one of the immortalized Four Horsemen of Notre Dame). The 1939 season ended with Notre Dame sporting an excellent record of 7-2-0 which qualified them to be ranked 13th in the nation. At 5-9, 185 pounds, Juzwik contributed greatly with good runs from scrimmage, excellent punt returns, and timely pass and run stops from his defensive halfback position. Steve took over the starting right halfback spot at the beginning of the 1940 campaign and kept it for the remainder of his college football career. He had an outstanding year which was highlighted by his 85-yard pass interception run against Army leading to a 7-0 Notre Dame victory. The 1940 team allowed their opponents the fewest touchdown passes for the season with Juzwik's defensive performance being one of the primary reasons for the Irish record. Steve also excelled on the offense by leading the team in rushing with 71 runs for 407 yards, and in scoring with seven touchdowns and one extra point kick for a total of 43 points. The 1940 campaign ended with a winning 7-2-0 record, and Juzwik was named an All-America halfback by United Press. Layden resigned as Notre Dame's coach to become the commissioner of the National Football League and was replaced by the legendary Frank Leahy. Juzwik was only one of two experienced backfield starters returning to begin the 1941 season. Leahy and Layden differed widely in their coaching methods which caused the players coached by Layden to make great adjustments to satisfy Leahy. Steve made the transition successfully and was the starting right halfback at the beginning of the '41 campaign. He was the outstanding back in the Georgia Tech game by scoring two touchdowns, one on a 67-yard reverse play. Steve scored twice against Illinois on a 12-yard run and a 13-yard pass reception. He kicked the winning point against Northwestern as Notre Dame won 7-6. Wally Ziemba blocked Northwestern's game-tying kick. Steve used his deceptive speed, strong, shifty running and good hands to lead the team in punt returns with 22 for 280 yards (average 12.7 yards per return), and in pass receiving with 18 catches for 307 yards and two touchdowns. The 1941 season ended for Notre Dame and introduced the Leahy era with an undefeated 8-0-1 record (marred only by a 0-0 tie with Army). The team was ranked third in the nation. Juzwik's contributions were recognized and he was chosen first team All-America halfback by *Football News*, and second team All-America by Jim Crowley and Hearst (International News Service). Steve was chosen to play in the East-West Shrine Classic in 1942 and was named the starting halfback in the 1942 College All-Star game versus the Chicago Bears. One of the highlights of the All-Star game was Juzwik's 91-yard run from scrimmage. He was drafted by Washington and played one year of professional football. After returning from service, Steve also played with Buffalo in 1946 and 1947, and with the Chicago Rockets in 1948.

Edward Modzelewski—Maryland—Running Back—1951

A native of West Natrona, Pennsylvania, Ed Modzelewski enrolled at the University of Maryland in 1948 to become one of the most powerful running fullbacks in Terrapin football history. One of his younger brothers, Dick, followed Ed to Maryland and became a College Hall of Fame tackle. Eugene, the youngest Modzelewski, was an excellent tackle at New Mexico State University. Ed was called "Big Mo" because he was the oldest, but the name was changed to "Mighty Mo" after the mighty battleship *Missouri*, when he displayed his fantastic, powerful running ability. Modzelewski started his varsity career as a halfback during the 1949 season which saw Maryland record and excellent 8-1-0 mark. They were ranked 16th in the country and beat

Missouri in the Gator Bowl to finish 9-1-0 under head coach Jim Tatum. Ed contributed greatly to this winning Terrapin season. In 1950, Modzelewski, still playing at halfback, really began to show what he was capable of accomplishing. In the Duke game, he missed out-gaining the entire Blue Devil team output by two yards, and missed the same feat by four yards in the North Carolina State game. Ed picked up 95 yards against Duke and 124 versus the Wolf pack. For the season, he picked up 553 yards in 119 carries for an average of 4.6 yards per carry. He caught eight passes for 110 yards and passed 12 times for 83 yards. Ed returned five kick-offs for 81 yards and scored 30 points. He missed two games because of injuries, but was selected to the All-Conference team and received All-America honorable mention. At the start of the 1951 campaign, Ed was moved to fullback to give the Terps that bull-dozing power lunge that was his specialty. At 6-0, 210 pounds, he was a big, strong, powerful runner and a terrific blocker. In the final spring practice game, Ed picked up 138 yards in 13 carries for an average of 10.6 yards per carry. He continued performing like that throughout the season and Maryland finished unbeaten, untied with a 9-0-0 record and received an invitation to the Sugar Bowl. Modzelewski was selected the Most Valuable Player in the bowl game with Tennessee by leading the Terps to a 28-13 victory. He went on to receive first team All-Conference honors and was chosen consensus All-America. Ed played as starting fullback in the College All-Star game and was the Pittsburgh Steelers No. 1 draft pick. He played professional football for eight years and lives in West Sedona, Arizona.

Robert Brudzinski—Ohio State—Defensive End—1976

A native of Fremont, Ohio, Robert Brudzinski was a four year letter winner and a two year starter at defensive end at Ohio State University under head coach Woody Hayes. In his freshman year, the Buckeyes began one of the most successful campaigns in the Woody Hayes era. They were the Big Ten Conference co-champions with a 10-0-1 record, ranked second nationally, and beat The University of Southern California in the Rose Bowl, 42-21. In 1974,

Ohio State was the Big Ten co-champion again with a 10-2-0 mark, ranked fourth in the country, and their only losses were to Michigan State in the regular season and to USC in the Rose Bowl. At 6-4, 228 pounds, Brudzinski contributed greatly in the Buckeye 1975 season which saw them in sole possession of the Big Ten championship. He had a total of 69 tackles with four for loss of 17 yards and recovered two fumbles. They were ranked fourth in the nation, and their only loss to UCLA in the Rose Bowl gave them a final record of 11-1-0 for the year. Brudzinski enjoyed an outstanding senior campaign, finishing third on the team with 70 unassisted and 56 assisted tackles for a combined total of 126 tackles. He also had 10 tackles for losses of 40 yards and tied for team lead in interceptions with four. In 1976, the Buckeyes were Big Ten co-champions, ranked sixth nationally with a 9-2-1 slate, and beat Colorado in the Orange Bowl. Robert's college career 209 tackles, which consisted of 117 solos and 92 assists, rank among the best in Ohio State football history. Brudzinski was a steady player who missed only four games during his Buckeye career. He played in 36 consecutive games in his final three seasons. In his four years, Ohio State finished with an outstanding, combined record of 40-5-2. Robert was an All-Big Ten Conference first team choice in 1975 and 1976, and Ohio State's Most Valuable Player in 1976. He was named honorable mention All-America in 1975 and consensus All-America defensive end in 1976. He was the Los Angeles Rams number one draft choice in 1977 and played four years with the Rams and five years with the Miami Dolphins.

Marvin Matuszak—Tulsa—Defensive End—1952

Marvin Matuszak was an outstanding athlete and football player at Washington High School in South Bend, Indiana. He went on to achieve greatness at the college and professional levels in football. Matuszak enrolled at the University of Tulsa in 1949 and showed early signs of becoming a great lineman. In 1950, Tulsa had an excellent 9-1-1 season under head coach J.O. Brothers and was ranked 19th in the nation due in some part to the line play of Matuszak. He was honored by being selected to the All-Missouri Valley Conference team. Another winning year followed in 1951 and there was little doubt that Tulsa's success was due to a great extent to Matuszak's stellar performances. His contributions were recognized on the national level and he was named All-America. He also repeated on the All-Missouri Valley Conference team. The 1952 season was very successful with Tulsa going 8-1-1 in regular play under coach Brothers and they were ranked 12th in the country. They lost to Florida in the Gator Bowl by a score of 14-13. Matuszak was captain of the Gator Bowl Tulsa squad and was selected the Most Valuable Player. In addition, Marvin was again named to the All-Missouri Valley Conference team and repeated as an All-America selection. Thus Matuszak became the first Golden Hurricane player to earn All-America honors for two consecutive years. He was chosen to play in the

College All-Star game in 1953. Marvin was the Pittsburgh Steelers third round draft choice and his professional career spanned from 1953 to 1964. He switched to linebacker and played with Pittsburgh, Buffalo and San Francisco. During that time, he was selected to the Pro Bowl three times. He also coached in the NFL for 13 years. Matuszak was inducted into the University of Tulsa Athletic Hall of Fame in 1983. Considered as possibly the top lineman in Tulsa's football history, Marvin's number 14 jersey has been retired. Being from South Bend, he was inducted into the Indiana (State) Football Hall of Fame in 1987. After retiring from pro ball, Matuszak was a building contractor and developer in Marietta, Georgia.

Raymond Frankowski—Washington—Def. Tackle—1941

Raymond Frankowski came to Seattle and the University of Washington from Hammond, Indiana in 1938, and became one of the greatest offensive and defensive linemen in the Huskies' college football history. He was a very gifted and versatile athlete who participated and excelled in three sports—football, wrestling and fencing. A three-year letter winner in football, Frankowski earned his first one during the 1939 season which saw Washington finish with a 5-4-0 record. He also won his first emblems in wrestling and fencing. In 1940, Washington, under head coach James Phelan, ended an excellent season with a 7-2-0 mark and was ranked 10th in the nation and second in the Pacific Coast Conference (now the Pacific-10 Conference). Frankowski contributed greatly to the success of the team, and his efforts were recognized and rewarded. He concluded the 1940 campaign by making every All-Opponent team. He was also selected first team All-Pacific Coast Conference and named first team All-America. Rudy Mucha, the Polish American All-America Husky center from Chicago, Illinois played with Frankowski on the 1939 and 1940 squads. The Huskies had another winning year in 1941 and were tied for second place in the conference. Raymond was selected Player of the Year at the University of Washington in 1940 and 1941. He was chosen consensus first team All-America in 1941, making him only the second Husky to be chosen an

All-American for two consecutive years. Frankowski also won the Pacific Coast Conference heavy-weight wrestling title and had a good year on the fencing team. He received his degree in General Studies in 1942 and was selected to play with the College All-Stars and in the East-West Shrine game. He was a second round draft pick of the Green Bay Packers and played five years of professional football with Green Bay and the Los Angeles Dons. As a distinguished two-time All-America football player and a wrestling title holder, Frankowski was inducted into the University of Washington Athletic Hall of Fame in 1986. The University of Washington inaugurated a Hall of Fame in 1979 to "honor and preserve the memory of those athletes, teams, coaches and members of the athletic staff who have contributed in a very outstanding and positive way to the promotion of the University of Washington athletic program." As of 1986, Raymond was the President/Executive Administrator for Teamsters Union 986 and lived in Diamond Bar, California.

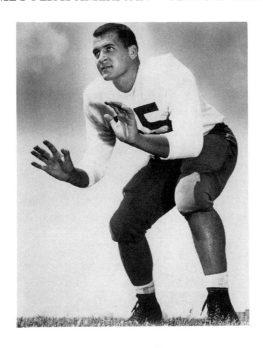

Johnny Guzik—Pittsburgh—Def. Tackle—1958

An outstanding scholar and athlete from Lawrence, Pennsylvania, Johnny Guzik enrolled at the University of Pittsburgh in 1955 and was a most welcome addition to the Panthers football team under the guidance of head coach John Michelosen. Coach Michelosen's prayers were answered in Guzik. He got not only a terrific football lineman but also an excellent scholar. In 1955, Pittsburgh had a good winning season with a 7-4-0 record and received the Lambert-Meadowlands Trophy awarded annually to the top Eastern Division I collegiate football team. Guzik began to show his offensive and defensive playing ability as a lineman on the 1956 squad. At 6-3, 223 pounds, John developed into a good blocker on offense and had excellent instincts on defense in stopping running attacks at or near his position. The Panthers finished the season with a 7-3-1 mark. The 1957 campaign proved to be a good one for Guzik but Pittsburgh finished on a losing note with a 4-6-0 record. Johnny became known as the "Bull" for the way he would hit the opponents on the field. He was named to the All-East team and received All-America honors. In 1958,

Guzik attracted more national media attention with his outstanding line play, and was honored by being selected consensus first team All-America. He was the only Panther to play over 400 minutes, averaging 42 minutes per game. That took a great deal of stamina and strength. Guzik was also chosen to the first team Academic All-America at the end of the season. He played in the 1958 East-West Shrine game and the 1959 College All-Star and Hula Bowl games. He was on the same team in the College All-Star game with Gene Selawski, the All-America tackle from Purdue. Johnny was a fourth round draft choice of the Los Angeles Rams and played professional football for two years with the Rams and one year with the Houston Oilers.

Frank Piekarski—Pennsylvania—Nose Guard—1904

The first college football player of Polish ancestry to be selected a first team All-America was Frank A. Piekarski, a four year letter winner at the University of Pennsylvania from 1901 through 1904. During the 1903 and 1904 seasons, the University of Pennsylvania front line was a collection of hard, tough and well-conditioned players which included Piekarski at guard and Tom Butkiewicz at tackle. Piekarski was Walter Camp's third team All-American in 1903, and consensus first team All-America selection in 1904. Butkiewicz was chosen third team All-American by Camp in 1904. The two Polish Americans were instrumental in leading the Quakers to an undefeated, untied season of 12-0-0 in 1904 and the national championship. Pennsylvania shut out eleven of their opponents and outscored all opposition 222 to 4—the only score was a field goal by Swarthmore which counted for four points in 1904. Piekarski was the only Pennsylvania lineman chosen first team All-America from the 1904 national championship squad. During his football career at Penn, the Quakers had a winning season each year and compiled an excellent four year record of 40-12-0. (Pennsylvania played 52 games during that four year period).

Stas Maliszewski—Princeton—Linebacker—1965

At 6-1, 215 pounds, Stas Maliszewski came from Davenport, Iowa to become one of Princeton University's leading gridiron greats in the modern college football era. Maliszewski was a three-year letter winner as an offensive guard and defensive linebacker on Princeton's football team from 1963 to 1965. The Tigers posted a 24-3 record in Maliszewski's three varsity seasons. In 1963, Princeton was upset by Dartmouth, 22-21, to share the Ivy League title with a 5-2 conference record. In 1964, the Tigers finished with their first undefeated season since 1951 and won the Ivy League championship with a 7-0 mark. They were ranked 13th in the country with a 9-0-0 overall record under head coach Dick Colman. Maliszewski was selected first team All-Ivy League linebacker in both 1964 and 1965, named All-East linebacker in 1964 and first team All-America in 1964. Stas was a consensus first team All-America selection at offensive guard in 1965 and awarded the Poe Memorial Trophy as Princeton's Most Valuable Player. He also received the Hooker Cup as the most valuable freshman wrestler and exhibited his athletic versatility by participating in rugby and lacrosse. Maliszewski graduated from Princeton with an A.B. degree in Philosophy. As an undergraduate, Stas was Director of the Princeton University Fund and Chairman of the University Lecture Series. He served as an assistant football coach at the Gillman School in Baltimore, Maryland under head coach Red Finney from 1966 to 1967. Maliszewski received his Master of Business Administration degree from Harvard University in 1970. Coaches, writers and sportscasters closely associated with Ivy League football during the first 17 years of formal league competition (1956-1972), picked an All-Time conference team in 1973. Selected to this All-Time team was the Princeton gridirom great, Stas Maliszewski. Selected with him was Chuck Matuszak, a 1967 grad of Dartmouth College, as the second team offensive center. In 1981, Maliszewski was named to the Ivy League Silver Anniversary All-Star football team. Stas has made a career in the field of Real Estate Investment Management. He is currently the Managing Director with the firm of Jones Lang Wootton Realty Advisors in New York City. Maliszewski serves on the National Board of Directors of the Pension Real Estate Association and is a member of the Princeton University Schools Committee in Chicago of which he was a former chairman. He is a member of the Board of the Princeton

Club in Chicago, and was the Princeton University Silver Anniversary Top Six Award Nominee in 1990.

Bill Romanowski—Boston College—Linebacker—1987

Considered by many to be the greatest linebacker ever to play at Boston College, Bill Romanowski was an All-Conference, All-State and All-America honorable mention football star at Rockville High School in Vernon, Connecticut. He was also named Greater Hartford Player of the Year as a senior. Bill was an excellent athlete, a two-year starter on the Rockville basketball team and a stand-out catcher in baseball. Romanowski enrolled at Boston College in 1984, and broke into the starting lineup in the seventh game against Penn State when he made 13 tackles. He followed that with 16 tackles versus Army, and interceptions in consecutive victories over Syracuse and Miami. Bill was a versatile athlete and filled in as fullback when the starter was injured. In only four starts as a freshman, Romanowski finished the regular season with 59 tackles (40 solo), two interceptions, one fumble recovery and two quarterback sacks. On top of that, he earned Defensive Most Valuable Player honors in the 1985 Cotton Bowl after registering 13 tackles (11 solo) in the Eagles' win over Houston. In 1985, Bill was the team leader with 150 tackles (94 solo) despite missing the Penn State game. He was outstanding with 20 tackles against Maryland, 18 against Pittsburgh, and season-high 22 versus West Virginia. He had his third career interception against Rutgers, and a quarterback sack and two fumble recoveries during the season. Romanowski earned All-East Coast Athletic Conference, Associated Press All-East and *Football News* All-Sophomore recognition at the end of the '85 campaign. Bill received All-America honorable mention honors for his junior season during which he had 123 tackles, four interceptions, 2.5 QB sacks, and two fumble recoveries. He had a season-high 19 tackles in the Hall of Fame Bowl with Georgia. He was also named to the All-New England, All-ECAC and Associated Press All-East teams for his performance during the 1986 season. At 6-3, 227 pounds, Bill had a spectacular 1987 season with a team and career high of 156 tackes (101 solo), two interceptions, one fumble cause, one QB sack and one tackle for loss. He earned All-New England, All-ECAC and All-East honors again and was selected All-America linebacker. Bill was also named an NCAA Scholarship winner during the 1987 campaign. Romanowski was a Butkus Award Finalist for the prize presented annually to the nation's most outstanding linebacker in college football. He received his General Management degree from Boston College in 1988, and was the San Francisco 49ers third round NFL draft choice. Bill was with the 49ers for six years and traded to the Philadelphia Eagles before the 1994 season. He was considered by many pro experts to be a top linebacker and was a starter for the Eagles in 1995.

Frank Rydzewski—Notre Dame—Linebacker—1917

The outstanding Polish American college football player in the 1910s was Frank X. Rydzewski, a three year letter winner at center for the University of Notre Dame in 1915, 1916 and 1917 under head coach Jesse Harper. At 6-1, 214 pounds, Frank was the starting center during the 1916 and 1917 campaigns. Rydzewski was selected an All-American in 1916, and chosen consensus first team All-America center after the 1917 season. (1917 was George "the Gipper" Gipp's first varsity season with Notre Dame). During his three year varsity career, Notre Dame compiled an excellent 23-3-1 record and outscored their opponents by an almost unbelievable 600 points, 664 to 68. Frank played professional football from 1920 through 1926 in the greater Chicago area. In 1939, Rydzewski was the state commander of the Illinois branch of the Polish Legion of American veterans. His greatness as a college football player was best illustrated in his selection by national sportswriters and sportscasters to the University of Notre Dame All-Time Team as a Defensive Lineman.

Edward Danowski—Fordham—Def. Back—1933

Edward Danowski saw the beginning of the golden era of Fordham University football emerge in 1932 under head coach Frank Cavanaugh, "the Iron Major," and continue onward and upward in 1933 under the guidance of head coach "Sleepy" Jim Crowley, one of the famed "Four Horsemen of Notre Dame." Danowski was a real triple-threat halfback who proved himself an excellent passer, runner and punter during his college career. In the 1932 campaign, Fordham finished with a winning 6-2-0 record, losing only to Michigan State and Boston College. Ed was elected captain of the 1933 squad which also had a winning 6-2-0 mark. The most memorable game of the 1933 campaign was a hard fought defensive battle which saw highly favored Alabama lose to the Rams by a score of 2-0, coming as a result of a blocked Alabama punt. Danowski distinguished himself during the entire season with his excellent passing, running, punting and defensive play. He won the Madow Trophy as the Most Valuable Player in the 1933 annual Fordham University-New York University classic. Danowski also became the first player in Fordham University football history to earn All-America honors in consecutive years, 1932 and 1933. Ed was selected to play in the East-West Shrine game in 1934. He went on to gain further fame as the professional quarterback who led the New York Giants to four NFL title games. On the strength of his efforts, the Giants won two chamionships.

He led the league in passing in 1935 and 1939 and was selected to the Pro Bowl in 1939. After coaching football briefly at Haverstraw High School in New York, he enlisted in the Navy. When Fordham resumed football after World War II, the head coaching job went to Danowski. Vince Lombardi, one of the famed Seven Blocks of Granite at Fordham, became one of his assistant coaches in 1947. Lombardi, who dreamed of becoming head coach at Fordham, was involved in a plot to oust Danowski and replace him. The plot failed, and Lombardi left Fordham to work as an assistant coach at Army under the legendary Earl "Red" Blaik. Danowski remained as Fordham's head coach until 1955 at which time the Rams dropped football until 1964. He was inducted into Fordham University's Sports Hall of Fame as a player and coach in 1970. In 1991, Fordham initiated the Edward F. Danowski Award. The award is presented annually to the senior football player who through his leadership, sacrifice and committment to excellence upon the field and within the University community, exemplifies the character of Danowski, a former player and head coach. The inscription on the front of the trophy reads: In honor of a son of Fordham, in recognition of his many significant contributions to the University as one of its greatest student-athletes and most-loved teachers whose love of the Lord, family and community exemplifies in the truest sense the fulfillment of self. Fulfillment done with grace, patience and courage; quietly with humor and humility.

Frank Dancewicz—Notre Dame—Def. Back—1945

Frank Dancewicz starred as a quarterback at Lynn Classical High School in Lynn, Massachusetts and led his team to state championships in 1940 and 1941, and the New England championship in 1941. He was named the top high school football player by the Eastern Massachusetts Sportswriters Association in 1940. The same year, Dancewicz was the unanimous choice for New England Interscholastic Football honors. Frank entered Notre Dame University in 1942, and was the starting quarterback in 1943 under head coach Frank Leahy. At 5-10, 180 pounds, Dancewicz was one of the fastest players on a Leahy coached team. Notre Dame finished the season with an excellent 9-1-0 record and was selected unanimous National Champions. Frank Leahy left Notre Dame to serve in the Navy in 1944 and Ed McKeever took over as head coach. Dancewicz and McKeever surprised the football world by going 8-2-0 during the 1944 campaign and were ranked number eight nationally. McKeever's coaching was so impressive that Cornell University offered him the head coaching job, and he left Notre Dame. Hugh Devore coached during the 1945 season and Dancewicz played excellent ball. He was outstanding in the Notre Dame victories over Illinois and Georgia Tech. He was not a flashy quarterback but an extremely intelligent, reliable, consistent player who got the job done game after game. He was a good leader on the field. Dancewicz was elected captain of the 1945 squad which finished with another winning 7-2-1 mark and was rated number nine in the nation. Frank was named first team All-America and finished sixth in the voting for the Heisman Trophy following the 1945 season. The Boston Yanks chose Dancewicz as their number one draft choice in 1946 and he played professional football with the Yanks for three years. In 1950, Frank was head coach at Salem High School and later served as an assistant coach at Lafayette College and then Boston University. He worked as a supervisor of physical education for the Lynn, Massachusetts school system at the time of his death at age 60 in July, 1985. Dancewicz was a member and supporter of many Polish American clubs such as the Polish National Alliance fraternal organization.

Walter Matuszczak—Cornell—Def. Back—1940

A graduate of Lowville Academy, Lowville, New York in 1936, Walter Matuszczak was captain of the football, baseball and basketball teams at the Academy. Matuszczak was a big offensive and defensive back at Cornell University for three years on the highly successful football teams of 1938, 1939 and 1940. Over the three years he was on the team, the Big Red compiled a record of 19-3-1, going 5-1-1 in 1938, 8-0 in 1939 and 6-2 in 1940. The 1939 team received the Lambert Trophy, one of the oldest and historically rich prizes in all of collegiate athletics awarded to recognize supremacy in Eastern football. Cornell finished the season as the number four team in the nation. In 1939, Matuszczak was an Associated Press All-America honorable mention selection, and was named to the New York Sun All-America team and the All-America Board of Football squad. In 1940, he was named first team All-Eastern and selected first team All-America. He was one of ten players receiving votes in the annual poll awarding the Heisman Trophy (won by Tom Harmon of Michigan that year). Matuszczak captained the 1940 Cornell football team. Walter was a tremendous blocking back, a first rate signal caller and an excellent defensive back. He played in the North-South All-Star game (co-captained the North squad) and also played in the Eastern College All-Star game against the New York Giants. He was the New York Giants sixth choice in the annual draft of college football players. Walter also excelled in baseball at Cornell playing as a right fielder in 1939 and 1941. He was one of the top hitters on the squad both years. The 1939 baseball team tied for the Eastern Intercollegiate League title, and the 1941 team finished second in the league. Matuszczak changed his name to Matuszak after graduating from Cornell University. Dr. Walter Matuszak graduated from Cornell University's Veterinary College in 1943. His son, Charles "Chuck" Matuszak, was an outstanding scholar and football player at Dartmouth College in the 1960s.

Chris Gardocki—Clemson—K/P—1991

A first team All-America prepster, Chris Gardocki set the Georgia state record for the longest field goal with a 59 yard boot and also played quarterback and defensive back at Redan High School in Stone Mountain, Georgia. He was an All-State soccer player who had 18 goals as a junior. Gardocki came to Clemson University in 1988 and began establishing all sorts of kicking records in his first varsity year with the Tigers. In 1988, he had the second best punting average by a freshman in Clemson football history, set a school record for field goal attempts with 32, was second team All-Atlantic Coast Conference place kicker, and honorable mention All-America as a punter. He finished the

1989 season as third team All-America place kicker, honorable mention All-America as punter, was the AC Conference punting champion with a 42.6 average, set the AC Conference record for kick-scoring in a season with 107 points, and won the AC Conference field goal and punting titles. In 1990, Gardocki was elected the Most Valuable Player on the Clemson squad. He was a first team All-AC Conference choice both as place kicker and punter for the 1989 and 1990 seasons, the first time in Conference history that the same player has been first team in both kicking areas. He averaged a Clemson record 44.48 yards as a punter in 1990, and connected on 22 of 28 field goals. Chris set a Tiger record for consecutive points after touchdown with 72 and 30 for 30 in 1990. Gardocki established seven Clemson records in the 1990 campaign, two in one game, and holds the record for 50-yard field goals in a season with three. He is second in Clemson football history in career kick-scoring and overall scoring with 261 points, and number one on Clemson's career punting list. Chris handled all punting and field goal attempts for the Tigers in the last three bowl games. He was named to the All-Bowl team after he booted three field goals in Clemson's 30-0 win over Illinois in the Hall of Fame Bowl. Gardocki was selected All-America at the completion of the 1990 season. Chris decided to enter the NFL draft with one year eligibility left at Clemson, and joined the Chicago Bears as a punter in 1991. As a free-agent signee from the Chicago Bears, Gardocki received a signing bonus to become the Indianapolis Colts' punter for the 1995 season.

CHAPTER III

ALL-TIME POLISH AMERICAN— THIRD TEAM

OFFENSE

Position	Name	School	Year
End	Troy Sadowski	Georgia	1988
End	Mark Chmura	Boston College	1991
Tackle	Robert Kula	Michigan State	1989
Tackle	Bruce Kozerski	Holy Cross	1983
Guard	Harry Olszewski	Clemson	1967
Guard	Henry Wisniewski	Fordham	1930
Center	Rudy Mucha	Washington	1940
Q.Back	Daniel Marino	Pittsburgh	1982
R.Back	Johnny Olszewski	California	1952
R.Back	Stanley Koslowski	Holy Cross	1945
R.Back	Stanley Kostka	Minnesota	1934
P.Kicker	Rick Ruszkiewicz	Edinboro	1982

DEFENSE

Position	Name	School	Year
End	Harry Jacunski	Fordham	1938
End	Peter Kwiatkowski	Boise State	1987
Tackle	Eugene Selawski	Purdue	1958
Tackle	John Matuszak	Tampa	1972
N.Guard	Jeff Zgonina	Purdue	1992
L.Backer	James Sniadecki	Indiana	1968
L.Backer	Mark Blazejewski	Fordham	1992
L.Backer	Leon Gajecki	Pennsylvania State	1940
D.Back	Steven Filipowicz	Fordham	1941
D.Back	Frank Kirkleski	Lafayette	1926
D.Back	Henry Toczylowski	Boston College	1940
Punter	Raymond Stachowicz	Michigan State	1980

Troy Sadowski—Georgia—Off. End—1988

A native of Chamblee, Georgia, Troy Sadowski came to the University of Georgia in 1984 from Chamblee High School where he was an outstanding football player who was honored as the Dekalb County Player of the Week, All-Dekalb County team end and Most Valuable Receiver on the team. He was red-shirted at Georgia in 1984. During the 1985 season, Sadowski showed surprising efficiency at tight end for a first year player, especially when called to start so early in the campaign. At 6-5, 243 pounds, Troy started seven games for the Bulldogs after a first stringer was lost to injury. He played in 11 games and made eight catches for 118 yards for an average of 14.8 yards per reception. In 1986, he solidified his hold on the number one tight end position during spring drills. Sadowski developed into a fine tight end over the course of the season. He showed the ability to catch the ball in clutch situations and in a crowd, and became a fine blocker. Troy caught 12 passes for 148 yards for an average of 12.3 per reception and scored two touchdowns. During the 1987 campaign, he started every game at tight end and used his size and strength to become an excellent receiver and blocker. His performance earned him first team honors on the All-Southeastern Conference squad. In 1988, Sadowski continued to perform as a great tight end, clutch receiver and a fine blocker. In the 44 games that he played during his college career, Troy caught 38 passes for 458 yards (average of 10.4 yards per reception) and scored five touchdowns. He was chosen All-Southeastern Conference first team member again and was also selected first team All-America. Sadowski was the Atlanta Falcons' sixth round NFL draft choice in 1989, but played with the Kansas City Chiefs as tight end. He was traded to the Cincinnati Bengals in time to start the 1994 season.

Mark Chmura—Boston College—Off. End—1991

Mark Chmura enrolled at Boston College in 1987 after starring as a versatile athlete at Frontier Regional High School in South Deerfield, Massachusetts. He played football under coach Myron Rokoszak and was a two-time Most Valuable Player and All-Western Massachusetts choice. Mark was also a three year selection in basketball, scoring over 1,000 points and grabbing over 1,000 rebounds in his schoolboy career. He still holds the school's 50-meter dash record. Chmura was red-shirted in 1987 at Boston College and was the Eagles' third leading receiver with 27 catches for 377 yards in 1988, his first year of varsity play. During the 1989 season, Mark was the most productive tight end in the nation in terms of pass receiving with 47 catches for a total of 522 yards (11.1 yards per catch average) and two touchdowns. His best day of the year was against Georgia Tech as he caught eight passes for 70 yards. Chmura led all Boston College receivers with 47 catches for 560 yards (an 11.9 average) and three touchdowns in 1990. His 53 yard touchdown reception against Navy was the Eagles' longest scoring play of the season, and Mark's 78-yard non-scoring catch at West Virginia was the Eagles' longest play from scrimmage. He was selected first team All-Big East tight end at the completion of the 1990 campaign. Chmura was a consistent performer, had good speed and size (6-6, 237 pounds) to become one of the best tight ends in college football in 1991. Early in the '91 season, Mark broke the Boston College career receiving record of 139, and then went on to establish a new Eagles' record of 164 catches by the end of the year. Chmura had an outstanding outing with 43 receptions for 587 yards and six touchdowns. He was Boston College's leading receiver and second highest scorer during the '91 campaign. Mark was again selected first team All-Big East Conference tight end by the Conference coaches and *Football News*. He was also named the 1991 Eastern College Athletic Conference, Division 1-A football all-star at tight end. In addition, he was chosen first team All-America by the Football Writers Association and Associated Press. He was chosen to play in the Senior Bowl and was drafted by the Green Bay Packers in 1992. Mark's brother, Matt, played football as tight end at the University of New Hampshire.

Robert Kula—Michigan State—Off. Tackle—1989

Robert Kula had a very successful prep career at Birmingham Brother Rice High School in West Bloomfield, Michigan. He was rated by many as the top offensive lineman in the state his senior year. A consensus All-State, he also won All-America honors. Kula was also a fine track and field performer in high school. Under head coach George Perles at Michigan State University, Robert was red-shirted in 1985 and lettered in 1986 by playing in 10 of 11 games as a substitute. In 1987, he started all 11 games at left guard after winning the position with a fine spring practice performance. Michigan State had a very good season with a 9-2-1 record in 1987. They beat USC in the Rose Bowl, were the Big Ten Conference champions and were ranked number eight in the nation. In 1988, Kula played the first three games at left tackle in place of Tony Mandarich. He was moved back to his normal position of left guard against Iowa. He got All-Big Ten Conference honors and was an honorable mention All-America. He also shared the Spartans' Outstanding Underclass Lineman Award with a teammate. Michigan State had a winning season again in 1988 but lost to Georgia in the Gator Bowl. At the start of the 1989 season, Kula moved from left guard to left tackle to replace All-American Tony Mandarich. He was voted a tri-captain by his teammates. Kula anchored the young offensive line and provided the leadership to make it into one of the finest units in the Big Ten. He was selected to the All-Big Ten Conference team and was named consensus first team All-America. The honors were unexpected because Kula was playing his first year at left tackle after three years at guard. In addition, Robert at 6-4½, 282 pounds, was given the Iron Man Award for strength and conditioning as well as the Up Front Award for the outstanding interior offensive lineman. At the end of the 1989 campaign, the Spartans were rated 16th in the nation and beat Hawaii in the Hula Bowl. He was Pittsburgh's top draft choice but apparently chose not to play pro ball.

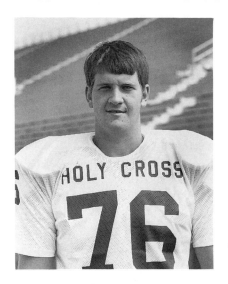

Bruce Kozerski—Holy Cross—Off. Tackle—1983

Winner of the Outstanding Scholar Athlete Award at James Coughlin High School in Plains, Pennsylvania in 1979, Bruce Kozerski went on to become an excellent scholar and athlete at the College of the Holy Cross during his football career from 1980 through 1983. Under new head coach Rick Carter, the Crusaders began their first season in Division 1-AA play in 1981 with a winning 6-5-0 record. They improved tremendously during the 1982 campaign, finishing with a 8-3-0 mark and giving Holy Cross the most victories in a season since 1952. Kozerski was selected first team All-Eastern College Athletic Conference, third team All-New England, and honorable mention All-America with the Crusaders ranked 11th in the nation in Division 1AA. In 1983, they finished with an excellent winning record of 9-2-1, won their first Lambert-Meadowlands Cup (awarded for supremacy in Eastern football), went to the Division 1-AA playoffs, were ranked third nationally and Rick Carter was named National Coach of the Year. Kozerski was acknowledged as being one of the leading players who helped Holy Cross to become a power-house in Division 1-AA. He received numerous honors in recognition of his tremendous contribution to Crusader football. In his senior year, Kozerski was selected first team All-America, first team Academic All-America, first team All-Eastern College Athletic Conference, first team All-New England and was awarded the NCAA Post Graduate Scholarship as one of the country's leading student athletes. Bruce also received the Davitt Award as the team's outstanding offensive lineman and the Judge Cooney Award as a senior letter winner who performed with courage, loyalty, and devotion. Kozerski was a National Honor Student at Holy Cross and graduated as a Physics major with a 3.7 grade point average. Bruce has carved out a fine professional football career after being a ninth-round draft choice of the Cincinnati Bengals in 1984. He has started at all five offensive line positions for the Bengals and was their starting center in Super Bowl XXIII. He finished his tenth year of pro ball in 1993, and was the offensive line leader at center at 6-4, 287 pounds. He calls the blocking assignments for the Bengals at the line of scrimmage and is one of their key players. Many pro experts feel that Bruce is one of the most under-rated players in the NFL. He was honored in March 1993 with a testimonial dinner in his home-town, Plains, Pennsylvania. He currently speaks to youth groups on the dangers of drugs and alcohol, and represents Hammer Strength in the New England area.

Harry Olszewski—Clemson—Off. Guard—1967

A native of Baltimore, Maryland, Harry Olszewski played football at Clemson University under head coach Frank Howard, the self-styled Baron of Barlow Bend, Alabama. Howard was known for his coaching success at Clemson from 1940 through 1969, as well as for his comic homespun oratory. Olszewski started all freshman games at offensive guard in 1964. He followed with 30 consecutive varsity games, becoming only one of two players to do so at Clemson. At 6-0, 237 pounds, he was quick and fast with good lateral movement and developed into Clemson's first consensus first team All-America in 1967. During his varsity seasons, the Tigers were Atlantic Coast Conference co-champions in 1965, champions in 1966 and again in 1967. Olszewski has the distinction of being Clemson's last offensive lineman to score a touchdown. He scored on a 12-yard run as an offensive guard after a fumbled snap fell into his arms in a 1966 game with South Carolina. Harry was the only unanimous choice to the All-Atlantic Coast Conference team for three consecutive years. The honors that Olszewski received attest to his brilliant performances game after game as a Clemson Tiger. He was unanimous All-State for three straight years and was voted the recipient of the Hamilton Award as the team's Most Valuable Player in 1967. Harry was awarded the Jacobs Blocking Trophy from the state of South Carolina and from the Atlantic Coast Conference. This trophy is presented annually to the outstanding blocker in the state and in the conference. Olszewski was voted the Outstanding Collegiate Athlete in South Carolina in 1967 and inducted into the state of South Carolina Hall of Fame in 1989. Harry was selected to the Silver Anniversary Atlantic Coast Conference first team honoring the top players who participated in the conference play during the first 25 years. He played in the East-West Shrine game in 1967 and the Senior Bowl and Coaches All-American games in 1968. Olszewski was the Cleveland Brown's third round draft choice in 1968, and played for the Brwns in 1968 and the Montreal Alouettes in 1969 and 1970. He was inducted into Clemson University's Athletic Hall of Fame in 1980. Harry lives in Florida.

Henry Wisniewski—Fordham—Off. Guard—1930

Henry Wisniewski had the honor of being the first Fordham University football player to be selected consensus first team All-America in 1930. He achieved this distinction by playing offensive and defensive guard under the coaching of the "Iron Major," Frank Cavanaugh, during the 1928, 1929 and 1930 football seasons. Cavanaugh was one of the coaching pioneers who believed that football was a game of conditioning and contact, and all his teams were in excellent physical condition. He instituted conditioning exercises that are still being used today. The "Iron Major" earned his major's commission and had half his face shot off during World War I. He was as tough on the football field as he was on the battlefield. It was under this strict regimen that Wisniewski joined the Fordham Rams' line. Fordham shocked the football world in 1929 by going 7-0-2 after a losing previous season. The squad posted six shutouts in nine games, and went 17 quarters at the start of the season before surrendering a single point. The two ties kept Fordham from earning a post-season bowl bid. Wisniewski was superb as a two-way guard and provided the team's line leadership. The staunch defense of the Rams' line inspired Fordham's Sports Information Director, Tim Cohane, to coin the famous phrase "The Seven Blocks of Granite." The 1929-1930 edition of the "Seven Blocks" did not capture the media attention as the later 1936-1937 edition, but they were the first ones. The 1936-1937 or Wojciechowicz and Jacunski version of the "Seven Blocks" was different from the earlier edition because it consisted of "three Poles, three Irishmen and Siano in the middle." On one side of Siano were Elecewicz, Miskinis, and Wisniewski. On the other side were Conroy, Foley, and Tracey. They were a collection of tough, superbly conditioned, hard hitting, unyielding defensive linemen with Wisniewski as their acknowledged leader. Fordham went 8-1-0 for the 1930 season, posting six shut-outs along the way. They opened the year by overwhelming Baltimore (73-0) and Buffalo (71-0), and entered the next to the last game with St. Mary's (California) with a 7-0 record. However, all hopes for a perfect season were dashed when St. Mary's came from behind to post a shocking 20-12 win. The first edition of one of the most fabled group of athletes then closed its chapter with a 12-0 victory over Bucknell. For his brilliant performances and leadership, playing in the midst of a fantastic group of linemen, Wisniewski was singled out and selected Fordham's first consensus first team All-America.

Rudy Mucha—Washington—Center—1940

Rudy Mucha traveled from Chicago, Illinois in 1937 to attend the University of Washington in Seattle and to play football under head coach Jimmy Phelan, the ex-Notre Dame quarterback. Rudy was the second Mucha to enroll at Washington. His older brother, Chuck, preceded him and was a three year letterman as a football guard from 1932 to 1934. Rudy was on the same varsity team in 1939 and 1940 as the two time All-America guard, Raymond Frankowski from Hammond, Indiana. At 6-2, 210 pounds, Mucha was a three year letter-winner from 1938 through 1940. His excellent offensive and defensive play at the center of the Husky line was evident and he was selected consensus first team All-America center in 1940. Mucha was only the eighth Washington player selected for the All-America honor, and the first Husky center to win it. Rudy was very effective as an offensive center but he was also impressive as a linebacker on defense. Mucha and Frankowski were very instrumental in leading the 1940 Husky football team to a second place conference finish with a 7-2-0 record and a number ten ranking in the nation. Rudy was chosen to the College All-Star team in 1941 and was in the starting line-up at center with Ed Rucinski, the All-America end from Indiana, and the Michigan mortals, Forest Evashevski at quarterback and Tom Harmon at halfback. Mucha was also selected to play in the East-West Shrine game. He played football at the Great Lakes Naval Training Station in 1942 and 1943 when he was in the service. His professional football career included stops at the Cleveland Rams in 1941 and the Chicago Bears from 1944 through 1947 where he started at guard during the Bears' 1946 championship season. Mucha was inducted into the University of Washington Athletic Hall of Fame in 1986 to "honor and preserve the memory of those athletes, teams, coaches and members of the athletic staff who have contributed in a very outstanding and positive way to the promotion of the University of Washington athletic program."

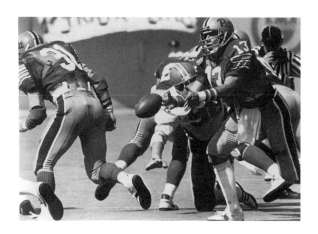

Daniel Marino—Pittsburgh—Quarterback—1982

Daniel Marino, Jr. is the only son of an Italian father, Dan Marino, and Polish mother, Veronica (Kolczynski) Marino. (Her parents were Polish immigrants—she grew up in the Polish Hill section of Pittsburgh.) Marino started playing quarterback in the fourth grade for the St. Regis School football team in the Oakland area of Pittsburgh. At Central Catholic High School, Danny starred as a football quarterback and baseball pitcher and short-stop. The Kansas City Royals selected him in the baseball draft, but the heavily recruited 6-3, 214 pounder accepted a football scholarship from the University of Pittsburgh to the delight of head coach Jackie Sherrill. In 1979, Marino led the Panthers to a Fiesta Bowl victory after replacing injured Rick Trocano in the season's seventh game. Pitt captured the Eastern title, finished sixth nationally, and Danny set a new Panther freshman record with 1,680 yards passing. As a sophomore in 1980, he was one of the country's leading passers until he was sidelined with a knee injury. He still finished with 1,513 yards, 14 touchdowns and was named to the All-East team. He had a sensational junior year and broke school career passing records with 2,876 yards and 37 touchdowns. He led Pitt to its third consecutive 11-1 record, and was named All-East and first team All-America quarterback. He also finished fourth in the voting for the Heisman Trophy. In the Sugar Bowl, Danny completed 26 of 41 passes for 261 yards and three touchdowns to defeat Georgia, 24-20. Marino's lackluster 1982 season probably cost him the Heisman Trophy (he was a candidate), and eliminated any All-America honors. He was captain of the 1982 squad, and did pass for 2,432 yards and 17 touchdowns, but unfortunately much more was expected of him. He finished as Pittsburgh's top total offense leader with 8,597 yards during his career and was the Panthers leading passer in 1979, 1980, 1981 and 1982. Danny graduated with a B.A. degree in Communications with a 3.0 cumulative grade point average. He played in the Senior and Hula Bowls and was the first round draft choice of the Miami Dolphins in 1983. He was the most exciting NFL rookie, completing 173 of 296 passes for 2,210 yards and 20 touchdowns. The first rookie ever named to start in the Pro Bowl, he received the team's MVP award and was named TSN Rookie of the Year. Marino shattered most NFL season passing records on his way to winning the 1984 MVP award, and was the first NFL quarterback to exceed 5,000 passing yards in one season. He was chosen to the Pro Bowl eight times, and was in his 12th pro year as the Dolphins quarterback in 1995. He is on his way to becoming the greatest passer in NFL history. Dan is second only to the NFL all-time passing leader, Fran Tarkenton, in four major career categories—touchdown passes, passing yards, attempts and completions. He should surpass Fran in 1996.

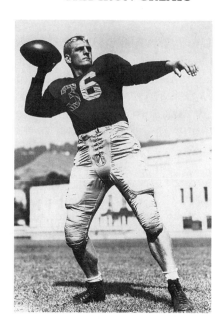

Johnny Olszewski—California—Running Back—1952

Johnny Olszewski enrolled at the University of California and was fortunate to play under the coaching of the legendary Pappy Waldorf. Waldorf brought an era of prosperity to the Berkley campus when he arrived from Northwestern. Prior to Waldorf, California had a reputation as a graveyard for coaches. Olszewski started his varsity play in 1950 and had the best day of his career in the Washington State game. He set two California single game marks. Johnny broke the single game rushing record of Jackie Jensen, an All-America fullback for California in 1948. Olszewski carried the ball 20 times that day and rolled up a net total of 269 yards while scoring two touchdowns on runs of 80 and 28 yards, shattering Jensen's record of 192 yards. The 269 yards was also good enough to set a new California total offense record. California finished the 1950 season with a 9-0-1 record. Coming into the Rose Bowl game with Michigan, the Golden Bears were unbeaten for the third straight year and had a 7-7 tie with Stanford. They lost the bowl game to Michigan, and were ranked number five nationally. In 1951, Johnny's career was cut short by a mid-season knee injury. Prior to the injury, Olszewski had given every indication that he was an All-America. Although he missed three games and saw only limited action in three others, he gained 651 yards for a 7.3 yard per carry average. Olszewski added much finesse to his powerful running when he took over as the Bears' starting back at the start of the 1951 season. This, combined with his natural power, caused backfield coach Wes Fry to comment that John was potentially the best back he had ever seen. Johnny's greatest assets were his running and blocking ability but he was also a good passer, a fair punter and an excellent defensive man. California finished the 1951 season with an 8-2-0 mark and was rated 12th in the country. Olszewski received the Ken Cotton Award at the end of the '51 season as the varsity player who displayed the most courage playing with a questionable knee. In 952, Olszewski's knee had healed and he went on to establish new California records with his fantastic running. He was named first team All-Pacific Coast Conference, was elected California's Most Valuable Player, and was also chosen first team All-America. John played in the College All-Star and East West Shrine games. He was a first round draft choice of the Chicago Cardinals and played 10 years of professional football. Olszewski was a Pro-Bowl team selection in 1954 and 1956. During his pro playing days, he was known as "Johnny O."

Stanley Koslowski—Holy Cross—Running Back—1945

Stanley Koslowski was one of the most versatile and out-standing backfield performers in college football in the 1940s era. He was the starting halfback for the Holy Cross Crusaders who ran, passed, punted, kicked field goals and points after touch-downs, and still had sufficient strength and stamina to star as a defensive back. His fantastic Holy Cross career started in 1943 when he established Crusader records for most yards gained rushing, most 200 yard games, best rushing yards average per game, most punts and longest yardage per game, most punt returns, and most returns for touchdowns. Koslowski starred on offense and defense all season and provided the primary back-field leadership. The Crusaders finished with an excellent win-ning record of 6-2-0 under head coach Anthony Scanlon. He was elected team captain for the 1945 squad, and once again began by establishing all sorts of Holy Cross records using his exceptional abilities. He set scoring (most points and most touchdowns), rushing (game, season and career yards), punting (best season and career average yards), and career punt return records that still rank among the best in Holy Cross football history. Koslowski's scoring and career points per game still are among the national leaders in college football. His most memorable performance of the 1945 season was against Villanova when Stanley scored two touchdowns, passed for another, and kicked two extra points in a 26-7 victory. He continued to play up to his excellent standards for the rest of the campaign which came to an end with a winning 8-1-0 record. Koslowski starred in a losing cause in the Orange Bowl game against the University of Miami. He passed for a 16 yard Holy Cross touchdown but Miami scored in the final seconds of the game to win 13-6. Stanley played in the College All-Star game in 1946, and was Washington's number two draft choice. Koslowski received the Bulger Lowe Trophy awarded annually to New England's outstanding player. He was also selected All-America at the end of the 1945 season. Stanley is a member of the Holy Cross Varsity Club Hall of Fame.

Stanley Kostka—Minnesota—Running Back—1934

Stanley Kostka became one of the University of Minnesota's most lethal football offensive weapons during the early 1930s. It was said in those days "when bigger, faster and better fullbacks are to be developed, Minnesota will get them as in the case of Joesting, Nagurski and Kostka." At 6-1, 230 pounds, the blonde, curly-haired, good-looking Pole followed in Nagurski's footsteps to keep Minnesota as a national football power. Under head coach Bernie Bierman, Minnesota had a very succesful season in 1933 to which Kostka's fantastic running contributed greatly. The ability of players such as Kostka at fullback was enough to ensure that the 1934 Minnesota team was one of the finest in the history of college football. The Gophers kept trying and were not to be denied the No. 1 national title by completing a perfect undefeated, untied 8-0-0 record. They achieved eight straight victories with a point spread of 270-38. The game of the year pitted Minnesota against a very powerful Pittsburgh team in which Kostka wore down the excellent Pitt squad by hammering the line again and again. He started the play of the game by lunging toward the line. The Panthers massed to stop him, but at the last moment Stan slipped the ball to Seidell. Seidell then lateraled it to Lund, who threw a long pass for the winning touchdown. The play was called the "buck lateral." The brilliant maneuver worked because of Kostka's numerous line plunges which constantly yielded good gains and caused the Pitt defense to concentrate on him. Kostka's playing was excellent and he was the star of the Gopher 13-7 victory over Pitt. Stan's outstanding features were the speed of his starting thrusts, the quickness of his cutbacks, and the terrific power of his legs that kept churning long after he had been nailed. He would concentrate on taking the ball and plowing his way through and over any opposition. He was raw power in the early 1930s. Stan was rated as the hardest man to stop in college football. During the 1934 campaign, he rushed 111 times for 665 yards for an average of six yards per carry and scored 10 touchdowns. He led the Minnesota team in scoring with 60 points. Kostka was selected All-America after the '34 season. *The New York Sun* rated Stan the best football player of 1934, and wrote that he may have been the mightiest of all Minnesota line smashers. Kostka was the starting fullback on the 1935 College All-Star football team, and played an outstanding game. He went on to play professional football for Brooklyn in the National Football League for two years.

Rick Ruszkiewicz—Edinboro—Kicker—1982

Rick Ruszkiewicz was a four year letter winner from 1979 through 1982 at Edinboro University of Pennsylvania as a place kicking specialist. He established numerous team and Pennsylvania State Athletic Conference place kicking records which still stand. Ruszkiewicz holds the Edinboro records for longest scoring plays on field goals with 49 yards against Clarion in 1982, 47 yards against Bloomsburg in 1981, and 47 yards against California University of Pennsylvania in 1979. Rick also holds the record in scoring with most field goals in an individual game with three against Shippensburg in 1980, three against California, and three against New Haven in 1981 and 1982. In addition, he has the record in scoring with the most field goals in a season with 15 in 1982, 12 in 1981 and 11 in 1980. Ruszkiewicz owns the career record of 43 field goals from 1979 through 1982. He is the leader in Edinboro football history in kick scoring with the most field goals of 43. He is a record holder in the PSAC for most field goals in a season with 15, and most kicking points of 70 in 1982. Rick also holds several career kicking records in the PSAC. Ruszkiewicz was the Division II National Annual Champion— All-Time Leader in scoring with field goals in 1982. His outstanding performances as a kicker earned him the first team Kodak All-America honors in 1982.

Harry Jacunski—Fordham—Defensive End—1938

A native of New Britain, Connecticut, Harry Jacunski attended New Britain High School and lettered in football, baseball and basketball. He was selected to the All-State football team in 1934. Jacunski received a scholarship to Fordham University in 1935, just in time to play on the best ever Ram football teams and to become a member of the immortal "Seven Blocks of Granite." He became a varsity player and a "Seven Blocks" member in 1936 by rotating at the end position with Leo Paquin. Harry actually recorded more playing time than Paquin during the '36 season, and caught the winning touchdown pass that beat St. Mary's of California, 7-6, in an exciting game at the Polo Grounds in New York City. Under the legendary head football coach, Jim Crowley, Fordham finished with a 5-1-2 record and was ranked number 15 in the nation. In 1937, the Rams finished with an undefeated 7-0-1 mark and were ranked third nationally. Unfortunately, they did not receive a post-season bowl bid because of their third consecutive tie with the University of Pittsburgh. Jacunski was impressive recovering fumbles and catching key passes in the Ram-Panther deadlock. Bill Krywicki was quarterback and Joe Woitkowski halfback on the '37 squad. Jacunski co-captained the 1938 Fordham football team with another Polish American, Mike Kochel (Kociel). The Rams finished the season with a 6-1-2 record—their lone loss was to Pittsburgh—and they were ranked 15th nationally. The Fordham defense allowed only 30 points in the nine games and posted seven shut-outs. The rushing offense averaged 297.1 yards per game, the best in the country. Jacunski and other members of the "Seven Blocks of Granite" made football history. Because they covered a couple of seasons, the "Seven Blocks" were, in reality, ten. In 1936 they included Druze and Paquin at ends, Babartsky and Franco at tackles, Lombardi and Pierce at guards and Wojciechowicz at center. In 1937, Berezny was at tackle, Kochel at guard and Jacunski had replaced Paquin at end. Four of the "Blocks" were Polish Americans. They were Harry Jacunski, Alex Wojciechowicz, Mike Kochel (Kociel) and Al Babartsky. The "Blocks of Granite" were good on offense but they were really a defensive unit. Jacunski was an outstanding member of the granite line and was selected All-America in 1938. He also received the Connie Murphy Award as Fordham's Outstanding Football Player. During his three varsity seasons, the Rams compiled an excellent 18-2-5 record. Jacunski graduated as an honor student with a B.S. degrees in Economics. He played with the College All-Stars in 1939 and was chosen to the Pro-Bowl in 1940. He was drafted by the Green Bay Packers and was with them for six years. After retiring from pro ball, Jacunski coached at Notre Dame (1945-'46) under Hugh Devore, at Harvard (1946-'47) under Dick Harlowe and began a 32 year coaching career at Yale in 1948 under Herman Hickman. He was the Yale varsity end coach and chief scout for 15 years and head coach of the freshman team for 17 years until retirement in 1980. During the Yale coaching years, he received the George Carens Award for his contribution to college football, and the Gold Key Award presented by the Connecticut Sports Writers for his contribution to athletics in the state of Connecticut. The Connecticut chapter of the National Football Foundation College Hall of Fame also honored him in 1970. He was selected to the Fordham University Football Hall of Fame in 1975 and the Green Bay Packers Hall of Fame in 1991. As of 1994 at age 78, Jacunski was an active owner of a specialties advertising business.

Peter Kwiatkowski—Boise State—Defensive End—1987

A native of Santa Barbara, California, Peter Kwiatkowski came to Boise State University in 1984 to become one of the best defensive linemen in Broncos' football history. Peter, at 6-3, 250 pounds, was a four year letterman and three year starter. He was equally effective at both the defensive end and tackle positions, but had the most experience at end. In 1984, he substituted at defensive end but played enough to earn a letter. He became a starter in 1985 and kept the first string position for the rest of his collegiate career. Kwiatkowski finished the '85 season with 68 tackles (20 for losses which included quarterback sacks and tackles behind the line of scrimmage) and recovered one fumble. In 1986, Pete made 91 tackles, 18 for losses and recovered two fumbles. He finished the 1987 season making a career high 101 tackles. He led the team in tackles for loss with 24 including a team high 15 quarterback sacks. Peter received Big Sky Conference Defensive Player of the Week honors after the Idaho game where he made 14 tackles, three quarterback sacks and forced two fumbles. He finished his four-year football career making 261 total tackles to rank seventh all-time at Boise State. He also finished his career with a school record of 62 tackles for loss. Kwiatkowski was a 1986 first team All-Big Sky Conference selection and was named honorable mention All-America by the Associated Press. Peter won three post-season honors for the 1987 campaign. He was selected first team All-America by the American Football Coaches Association for the University 1-AA class, the Most Valuable Defensive Player in the Big Sky Conference and first team All-Big Sky Conference. Kwiatkowski's selection marks only the 11th time a Boise State player has been selected to a Kodak All-America team by the American Football Coaches Association. He was the first Bronco player to earn the Kodak award since 1985. Peter completed his degree work in physical and secondary education at Boise State University, and entered the professional football ranks. He played three years of pro ball with the Miami Dolphins and the Calgary Stampeders. Kwiatkowski returned to his alma mater in 1991 to become a defensive assistant football coach.

Eugene Selawski—Purdue—Def. Tackle—1958

Eugene Selawski played only two years for Purdue University, but head coach Jack Mollenkopf learned quickly that he inherited a treasure. Selawski turned out to be not only one of the greatest tackles at Purdue, but also one of the hardest working and intelligent ones on the gridiron and in the classroom. He was Mollenkopf's dream come true. At the beginning of the 1957 season, Gene was used primarily as a back-up for the starting tackle. But he quickly showed that he had a combination of strength, agility and ability to think and play under pressure. He was a hard hitter and an excellent blocker. Selawski was particularly impressive in the 1957 game with Illinois which Purdue won 21-6. He nailed down the starting tackle position and held it for the rest of the season through the 1958 campaign. Gene was elected co-captain of the 1958 Purdue squad in recognition of his leadership qualities. He played extremely well during his senior season which Purdue finished with a 6-1-2 record and a national ranking of thirteen. Selawski's outstanding contributions were recognized and he was selected first team All-Big Ten Conference tackle and chosen first team All-America. In addition, Gene was selected first team Academic All-Big Ten Conference, and was the first Purdue football player to be chosen to receive the Noble E. Kizer Award. This award is presented annually to the football

112

junior or senior letterman with the highest academic excellence for the previous two terms. Selawski was chosen to play in the Blue-Gray, the Senior Bowl and the College All-Star games. He played pro ball for three years.

John Matuszak—Tampa—Def. Tackle—1972

An excellent football player at Oak Creek High School, Oak Creek, Wisconsin, John Matuszak was recruited by many colleges and universities during his senior year. Never an outstanding student, John learned that his grades were not up to Big Ten Conference standards and he could not attend Iowa. As suggested to him, Matuszak attended Fort Dodge Junior College in Iowa in an effort to improve his scholastic record. He got a B average, played good football, was chosen All-Conference tight end and named honorable mention All-America. Coach Dan Devine convinced Matuszak to enroll at Missouri where John was a starting tight end for the Tigers in his sophomore year. An unfortunate personal problem unrelated to football, caused Matuszak to transfer from the University of Missouri to the University of Tampa. John fit in beautifully with Tampa's football program in 1971 and 1972 under head coach Earl Bruce. At 6-8, 280 pounds, the Polish husky was the strongest and biggest player on the

Tampa team. He had good speed, and clocked at 4.8 in the 40. During the 1971 season, John started at tight end on the offensive unit, but was moved to defensive tackle where he found a home. He was an outstanding defensive tackle and finished as the leading tackler on the team during the '71 campaign. His great size and strength made him one of the best in the country at his position and he demonstrated that during the 1972 season. John was a consistent player who was good in all phases of the game. He had an excellent year and played a superb game in the Florida Citrus Bowl. He contributed greatly to Tampa's bowl victory over Kent State. After the 1972 campaign, he was named the Southeastern Defensive Player of the Week and selected All-America tackle. He was also runner-up to Gary Huff as the Florida Amateur Athlete of the Year. John was in the starting line-up on defense in the College All-Star game in 1973. He was voted the Most Valuable Player in the American Bowl, a North-South all-star game. He was predicted to be one of the top NF draft choices in the country and turned out to be the Houston Oilers' No. 1 draft choice. He played professional football for nine years, six of them with the Oakland Raiders. John had one of the most outstanding professional football careers—especially with the Raiders. He lived life to the fullest and even took on Hollywood's silver screen. He performed in films such as *North Dallas Forty*, *Caveman*, *Goonies* and HBO's smash football sitcom, *First and 10*. The late John "the Tooz" Matuszak was a rollicking individualist who had his own outlook on life.

Jeff Zgonina—Purdue—Nose Guard—1992

Jeff Zgonina was a star athlete at Carmel High School in Long Grove, Illinois before coming to Purdue University in 1988. He was All-State, All-Area, All-County and All-Catholic League as a prep football senior. He was an excellent shot putter in track and also played basketball and hockey. Zgonina was red shirted at Purdue in 1988. He began as a linebacker, but his increased size and strength caused him to move to the defensive tackle position. In 1989, Jeff was *Football News* Freshman All-America, honorable mention All-Big Ten Conference and ranked third in the conference in tackles for loss. He ranked third on the team with 82 tackles and second with quarterback sacks. Zgonina started at defensive tackle again for the 1990 season and was a second team All-Big Ten selection. He led the conference linemen in tackles and ranked second in tackles for loss. Jeff won the team's Pop Doan Award as the outstanding defender versus the Hoosiers of Indiana. In 1991, Zgonina had another excellent outing playing the nose guard position. He made 76 tackles despite constant double and triple teaming. He was selected first team All-Big Ten defensive lineman. He was also chosen as an honorable mention All-America and was the *Football News* pick for an Almost All-America. At 6-2, 270 pounds, Zgonina had a spectacular season in 1992. He was named one of 12 semifinalists for the Lombardi Award as the outstanding lineman of the year and a top candidate for the Outland Trophy as the outstanding interior lineman in the nation. He was chosen first team All-Big Ten and selected All-America. *Sporting News* called Zgonina the 1992 Big Ten Defensive Player of the Year and the NCAA's second best interior lineman. Jeff finished his career at Purdue by being ranked first on the all-time list with tackles for loss and sixth in total tackles. His career statistics show 266 solo tackles, 116 assisted for a total of 382 tackles. He also had 72 tackles for a loss of 244 yards. Zgonina was chosen to the East-West Shrine, Hula Bowl and Japan Bowl teams. Jeff was the Pittsburgh Steelers NFL draft choice as a defensive tackle in 1993.

James Sniadecki—Indiana—Linebacker—1968

James Sniadecki was an All-State linebacker and offensive end at St. Joseph's High School, South Bend, Indiana in 1963 and 1964. He was an outstanding player and team leader on St. Joseph's 1964 squad which won the mythical state championship. Jim was also an excellent basketball player and was selected to the Catholic All-Round Athlete team as a senior. He enrolled at the University of Indiana in 1965 and played under head coach Johnny Pont. He was a three-year starting linebacker and was an All-Big Ten Conference performer in 1966. He made 84 tackles (59 solo) to rank second on the squad to his line backing teammate, Ken Kaczmarek. Sniadecki had the ability to diagnose plays well and to react quickly. He was a top defensive player on the team, strong enough at 214 pounds to handle inside plays and fast enough to cover outside. Jim shared in the glories and honors that were earned by Indiana in 1967. The team won its first five games, and Hoosier fans all over the state greeted each other with "keep the big red ball rolling" while passing a little red ball. Indiana finished with a 9-1-0 record and received a first ever invitation to appear in the Rose Bowl against the University of Southern California. Unfortunately, they lost to USC, 14-3, but the team and especially Sniadecki performed very well. Indiana shared the Big Ten Conference title with Purdue and Minnesota and were ranked fourth in the country. For turning the Hoosiers around from 1-8-1 to 9-2-0, Coach Pont was chosen National Coach of the Year. Jim was selected to the All-Big Ten Conference team as linebacker. Indiana had a winning 1968 season— Sniadecki's performances were extremely impressive and he was named All-Big Ten Conference again and selected All-America. Many football authorities considered Jim Sniadecki and Ken Kaczmarek to have been the best line backing duo in the country. Jim was chosen to play in the East-West Shrine and the Hula Bowl games in 1968. Sniadecki played professional football with the San Francisco 49ers from 1969 through 1973 and was captain of the San Francisco specialty teams. He also played two years in the World Football League. After retiring from pro ball, Jim became a restaurant owner in Redwood City, California. He was inducted into the Indiana (State) Football Hall of Fame in 1987.

Mark Blazejewski—Fordham—Linebacker—1992

Born in Poland, Blazejewski came to the United States at the age of six with his mother and brother. He attended Bishop Hoban High School in Plains, Pennsylvania and received All-State, All-League and All-America honors in football. Mark received a Leadership Scholarship to Fordham University which he entered in 1988. He played in all 10 games as a back-up linebacker in his freshman year. In 1989, Mark, at 6-0, 225 pounds, finished the year averaging a terrific 15.5 tackles per game. He did not start the season opener, but came on strong to start each of the last seven games. His best effort was 23 tackles against Princeton. Mark was named captain of the 1990 Ram squad, but missed the entire season after suffering a torn anterior cruciate ligament in his left knee. However, he was selected All-America by the Sports Information Directors Association. Mark returned for the 1991 campaign and served as one of the Rams' captains. He proved to be the "heart and soul" of Fordham's defense. He started all 10 games and finished the year as the top tackler in the Patriot League with 14.5 tackles per game. He was named co-defensive Player of the Week in games against Bucknell and Villanova. Blazejewski was also honored by the Eastern College Athletic Conference as its co-defensive Player of the Week after the Villanova game. He was named to the first team All-Patriot League and All-ECAC as a linebacker at the end of the '91 season.

He was also selected second team All-America linebacker by Associated Press. During the 1992 campaign, Mark was once again elected one of the Rams' tri-captains. He had another fantastic outing. He was selected for the Patriot League Defensive Award for 1992 by the league's head football coaches. He was also named to the All-Patriot League and All-ECAC first teams as linebacker. In his four year career at Fordham, Mark finished with a total of 409 tackles of which 205 were solos and 204 assisted. He intercepted three passes his senior year for 65 yards and scored one touchdown. He was considered to be a complete linebacker by football experts. In addition to all the honors he received, Blazejewski was selected first team All-America in 1992. If the All-America honor he got for the 1990 season, in which he did not play, was to be counted, Mark would have been All-America for three consecutive years. He plans to use his degree toward a career in physical therapy.

Leon Gajecki—Pennsylvania State—Linebacker—1940

Leon Gajecki began his football career at Ebensburg High School in the tiny coal mining town of Colver, Pennsylvania as a small 96-pounder. In one summer he went from 96 to 160 pounds and continued growing until he reached 6 feet and 225 pounds in his senior year at Pennsylvania State University. Gajecki enrolled at Penn State in 1937 primarily because his high school mentor became an assistant coach for the Nittany Lions football team. The 1938 Penn State team, with only 10 passes completed against them all season, set three NCAA pass defense records including fewest yards passing allowed and lowest completion percentage. Among the defensive standouts were Gajecki, Carl Stravinski and Walter Kniaz. Under head coach Bob Higgins, Gajecki saw the Nittany Lions welcome an era of football prosperity. He was considered the key to Penn State's returning respectability in eastern college football. At 180 pounds, Leon was the smallest man on the squad, but he averaged 58 minutes a game playing both offensive and defensive center. What he lacked in size, he made up in determination and helped the Nittany Lions to a winning 1939 season with a 5-1-2 record.

Gajecki was elected captain of the 1940 team, and at 225 pounds, led them to a very successful 6-1-1 season. The forward wall, an awesome seven, was called "The Seven Mountains," a nickname suggested by an alumnus and referring to a mountain range northeast of the campus. The line had Leon, Carl Stravinski, Mike Garbinski and Walter Kniaz. The 1940 campaign was Penn State's best in 19 years. Gajecki was acknowledged as one of the best centers in the country and was selected first team All-America. He played in the East-West Shrine game and was drafted by the Pittsburgh Steelers. Leon decided against pro ball and World War II put a stop to any football plans. After the war, he joined the Humble Oil and Refinery Company in Pitman, New Jersey and was with them until retirement. His love for Penn State continued and he began scouting players for the Nittany Lions. He helped produce such stars as Milt Plum, Dave Rowe, Dave Robinson, Lydell Mitchell, and Franco Harris. Gajecki helped to resurrect the Glassboro State College football program, officiated games, and worked with youngsters. He suffered a stroke in 1968, but got back on his feet and became active again. Gajecki was honored by being inducted into the All-Sports Hall of Fame in Johnstown, Pennsylvania.

Steven Filipowicz—Fordham—Def. Back—1942

Steven Filipowicz started his varsity career at Fordham University in 1939 under the coaching of the legendary "Sleepy" Jim Crowley. Filipowicz played in his first game as a substitute back in the first-ever televised college football game against Waynesburg College as part of New York's World Fair demonstration of this new medium. The Rams' 1939 team was captained by the backfield star, William Krywicki, and finished with a winning 6-2-0 record to be ranked number 17 in the country. In the first game of the 1940 season against West Virginia, Filipowicz scored two touchdowns to lead Fordham to a 20-7 win. With a post-season bid on the line, the Rams entered the season finale with New York University, their local nemesis. Filipowicz starred again by running for three touchdowns, passing for another one as Fordham rolled to a 26-0 victory and a Cotton Bowl invitation. Steve scored Fordham's first touchdown against Texas A&M in the bowl game to put the Rams ahead, but the Aggies rallied to beat them, 13-12. The season ended with a 7-2-0 record and number 12 national ranking. He was an outstanding athlete with great speed, physical abilities and a constant two way offensive threat with his excellent running and passing. He was a fast, intelligent, aggressive back who was very hard to stop. In addition, Steve

120

was a fine blocker and an outstanding defensive back. The 1941 season was an excellent one for him and the Rams, who finished with a good 8-1-0 record, were ranked sixth in the nation, and beat Missouri in the Sugar Bowl. Steve was a one man ram for Fordham against West Virginia during the 1942 campaign for a 23 to 14 victory. He passed 40 yards for one touchdown and then ran a beautiful 71-yard sprint for another TD. Filipowicz was awarded the Madow Trophy for his superior performance in the 1940 game with N.Y.U., and was selected All-America back after the 1941 season. Steve was the best offensive and defensive back Fordham produced in a decade. He was also an excellent baseball player at Fordham. Steve was chosen to play in the College All-Star and the East-West Shrine games. He was the New York Giants first round draft choice and, after service in World War II, played pro ball with the Giants in 1945 and 1946. Filipowicz was the first athlete to play two sports in the same city on the same field. He played outfield with the baseball Giants and running back with the football Giants in the Polo Grounds in 1945. In 1971, the Fordham University athletic department began honoring former athletes, coaches, and administrators for their past athletic achievements. Steve Filipowicz was selected to the Hall of Fame in 1976 for his contribution to the Fordham football and baseball teams.

Frank Kirkleski—Lafayette—Def. Back—1926

Frank Kirkleski was an outstanding offensive and defensive halfback at Lafayette College in 1924. Frank was the leading scorer for Lafayette in 1925, and was elected Captain of the 1926 squad which finished the season with a perfect undefeated, untied record of 9-0-0. They were successful in beating the University of Pittsburgh for the third straight year. Kirkleski was not only a remarkable triple-threat performer who excelled in broken field running, passing and punting, but also was a good, fast, intelligent defensive back. During his three-year college football career, Lafayette finished with an excellent 23-3-1 record, including the perfect 9-0-0 slate during Frank's senior year. He was the acknowledged offensive and defensive backfield leader and an inspirational player for Lafayette during three good, winning seasons. He had the natural athletic ability required for a good backfield performer. His spectacular performances earned him first team All-America honors as a back in 1926. Kirkleski was selected to play in the East West Shrine game in 1927, and professional football with Pottsville (Pennsylvania) in 1927 and 1928.

Henry Toczylowski—Boston College—Def. Back—1940

Henry "Tarzan" Toczylowski was a three year letter winner at Boston College under head coach Frank Leahy in 1938, 1939 and 1940. He was elected captain of the 1940 squad which is still rated as one of the best gridiron teams in Boston College history. In 1938, Toczylowski was the starting halfback. He was a strong, powerful runner and trying to stop him was comparable to stopping a tank. The Eagles enjoyed a winning 1939 season, finished with an impressive 9-2-0 record, were ranked 11th in the nation, and received their first ever bowl bid to play Clemson in the Cotton Bowl. The Boston College-Clemson classic turned into a fierce defensive struggle. The Eagles' defense held the Tigers to only 11 first downs, allowed them only 51 plays and only two pass completions, due in great part to Toczylowski's excellent play at defensive back. Boston College also forced five Clemson fumbles, but the Tigers won, 6-3. Toczylowski passed four times for 73 yards but the Eagles could not score a touchdown. During the 1940 season, Toczylowski performed as an excellent blocker, constantly clearing the way for the ball carrying backs. The squad was strengthened by the addition of an outstanding back, Mike Holovak, who became a College Hall of Famer. Henry played an inspiring game on offense and defense against Georgetown in the last game of the year. Georgetown's unbeaten streak of 23 games ended as Boston College handed the Hoyas their first loss in three years. The Eagles finished with an unbeaten, untied 10-0-0 record, were ranked fifth nationally, and received a Sugar Bowl invitation to play Tennessee. The Volunteers were ranked fourth in the country, and were heavily favored to beat the Eagles. However, Boston College, led by the fantastic backfield consisting of Toczylowski, Holovak, Maznicki and O'Rourke, rose to the challenge. The final score was 19-13. Toczylowski was chosen an All-America back by several selectors in 1940 and was Brooklyn's seventh round NFL pro choice in 1941. Henry was inducted into the Boston College Varsity Club Hall of Fame in 1971.

Charles Toczylowski was a member of the Boston College football team in 1969 and Martin Toczylowski in 1972.

Raymond Stachowicz—Michigan State—Punter—1980

Raymond Stachowicz was an outstanding athlete and punter on the Brecksville High School football team in Broadview Heights, Ohio, and came to Michigan State University in 1977 with excellent credentials. He established his mark early by taking over the Spartan starting punting role in his freshman year, and holding it for the rest of his college career. He was a four year letter winner from 1977 through 1980, and did so well that no one could challenge his starting position. He proved to be not only the leading Spartan punter, but also was the Big Ten's first four time All-Conference selection. He was the first team choice each of of the four years—an outstanding accomplishment. As the Spartan and Big Ten four-year punting leader, he got off his longest kick of 75 yards in 1978 against Notre Dame. To prove that this was no fluke, he followed with 73 yards against Wisconsin in 1980, 72 yards against Purdue in 1979 and again in 1980. He punted 71 times in 1980, 62 times in 1979, 42 in 1978 and 58 in 1977 for a career total of 230 punts. He improved his punting average each year starting with 43.1 yards per punt and finishing with an average of 46.2 in 1980. This average of 46.2 ranks second highest in Spartan gridiron history. Stachowicz was selected All-America in 1979, and was named consensus All-America in 1980. Raymond was the Green Bay Packers' NFL draft choice in 1981 and played with them two years. He also played professional football with the Chicago Bears and the Detroit Lions.

CHAPTER IV

ALL-AMERICANS—ALTERNATES

Donald Aleksiewicz—Hobart—Back—1972
Joseph Bogdanski—Colgate—End—1934
Kevin Graslewicz—Hamline—End—1984
Ken Kaczmarek—Indiana—Linebacker—1967
Ted Kluszewski—Indiana—End—1947
Richard Kowalski—Hobart—Back—1975
Edmund Kulakowski—West Virginia—Tackle—1947
John Kulakowski—Northwestern State—End—1987
Mark Lagowski—Salisbury State—Linebacker—1982
Albin Lezouski—Pittsburgh—Guard—1938
Ed Mioduszewski—William & Mary—Back—1952
Mark Obuszewski—Alfred—Def. Back—1992
Jerry Ostroski—Tulsa—Guard—1991
Thomas Pierzga—Boston University—Tackle—1979
Robert Pietuszka—Delaware—Def. Back—1976
John Rapacz—Oklahoma—Center—1946
Charles Sieminski—Pennsylvania State—Tackle—1962
Bobby Spitulski—Central Florida—Linebacker—1991
Joseph Stanowicz—Army—Guard—1944
David Suminski—Wisconsin—Tackle—1952
Walter Trojanowski—Connecticut—Back—1949
Todd Wilkowski—Ithaca College—Quarterback—1991
John Witkowski—Columbia—Quarterback—1983
Steve Wojciechowski—Buffalo—Linebacker—1987
Dan Zakashefski—Montclair State—Def. Tackle—1986

Donald Aleksiewicz—Hobart—Back—1972

Donald Aleksiewicz was a four-year letter winner in football at Hobart College, Geneva, New York from 1969 through 1972. He was an outstanding athlete and record-setting running back whose accomplishments are still included in the NCAA Division II individual record books. During the 1971 season, Aleksiewicz was in nine games, 276 plays in which he ran for 1,616 yards, 19 touchdowns and finished the year with a record of 179.6 yards per game. He also set a record all-purpose running career yards of 6,063 from 1969 through 1972. He accomplished this feat by rushing for 4,525 yards, running for 470 yards after pass receptions, returning punts for 320 yards, and returning kick-offs for 748 yards. Aleksiewicz is also one of the Division II college Annual Champions, All-Time Leaders in rushing career yards of 4,525 on 819 plays for an average of 5.53 yards per carry, and rushing season yards of 1,616 on 276 plays for a 5.86 average yards. In addition, he is among the All-Time Leaders in career yards per game of 133.1 from 1969 through 1972, and season yards per game of 179.6 for 1971. He was the NCAA Division II Annual Champion in Rushing for the 1971 season. Donald was awarded the Vincent S. Welch Memorial Trophy by Hobart College in 1972 for scholarship, leadership and being selected the football team's Most Valuable Player. He was the first player ever selected for All-America honors from Hobart when he was chosen first team All-America running back in 1972 by the Associated Press and the American Football Coaches Association. Aleksiewicz was a Hobart College Athletic Hall of Fame charter class inductee in 1986 in recognition of his outstanding contributions to Hobart athletics in the fields of football and lacrosse.

Joseph Bogdanski—Colgate—End—1934

Joseph Bogdanski was a three-year letter winner as an offensive and defensive end at Colgate University during the 1932, 1933 and 1934 seasons. This period in Colgate's football history was its shining hour under the legendary head coach Andy Kerr. The 1932 squad was Kerr's showpiece, for it was unbeaten, untied and unscored on, to finish with a perfect 9-0-0 record. This terrific

126

unit was also known as the 4-U team because it was uninvited to the Rose Bowl. Bogdanski was an excellent athlete with good speed and good hands, and was an intelligent player who knew what to do with the ball when he caught it. He captured the starting end position early in the 1932 season and kept it for the rest of his varsity career. During the '32 campaign, Kerr introduced the downfield lateral, a play which swept the country for the next few years. The Colgate Red Raiders had an outstanding line that included Bogdanski at end and Ed Prondecki at tackle. In 1933, Colgate continued with their successful winning seasons and finished with a 6-1-1 mark. Joe had an excellent outing and was selected to the first team All- East Conference. He continued to star game after game and the Red Raiders finished with another winning season of 7-1-0 during the 1934 campaign. Bogdanski repeated as a first team All-East Conference member and was also selected All-America. Grantland Rice paid Bogdanski one of the greatest compliments by naming him one of the East's most capable ends and comparing him with the immortal Larry Kelly of Yale. Joe played in the College All-Star and the East-West Shrine games. In the All-Star game, he started with the All-America fullback from Minnesota, Stan Kostka. Later, Bogdanski was the Director of Athletics at Arnold College.

Kevin Graslewicz—Hamline—End—1984

A native of Columbia Heights, Minnesota, Kevin Graslewicz enrolled at Hamline University in 1981 and established all sorts of football reception records that have not been broken. Head football coach, Richard Tressel, described Kevin as "an outstanding athlete and great player—insightful student of the game of football." Graslewicz was a three-year starter and alternated as a play messenger in his freshman year. As a freshman, he caught seven passes for 131 yards (18.7 yds./catch) and scored one touchdown. In 1982, Kevin had 41 receptions for 583 yards (14.2 yds./catch) and scored four TDs. In his junior year, he finished with 48 catches for 791 yards (16.5 yds./catch) and had three TDs. As a senior, Kevin excelled by catching 71 passes for 996 yards (13.5 yds./catch) and five TDs. He was a meticulous pattern runner with tremendous concentration and toughness who broke tackles to gain extra yards after catching the ball. In addition, Graslewicz, at 6-2, 190 pounds, was a tenacious blocker in Hamline's option attack. He holds the University season and career reception records, and season and career reception yardage records. He was honorable mention All-Minnesota Intercollegiate Conference in 1982, and was named first team All-Conference in 1983 and 1984. In 1982 and 1983, he was Conference Player of the Week and Hamline's Offensive Player of the Year in 1983 and 1984. Kevin was selected Kodak first team All-America by the American Football Coaches Association in 1984. Graslewicz was a versatile athlete and a letter winner in hockey and baseball in addition to football.

Ken Kaczmarek—Indiana—Linebacker—1967

Ken Kaczmarek earned All-State honors at St. Joseph High School, South Bend, Indiana in 1962 and 1963 when the team was 9-1-0 and 8-1-0. He played linebacker on defense, end on offense and graduated at the top quarter of his class. Kaczmarek enrolled at the University of Indiana in 1964 to become not only one of the Hoosiers' but also one of Big Ten's best ever linebackers. At 6-0, 225 pounds, he was a free-wheeler at his position, and one of the best tacklers on the team. During the 1966 season, he led the Hoosiers in tackles with 92 including 45 solos. Ken was an All-Big Ten performer at the end of the '66 campaign. Kaczmarek teamed up with his schoolmate from St. Joseph High, Jim Sniadecki, to become the best line backing duo at Indiana, the Big Ten Conference, and according to some authorities, in the country, during the Hoosiers' 1967 season. Kaczmarek and Sniadecki provided the defensive leadership that led Indiana to a Big Ten Conference championship and a first ever Rose Bowl bid. Kaczmarek called the defensive signals for the Hoosiers during the '67 campaign. The two Polish Americans led the team in tackles during the 1966 and 1967 seasons. Opponents tried to run away from them but met with little success. Kaczmarek was selected first team All-Big Ten Conference linebacker and was also honored by being named All-America in 1967 and chosen to play in the Hula Bowl game in 1968. Ken was named a member of the Indiana (State) Football Hall of Fame.

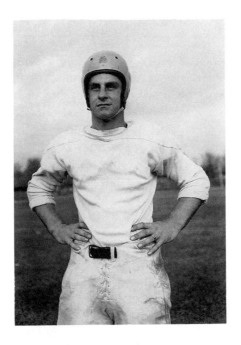

Ted Kluszewski—Indiana—End—1947

A native of Argo, Illinois, Ted Kluszewski was a high school three-sport letter winner in football, baseball and basketball. He enrolled at the University of Indiana and was the Hoosiers' leading pass-catcher as a freshman in 1944. He became a starting end, playing offense and defense, and kept that position for the rest of his college career. The 1945 season saw Ted emerge as a gridiron star. Kluszewski was devastating in the annual battle with Purdue for the Old Oaken Bucket. He stole an airborne fumble deep in Purdue territory and Indiana scored from a yard out. Ted later caught a clutch pass for a touchdown and led the Hoosiers to a victory over the Boilermakers. Purdue, under head coach Bo McMillan, finished the season with a 9-0-1 record and were ranked fourth nationally. For his contribution during the '45 campaign, Kluszewski was named by W.B.Patton to the All-Indiana team, and the Associated and United Presses selected him

129

first team All-Big Ten Conference end. He was also selected to the All-America squad by Grantland Rice and the Football Digest. Ted had very good years in 1946 and 1947, but neither Indiana nor he could top the '45 campaign. After graduating from Indiana, Ted chose to pursue a professional baseball career and went on to make baseball history with the Cincinnati Reds as both a player and a coach. He was a starter and star baseball player who led the Big Nine Conference in runs batted in his freshman year at Indiana. Kluszewski led the National League with 49 homers and 141 RBIs in 1954, and averaged 43 HRs and 116 RBIs from 1953 to 1956. He also set NL records for scoring runs in 17 straight games and for fielding as a first baseman for five years. Ted was selected to the NL All-Star team from 1953 through 1956. Kluszewski was elected to the National Polish-American Sports Hall of Fame in 1974. Ted died in 1988 at age 64.

Richard Kowalski—Hobart—Back—1975

Richard Kowalski was a four-year letter winner in football at Hobart College from 1972 through 1975. As a freshman, he was used as a substitute for Donald Aleksiewicz, the All-America running back. When Aleksiewicz graduated, Kowalski replaced him in the backfield in 1973 and went on to become another record-setting running back. He was among the Division III Annual Champions, All-Time Leaders in rushing career yards from 1972 through 1975 of 4,631 on 907 plays for an average of 5.11 yards per play. He was also one of the All-Time Leaders in rushing career yards per game of 128.6 in 36 games. Dick holds the Hobart College career scoring record with 308 points, and the career total offense record with 4,760 yards. Kowalski was co-captain of the 1975 Hobart squad. He was awarded the Vincent S. Welch Trophy for scholarship, leadership and being elected the team's Most Valuable Player. He also received the Murray Bartlett Trophy for his sportsmanship and love of the game. Kowalski was the second Hobart College player to be chosen first team All-America below Division I-A by the Associated Press and the American Football Coaches Association in 1975. Richard was inducted into the Hobart College Athletic Hall of Fame in 1987.

Edmund Kulakowski—West Virginia—Tackle—1947

Edmund Kulakowski attended Kingston High School in Wilkes-Barre, Pennsylvania where he was an "All-Scholastic" football player and a member of the school's State and Wyoming Valley Conference championship teams from 1936 through 1939. He left the coal mines of Wilkes-Barre in 1940 to enroll at the University of West Virginia where he was a four-year starter and letterman in 1941, 1942, 1946 and 1947. Kulakowski served in the Marines in World War II and was wounded in the Pacific on Saipan and Okinawa. His wartime wounds did not stop him from resuming his studies and football career at West Virginia in 1946 and 1947. At 6-5, 210 pounds, Ed played offensive and defensive tackle. During the 1946 season, the Mountaineers were 7-3-0 and played Army against Davis and Blanchard but lost, 14-7. In the Penn State game, Kulakowski blocked three punts and three extra point kicks. He played four seasons, never missed a game and spent 60 minutes of each game as a two-way tackle. He was named to Street and Smith's football magazine All-Star team and was selected All-America in 1947. Being an outstanding scholar, he was named in "Who's Who in American Universities and Colleges." Ed was chosen to the Blue-Gray team in 1946 and 1947. He was also selected to the West Virginia All-Time 1940-1949 Team and the Decade All-Time offensive and defensive tackle. From 1948 through 1951, Kulakowski was an assistant professor and football line coach at Austin College. He quit coaching and moved to Florida in 1951 where he taught basic sciences, chemistry, physics and astronomy at Edison Community College until retirement in 1983 as an astronomy and geology instructor. During his tenure at Edison, Ed received 17 grants and fellowships from the Atomic Energy Commission, National Science Foundation and the U.S. Department of Energy. Most of his research was in the fields of nuclear structure and chemical radiation as they related to the fields of chemistry and physics. Kulakowski was president of the Fort Meyers Kiwanis Club and the local chapter of Phi Delta Kappa, the national honorary educational fraternity. He is a member of the Disabled American Veterans, American Legion and Florida Academy of Sciences. Edison Community College built an astronomical observatory on campus which they named the Edmund A. Kulakowski Observatory in his honor. The Kulakowski Observatory is the largest and most extensive astronomical observatory in Southwest Florida, and is used by science classes and various community organizations. Ed's wife, also a West Virginia graduate, retired in 1984 as supervisor in health and rehabilitation services in the state of Florida. Their three sons are college graduates and pursuing professional careers.

John Kulakowski—Northwestern State—End—1987

A star football linebacker at Bonnabel High School in Kenner, Louisiana, John Kulakowski was an All-East Bank, All- District performer and named team's Most Valuable Player in his senior year. He enrolled at Northwestern State University, Louisiana in 1984 and became a starting defensive end in the third game of his freshman year. At 6-2, 229 pounds, John had an excellent four-year career as starting defensive end. He closed his college career by setting a new season record for quarterback sacks, and placed third among all players and first among defensive linemen with 96 tackles, nine of them for losses. John was the squad spokesman and often met with the coaches to discuss team problems. Head coach Sam Goodwin said that John led the best team defense of any he ever had at Northwestern. Kulakowski was named All-Southland Conference in 1986 and 1987. At the end of the 1987 season, John was named as Defensive Most Valuable Player by his teammates and was also awarded the Joe Delaney Leadership Trophy, named permanent team captain and honored with the Lester Lation Memorial Award given annually to the player who shows the most determination, dedication, effort and desire. He was also selected Kodak first team All-America by the Associated Press and American Football Coaches Association. John is listed in "Who's Who in American Colleges and Universities," and graduated with a degree in public relations with a minor in marketing. Kulakowski comes from an outstanding college football family including his father Ed, uncle Bob, brother Chris and great-uncle Edmund.

Mark Lagowski—Salisbury State—Linebacker—1982

Mark Lagowski played football at Laurel High School in Laurel, Maryland where he was chosen All-State in his senior year. He enrolled at Salisbury State University, Maryland in 1979 and became one of the most outstanding defensive players in Salisbury College football history. Mark had the natural talents and the athletic ability to make his presence known early in his college career. At 6-2, 210 pounds, Lagowski became a starter on the defensive squad early during his freshman year. He started as a defensive end and rotated as linebacker when needed. Mark was finally established in his permanent spot as a linebacker who developed into a great team leader and a punishing defender. He had the size, strength, intelligence and aggresiveness required for that position. As an example of his leadership qualities, Lagowski was elected team captain during his junior and senior years. He finished his college career with seven interceptions which went for 62 yards. Mark was named the team's Most Valuable Player as a senior in 1982. In recognition of his outstanding football performances at Salisbury, Lagowski was selected College Division Kodak first team All-America linebacker in 1982 by the Associated Press and American Football Coaches Association.

Albin Lezouski—Pittsburgh—Guard—1938

Albin Lezouski (Al Leeson) was a three-year football letter winner at the University of Pittsburgh from 1936 to 1938, and played offensive and defensive guard under head coach Jock Sutherland. During the 1936 season, Pitt finished with an 8-1-1 record, was ranked third in the nation, beat Washington in the Rose Bowl, lost to Duquesne and tied Fordham. The tie with Fordham was one of those classic contests that have gone down in college history as a perfect example of football's defensive battles. Lezouski played 60 minutes of each game, blocking on offense and tackling on defense. In 1937, Pitt's perfect record was marred only by a tie with Fordham in another titanic struggle that ended in a scoreless tie. Panther fumbles in the fourth quarter kept their defense on the field, and the Pitt line led by Lezouski would not allow the Rams to advance the ball closer than the

Panther 41 yard line. The "Blocks of Granite" held Pitt scoreless in 1936 and 1937, but the Panther defense was also outstanding by holding Fordham scoreless during these classic encounters. Lezouski contributed greatly to the Panthers' defensive efforts. Pitt finished the season ranked No. 1 in the country. Finally in 1938, Pittsburgh beat Fordham, 24-13, finished with an 8-2-0 record, and were ranked eighth nationally. For his excellent line play, Lezouski was selected All-America in 1938. He was drafted by the NFL Pittsburgh Steelers in 1939, but chose to remain at Pitt as an assistant coach from 1939 to 1942.

Albin's son, Rick Leeson, was also a three-year football letterman at Pitt and starred as a fullback during the 1961, 1962 and 1963 seasons. Rick played with quarterback, Fred Mazurek, and was the Panther rushing leader in 1961 and 1962 and scoring leader in 1962. Rick is a dentist in Monroeville, Pennsylvania.

Ed Mioduszewski—William and Mary—Back—1952

Ed Mioduszewski lettered in football at The College of William and Mary in 1950, 1951 and 1952. Ed was an outstanding backfield star who played under three different coaches during his three-year football varsity career. Mioduszewski was chosen first team All-Southern Conference back following the 1951 season, and the Associated Press named him Honorable Mention All-America. Ed was elected co-captain of the 1952 squad and had a fantastic year as a backfield star and team leader. He was a repeat first team All-Southern Conference selection and was also chosen second team All-America by the Associated Press. Mioduszewski was selected to play in the Blue-Gray All-Star Football classic in 1952 and the Senior Bowl in 1953. After graduation, Ed was picked by the professional Detroit Lions in the 1953 NFL draft.

Mark Obuszewski—Alfred—Def. Back—1992

An outstanding scholar-athlete at Allegany High School in Allegany, N.Y., Mark Obuszewski enrolled at Alfred University in 1988 and earned his first letter in football during the Saxons' 1989 season as a free safety. He played a key role on the Eastern

College Athletic Conference Northeast Championship team of 1989, and was selected District GTE Academic All-America. Mark missed the entire 1990 season with a knee injury, but at 6-1, 195 pounds, came back strong to finish as Alfred's second leading tackler during the 1991 campaign. He also completed three of three passes for 65 yards, returned three punts for 28 yards, and was team leader with six pass interceptions for 54 yards. Obuszewski was elected captain of the 1991 squad and voted Most Valuable Player for the season. He was re-elected captain for the 1992 season and had a remarkable outing. Mark finished as team leader in total tackles, solo tackles, pass breakups, pass interceptions, fumble recoveries and punt returns. He was again voted the team's MVP, showing the respect his coaches and teammates had for him. Obuszewski, a Dean's List electrical engineering student, was named Kodak first team All-America by the American Football Coaches Association at the end of the 1992 season. He was honored on their Division II team, made up of the best players in the country from NCAA Division III and NAIA Division II colleges and universities. Mark was also honored on the first team of the ECAC Division III team, one of only two defensive secondary players on the squad. He also received All-America honors from the College Sports Information Directors of America. Obuszewski graduated in December of 1992 with a GPA of 2.94 in Electrical Engineering. Alfred University was ranked fourth academically among Northeast regional schools in U.S. News and World Report college rankings. Alfred boasts of over 50 academic and athletic All-Americans in the last decade. Among them are Mark Szynkowski, class of 1989, and Mark Obuszewski, class of 1992.

Jerry Ostroski—Tulsa—Guard—1991

Jerry Ostroski was a two-way tackle at Owen J. Roberts High School in Collegeville, Pennsylvania who earned first team all-conference, all-area, and all-suburban Philadelphia honors in his senior year. He was also an honorable mention selection to the Southeastern Pennsylvania tri-state area, including Pennsylvania, New Jersey and Delaware. Ostroski enrolled at the University of Tulsa in 1988 and wrote football history as an outstanding offensive guard. Jerry was a four-year letter winner and a three-year starter in football. He was a part-time starter at tackle as a true freshman and the only freshman to earn a letter during the 1988 season. He was graded highly for his performance as a sophomore and was an athletic academic achievement award recipient. He made the switch from strong tackle to quick guard during spring drills before the 1990 campaign. Jerry was selected the offensive lineman of the game four times during the '90 season and the coaches rated his overall performance very highly. He also repeated as an athletic academic achievement award winner. At 6-4, 305 pounds, Ostroski had good size and strength, was a dominant player and possessed good speed for his size. He had an excellent 1991 season and was greatly responsible for the Hurricanes' winning year with a 10-2-0 record. He was particularly effective in the Freedom Bowl game in which Tulsa upset San Diego State, 28-17. For his performance in the bowl game, Jerry was selected first team offensive guard to the 1991 All-Bowl team. He received greater honors by being chosen first team consensus All-America offensive guard by major selectors. He was also selected to play in the Senior Bowl game. In 1995 he was a starting guard with the Buffalo Bills. Ostroski plans to become an athletic trainer.

Thomas Pierzga—Boston University—Tackle—1979

Thomas Pierzga was a four-year starting tackle at Massapequa High School in Massapequa, New York and was All-Division and All-County team selectee. He was also All-Division and All-County in wrestling and finished second in New York State. He finished fourth in the County in both the shot-put and discus throw in track. Pierzga began his football career in his sophomore year at Boston University as an offensive tackle on the varsity squad but was moved to defense for the 1978 season as a junior. At 6-4, 250 pounds, he found himself a home at the defensive tackle position, and finished fourth on the team in total tackles during the 1978 campaign. He excelled in the games against Rhode Island, Dartmouth, Holy Cross and Bucknell. Tom blocked a Holy Cross punt and intercepted a Bucknell pass for a touchdown. He made several weekly All-East teams. Pierzga was elected co-captain of the 1979 team which finished with an excellent 8-1-1 record and a 4-1-0 mark in the Yankee Conference. Tom starred as one of the leading tacklers, led the team in fumble recoveries, and was second in quarterback sacks. He was named to the weekly All-East and All-Yankee Conference teams after their victory over Harvard. He was given the Jim Meredith Award in 1979 which Boston University presents annually to the top player for competitiveness. Pierzga was selected first team All-Yankee Conference defensive tackle. He was also honored by being selected first team All-America, below Division I-A, by the Associated Press and the American Football Coaches Association.

Robert Pietuszka—Delaware—Def. Back—1976

Robert Pietuszka starred in football at St. Elizabeth High School in Wilmington, Delaware and enrolled at the University of Delaware in 1973. He was an excellent football player at Delaware, and was a three-year varsity letter winner at cornerback in 1974, 1975 and 1976. During his first varsity year in 1974, Robert was a reserve defensive back but graduated to a starter before the season ended. The '74 Blue Hen squad went 12-2-0 and advanced to the NCAA Division II title championship before falling to Central Michigan in the Camelia Bowl in Sacramento, California. Pietuszka was the starting safety for the 1975 team that went 8-3-0 but did not qualify for postseason play. He started at cornerback for the 1976 squad that finished with an 8-3-1 record and lost in the NCAA Division II quarter-finals to Northern Michigan. As a sophomore, Pietuszka intercepted one pass and had 25 tackles. In his junior year, he led the team with three interceptions for 28 yards, was fourth on the squad with 71 tackles, and showed outstanding playing abilities in the Virginia Military Institute game with a career high 18 tackles. As a senior, Robert led the team with seven interceptions for 25 yards and returned six punts for 45 yards. During his three-year varsity career, he intercepted eleven passes and currently ranks among the University of Delaware leaders. Pietuszka was honored by the Newark and Wilmington TD Clubs as the Defensive Player of the Year. He was also chosen first team Kodak All-America by the Associated Press and the American Football Coaches Association in 1976.

John Rapacz—Oklahoma—Center—1947

John Rapacz enrolled at the University of Oklahoma after wartime service in the Marines. He was selected All-America center in 1946 during a season that Oklahoma, under head coach Jim Tatum, finished with an 8-3-0 record including a Gator Bowl victory over North Carolina State, and were ranked 14th in the nation. Rapacz was a tireless, highly regarded two-way player who excelled at center on offense and as linebacker on defense. He provided mature leadership to the Oklahoma line and had the instinctive all around skills. John had an excellent 1947 season under new head coach, Bud Wilkinson. The year ended with a winning 7-2-1 mark which earned the Sooners 16th ranking nationally. Rapacz left school after the '47 season and played with the College All-Stars in 1948. He then played professional football with the Chicago Rockets of the All-America Football Conference in 1948 and the Chicago Hornets in 1949 before joining the New York Giants in 1950. Two broken legs led to his retirement as a pro player following the 1954 season. He returned to his hometown of Kalamazoo, Michigan in 1957 to become an assistant high school football coach. Rapacz completed work toward his college degree at Western Michigan University and continued to teach and coach following open-heart surgery in 1981. John died on January 2, 1991 at age 66 following a heart attack while visiting his son in Oklahoma. He was the University of Oklahoma's first post-World War II football All-America. Rapacz was a two-year letter winner at Oklahoma and was selected first team All-Big Six Conference center in 1946 and 1947.

Charles Sieminski—Pennsylvania State—Tackle—1962

Charles Sieminski enrolled at Pennsylvania State University in 1959, and played starting varsity tackle for three years from 1960 through 1962 under head coach Rip Engle. During these years, Penn State had a good winning record, greatly due to Sieminski's strong team contribution at tackle. In 1960, the Nittany Lions finished with a 7-3-0 record, including a Liberty Bowl win over Oregon. They were ranked 16th in the country. The 1961 campaign was equally effective with a 8-3-0 mark, a Gator Bowl victory over Georgia Tech, and number 17 ranking nationally. Sieminski became the team line leader in 1962 and was the defensive stand-out. The three-year letterman was a very strong, aggressive and agile lineman. Led by Sieminski, the Nittany Lions went 9-2-0 with losses only to Army and to Florida in the Gator Bowl. This was the fourth straight year that Penn State was in a bowl game and finished the '62 season ranked ninth in the nation. Sieminski was selected All-America by the Newspaper Enterprise Association and also received All-America honors from the Associated and United Presses. Chuck was chosen to play in the East-West Shrine and College All-Star games in 1963. He helped the College All-Stars beat the Green Bay Packers,

20-17, by his outstanding performance at defensive tackle. The San Francisco 49ers selected Sieminski as their fourth round NFL draft choice in 1963 and he played with them, the Atlanta Falcons, and the Detroit Lions for six years. In 1987, Chuck Sieminski was teaching high school and coaching football at Mountain Top, Pennsylvania.

Bobby Spitulski—Central Florida—Linebacker—1991

A native of Orlando, Florida, Bobby Spitulski was an All-State choice in football and wrestling at Bishop Moore High School. He lettered three times in football and baseball, and twice in wrestling and weight lifting. Spitulski was named the school's Most Athletic Student as a senior. He also excelled in academics, graduating in the top five percent of his class. Bobby enrolled at the University of Central Florida in 1987 and was red-shirted his freshman year. He played his first varsity game in 1988 as a defensive tackle making 72 tackles, three sacks and eight stops for 31 yards in losses. During the 1989 season, Spitulski turned in another excellent performance. In 1990, Central Florida's defense, which held opponents to very few yards, was led by Spitulski. He was chosen second team All-America after starting 13 games at outside linebacker. He made 97 tackles and led the team with 13 quarterback sacks and 18 stops for loss of 105 yards. Bobby was named National Defensive Player of the Week after the Savannah State game during the 1991 campaign. He performed well all season and was chosen All-America by the Associated Press. Bob was also first team All-Independent Conference outside linebacker. Spitulski finished his college football career with 280 tackles, and was selected to play in the East-West Shrine game. At 6-3, 232 pounds, Bobby was the Seattle Seahawks third round choice in the 1992 NFL draft, and has played pro ball for four years with them as a linebacker through the 1995 season. His brother, Jimmy, was a linebacker at the University of Central Florida in 1992.

Joseph Stanowicz—Army—Guard—1944

Joseph Stanowicz began playing varsity football at Army in 1942, just in time to become part of one of the greatest teams in college football history. Stanowicz was a starter at guard and contributed greatly to Army's winning 1942 campaign. The '42 season was head coach Earl Blaik's warning to the football world of the great things to come. The first sign of trouble from the Military Academy came in 1943 when Army finished with a 7-2-1 record and were ranked number 11 in the country. Joe, as one of the starting guards, played along-side the All-America center, Casimir Myslinski. In the '43 Army-Navy game, Stanowicz blocked a Navy kick for a safety that gave Army a 9-0 lead in the third quarter. Army went on to beat Navy, 23-7. The 1944 team was like a Loch Ness monster emerging from the depths of the Hudson River along the palisades of West Point. Coach Blaik had so many men on his squad that he used two separate teams. It was not a two-platoon system with separate offensive and defensive units, but an organization with two complete two-way squads. Stanowicz provided the line leadership on one of the teams, and Glenn Davis and Doc Blanchard were the backfield leaders on the other team. Army's beating of the Irish in 1944 was the worst defeat in Notre Dame history. The Cadets went on to record a perfect undefeated, untied 9-0-0 season and they were ranked number one in the nation. Army also finished first in scoring defense and rushing offense. Stanowicz contributed in a great measure to the success of the Army team and was selected first team All-America in 1944.

David Suminski—Wisconsin—Tackle—1952

A native of Ashland, Wisconsin, David Suminski enrolled at the University of Wisconsin to play football under head coach Ivy Williamson. Suminski's football talents were based on his long experience in playing tackle. In high school he won four letters at this line position, earning such honors as being selected on the All-State squad, being named captain of the Wisconsin-Michigan All-Conference team, and playing in the 1949 North-South high school All-Star game. In his sophomore year at Wisconsin, Suminski was moved from second to first string varsity offensive tackle and held that starting position for the rest of his college career. He had a very good season in 1951, showing fast and steady improvements in his aggressiveness, speed in getting off the line, and blocking assignments. The Badgers finished the season with an excellent 7-1-1 mark, were ranked eighth nationally, and Suminski was named honorable mention All-Big Nine Conference. During the 1952 campaign, David was firmly established as the Wisconsin offensive line leader and his performance was superb. He was particularly impressive in the

Wisconsin Rose Bowl game with the University of Southern California. The Wisconsin starting line-up included Simkowski at center and Andryhowski at end in addition to Suminski. The Badgers finished with a 6-3-1 record, shared the Big-Nine title and were ranked 11th nationally. Suminski's contributions were evident and he was named Wisconsin's MVP, chosen first team All-Big Nine Conference, and selected first team All-America. He played professional football with Washington.

Walter Trojanowski—Connecticut—Back—1949

Walter Trojanowski played four seasons as a starting halfback for the University of Connecticut. Because of military duties, Walt played at U Conn in 1942, 1945, 1946 and 1949. Trojanowski is the all-time leader with 25 career rushing touchdowns, and he is also on the Yankee Conference All-Time Top Ten list with 25 rushing touchdowns during his college football career. In 1945, Walt rushed for 22 touchdowns and scored 132 points. He was the Major College Champion in Scoring and Touchdowns for that year. Trojanowski's top season at U Conn in terms of rushing yards was 1945 when he gained 761 yards on 158 carries. The Huskies finished with an excellent 7-1-0 season for the year. For his entire college football career, Trojanowski ran the ball 311 times for 1,356 yards. He holds the U Conn touchdown records for single games with six TDs vs Worcester Tech, four vs Boston University and four vs Maine during the 1945 campaign. Walt was an excellent athlete, well conditioned, had good hands and was a fast, elusive runner. He had the natural speed and power to run around or over the opposition. He was also a good pass receiver and developed into a very good blocker. Trojanowski was selected to play in the East-West Shrine game in 1946 and was Washington's fourth round pro draft choice that year. He decided not to pursue a professional football career. Walt completed his military obligations and returned to U Conn to play in 1949 and finish his college education. The Associated Press selected Trojanowski first Team All-America for his performance in 1945.

Todd Wilkowski—Ithaca College—Quarterback—1991

A native of Depew, New York, Todd Wilkowski played football at Depew High School and was a third team All-State selection at quarterback. He enrolled at Ithaca College in 1988 and has become the most celebrated quarterback in the Bombers' football history which dates back to 1930. Todd became the starting quarterback during his freshman year in 1988, and was the only signal caller to start in four different seasons at Ithaca. Wilkowski's first collegiate carry was memorable—a 51-yard sprint for a touchdown against St. Lawrence in 1988. He threw for 279 yards and three touchdowns against American International during the 1990 campaign in one of his top performances with the Bombers. He also led Ithaca to a 34-20 win over Dayton for a victory in the Amos Alonzo Stagg Bowl and the NCAA Division III Championship in 1991. Wilkowski had a fantastic college football career and finished with amazing regular season statistics of 3,339 yards passing for 30 touchdowns, plus 976 yards rushing for 16 more touchdowns. In post-season games, Wilkowski passed for 1,192 yards and eight touchdowns and ran for 387 yards and four more touchdowns. During his four-year football career, Todd established 11 Ithaca College regular season and 12 playoff records in passing yards and total offense. He led Ithaca to an outstanding four-year career over-all record of 40-7-0. Wilkowski played on two NCAA Division III Championship teams (1988 and 1991). He was selected to the Champion U.S.A. Division III All-America team in 1991. He graduated with a 3.0 GPA in Physical Therapy.

John Witkowski—Columbia—Quarterback—1983

John Witkowski had one of the most unusual college football careers at Columbia University. While quarter backing Columbia's football team during three losing seasons (1-9-0, 1-9-0, and 1-7-2), Witkowski went on to establish all sorts of passing and total offense records for which he received numerous honors including All-America selection. He lettered in 1981, 1982 and 1983 and captained the 1983 squad. During the 1981 season, Witkowski attempted 294 passes, completed 129 for 1,647 yards and four touchdowns. In 1982, he attempted 453 passes, completed 250 for 3,050 yards and 29 touchdowns. During the 1983 campaign, John attempted 429 passes, completed 234 for 3,152 yards and 23 touchdowns. His longest play in passing was a 93 yarder in 1983 against Bucknell. Witkowski holds Ivy League and Columbia University football records for touchdown passes in a game, season and career; total offense in total plays for a game, season and career; total offense in total yards in all three categories; and passing attempts, completions and passing yards for a game, season and career. For his accomplishments in an unfortunate losing cause, Columbia awarded Witkowski with the David W. Smyth Cup in 1982 and 1983. This cup is presented annually to the outstanding varsity football player for spirit, leadership, sportsmanship and loyalty. He was also the recipient of the Asa S. Bushnell Cup as the Ivy League Player of the Year. Witkowski holds 14 Ivy League records and numerous Columbia University records including total offense with 3,167 yards in 1983, 2,947 yards in 1982 and 7,748 yards for career from 1981 through 1983. John was selected to the All-Ivy League team in 1982 and 1983, Eastern College Athletic Conference Player of the Year for 1982 and 1983, and Ivy League Player of the Year for 1982 and 1983. He was also named an Honorable Mention All-America in 1982 and chosen All-America in 1983. Witkowski was the Detroit Lions NFL pro draft choice in 1983 and quarterbacked the Lions, Houston Oilers and the WLAF champion London Monarchs.

Steve Wojciechowski—Buffalo—Linebacker—1987

A graduate of Bishop Timon High School in Buffalo, New York, Steve Wojciechowski attended St. Lawrence University before transferring to the State University of Buffalo in 1985. He had an outstanding three-year football career at Buffalo as a starting inside linebacker at 6-1, 235 pounds. Steve set UB season records for unassisted and total tackles during the 1987 campaign and tied the school mark for assisted tackles. He also established the Buffalo game standards for solo and total tackles against Connecticut State University, and tied the game mark for assisted tackles against Albany State. In his three-year college football career at UB, Wojciechowski made 279 tackles (106 solo and 173 assisted), intercepted two passes and had six pass breakups. Buffalo head coach Bill Dando said of Wojciechowski: "He's as fine a linebacker as we've had since we brought the program back in 1977, and that includes three All-Americans. With his size and quickness, he could have played on our Division I teams of the 1960s. Steve is tough, has an instinct for the ball, pursues well and he sticks people when he gets there." Steve was the UB 1987 team captain and received the Outstanding Linebacker Award at the end of the season. Wojciechowski was only the second University of Buffalo football player to be selected Kodak first team All-America by the Associated Press and the American Football Coaches Association.

Dan Zakashefski—Montclair State—Def. Tackle—1986

A native of Middlesex, New Jersey, Dan Zakashefski was a three-year football letter winner as an offensive tackle at Montclair State College in New Jersey from 1984 through 1986. He became the only two-time Kodak first team All-American in Montclair State College football history. Dan was used sparingly during his freshman year in 1983 and was credited with five total tackles. He became a starter during the 1984 season and had an excellent year. He finished with 45 total tackles (24 unassisted and 21 assisted) and had eight sacks. His performance earned him honorable mention on the New Jersey Athletic Conference. During the 1985 campaign, Zakashefski was an excellent defensive lineman with 70 total tackles (41 solo and 29 assists) and 14 sacks. Montclair State was in the Division III Championship playoffs and beat Western Connecticut State in the first round but lost to Ithaca College in the quarterfinals. Dan was singled out for individual honors by being selected to the first team All-New Jersey Athletic Conference and All-Eastern College Athletic Conference. He was also selected Kodak first team All-America by the Associated Press and the American Football Coaches Association. The 1986 season was another good one for Zakashefski and Montclair State. Dan was credited with 74 total tackles (37 solos and 37 assists) and six sacks. The Red Hawks were in the Division Championship playoffs again and beat Hofstra in the first round only to lose to Ithaca College in the quarterfinals. Zakashefski repeated as a first team defensive lineman on the All-NJAC and the All-ECAC. He was also selected first team Pizza Hut Division III All-America and the prestigous Kodak All-America. At the time of Dan's graduation, he was the only two-time Kodak first team All-America and the all-time sack leader at Montclair State College.

CHAPTER V

HONORABLE MENTION ALL-AMERICANS

Jason Bednarz—Southern Methodist—Linebacker—1992
Dave Bielinski—Bowling Green—Def. Back—1992
Richard Bielski—Maryland—Fullback—1954
John Biskup—Syracuse—Kicker—1992
Michael Chalenski—UCLA—Def. End—1992
Kevin Czarnecki—Army—Linebacker—1993
Arden Czyzewski—Florida—Kicker—1991
Eddie Jankowski—Wisconsin—Fullback—1937
Joseph Klecko—Temple—Guard—1976
Edward Klewicki—Michigan State—End—1934
Scott Kowalkowski—Notre Dame—Linebacker—1990
Robert Kuberski—Navy—Def. Tackle—1992
Ed Kulakowski—Austin Peay State—Guard—1955
Charles Matuszak—Dartmouth—Center—1966
Fred Mazurek—Pittsburgh—Quarterback—1964
Mike Munchak—Pennsylvania State—Off. Guard—1981
James Ninowski—Michigan State--Quarterback—1957
Frank Nowak—Lafayette—Quarterback—1983
Steve Ostrowski—Northwestern—Linebacker—1993
John Pirog—Army—Off. Guard—1992
Mark Rypien—Washington State—Quarterback—1985
John Strzykalski—Marquette—Halfback—1944
Mark Szlachcic—Bowling Green—Wide Receiver—1992
Dick Szymanski—Notre Dame—Center—1954
Scott Zolak—Maryland—Quarterback—1990

Jason Bednarz—Southern Methodist—Linebacker—1992

Jason Bednarz was an outstanding scholar-athlete at Slaton High School in Slaton, Texas as a National Honor Society vice-president, honor roll student and student council vice-president. He was also a three-year football letterman and honorable mention all-district quarterback in 1985. In addition, Jason was a punter and linebacker during the 1987 season. Bednarz was red-shirted in 1988 as a freshman at Southern Methodist University, but was one of their biggest surprises in 1989. He tried out as a walk-on quarterback but was switched to an interior linebacker where he flourished. Jason started nine games and was awarded a football scholarship. He finished third on the team with 81 tackles (58 solos and four for losses). Bednarz underwent knee surgery in the off-season and saw only limited action in the 1990 spring practice. However, he started all 11 games at inside linebacker during the 1990 season, and finished third on the team with 99 tackles of which 59 were unassisted. Most players would have been sidelined with the assortment of injuries that beset Jason during the 1991 season. Despite a bad turf toe, broken finger and other ailments, he finished second on the team with 117 tackles. He was named SMU's Unsung Hero of 1991. He also received the Lettermen's Association Award which is presented to the player who best shows the characteristics of hard work, determination and team spirit typical of a letterman. In addition, Jason was an Honorable Mention All-America selection at the end of the season. At 6-2, 235 pounds, Bednarz continued to star during the 1992 campaign and led the team with 126 tackles. He received the Christian-Terrell Award presented to the defensive player who is voted Most Valuable by his teammates, and the Mustang Club Award presented to the Most Valuable Defensive Player as chosen by the coaching staff. Once again, Jason was selected Honorable Mention All-America linebacker at the end of the season. He finished his four-year college football career with 423 tackles of which 258 were solos. Bednarz graduated with a major in public relations. His brother, Devin, played football at Northeast Oklahoma State University.

Dave Bielinski—Bowling Green—Def. Back—1992

A four-year football letterman at Trinity High School in North Royalton, Ohio, Dave Bielinski played wide receiver and defensive back on the league championship team, earned all-state and all-district honors twice and all-league honors three times. Bielinski was red-shirted as a freshman in 1988 at Bowling Green State University. He won his first letter during the 1989 season as a back-up free safety. He finished with 28 tackles and tied for the team lead with two pass interceptions. Dave started all ten games at defensive back during the 1990 campaign and finished ninth in the nation, third in the Mid-American Conference and first on the team with six pass interceptions. He was third on the team with 102 tackles, and was the Falcon's Player of the Week twice. Bielinski earned Honorable Mention All-Mid-American Conference honors and was an All-MAC choice on *Football News'* all conference team. At 6-3, 215 pounds, Dave had another outstanding year in 1991. He intercepted four passes and was third on the team with 96 tackles. He ranked with the best hard tacklers in the country and was named MAC Player of the Week for his performance against West Virginia. Bielinski was chosen Honorable Mention All-America defensive back and was the choice of MAC coaches and *Football News* as a first team All-MAC defensive back. Dave finished with an excellent 1992 season and was again named All-MAC defensive back. During his career at Bowling Green, Bielinski made 295 tackles and 14 pass interceptions. A communications graduate, Dave was presented with the Carlos Jackson Memorial Award at the completion of the 1992 campaign. This honor is given to the player who makes the biggest contribution to the team in the areas of leadership, inspiration and extra effort.

Richard Bielski—Maryland—Fullback—1954

Richard Bielski starred as an offensive and defensive back at Patterson Park High School in Baltimore, Maryland, and was selected all-state in his senior year. He enrolled at the University of Maryland in 1951 and played football under head coach Jim Tatum. During his first varsity year in 1952, Bielski had an excellent outing against Georgia when he bulled his way through the Bulldogs for 67 yards in nine carries. He was used sparingly during the season but rushed 28 times for 154 yards, finishing with a 5.5 yards per carry average. The Terps had a 7-2-0 season record and were ranked 13th nationally. Dick lived up to his expectations during the 1953 campaign by nailing down the starting fullback and place kicker positions. At 6-0, 200 pounds, Bielski was very strong, had good speed and developed into an outstanding blocker. He helped Maryland finish with a 10-1-0 record and a No. 1 national ranking. He was the backfield and kicking star for Maryland in 1954 and led them to a 7-2-0 season and number eight national ranking. He was selected first team All-Atlantic Coast Conference fullback and named Honorable Mention All-America after the 1954 season. Dick was chosen to play with the College All-Stars in 1955. Philadelphia selected Bielski as their first round NFL draft choice in 1955. He played with them for five years, followed by two years with Dallas and two years with Baltimore. He was a Pro Bowl selection as an end in 1962. As a pro, Bielski caught 107 passes for 1,035 yards and 12 touchdowns. He also kicked 58 PATS and 26 field goals. He was receiver coach for Baltimore from 1964 through 1972, and joined Washington in a similar capacity in 1973.

John Biskup—Syracuse—Kicker—1992

An outstanding football place kicker at East Islip High School in East Islip, New York, John Biskup was named All-America, All-State, All-Long Island, and All-County. He also played tail back and defensive back and was team captain in his senior year. Biskup was red-shirted as a freshman in 1988 at the University of Syracuse. After a slow start in 1989, he finished with the sixth best field goal percentage in Syracuse football history. He won the East Carolina game with a 24-yard field goal with only four seconds left to play, and was named Most Valuable Player. He was also given the game ball and was named Eastern College Athletic Conference Rookie of the Week. John was named Special Teams Player of the Week for his performance in the game with Florida State. He won the Peach Bowl game for Syracuse by kicking a 26-yard field goal against Georgia with only seconds left to play. He finished the season leading the team in scoring with 67 points. In 1990, John led the team in scoring again with 63 points and tied the Syracuse single game record with seven PATS against Vanderbilt. Biskup's team leading 85 points made during the 1991 campaign were the seventh highest in Syracuse football history. He was named the Big East Special Teams Player of the Week once, and Syracuse Special Teams Player of the Week three times. John tied the Big East record in field goals and was second in scoring. At 5-9, 187 pounds, Biskup became the most accurate field goal kicker in Syracuse football history and all-time leader in PATS. He was instrumental in Syracuse's win over Ohio State in the Hall of Fame Bowl. He received Big East and ECAC honors at the end of the '91 season. During the 1992 campaign, Biskup led the team with 81 points and established a new SU all-time career scoring record with 295 points. He helped Syracuse win several games with field goals, and led the Big East in scoring. He was named SU's Special Teams Player of the Year. John was selected first team All-Big East and All-Eastern College Athletic Conferences as place kicker. Biskup was also named an Honorable Mention All-America at the completion of the 1992 season.

Michael Chalenski—Pittsburgh and UCLA—Def. End—1992

An outstanding athlete at Brearly Regional High School in Kenilworth, New Jersey, Michael Chalenski starred in football, baseball and track. As linebacker and fullback, Mike was selected first team All-America and 1988 New Jersey Player of the Year. He enrolled at the University of Pittsburgh in 1988 and played in 10 of 12 games as a freshman. He made 50 tackles including five for loss. Mike had a career-high ten tackles against Notre Dame and was selected to the *Sporting News* Freshman Honor Roll. Chalenski was red-shirted during the 1989 season after transferring to UCLA. In 1990, he started six games at defensive end and appeared in just seven overall because of a shoulder injury. He recorded eight tackles against Oregon State, and finished with 27 for the year. During the 1991 season, Mike had an outstanding outing having recovered from shoulder surgery. At 6-5, 260 pounds, he finished with 36 tackles of which 23 were solos. He helped UCLA to a good, winning 9-3-0 season in which they defeated Illinois in the John Hancock Bowl. Chalenski was selected All-PAC-10 defensive lineman and to the *Football News* "Almost All-America" team. Mike had an excellent 1992 season finishing with 42 tackles of which 27 were unassisted. He was chosen again to the All-PAC-10 team and named Honorable Mention All-America defensive end. He was selected to play in the East-West Shrine and the Hula Bowl games at the end of the season. Chalenski was drafted by the NFL Philadelphia Eagles and was their defensive lineman during the 1995 season.

Kevin Czarnecki—Army—Linebacker—1993

An excellent student-athlete at West Catholic High School in Grand Rapids, Michigan, Kevin Czarnecki played linebacker and fullback in football. He was captain of the football and wrestling teams his senior year, and was named All-City, All-Area and All-State in football. Son of a retired sergeant major who served 26 years in the Army, Kevin considered the football and educational opportunities before choosing West Point. He was nearly forced to give up football his freshman year because of a pinched neck nerve. However, a special neck brace designed to eliminate the "stingers" enabled him to play during the 1991 season and he proved to be a valuable asset to the Army team. At 6-1, 235 pounds, Czarnecki became a starter at inside linebacker and finished third on the squad with 99 tackles while sharing the lead with two interceptions. He had a high of 14 tackles against Boston College and followed with 13 versus North Carolina. During the 1992 campaign, Kevin proved that he was one of the East's best linebackers. He turned in an impressive performance with career-high 21 tackles in the annual Army-Navy game. In the classic battle with Navy, Kevin's outstanding play caused one of the television commentators to state that every team needs Czarnecki at linebacker. His 131 season tackles earned him the coaches' choice for an Outstanding Performance Award. He was also selected All-East linebacker for 1992. Kevin was firmly established as Army's defensive leader at the start of the 1993 season, and he lived up to everyone's expectations. He was ranked first in tackles and proved to be an inspirational defensive leader. Czarnecki again performed magnificently in the annual Army-Navy game, and was chosen game's Most Valuable Player for Army. (Jim Kubiak was MVP for Navy). Kevin received the coaches' Outstanding Performance Award again, and was named for All-East honors. He was also chosen Honorable Mention All-America linebacker for 1993.

Arden Czyzewski—Florida—Kicker—1991

Arden Czyzewski was a first team All-State place kicker in 1986 at Tampa King High School before enrolling at the University of Florida. He was red-shirted as a freshman in 1987 at Florida, and saw limited action as a back-up place kicker during the 1988 season. In 1989, Czyzewski made nine out of nine PAT attempts and was seven for seven in field goals. He kicked a 41-yard game winning field goal to beat Louisiana State 16-13. His kick was named the Southeast Conference Play of the Week. Czyzewski sustained a torn anterior cruciate ligament to his left knee and missed the final four games of the year. The 1990 campaign was an outstanding one for Arden. He made 15 of 19 field goal attempts, the longest being 46 yards against Mississippi State. He made 42 of 45 PAT tries which set a single season Gator school record. Czyzewski also took over the punting chores in the fourth game of the '90 season. Only six of his 32 punts were returned and 10 were placed inside the 20 yard line. Arden led the Gator squad and was fourth in the Southeastern Conference in scoring. He was selected the special team's Most Valuable Player for 1990. He continued to another record scoring season in 1991 and finished leading the Gator squad for the second year. Czyzewski set the Sugar Bowl record with five field goals in Notre Dame's upset victory over Florida. He was selected first team Southeastern Conference place kicker, chosen first team on the 1991 All-Bowl team, and named Honorable Mention All-America place kicker. He was also selected to play in the Senior Bowl game.

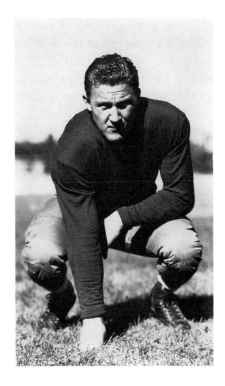

Eddie Jankowski—Wisconsin—Fullback—1936

A native of Milwaukee, Eddie Jankowski was a three-year football letterman as an outstanding player at the University of Wisconsin from 1934 through 1936. Playing as a fullback and linebacker, Jankowski was elected Wisconsin's Most Valuable Player by leading the Badgers on offense and defense in his junior year during the 1935 season. He received the Jimmy Demetral Award which is presented annually to the player most instrumental to the success of the team as chosen by his teammates. In 1936, Ed was chosen for the Jimmy Demetral Award again as the Badgers' MVP. He was one of ten candidates for the Chicago Tribune Big Ten Conference MVP Award as a junior and senior. He finished tied for third place as a senior in 1936. Jankowski was selected All-Big Ten fullback, named an Honorable Mention All-America, and chosen to the College All-Star and East-West Shrine teams. A first round NFL draft pick in 1937, Ed played pro ball with the Green Bay Packers for five years, and was All-Pro

156

in 1940. He was inducted into the University of Wisconsin W Club Hall of Fame in 1992.

Joseph Klecko—Temple—Guard—1976

Joseph Klecko starred for the Temple University football team from 1973 to 1976 where he displayed the defensive talents that led him to professional football stardom. As a freshman, he was the Eastern College Athletic Conference Rookie of the Week after the 1973 Delaware game when he had 15 tackles and five quarterback sacks. The Owls finished the '73 season with an excellent 9-1-0 record under head coach Wayne Hardin. Klecko became the Temple defensive leader during the 1974 campaign with 114 tackles. He repeated as the leading tackler during the 1975 season with 104 tackles of which 57 were solos. Klecko helped Temple to another winning 8-2-0 record. In recognition of his performance, he was selected to the All-ECAC team and named Honorable Mention All-America. Once again, he was the Owls' leading tackler in 1976 and was selected first team All-East middle guard. He also repeated as an Honorable Mention All-America. Klecko is the Temple defensive leader with 373 career tackles of which 152 were unassisted and 221 assisted. He was drafted by the New York Jets, became a starter in the ninth game of his rookie season and had more sacks than any other NFL freshman. He was chosen All-Pro three times and became the first defensive player ever to be picked to the Pro Bowl at three different positions. In 1981, Klecko was selected the NFL Defensive Player of the Year, and played professional football for 12 years. Joe was inducted into the Temple University Hall of Fame in 1987, and has been a candidate for election to the Polish-American Sports Hall of Fame.

Edward Klewicki—Michigan State—End—1934

Edward Klewicki starred in football at Hamtramck High School, Hamtramck, Michigan before becoming an outstanding end at Michigan State University. He lettered in football in 1932, 1933 and 1934 during which period the Spartans compiled an excellent 19-4-2 record. As a sophomore in 1932, Klewicki set up Michigan State's first score by blocking a Syracuse punt. In 1933, the Spartans lost Jim Crowley to Fordham and Charley Bachman became the new head coach. In the Marquette game, Ed enabled the Spartans to make the winning touchdown by causing the opposing punter to fumble the ball which Michigan State recovered and scored. In the 27-3 win over Syracuse, Klewicki caught a pass for a touchdown and played an outstanding game on defense. During the 1934 season, Ed starred in the 16-0 win over the Wolverines by catching three straight passes for sizable gains. He also had good games against Carnegie Tech and helped in scoring against Marquette with his timely pass catches. He received the Governor of Michigan Award in 1934. This award is presented annually to the player who is voted the most valuable performer on the team by the men on the football squad. The presentation is made each year by the governor of Michigan. In addition, Klewicki was honored by Michigan State by being selected as an end on the Old Timers team consisting of pre-1940 players only. He was also named an Honorable Mention All-America in 1934. Klewicki was drafted by the Detroit Lions in 1935 and played four years of pro ball. Ed was elected to the National Polish-American Sports Hall of Fame in 1982.

Scott Kowalkowski—Notre Dame—Linebacker—1990

A star athlete at St. Mary's High School in Orchard Lake, Michigan, Scott Kowalkowski earned four letters in football, two in track and one in baseball. He won all sorts of local, state and national honors in football, and captained the football team as a senior before enrolling at the University of Notre Dame in 1987. As a freshman at Notre Dame, Scott was used as a reserve linebacker but earned most of his playing time with the special teams. During the 1988 season, he was the top back-up for a senior linebacker and a member of the kicking teams. He was a solid fundamental player, hard-hitting, aggresive defender who helped Notre Dame to improve their pass rush. Scott excelled in the Purdue, Air Force and West Virginia (Fiesta Bowl) games. He captured the starting linebacker job during the 1989 spring drills and started all but one game during the season. He turned in an outstanding performance in '89 and was selected Honorable Mention All-America. Scott made 150 special team appearances, led both teams with 11 tackles in the Orange Bowl against Colorado, and had a total of 29 tackles versus Air Force, Michigan, Stanford and Navy. He started every game in 1990 and was named Honorable Mention All-America again. At 6-2, 230 pounds, Scott was a versatile performer who was the only Notre Dame player to see action in every game over his four-year career, including the Senior Bowl. In 1995, Scott was a linebacker with the Detroit Lions.

His father, Robert, played football at the University of Virginia and pro ball for 11 years with the Detroit Lions.

Robert Kuberski—Navy—Def. Tackle—1992

A scholar-athlete at Ridley High School in Folsom, Pennsylvania, Robert Kuberski played on the league championship football team and was captain of the west squad in the Hero Bowl All-Star prep game. He was chosen all-league, all-county and

All-Southeastern Pennsylvania in football. Bob was also on the state runner-up team in lacrosse. Kuberski entered the U.S. Naval Academy in 1989 and played on the plebe junior varsity team. In 1990, he started the final seven games of the season at defensive tackle and finished third on the team with 74 tackles. Kuberski received the Eastern College Athletic Conference All-East weekly honor roll citation for his performance in the James Madison game. During the 1991 season, Bob led the Navy defensive line in tackles with 86 and five tackles for losses of 13 yards. He was given the ECAC All-East weekly honor roll citation again for his performance against Delaware. At the end of the '91 campaign, he was selected first team All-East by the Associated Press and Eastern College Athletic Conference as defensive lineman. At 6-4, 281 pounds, Kuberski had excellent quickness and size which enabled him to make the big plays. He had an excellent outing during the 1992 season and provided the defensive line leadership for Navy. In his three-year varsity career at Navy, Bob finished with 240 total tackles of which 152 were unassisted. Kuberski was selected first team All-East defensive lineman by the Eastern College Athletic Conference. He was also named Honorable Mention All-America defensive lineman for 1992.

Ed Kulakowski—Austin Peay State—Guard—1955

An outstanding student-athlete at Edwardsville High School in Edwardsville, Pennsylvania, Ed Kulakowski played football and basketball and was active in wrestling and track. He enrolled at the Virginia Polytechnic Institute and played football for one year. He had to leave Virginia Tech the following year to help support his family by working in the coal mines. Ed resumed his college education and football career in 1953 by enrolling at Austin Peay State University in Clarksville, Tennessee. He played as an offensive and defensive guard who did not miss a game during his three years of varsity football. Ed was chosen all-state and all-conference guard and was also named Honorable Mention All-America in recognition of his excellent performances. In addition, he was a three year letterman in track. Kulakowski was an honor graduate with a bachelor of science degree in mathemathics. He coached football at Austin Peay for two years and then became engineer and operations manager in network planning and engineering with South Central Bell in New Orleans.

His son, Ed, Jr., starred in football and graduated from Northwestern Louisiana State University and the University of New Orleans. He did graduate work in computer science at St. Regis Jesuit College. Son, Chris, also played football and graduated from Southeastern Louisiana State University with a B.S. degree in industrial engineering. Another son, John, was an All-American and an honor student at Northwestern Louisiana State University. Ed's great-uncle, Edmund, was an outstanding scholar-athlete, and All-America at West Virginia University.

Charles Matuszak—Dartmouth—Center—1966

An outstanding scholar-athlete, Charles "Chuck" Matuszak graduated from Jamesville-Dewitt High School in Fayetteville, New York where he was in the top fifth of his class. He was named to the all-county football teams his junior and senior years, and played on teams which won the county championships. Chuck was also a key member and captain of the baseball team. He was a member of the National Honor Society and received a National Merit Letter of Commendation. Matuszak enrolled at Dartmouth College in 1963 and had a fantastic football career. After helping Dartmouth to an undefeated season in 1965, Chuck was a unanimous All-Ivy League selection at center. A consistent standout, Matuszak led the Indians to their successful defense of the Ivy League title and to another excellent, winning year with a 7-2-0 record during the 1966 campaign. He was chosen All-Ivy League center again and received a host of other honors. Chuck was selected first team All-New England, first team All-East and Associated Press Honorable Mention All-America center. His father, Dr. Walter Matuszak (formerly Matuszczak), was an All-America and captain of the 1940 Cornell University football team which defeated Dartmouth in the famous "fifth down" game. Chuck followed in his father's footsteps, studied medicine after graduation and went into private practice. In 1973, coaches, writers and sportscasters associated with Ivy League football picked an All-Time Conference team. Selected to this All-Time squad was Chuck Matuszak as the second team offensive center. Stas Maliszewski of Princeton was first team offensive guard.

Fred Mazurek—Pittsburgh—Quarterback—1964

Fred Mazurek came to the University of Pittsburgh in 1961 from Redstone High School where he was an outstanding athlete excelling in football and baseball. He was a three-year letter winner at Pitt and a very effective offensive leader for the Panthers. He had an excellent season in 1963 when Pitt finished with a 9-1-0 record under head coach John Michelosen and was ranked fourth in the nation. During the '63 campaign, Michelosen kept the two deep backs in single wing formation, but he added a quarterback, Mazurek, under the center and an end spaced 15 yards from the tackle with a wing back in the slot between them. The result was a wide open attack combining power, passing and deception. Against Washington, Mazurek hit on 11 of 16 passes, then intercepted a fourth period pass on the Pitt 13 yard line to stop the Huskies, 13-6. In the game with West Virginia, Fred caught an 11-yard touchdown pass from the tail back to beat the Mountaineers, 13-10. Mazurek was an excellent, versatile performer who could pass, run and catch and kept the opposing defense bewildered. He was the Pitt career passing leader from 1962 through 1964 and had the best total offensive careers for those years. Fred was the Panthers annual leader in passing (1963 and 1964), rushing (1963), scoring (1963) and total yards (1963 and 1964). He broke the school record (prior to 1982) at Pitt for yards gained in one season by passing for 949 yards and running for 646 for a total of 1,595 yards. Mazurek was a big man on campus in 1964 when he courted the coach's daughter, Sue Michelosen. (They later married and had a son who was a highly rated prep quarterback). Mazurek was named Honorable Mention All-America, and selected to play in the East-West Shrine game. He played professional football as a flanker for several years with the Washington Redskins. Mazurek became an attorney and was the director of corporate taxes for Avery International Corporation in California.

Mike Munchak—Pennsylvania State—Off. Guard—1981

Mike Munchak starred in football as fullback and defensive end at Central High School in Scranton, Pennsylvania. He became an offensive lineman at Pennsylvania State University and played both tackle and guard, but started every game at offensive guard in his senior year. The Nittany Lions, under head coach Joe Paterno, compiled an excellent 28-8-0 record during Munchak's three years. They won the Liberty Bowl in 1979 and were ranked 20th in the country, then beat Ohio State in the 1980 Fiesta Bowl to finish number eight nationally. The 1981 season saw Penn State's high power offense operate with Munchak and Leo Wisniewski leading the offensive linemen. Mike performed like a well-oiled machine helping Penn State to beat the University of Southern California in the Fiesta Bowl and rank third in the nation with a 10-2-0 record. He had a brilliant season as an offensive guard who devoted much of his time blocking for Curt Warner and other backs. In recognition of his contribution to Penn State's success, Mike was named an Honorable Mention All-America after the 1981 campaign. He was eligible to play for Penn State in 1982 because he was red-shirted in 1978. But he received his B.S. degree in business logistics and decided to enter the 1982 NFL draft. Mike was the Houston Oilers' first round selection, and as of 1993, had played 12 years as an Oiler. He was selected a Pro Bowler eight times and was a Pro Bowl starter six times. Munchak was chosen to the NFL's "Team of the Decade" for the 1980s, and to the Oilers' 30th Anniversary "Dream Team" in 1989. Football experts feel that Mike will be elected to the Pro Football Hall of Fame when he retires.

James Ninowski—Michigan State—Quarterback—1957

One of the most under-rated quarterbacks in college football, Jim Ninowski came to Michigan State University from Pershing High School, Detroit, Michigan in 1954. He was a three year football letter winner from 1955 through 1957 under head coach Duffy Daugherty. Jim was selected the Spartans' Spring Game Outstanding Player in 1955 and was used as a substitute quarterback for the season. During the 1956 campaign, Wilson was the starting quarterback and Ninowski was delegated to a back-up role. He was again selected the Spring Game Outstanding Player in 1957 and took over as the starting quarterback at the beginning of the regular season. Jim turned in an excellent performance for the year. For example, he threw six straight touchdown passes in the game with Indiana to beat them 54-0. Against California, Ninowski completed nine of 14 passes for 151 yards and passed for three touchdowns to win 19-0. Jim finished the 1957 campaign with a completion percentage of .570 average, having completed 45 of 79 attempts. Michigan State ended the season with a 8-1-0 record, were number two in the Big Ten Conference and number three in the nation. He was selected first team consensus All-Big Ten Conference and Honorable Mention All-America. He was named the Most Valuable Player in the North-South game in 1957 and also played in the Hula and Senior Bowl games. Jim really distinguished himself during the College All-Star game in 1958 when he threw two touchdown passes and, with Walt Kowalczyk, led the All-Stars to a 35-19 victory over the Detroit Lions. For his contribution, Ninowski was selected the All-Stars Most Valuable Player. He received the Danziger Award in 1957 as the player from the Detroit area who made the most outstanding contribution to the Michigan State football team. He was the fourth round NFL draft choice of the Cleveland Browns in 1958 and had a fantastic 12 year professional football career. In 1959, Ninowski was the Old Timers' Spring Game Outstanding Player at Michigan State University. Jim was presented with the prestigous Daugherty Award in 1979 which goes annually to the Michigan State University football alumnus who has distinguished himself in endeavors on and off the football field since his graduation. Ninowski was honored as an outstanding professional football player and a successful business executive.

Frank Nowak—Lafayette—Quarterback—1983

One of the most outstanding quarterbacks in Lafayette College football history, Frank Nowak led the Leopards to excellent winning seasons during his three-year varsity career in 1981, 1982 and 1983. He showed his leadership, passing and quarter backing abilities early and was elected the team's Most Valuable Player after the 1981 campaign. That year, Frank threw 251 passes and completed 132 for 1,765 yards and 12 touchdowns. His best game was against Central Connecticut when he completed 12 of 19 passes for 270 yards. For his performance during the 1982 season, Nowak was the Associated Press Honorable Mention All-America quarterback selection. He attempted 257 passes and completed 154 for 2,257 yards and 20 touchdowns. His best games of the campaign were against Bucknell, Columbia and Princeton. Nowak was elected co-captain of the 1983 squad and guided the Leopards to another winning year. During the 1983 season, he attempted 326 passes and completed 192 for 2,356 yards and 19 touchdowns. He turned in his best performances versus Columbia, Colgate and Bucknell. Nowak was the Leopards' passing leader in 1981, '82 and '83, and his career passing record ranks second in Lafayette College football history. During his three-year career, Frank attempted 834 passes, completed 478 for 6,378 yards and 51 touchdowns, finishing with a 57.3 percent passing average. As one of the highlights of his college football career, Nowak was selected the Most Valuable Player of the 1981 Lafayette-Lehigh game in which he led the Leopards to victory by a score of 10-3. The Lafayette College-Lehigh University series dates back to 1884, and in 1993 the schools played the 129th game of this classic, bitterly contested "College Football's Most-Played Rivalry."

Steve Ostrowski—Northwestern—Linebacker—1993

A top scholar-athlete at Joliet Catholic High School in Bolingbrook, Illinois, Steve Ostrowski was a prep Honorable Mention All-America pick in football. He was the conference defensive Most Valuable Player, team captain and the squad's leading tackler his senior year. Steve was also a member of the National Honor Society and President of the Student Council. Ostrowski earned his first letter at Northwestern University by playing in 10 games as a reserve linebacker and special teams player. He collected six solo tackles and nine assists for the season. He was named Northwestern Gridiron Network's Defensive Newcomer of the Year at the end of the 1990 campaign. In 1991, Steve started 8 of 11 games at linebacker position, and finished third on the team with 74 tackles, 36 of which were solos. He collected a career best 12 tackles at Michigan, and recorded 10 against Illinois and Iowa. Ostrowski was the starting linebacker for the 1992 season, and, at 6-0, 225 pounds, had an excellent outing. He had a career high 14 tackles and a quarterback sack against Stanford. Steve was Northwestern's top tackler with 125 stops for the season. His 79 solo tackles were the most on the Wildcats' squad and ranked eighth in the Big Ten Conference. He was chosen All-Big Ten Conference linebacker and Football News' "Almost All-America." Established as the team's defensive leader, Steve had another excellent year in 1993 with his best of 15 tackles against Illinois. He finished as the Wildcats' leading tackler and was named All-Big Ten and Honorable Mention All-America.

John Pirog—Army—Off. Guard—1992

John Pirog played football as an offensive and defensive guard at Saratoga Springs High School, Saratoga Springs, New York where he lettered twice and was elected team captain in his senior year. He also lettered three times in lacrosse. John attended the USMA Prep School after graduating from high school and was an offensive guard on the football team. Pirog was on the junior varsity team as a plebe at the U.S. Military Academy in 1989. In 1990, he earned his first letter by getting sufficient playing time in seven games as a back-up offensive guard. John opened the 1991 campaign as the starter at right guard and played four games before being sidelined with a concussion. He returned to active duty in a reserve capacity against the Air Force and was again a starter against Akron and the season-ending classic with Navy. Although a starter in six of ten games during the 1991 campaign, Pirog played well and was impressive enough to be selected a second team All-East offensive lineman. John had an excellent outing during the 1992 season and proved that he had the size at 6-6, 270 pounds, the strength, and the ability to rank with the East's top linemen. He was selected first team All-East offensive lineman, and *Football News* named him an "Almost All-America" offensive guard for the 1992 season.

Mark Rypien—Washington State—Quarterback—1985

Mark Rypien was born in Calgary, Alberta (Canada), but grew up in Spokane, Washington. He attended Shadle Park High School and was one of the nation's top ten prep career passers (423 of 849 for 6,460 yards and 65 TDs), named All-America, and chosen the state's outstanding high school athlete. Rypien enrolled at Washington State University in 1981 and saw limited varsity duty. He injured his knee in 1982, had surgery and was red-shirted for the year. In 1984, he capped a brilliant campaign by being named All-Pacific 10 first team quarterback, also named All-West Coast second team by UPI and an All-America Honorable Mention by Associated Press. He completed 134 of his 271 passes for 1,927 yards and 14 touchdowns during the '84 season. He also rushed for 275 yards and had 2,202 yards in total offense, averaging nearly six yards every time he touched the football. Mark saved the best for his last season in 1985, throwing and running for 2,417 yards as a senior. He set two single game records in 1985, and guided the Cougars to a single game team record and several total offense marks. He was elected team co-captain prior to the Washington game. Rypien finished his college football career with over 5,000 yards in total offense and over 4,500 yards passing, the second best total in the Cougars' football history. He was selected to the AP Honorable Mention All-America team for the second straight year. He also received All-PAC 10 honors. Mark played in the East-West Shrine game and starred in the Senior Bowl by leading the North squad to a 31-17 win over the South. He was the Washington Redskins' sixth-round pick in 1986 and, as of 1993, had been with the Redskins for seven years. In 1990, Mark led Washington to a play-off win over Philadelphia by throwing two touchdown passes. He passed for 2,070 yards and 16 TDs in regular season play. Rypien was outstanding during the 1991 season—his best in the pros—and led the Redskins to a 15-2-0 record. He was named NFL Most Valuable Player for the Year, and was selected NFC Pro Bowl starting quarterback. During the NFC Championship game, he led the Redskins to a 41-10 victory over the Detroit Lions completing 12 of 17 passes for 228 yards and throwing for two touchdowns. Rypien led Washington to a 37-24 win over the Buffalo Bills in Super Bowl XXVI. He passed for 292 yards, two touchdowns and was named Super Bowl's Most Valuable Player.

John Strzykalski—Marquette—Halfback—1944

John Strzykalski was a four-year football-letter winner at Marquette University from 1941 through 1944. The Warriors' 1942 team, coached by Tom Stidham, was one of the best in their gridiron history. Strzykalski, the only sophomore on the starting eleven, was the triple-threat star of the team. He was an outstanding runner at halfback, an accurate, dependable passer and an excellent kicker. Marquette opened the 1942 season with an impressive 14-0 win over the Kansas Jayhawks. Strzykalski scored one of the touchdowns and led the Warriors on offense and defense. They lost the second game against the national champions, Wisconsin, but Johnny guided Marquette to a scoring drive in the third quarter, running over from the three yard line for their only touchdown. Iowa State fell to the Warriors in their next game which had Strzykalski racing 90 yards with the second half kick-off for a touchdown. John was unstoppable against Michigan State. While he was running, passing and kicking with brilliant effectiveness, Marquette dominated the game through most of the 60 minutes of play. Johnny was responsible for all four of the Warriors' scores. He ran for two touchdowns, one for 53 yards, and passed for two other TDs. Strzykalski passed for three touchdowns in the Warriors next victory over Arizona. He guided Marquette to a victory over Detroit, and returned a kick-off for 93 yards against Manhattan to put the game out of reach. Marquette held Great Lakes Naval Training Station scoreless through most of the first half with the aid of Strzykalski's 93-yard quick kick, which put the Sailors in a hole. However, Great Lakes went on to win with touchdowns in the second half. Marquette defeated Camp Grant (Illinois) with Strzykalski scoring a touchdown. The Warriors finished the season with an excellent 7-2-0 record and were ranked 19th in the country. Strzykalski compiled a 41.9 yard punting average for the year which was third best in the nation. Johnny continued to play outstanding football during the 1943 and 1944 campaigns, but Marquette could not repeat the winning season's performance. Strzykalski was named an Honorable Mention All-America and was chosen to play for the College All-Stars in 1945. Johnny was a first round draft choice in 1945 and played seven years of professional football with San Francisco.

Mark Szlachcic—Bowling Green—Wide Receiver—1992

A three-year football letter winner at Whitmer High School in Toledo, Ohio, Mark Szlachcic played split end on two Great Lakes League Championship teams, and was named first team All-Ohio. Szlachcic was red-shirted during his freshman year in 1988 at Bowling Green State University. He earned his first letter in 1989 serving as a back-up receiver. Mark led the team in receptions with 46 for 582 yards and two touchdowns during the 1990 campaign. His average of 4.6 catches per game was second best in the Mid-American Conference. At 6-4, 205 pounds, Mark made a good target for the Falcon passers, had good hands and deceptive speed. At the end of the 1991 season, Szlachcic had caught a pass in 25 consecutive games. Mark was a unanimous All-MAC selection after catching 65 passes during the regular season, and 11 more in the California Raisin Bowl to earn game Most Valuable Player honors. His 189 receiving yards in the bowl game set a school record. He was named Honorable Mention All-America and also the 1991 All-Bowl team receiver. Mark also became a punt returner during the 1992 campaign. He finished the year leading Bowling Green and the MAC in receiving with 62 catches for 834 yards and seven TDs. He also led the Falcons in punt returns with 139 yards and was second in scoring with 42 points. Szlachcic was fifth in the MAC in punt returns and 10th, in scoring. Mark became the All-Time Mid-America Conference pass catcher, and set a Mid-America Conference career record with 182 receptions for 2,570 yards. He was the conference coaches' unanimous choice for the 1992 All-Mid America Conference first team and repeated as an Honorable Mention All-America. A Business Administration graduate, Szlachcic was chosen to play in the Blue-Gray All-Star classic.

Dick Szymanski—Notre Dame—Center—1954

Dick Szymanski was a 6-2, 210 pound football star at Libbey High School in Toledo, Ohio where he became an All-City and All-State center selection in 1949 and 1950 as well as a member of the 1950 high school All-America team. He won two letters in football, three in baseball and two in basketball. Dick enrolled at the University of Notre Dame in 1951 and won the starting linebacker position in his freshman year. Szymanski did an outstanding job at line backing and was a great addition to one of the best Notre Dame defensive units in many years. Against Navy, Dick intercepted two Middie passes to stop their offensive drives. He was also instrumental in stopping Oklahoma ball carriers time after time to help Notre Dame to a 27-21 upset victory. He played his best game of the year against Michigan State by constantly stopping Spartan runners for loss of yardage or little or no gain. The Notre Dame defensive effort led by Szymanski was so effective that Michigan State was held to only

171

169 yards rushing and passing whereas they had been averaging more than 400 yards per game. Notre Dame finished with an excellent 7-2-1 record and was ranked 13th in the country. Szymanski was a starting linebacker again during the 1952 campaign and turned in an even better performance than he had the previous year. He helped Notre Dame to another winning season and number three rank nationally. The one platoon rule cut down his playing time during the 1953 campaign, and Dick backed up at center and linebacker. In 1954, Szymanski started at center and linebacker and had a fantastic season through the first six games. He sustained an injury (ruptured spleen) and was lost for the year after a successful emergency operation. Dick finished as a four-year letter winner at Notre Dame playing center on offense and linebacker on defense. He was named an Honorable Mention All-America and selected to the East-West Shrine and College All-Star teams. The Baltimore Colts selected Szymanski as their second round draft choice in 1955. He played 4 years with the Colts and was chosen to the Pro Bowl in 1956, 1963 and 1965. Dick contributed greatly to the Colts' NFL titles in 1958, 1959 and 1960. He ended his playing career in 1968 and spent 14 years in various management positions including general manager of the Baltimore Colts. He was also the president of the NFL Alumni Association and is currently VP/Chapter Operations in Ft. Lauderdale, Florida. Szymanski was inducted into the National Polish-American Sports Hall of Fame in 1994.

Scott Zolak—Maryland—Quarterback—1990

Scott Zolak earned All-State and All-Conference honors as a senior quarterback at Ringgold High School in Monongahela, Pennsylvania. He was a four-year letter winner who also handled the punting duties. His father was athletic director and coached Joe Montana at Ringgold High. Scott was water boy for Montana's team during one season. Zolak was red-shirted as a freshman at the University of Maryland in 1986. He saw no action in 1987 and played in four games in 1988. In 1989, Scott played in eight games as a back-up quarterback and completed 33 of 69 passes for 407 yards and two touchdowns. He finally became a starter as a senior during the 1990 season. Despite only one year as a starter at Maryland, his performance was so outstanding that he ranks fifth on the Terrapins' all-time list with 270 completions and seventh with 3,124 passing yards. He was ranked second in the Atlantic Coast Conference in total offense, averaging 217.5 yards per game. He completed 225 of 418 passes for 2,589 yards and 10 touchdowns in his senior year, breaking the school season record of 196 completions. His 2,589 season passing yards ranks second on Maryland's all-time list. Zolak was named ACC Offen-

173

sive Back of the Week for his performance in four games. He set a single-game school record by completing 28 passes of 46 attempts for 303 yards and two touchdowns against Virginia Tech. He broke his own record against Michigan by completing 29 of 45 attempts for 264 yards. For his amazing one season performance, Scott earned Honorable Mention All-America honors after the senior campaign. Zolak was drafted by the New England Patriots in 1991. He played in six games with four starts in 1992 and completed 52 of 100 passes for 561 yards and two touchdowns. In his first ever start against Indianapolis, he earned AFC Offensive Player of the Week honors by completing 20 of 29 passes for 261 yards and two touchdowns to lead the Patriots to their first win of the season. Scott started several games for the Patriots during the 1995 season and turned in excellent performances.

CHAPTER VI

ACADEMIC AWARD WINNERS

Chris Baniszewski—Northern Arizona—Wide Receiver—1989
Robert Chudzinski—Miami (Fla.)—Tight End—1990
Bruce Filarski—Pacific—Off. Guard—1979
Mike Franckowiak—Central Michigan—Quarterback—1974
Chester Gladchuk, Jr.—Boston College—Center—1972
Rich Kacmarynski—Central College—Fullback—1991
John Kasperski—Tulsa—Off. Guard—1984
Gary Kasprzak—Columbia—Def. Tackle—1992
Steve Koproski—Kent State—Tight End—1993
Scott Kozak—Oregon—Linebacker—1988
James Kubacki—Harvard—Quarterback—1976
Jeffrey Kubiak—Air Force Academy—Punter—1984
Frank Lewandowski—Northern Illinois—Linebacker—1979
Tom Myslinski—Tennessee—Off. Guard—1991
Jason Olejniczak—Iowa—Def. Back—1993
Mike Pawlawski—California—Quarterback—1991
Joseph Restic,Jr.—Notre Dame—Def. Back—1978
John Skibinski—Purdue—Fullback—1977
Joe Staysniak—Ohio State—Off. Tackle—1989
Robert Stefanski—Northern Michigan—Wide Receiver—1984
Mark Szynkowski—Alfred—Off. Tackle—1989
Michael Tomczak—Ohio State—Quarterback—1984
Steve Tomczak—St. Francis—Quarterback—1993
Gregory Worsowicz—Sewanee—Def. Back—1981
Joseph Zeszotarski—Muhlenberg—Def. End—1990

Chris Baniszewski—Northern Arizona—Wide Receiver—1989

An excellent scholar-athlete at McClintock High School in Tempe, Arizona, Chris Baniszewski earned All-League, All-State and All-Arizona football honors as a prep senior. He enrolled at Northern Arizona University in 1986 and played as a substitute wide receiver in his freshman year. Chris was in nine games and caught 10 passes for 161 yards. As a sophomore in 1987, Baniszewski played in nine games again and caught 21 passes for 237 yards and three touchdowns. He finished high on the ballot for All-District 8 College Sports Information Directors Association Academic team at the end of the season. Chris saw action in 11 games during the 1988 campaign and made 240 yards with 21 pass receptions. As an outstanding scholar athlete majoring in political science, Baniszewski was again top man for All-District 8 Cosida Academic team. During the 1989 season, Chris started all 11 games as a wide receiver and finished leading the team with 40 catches for 390 yards and one touchdown. He averaged 9.8 yards per pass reception. At the end of the season, Baniszewski was named first team Academic All-America wide receiver by the College Sports Information Directors Association.

Robert Chudzinski—Miami (Fla)—Tight End—1990

A native of Toledo, Ohio, Robert Chudzinski was a scholar-athlete at St. John's High School where he won All-City football honors as tight end and linebacker, and was chosen Honorable Mention All-Ohio National Football Foundation's Hall of Fame in 1985. Chudzinski finished with a 3.6 grade point average and was named to the Toledo All-City Academic Team. He was redshirted at the University of Miami (Florida) in 1986. Robert was a reserve tight end in 1987 and saw a lot game action in short yardage situations. He proved to be the key performer in Miami's Orange Bowl victory over Oklahoma. As a starter in 1988, he quickly earned a reputation of being a clutch third down receiver. He came up with his best performances in big games against Florida State, Michigan, Arkansas and Notre Dame when he made 23 receptions which were good for 295 yards. Chudzinski had an outstanding first season as a starter and was chosen All-South Independent tight end. In addition, he was also selected Honorable Mention All-America. As a junior in 1989, Robert closed out the season in big-time fashion, making two acrobatic catches for 21 yards and one touchdown in Miami's Sugar Bowl victory over Alabama. He was the Ryder Offensive Player of the Game against Missouri after catching a career-high eight passes for another career best 101 yards and a touchdown. He finished the season with 20 pass catches for 207 yards. At 6-4, 235 pounds, Chudzinski was a player who could find the opening in a secondary and hold on to just about anything thrown in his direction. He had good hands and was an intelligent player, but was hampered by injuries throughout his career. Robert had an excellent 1990 campaign and repeated as an All-South Independent tight end selection. Chudzinski was named the National Collegiate Athletic Association Postgraduate Scholarship Winner in his senior year at Miami.

Bruce Filarski—Pacific—Off. Guard—1979

Bruce Filarski was a high school football All-America at Cabrillo High in Lompoc, California. He won five letters in football, wrestling and track. Filarski enrolled at the University of California—Riverside, but transferred to the University of the Pacific when U.C.—Riverside dropped football. Pacific obtained not only an outstanding football player but also an excellent scholar. Bruce started on the defensive line as a freshman, and finished with 37 tackles and three quarterback sacks. The switch from defensive lineman to offensive guard in his sophomore year proved to be very successful. He was an aggressive, hard-hitting blocker, excellent on sweeps and started all games during his four year college career. Filarski was selected first team Academic All-America by the College Sports Information Directors Association at the end of the 1978 season. He was the first UOP player to earn this honor having a fantastic 3.89 grade point average. He was also named National Football Foundation's Hall of Fame Scholar-Athlete for 1979. The honors that Filarski received seem to be endless. He was a member of Phi Kappa Phi Honor Society,

Dean's List, PCAA Scholar Athlete, and received the Eddie Le Baron Award in 1977 and 1978 presented annually to a football player for outstanding scholarship. In addition, Bruce was awarded the NCAA Postgraduate Scholarship of $2,000 for postgraduate study. Filarski was also awarded a $3,000 Fellowship for graduate study by the Honor Society of Phi Kappa Phi. The graduate work was done in medicine at the University of California, San Francisco School of Medicine.

Mike Franckowiak—Central Michigan— Quarterback—1974

A scholar-athlete and an excellent football player at West Catholic High School in Grand Rapids, Michigan, Franckowiak was named the Grand Rapids high school Athlete of the Year and ranked academically in the top one-sixth of his graduating class. When Franckowiak enrolled at Central Michigan University in 1971, the Chippewas obtained not only an outstanding, versatile football performer but also an excellent student. In 1972, he was the Mid-America Conference top punter and a back-up quarterback for Central Michigan. He improved his punting during the 1973 season and became the starting quarterback. At 6-4, 215 pounds, Mike had good speed, was a strong runner and ran the option plays to perfection. He also had an extremely strong and accurate passing arm and completed over 50% of his passes. He led the Chippewas to 17 wins in 20 starts and the Division II championship in 1974. He climaxed his career by being chosen as the Outstanding Offensive Player in both the Pioneer and Camellia Bowls, hitting on 11 of 13 passes for 186 yards and one touchdown in the title game. Mike was selected Central Michigan's Most Valuable Player and Outstanding Offensive Back in 1974. He was chosen to the Mid-American Conference All-Academic football team and was named Academic All-America following the 1974 season. He was also selected All-America. Franckowiak was chosen to play in the East-West Shrine game and was a member of the East team in the annual Coaches All-America game. Mike was the third round NFL draft choice of the Denver Broncos in 1975.

Chester Gladchuk, Jr.—Boston College—Center—1972

Son of the Boston College Hall of Fame center and linebacker in 1940, Chester Gladchuk, Jr. was also a letter winning center with the Eagle football team from 1969 through 1972 under head coach Joe Yukica. In addition to being a scholarship football player, Gladchuk was a Dean's List student in business management. In his senior year, Chet received the "Unsung Hero" award given by the New England Football Writers' Association and the Tim Mara Scholarship Award presented by the N.Y. Giants football club. He earned his bachelor degree from Boston College in 1973, and a master's degree in sports administration from the University of Massachusetts in 1974. Gladchuk spent the next four years as director of athletics and physical education and head football coach at New Hampshire Prep School. In 1978, he became the assistant director of athletics and director of General Physical Education at the University of Massachusetts. From 1985 to 1988, Chet served as associate athletic director at Syracuse University. He became athletic director at Tulane University in 1988 and was instrumental in improving the fund raising and basketball programs. Gladchuk replaced the retiring William J.

Flynn as the Boston College athletic director in 1990. In three short years, at age 43, Chet has succeeded in keeping Boston College competitive in intercollegiate sports while upholding its academic and spiritual values. He was named chairman of the Big East Conference Finance Committee, and serves on two NCAA committees, the College Football Association's Athletic Directors Committee and the ECAC Finance Committee.

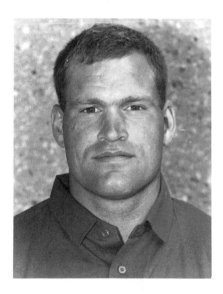

Rich Kacmarynski—Central College—Fullback—1991

Rich Kacmarynski ended his first season as an assistant football coach at Central College in 1993 after an outstanding four-year career as a Flying Dutchman. A native of Mallard, Iowa, Rich played fullback during his freshman year at Central in 1988. The Flying Dutchmen, under head coach Ron Schipper, finished with an 11-2-0 record, were Iowa Conference champions, and Kacmarynski received the O'Donell Award as Central's outstanding football freshman. In 1989, Central won the Iowa Conference championship again with a 10-1-0 mark, were NCAA Division III play-off qualifiers, and Rich received the Mentik Award for football leadership. He was also first team All-Iowa Conference fullback selection after leading Central in rushing yardage. In 1990, Kacmarynski carried the ball 170 times for 823 yards, caught seven passes for 112 yards and had five kickoff returns for 76 yards. Central finished with a 10-2-0 record, were champions of the Iowa Conference, and were in the NCAA Division III play-offs. Rich was again selected first team All-Iowa Conference fullback, received the Lankelma Award as the outstanding football underclassman, and was named to the GTE Academic All-Region team with a fantastic 3.87 grade point average. He was also one of four Division III athletes chosen to serve on the NCAA's Student-Athlete Advisory Committee. He was elected co-captain of the 1991 football squad. Rich finished with 178 rushes for 922 yards and 11 touchdowns, and caught seven passes for 50 yards and one touchdown. He was named Iowa Conference and team Most Valuable Player, chosen first team GTE Academic All-America, and an NCAA Postgraduate Scholarship winner. He is the third leading rusher in Central College football history with 2,725 yards, and holds the all time career record for rushing touchdowns with 36. In 1992, Phil Kacmarynski was a senior fullback, and Mark Kacmarynski a freshman tail back on the Central College football team.

John Kasperski—Tulsa—Off. Guard—1984

John Kasperski received All-Metro, All-Conference and All-District football honors in leading Hazelwood Central High in Florissant, Missouri to the top ranking in the Greater St. Louis area. He enrolled at the University of Tulsa in 1981 and very quickly nailed down the starting offensive guard position which he held through his senior year. During the 1982 season, John was credited with making the key block in a 41-yard touchdown run that put Tulsa ahead to stay in the victory over Oklahoma State. His outstanding performance in the 1983 season-opener against San Diego State earned him Missouri Valley Conference Player of the Week honors. He had an excellent campaign and was first team All-Missouri Valley Conference, named to the Conference All-Academic team, and chosen Honorable Mention All-America by the Associated Press. At 6-4, 240 pounds, Kasperski continued his fine performances during the 1984 season, and repeated as first team All-Conference and Honorable Mention All-America. John was also selected to the conference first team All-Academic. Kasperski's brother, Donald, played quarterback for the Air Force Academy in Colorado.

Gary Kasprzak—Columbia—Def. Tackle—1992

Gary Kasprzak graduated Tonawanda High School in Tonawanda, N.Y. in 1989 as a two-year football letter winner and received a National Merit Commendation. He was selected Western N.Y. All-Star team's Most Valuable Lineman and Most Valuable Player of the 1988 Tonawanda-North Tonawanda football game. Gary was also All-Western N.Y. Academic team member and Tonawanda's top science student as a junior and senior. Kasprzak began his varsity career at Columbia University playing nose tackle as a sophomore in 1990. His first start was in the season-opener against Harvard when he registered eight tackles, a sack and a fumble recovery to set up a field goal. He finished the campaign with 46 tackles, 29 solos, and led the team with five sacks and ten tackles for loss. Gary proved to be a very good athlete who could play tackle, end or outside linebacker. His unusual quickness allowed him to get the jump on the offensive linemen. Kasprzak was 6-0, 220 pounds as a junior in 1991, and finished with 37 tackles of which 26 were unassisted. He tied for the team lead in sacks with six and had six tackles for loss. His career-high 57 tackles as a senior during the 1992 season were a defensive gem. Of the 57 tackles, 36 were solos and ten for loss of yards. Kasprzak was an engineering major who was on the Dean's List, and the Columbia scholar-athlete was named first team Academic All-Ivy League at the end of the 1992 season. Gary's third cousin, Don Kasprzak, was an excellent football player and captain of the 1946 Columbia University football team.

Steve Koproski—Kent State—Tight End—1993

An excellent scholar-athlete, Steve Koproski was a member of the National Honor Society at St. John High School in Ashtabula, Ohio. He was the football team's Most Valuable Player, earned special mention on the All-Ohio squad, and was a first team All-District choice. Steve was named offensive and defensive lineman of Ashtabula County. Koproski enrolled at Kent State University in 1989 and started as a linebacker but was moved to tight end in freshman fall drills. He was red-shirted in his first year with the Golden Flashes. In 1990, he started in his first game against West Virginia and kept the starting position for the rest of the season. Although used primarily as a blocker, Steve caught three passes for 45 yards. He received Honorable Mention on the Academic All-Mid American Conference team. During the 1991 campaign, Steve played in all 11 games and was a starter nine times. He caught five passes for 44 yards with season-high two receptions good for 23 yards against Ohio University. He also saw some action on the special teams. Koproski was selected to the Academic All-MAC first team by the conference faculty representatives. Steve was a starting tight end during the 1992 season. He caught 12 passes for 123 yards and proved to be a consistently dependable blocker. He was selected to the Academic All-MAC first team again at the end of the season. Koproski received All-MAC honors for his performance as a graduate student during the 1993 season. An accounting major, Steve was chosen to the Academic All-MAC team for the third time in 1993.

Scott Kozak—Oregon—Linebacker—1988

Scott Kozak attended Colton High School in Colton, Oregon and lettered in football, baseball and track. Scott played linebacker, tail back, safety and also punted. He won many awards for leadership and scholarship, including election to the National Honor Society. Kozak enrolled at the University of Oregon in 1984 and was red-shirted his freshman year. Scott became a four-year letter winner playing outside linebacker from 1985 through 1988. He was an explosive player who had the speed to overcome the rare occurances when he was caught out of position. He received the Higdon Award which is presented to the top sophomore student-athlete at Oregon based on his athletic performance and outstanding academic record. As a junior, Scott had the team high tackles for losses and sacks in ten games. He was named the

Honda Scholar-Athlete of the Week in 1987 for his play against Washington combined with his high academic standing. As a senior, Scott was named second team All-PAC-10, was Oregon's Player of the Year, received Academic All-Conference honors, and earned GTE Academic All-America honors. He was also a finalist for the Butkus Award which is given annually to the nation's top linebacker. His four-year career totals included 206 tackles (156 solos and 50 assisted), two interceptions, ten quarterback sacks and four forced fumbles. Kozak was chosen to play in the Senior and Japan Bowls, and was drafted by the Houston Oilers in the second round in 1989. As of 1992, he has not missed a game in his four-year pro career, and was the leading special teams tackler during the 1991 and 1992 seasons. He has been used as a reserve linebacker. Scott owns his own Portland, Oregon based contracting company called Kozak Enterprises and works there after the football season.

James Kubacki—Harvard—Quarterback—1976

A three-year football letterman at St. Ignatius High School in Fairview Park, Ohio, James Kubacki captained the team in his senior year and was chosen All-Scholastic. Jim also participated in basketball and track. Kubacki enrolled at Harvard University in 1973 and spent his first two years playing with the junior varsity. He established himself quickly in his first start as a junior by setting a single game total offense record against Columbia with 310 yards despite a jammed finger on his passing hand. He completed 15 of 18 passes for 289 yards and three touchdowns against Brown and was selected ABC-TV Offensive Player of the Game. His excellent outing against Yale gave Harvard its first undisputed Ivy League championship in 20 years. Kubacki set a new Harvard total offense record in 1975 with 1,701 yards. He was selected All-East, All-New England, All-Ivy League, All-Eastern College Athletic Conference, Coaches' Player of the Week (three times), ECAC Player of the Week, Ivy League Player of the Week (twice), New England Player of the Week, and chosen to the ECAC weekly team three times. Kubacki was also named the NCAA Scholarship Award Winner for 1975 to certify his qualifications as an outstanding scholar and athlete. Jim was the first Harvard University junior to win the Frederick Greeley Crocker Award. This award is given annually to the Harvard football letterman who is elected the squad's Most Valuable Player by his teammates. Jim went on to have another excellent year in 1976. He rushed for 396 yards and eight touchdowns, passed for 945 yards and eight TDs to finish as Harvard's total offense leader with 1,341 yards and 16 TDs. He was chosen Coaches' All-Ivy League, UPI All-New England and ABC-TV Offensive Player of the Game vs. Massachusetts. He set the Harvard record for most total yards in a career at 3,042 for 1975 and 1976. Kubacki came from an athletic family. His brother, Ray, was a quarterback at Harvard in 1967, and brother, Bob, was a quarterback at Bowdoin College.

Jeffrey Kubiak—Air Force Academy—Punter—1983

Jeffrey Kubiak played football at Preble High School in Green Bay, Wisconsin as right guard on offense and nose guard on defense. He was selected to all-league and all-state football teams and was a two-year letter winner. Kubiak entered the U.S. Air Force Academy in Colorado Springs, Colorado in 1980 and became an excellent punter at the Academy and in the Western Athletic Conference. He was also an outstanding scholar and was selected first team Academic All-America in 1982. To be eligible, student athletes must be regular performers and have at least a 3.20 grade point average (on a 4.00 scale) during their college careers. The football players are chosen by the Sports Information Directors of America. Kubiak was also picked second team punter on the All-Western Athletic Conference at the end of the 1982 season. At 6-1, 209 pounds, Jeff was chosen for All-Western Athletic Conference honors in 1983, and was again named first team Academic All-America for the second year. Kubiak was also named an NCAA Postgraduate Scholarship Winner. To qualify, student-athletes must maintain a 3.00 grade point average during their collegiate career and perform with distinction in varsity football.

Frank Lewandowski—Northern Illinois— Linebacker—1979

Frank Lewandowski won first team All-State football honors as a senior at Muskegon Catholic Central High School in Muskegon, Michigan in 1975. He enrolled at Northern Illinois University in 1976 to become one of the greatest linebackers in their football history. At 6-0, 225 pounds, Frank was a four-year letter winner. He has the school record for most career tackles (616 in 42 games), best tackle per-game career average (14.7), and most single game tackles (33). He became the first player in Mid-America Conference to compile 600 or more career stops. He owns the MAC single game tackle record of 33, and led the Huskies in tackles for four consecutive seasons. Frank was AP Honorable Mention All-America in 1977 and 1979. He was named second team All-MAC in 1976 and first team in 1977 and 1979. Lewandowski was selected first team Academic All-MAC in 1977. He was selected MAC Defensive Player of the Year as a senior, and was voted MAC Defensive Player of the Week four times during his career. Frank was a two-time Northern Illinois team defensive Most Valuable Player in 1977 and 1979, and was voted team co-captain in 1979. Lewandowski was inducted into the Northern Illinois University Athletic Hall of Fame in 1992.

Tom Myslinski—Tennessee—Off. Guard—1991

An All-State football center at the Free Academy High School in Rome, N.Y., Tom Myslinski led the Academy to an undefeated season and the state championship in 1986. He was a highly recruited high school lineman who chose Tennessee over Notre Dame and other leading colleges. Red-shirted in 1987, Tom played in six games during the 1988 campaign. Myslinski was named Academic All-Southeastern Conference after the '88 season. He started all 12 games at right guard in 1989 and helped the Vols to a record-setting offensive production that averaged 408.5 yards per game. In 1990, Myslinski started in all 13 games. At 6-3, 285 pounds, Tom was excellent at both run blocking and pass protection. He was outstanding against Notre Dame as the Vols piled up 516 yards in total offense. He provided the offensive line leadership for Tennessee in 1991. Tennessee finished the '91 campaign with a 9-3-0 record, was ranked 15th in the nation, but lost to Penn State in the Fiesta Bowl. Myslinski was chosen first team All-SEC offensive guard by the conference coaches, and named "Almost All-America" by *Football News*. He was also named to the SEC Academic Honor Roll. Tom played for the East squad in the 1992 Japan Bowl. He was a fourth round draft choice of the Dallas Cowboys in 1992. His father Tom, Sr., played football for Maryland and the N.Y. Jets. He coached football at Rome's Free Academy.

Jason Olejniczak—Iowa—Defensive Back—1993

An Honorable Mention All-America quarterback at Decorah High School in Decorah, Iowa, Jason Olejniczak was also a two time All-State and three time All-Conference quarterback and defensive back. He led the team to a 31-2-0 mark and two state titles as starting QB, and set school record for total offense passing for 901 yards and rushing for 890 as a senior. An excellent scholar-athlete, Jason was a member of the National Honor Society. In 1989, he was red-shirted as a freshman at the University of Iowa. He played in all 12 games as a backup defensive back in 1990 recording 40 tackles and three interceptions. He had season-high seven stops at Michigan State and finished tied for sixth in Big Ten with interceptions. Jason was named to the Big Ten Conference All-Academic squad at the end of the season. Olejniczak started in all 12 games in 1991, and his interception in the Wisconsin game led to Iowa's game winning scoring drive. He also excelled in the Holiday Bowl with key tackles and interceptions against Brigham Young. He repeated as Big Ten All-Academic at the end of the season. At 6-0, 198 pounds, Olejniczak was a starting defensive back in 1992. He led the team with 104 tackles, including 15 tackles and a forced fumble versus Miami (FL) for which he was named defensive game Most Valuable Player. Jason was chosen Chevrolet Scholarship Player of the Game after making 12 tackles and breaking up a pass at Michigan. He was an Honorable Mention All-Big Ten pick in addition to being named Big Ten Academic for the third time. He was also named to the GTE Academic All-America second team, and was a two-time Dean's List honoree. Olejniczak finished his collegiate career in grand style by being selected for All-Big Ten Conference honors for his athletic and academic achievements. He also received GTE Academic All-America honors, and was named Honorable Mention All-America. The University of Iowa considers Olejniczak "an example of the quintessential student-athlete whose list of academic achievements was as lengthy as his accomplishments on the gridiron." He had a 3.00 grade point average three consecutive years and graduated with a 3.30 GPA as a marketing major. The 1993 University of Iowa Football Media Guide lists Jason Olejniczak as the Definition of the Student-Athlete. Jason's brother, Lon, played football at the University of Iowa from 1979-1982.

Mike Pawlawski—California—Quarterback—1991

Mike Pawlawski came to the University of California in 1987 from Troy High School in Yorba Linda, California where he starred in football and baseball. He was a place kicker, receiver, defensive back, and, finally, a quarterback in his senior prep year. Mike was chosen Freeway League Player of the Year and received All-Orange County and CIF honors as quarterback and defensive back. Pawlawski was red-shirted as a freshman in 1987 at the University of California. He was a substitute quarterback during the 1988 and 1989 seasons, and also played on California's kick coverage squad. Mike saw action at quarterback in only two games in 1989 against Miami and Wisconsin. He nailed down the starting quarterback position during fall camp in 1990. At 6-1, 205 pounds, Pawlawski developed into an excellent leader who completed 179 passes of 299 attempts (59.9%) for 2,069 yards and 17 touchdowns. He was selected PAC-10 Offensive Player of the Week after completing 19 of 29 passes for two touchdowns, and scoring one himself in rallying the Bears for a tie with Southern California. He also guided California to a 17-15 defeat of Wisconsin in the Copper Bowl. It was the Bears' first bowl bid in 11 years, and Mike was named the Bowl's Most Valuable Player. Pawlawski was chosen Honorable Mention All-America, and earned

All-PAC-10 honors as a junior in 1990. He also received an Academic Award by being selected the National Football Foundation Scholarship Award Winner. Mike had a fantastic season in 1991 completing 191 of 316 pass attempts (60.4%) for 2,517 yards and set a new single season record at California by throwing 21 touchdown passes. He finished his collegiate career in impressive fashion by leading the Bears to a 37-14 victory over Clemson University in the Citrus Bowl with 21 completions in 32 attempts for 230 yards. Pawlawski was chosen the Bowl's Most Valuable Player. He ranks second on the University of California's career list with 38 touchdown passes and is fourth with 4,779 yards in passing. Mike shared Offensive Player of the Year honors in the PAC-10, and was named first team All-PAC-10 quarterback. He was also named Honorable Mention All-America by Associated Press and *Football News*. He was one of seven finalists for the Johnny Unitas Award which is given annually to the nation's top senior quarterback. He was drafted by Tampa Bay in 1992.

Joe Restic, Jr.—Notre Dame—Def. Back/Punter—1978

Joe Restic, Jr. was the son of Harvard University's head football coach and an outstanding quarterback, defensive back and punter at Milford High School in Milford, Massachusetts. He was Honorable Mention High School All-America and a member of the National Honor Society. Restic was used primarily as a punter during his freshman year in 1975 at the University of Notre Dame. He punted 40 times for 1,739 yards to finish with an average of 43.7 yards per punt which ranked seventh in the nation. He established the Notre Dame record for punting average in a single game with a 51.6 mark against Air Force. Joe also completed a 10-yard touchdown pass against Miami. He became a starting defensive back early in his sophomore year. As a punter, he averaged 41.7 yards on 63 kicks, including a 63-yarder. He was named Honorable Mention All-America as both punter and defensive back in 1976. In 1977, Restic performed as an amazing defensive back. He denied Clemson a touchdown with a diving interception deep in Notre Dame territory. Joe made eight tackles, five of them solo, in a 49-19 victory over USC and intercepted a

Trojan pass. He led the team with six interceptions and made 41 tackles. He also punted 45 times for 1,713 yards (average 38.1 yards per punt). Notre Dame finished the '77 campaign with a 10-1-0 record including a Cotton Bowl victory. Restic was again named Honorable Mention All-America and was also selected first team Academic All-America by the College Sports Information Directors of America. Joe had another fantastic season in 1978 with 51 tackles, eight broken up passes, two fumble recoveries, three interceptions for 59 yards and one touchdown. He also punted 61 times for 2,330 yards for an average of 38.2 yards per punt. Once again he was chosen Honorable Mention All-America, and also repeated as a first team Academic All-America selection. In addition, Restic was named an Honor Student-Athlete by the NCAA and presented with a $2,000 post-graduate scholarship. The National Football Foundation and Hall of Fame also honored Joe as a Scholar-Athlete with a $3,000 scholarship for post-graduate study. He played professional football for three years in the U.S. Football League, and then graduated from the University of Pennsylvania School of Dental Medicine with a doctorate degree.

John Skibinski—Purdue—Fullback—1974

A three-sport star at LaSalle High School in Peru, Illinois, John Skibinski won four letters each in football, track and wrestling. He was an All-State selection in football after gaining 1,200 yards rushing his senior year. Skibinski was redshirted his freshman year in 1974 at Purdue University, and was used primarily as a blocking back during the 1975 season. He became a starting fullback in 1976 and rushed for 871 yards in 173 carries for a 5.0 yard average (second highest on the team). He was also Purdue's second leading receiver with 13 receptions for 118 yards and scored four touchdowns. John turned out to be a strong back at 6-1, 219 pounds who topped 100-yard rushing marks twice with 133 against Wisconsin and 121 against Miami. He ran for at least 70 yards on six other occasions. Skibinski had his most outstanding day in Purdue's 16-14 upset of top ranked Michigan with 84 rushing yards on 17 carries and four pass receptions for 39 yards. John did not lose a yard from scrimmage during the season. In recognition of his magnificent junior year campaign, Skibinski was given the Jack Mollenkopf Award by the Purdue Club of Chicago. This award is based on qualities of dedication, loyalty and devotion personified by the late Boilermaker head football coach. John did not let down for a minute during the 1977 campaign and finished with another outstanding year. He was selected for All-Big Ten Conference honors and was also an Honorable Mention All-America. Skibinski was also an NCAA Scholarship Award Winner to certify his qualifications as an excellent scholar and athlete. He was chosen to play in the Hula Bowl and the East-West Shrine game. John was drafted by the Chicago Bears in 1978 and played with them for five years. He also played pro ball for two years in the USFL. He was only one of several Skibinskis who played football for Purdue. His father, Joseph, lettered from 1949 through 1951, and uncle, Dick, lettered from 1953 to 1955. Both of them were excellent guards. The youngest, Rick, was an offensive lineman during the 1984 and 1985 seasons.

Joe Staysniak—Ohio State—Off. Tackle—1989

An Ohio native, Joe Staysniak was an exceptional scholar-athlete at Midview High School in Elyria, Ohio where he won first team All-Ohio honors as a two-way tackle. He was third in his class with an excellent 3.9 grade point average. Joe enrolled at Ohio State University in 1986, and started all 12 games at offensive tackle as a freshman. He helped the team to a 10-3-0 record and a Cotton Bowl victory over Texas A&M. He was named to the Big Ten All-Academic team at the end of the season. As a sophomore, he started in all 11 games and was again Big Ten's All-Academic. Joe combined physical skills with a thorough understanding of the game. At 6-5, 287 pounds, he had excellent mobility which enabled him to be a good pass protector. Staysniak recuperated from mono and worked himself into condition to start nine of 11 games as a junior. After another outstanding outing, he received All-Big Ten Conference team honors and was again selected to the Big Ten All-Academic team for the third straight year. Joe was appointed team captain for his senior year, and started all 12 games at tackle to help lead the team to a 8-4-0 mark and the Hall of Fame Bowl victory. At the end of the season, he was named first team All-Big Ten Conference, first team Big Ten Conference All-Academic, second team All-America and first team Academic All-America. He was one of eleven 1989 National Football Foundation and Hall of Fame Post Graduate Scholarship recipients. Staysniak graduated Ohio State University cum laude with a degree in marketing. Joe was the San Diego Chargers NFL draft selection in 1990 but played for the Buffalo Bills during the 1990 and 1991 seasons. He was a reserve offensive lineman with the Kansas City Chiefs in 1992 and became an offensive lineman for the Indianapolis Colts in 1993. Joe was a starting right guard for the Colts at the beginning of the 1995 season.

Robert Stefanski—Northern Michigan—Wide Receiver—1984

Robert Stefanski played high school football at Grand Blanc, Michigan and was an all-conference wide receiver and quarterback. In addition, he was an all-conference and twice MVP in basketball, played baseball and competed in track and field. Stefanski enrolled at Northern Michigan University in 1980 and was red-shirted his freshman year. He played in three games as a reserve wide receiver in 1981 and caught four passes for 100 yards. Bob earned his first varsity letter for the 1982 campaign when he played in eight games and caught nine passes for 199 yards and one touchdown. At 6-2, 183 pounds, Stefanski had the intelligence, speed, good hands and athletic ability to develop into an outstanding receiver, which he did during the 1983 season. He was the starting wide receiver in all games, and established a Wildcat pass receiving record with three touchdown catches in each of the games against Michigan Tech, Saginaw Valley and Northern Iowa. Stefanski led the Wildcats in pass receiving in 1983 with 56 catches for 1,019 yards and scored 10 touchdowns. Bob had a 3.80 grade point average as a computer math major and was chosen first team Academic All-America. Stefanski continued to set pass receiving records in 1984 by scoring 11 touchdowns on passes and led the team with 47 catches for 809 yards. He was also the scoring leader for Northern Michigan with 66 points in 1984 and holds the Wildcat football career touchdown pass receiving record with 22. Bob went to law school and became a successful lawyer. He was selected as an Outstanding alumni of Northern Michigan University.

Mark Szynkowski—Alfred—Off. Tackle—1989

A graduate of North Tonawanda High School in North Tonawand, New York, Mark Szynkowski enrolled at Alfred University to become a four-year letter winner in football from 1986 to 1989. He was one of the most outstanding scholar-athletes to attend Alfred. At 6-4, 285 pounds, Mark started at offensive tackle a major part of his sophomore year and all of his junior and senior seasons. Following the 1988 campaign, Szynkowski was named to the GTE College Division Academic All-America second team by the College Sports Information Directors of America. To be eligible for this academic honor, a student athlete must be a starter or important reserve and carry at least a 3.20 cumulative grade point average. Szynkowski had a 3.83 grade point average in business administration, was an Honor Student and a member of the Business Dean's Student Advisory Council. He was one of four Alfred University student athletes to be named to the District I team. Szynkowski was the Saxons top offensive lineman and was elected one of the team captains. Alfred finished the 1989 season with a 9-2 mark and won the Eastern College Athletic Conference North Championship when they beat Bridgewater State. In recognition of his football performance, Mark was named to the Division III All-America team. In addition, he was chosen a GTE Academic All-America first team member, becoming the first Alfred student athlete to earn this honor. Szynkowski had a 3.74 grade point average in accounting, was on the Dean's List, a member of the University Honors Program and on the Dean's Advisory Council.

Michael Tomczak—Ohio State—Quarterback—1984

A Chicago native, Michael Tomczak lettered in football at Ohio State University as quarterback from 1981 to 1984 under head coach Earle Bruce. He started as a back-up to quarterback Art Schlichter during the 1981 season, and the Buckeyes finished with a 9-3-0 record, were the Big Ten Conference champions, and beat Navy in the Liberty Bowl. Tomczak took over as the starting quarterback for the 1982 campaign and showed his inexperience in the first game with Baylor, completing only 6 of 15 passes for 93 yards. But he was great against Illinois, completing a 74 yard pass for the game's first touchdown and throwing effective short passes when his team needed them most. The Buckeyes beat Illinois 26-21, and then Tomczak led them to victories against Indiana, Purdue, Northwestern, Minnesota and Michigan. Mike directed an efficient offensive assault against Brigham Young, the Western Athletic Conference champs, in the Holiday Bowl and outclassed the highpowered offense led by Cougar quarterback, Steve Young. In 1983, Tomczak led the attack that beat Oregon and No. 2 Oklahoma. He completed 15 of 25 passes for 234 yards in a 24-14 win over Oklahoma. Ohio State finished the regular season with an 8-3-0 mark and then met Pittsburgh in the Fiesta Bowl. At 6-1, 204 pounds, Tomczak threw a 39 yard touchdown pass with 39 seconds left to beat Pitt 28-23. Mike was named the NCAA Scholarship Winner in 1983 to certify his qualifications as an excellent scholar and athlete. He suffered a broken leg in 1984 spring practice which prevented him from starting the first game of the season against Oregon. He returned for the second game and in the following weeks directed Ohio State wins over Washington State, Iowa and Minnesota. Mike passed for 280 yards against Purdue but in a losing cause. The Buckeyes finished with a 9-3-0 record, were Big Ten champs but lost to USC in the Rose Bowl 20-17. Tomczak started at quarterback for three years and passed for more yards, 5,569, than all other Ohio State quarterbacks except Art Schlichter. Mike was drafted by the Chicago Bears in 1985 and played with them until 1991. He is still the only Chicago quarterback to win a play-off game, over Philadelphia in 1988 and New Orleans in 1990, since the Super Bowl season of 1985. He left the Bears with a 23-11 record as a starter. The Green Bay Packers signed him to back up another Polish American quarterback, Don Majkowski. Tomczak played his seventh year of pro ball with Green Bay and replaced injured Cleveland Brown's quarterback, Bernie Kosar, during the 1992 season. Mike was a back up quarterback during the 1993 campaign with the Pittsburgh Steelers. When not playing football, he devotes time to his furniture business in the Chicago area.

Steve Tomczak—St. Francis—Halfback/ Quarterback—1993

Steve Tomczak broke 14 football passing records as quarterback at Lincoln-Way High School in Frankfort, Illinois. As a senior, he completed 102 of 178 passes for 1,429 yards. Steve enrolled at Indiana University as a walk-on, hoping to become a Big Ten quarterback as older brother, Mike, had done at Ohio State University. He transferred to the College of St. Francis because of questions concerning his scholarship and quarterbacking. He chose St. Francis primarily to play again with his former high school teammates. Tomczak platooned Ed with Paul Myszka at quarterback as a freshman and for part of his sophomore season before taking over the right halfback position. Steve chose to play halfback giving St. Francis a triple threat who could run, catch passes and throw from the halfback spot. As an example, he caught a 16 yard touchdown pass from Myszka with 59 seconds left to give St. Francis an 18-17 win over Hillsdale College. As a senior at 6-0, 185 pounds, Steve quarterbacked part of the Northern Michigan game after Myszka left with a concussion. After Myszka sustained a severe injury in the Ferris State game, Tomczak took over again and did an incredible job. He completed 17 of 27 passes for 275 yards and four touchdowns to beat Saginaw Valley State 54-33. He was named NAIA Division I Offensive Player of the Week for his play against Saginaw Valley. Starting four of the final five games, Steve finished the year completing 85 of 147 passes for 1,281 yards with a school record-tying 11 touchdown passes. He set or tied 13 school single-game and season records, among them most consecutive games passing 200 yards or more (four) and most yards passing in a single game (288). Tomczak was selected to the NAIA All-District 20 first team as a quarterback, and was a unanimous choice to the Midwest Intercollegiate Football Conference 1993 first team All-Academic. Steve graduated in December 1993 with a degree in business management and planned to play professional football before entering the business world.

Gregory Worsowicz—Sewanee—Def. Back—1981

From 1978 through 1981 Gregory Worsowicz was a four-year letter winner, an outstanding football player, and an excellent student at Sewanee, now known as The University of the South, in Sewanee, Tenn. Playing as defensive back, Worsowicz gained the reputation as one of the hardest hitters of all time at Sewanee. In recognition of his great achievements on the gridiron, Gregory was named College Athletic Conference first team defensive back in 1980 and again in 1981. In addition, he was also selected Kodak Little All-America first team as defensive back in 1981. Worsowicz was the perfect example of a Division III All-America football scholar-athlete by being chosen the NCAA Postgraduate Scholarship Winner in 1982. To qualify for the Postgraduate Scholarship, student-athletes must maintain a 3.0 grade point average (on a 4.0 scale) during their collegiate careers and perform with distinction in varsity football. In the 1980s, Sewanee was not the football power it had been in 1899 when it won all 12 games and was ranked No. 2 in the nation. That season Sewanee defeated and held scoreless Georgia, Georgia Tech, Tennessee, Southwestern, Texas, Tulane, Texas A&M, Louisiana State, Mississippi, Cumberland and North Carolina. Auburn, coached by John Heisman, was the only team able to score any points. However, Sewanee was a good Division III team and turned out an outstanding player, Worsowicz, who was offered a contract to play pro ball with the Seattle Seahawks. Gregory turned down the contract offer to attend medical school and become a doctor.

Joseph Zeszotarski—Muhlenberg—Def. End—1990

Joseph Zeszotarski was a scholar-athlete at Green Brook High School in Green Brook, New Jersey, who participated in football, basketball and track. Joe enrolled at Muhlenberg College in 1987 and was a letter winner in football during his freshman year. He was used primarily as a defensive end and recorded four tackles. Zeszotarski became a starter at defensive end in 1988 and was third on the team with 64 tackles of which 33 were solos and five for losses. Joe led the Mules with 78 tackles (34 solos), six pass break ups and two fumble recoveries during the 1989 season. He was selected first team GTE Academic All-America defensive end by the College Sports Information Directors of America. To be eligible, student-athletes must be regular football performers and have at least a 3.20 grade point average (on a 4.00 scale) during their collegiate careers. At 6-2, 198 pounds, Zeszotarski was elected the Muhlenberg football team captain at the start of the 1990 season. He proved to be an excellent team leader and was second on the team with 84 tackles. In recognition of his scholastic and football achievements, he was again selected Academic All-America. In addition, having a fantastic 3.86 grade point average in his senior year, Joe was chosen to the Academic All-Centennial Conference at the end of the 1990 campaign. He was a four-year letter winner, had 230 tackles, made three sacks, 11 pass break ups, two interceptions and four fumble recoveries. He was an economics major, member of Phi Kappa Tau fraternity, and an outstanding scholar-athlete at Muhlenberg College.

CHAPTER VII

COLLEGE ALL-STARS

Daniel Abramowicz—Xavier—Wide Receiver—1966
Paul Andrzejewski—Army—Split End—1993
Pete Banaszak—Miami (Fla.)—Running Back—1965
John Brzezinski—Harvard—Def. Tackle—1990
Frank Gatski—Marshall & Auburn—Center—1945
Doug Helkowski—Pennsylvania State—Punter—1991
Henry Hynoski—Temple—Fullback—1974
Bruce Jankowski—Ohio State—End—1970
Ron Jaworski—Youngstown State—Quarterback—1972
Robert Kowalkowski—Virginia—Def. Tackle—1965
Glen Kozlowski—Brigham Young—Wide Receiver—1985
Larry Krutko—West Virginia—Fullback—1957
Donald Majkowski—Virginia—Quarterback—1986
Walter Michaels—Washington & Lee—Fullback—1950
Eugene Modzelewski—New Mexico State—Def. Tackle—1965
John Niemiec—Notre Dame—Halfback—1928
Steve Pisarkiewicz—Missouri—Quarterback—1976
Joseph Pliska—Notre Dame—Halfback—1914
Paul Romanowski—Butler—Quarterback—1991
Robert Skoronski—Indiana—Tackle—1955
Joe Tereshinski—Georgia—End—1946
Frank Tripucka—Notre Dame—Quarterback—1948
Harry Ulinski—Kentucky—Center—1949
John Wojciechowski—Michigan State—Off. Guard—1985
Bill Wolski—Notre Dame—Halfback—1965

Daniel Abramowicz—Xavier—Wide Receiver—1966

A native of Steubenville, Ohio, Danny Abramowicz had an outstanding collegiate football career as a three year letter winner as wide receiver at Xavier University in Ohio. At 6-0, 198 pounds, Danny caught 18 passes for 257 yards in his first varsity campaign in 1964. As a junior, Abramowicz finished with 50 catches for 738 yards and eight touchdowns, helping Xavier to an 8-2-0 season. He was named to the All-Catholic All-America team at the end of the year. Although facing double coverage his senior season, he caught 34 passes for 585 yards and three touchdowns. Abramowicz did not have great speed, but his intelligent running of pass patterns and deceptive moves created openings. He was also gifted with good hands. Danny holds Xavier University records for passes caught in a season (50 in 1965), in a career (102 in 1964-1966), yards gained through passes caught in a career (1,470), as well as touchdown passes caught in a season (eight in 1965) and in a career (13). Abramowicz graduated Xavier with a 3.0 grade point average with a degree in Economics and Education. He was selected a member of the prestigous Xavier University Legion of Honor which was the highest award that could be bestowed upon a football player for sportsmanship, leadership and scholarship. He was drafted in the 17th-round by the NFL New Orleans Saints and made the team on sheer courage and determination. Danny led the NFL in pass receptions with 73 in 1969 for 1,015 yards and seven touchdowns. He was the third man in NFL history to make 50 or more receptions in each of his first four pro seasons (50 in '67, 54 in '68, 73 in '69, and 55 in '70).

In six seasons, 1967-1972, Abramowicz finished second in Saints' history in catches (307), receiving yards (4,875) and touchdowns (37). He also caught passes in 105 consecutive games, an NFL record which stood until 1982. Danny finished his pro career with the San Francisco 49ers in 1974 and went into private business. He returned to football in 1989 as head coach at Jesuit High School in New Orlean. He joined the NFL Chicago Bears in 1992 as their special teams coach. Abramowicz was inducted into the Xavier University Athletic Hall of Fame in 1981 and the State of Louisiana Sports Hall of Fame in 1992. He is also a member of the New Orleans Saints' Hall of Fame. In June 1992, Abramowicz was elected to the National Polish-American Sports Hall of Fame. Danny's son, Andrew, was a football center and an excellent scholar at Tulane University in 1992.

Paul Andrzejewski—Army—Split End—1993

Paul Andrzejewski had an outstanding athletic and scholastic career at Orchard Park High School in New York. He earned three letters each in football and baseball, and four in basketball. Paul was named to All-Western New York teams in football and baseball. As a wide receiver in football, he set the school record in 1989 for most passes caught in a single game. As a plebe at West Point in 1990, Andrzejewski played in one game against Lafayette. He moved into the No. 2 split end spot late in his second year where he saw reserve duty in three of the final four games. Paul moved into the starting split end position during preseason work in his junior year, and never let go of that job once the season began. He finished it as Army's leading receiver, catching 17 more passes than the second ranked end. His 27 receptions were the most by an Army player since the Cadets switched to the ground-dominated wishbone offense in 1984. He caught at least one pass in all 11 games. His season best was six catches in the victory over Lafayette, and he also had four receptions in the come-from-behind win over Navy. His coaches rated him high for "excellent hands, very good routes, and great attitude." At 6-0, 183 pounds, Andrzejewski was again Army's leading receiver during the 1993 campaign.

Pete Banaszak—Miami (Fla.)—Running Back—1965

An excellent athlete and scholar at Marinette High School in Wisconsin, Pete Banaszak starred in football, basketball, baseball and track. He won the state prep discus championship in his senior year. Banaszak enrolled at the University of Miami in Florida in 1962, and developed into an exceptional running back for the Hurricane football squad under head coaches Andy Gustafson in 1962 and '63, and Charlie Tate in 1964 and '65. Pete was the Hurricanes' individual record holder in rushing during the 1963 campaign with 97 carries for 461 yards (average 4.8 yards per carry), and three touchdowns. He was Miami's leading rusher again during the 1965 season with 111 runs for 473 yards (4.7 yards per run) and four touchdowns. Banaszak ran for a Hurricane high of 27 carries in 1965 against the University of Florida. Pete was selected Miami's Most Valuable Player in his senior year, and also managed to be on the Dean's List as an outstanding student. He was a fifth round NFL draft choice of the Oakland Raiders in 1966 and had a terrific 13-year professional football career. At 6-0, 210 pounds, he was an excellent running back and a powerful, punishing blocker. He is on the Oakland record books for career rushing yards, points scored by touchdowns, yards gained after pass catches, and total yards rushing and pass receiving. Pete was elected to the National Polish-American Sports Hall of Fame in 1990. Banaszak lives in Ponte Verda, Florida and is vice-president of Crowley Maritime corporation in Jacksonville, Florida.

John Brzezenski—Harvard—Def. Tackle—1990

John Brzezenski captained the 1986 football team at Lexington High School in Lexington, Massachusetts, and was selected All-League, Honorable Mention All-America, and National Football Foundation and Hall of Fame Scholar-Athlete in his senior year. He was also All-League in track and field for three years. Brzezenski enrolled at Harvard University in 1987 and became an outstanding football and track performer. When John arrived at Harvard, his future appeared to be on the offensive line. However, he gained his second varsity letter during the 1989 season after making the switch from offensive to defensive tackle following the 1988 campaign. John had good speed and quickness for his size, and had a tremendous desire to succeed. After the initial adjustment period, Brzezenski established himself as a legitimate defensive tackle. During the 1989 season, he recorded 22 solo tackles in 10 games including a fourth-quarter sack against Yale in Harvard's 37-20 upset at the Yale Bowl. He took over as the defensive line leader during the 1990 campaign and turned in a magnificent performance. John was chosen for All-Ivy League honors after his senior season. At 6-4, 250 pounds, Brzezenski was an imposing figure both on the gridiron and in the throwing circle, where he tossed the 35-pound weight for the Crimson track and field team. He also earned All-Ivy League honors with a record toss which qualified him for the NCAA championship. Brzezenski graduated Harvard University with honors as an Economics major in 1990.

Frank Gatski—Marshall and Auburn—Center—1945

Frank Gatski was the son of a coal miner and grew up in Number Nine Coal Camp in West Virginia where he also worked in the mines for one year. Frank played four years of football as center at Farmington High School, Farmington, West Virginia where he learned early that he had to be tough to play and succeed in football. He survived a rugged pre-season tryout at Marshall University and received a football scholarship in 1940. Gatski started at center for the freshman team during the 1940 season. He graduated to the varsity squad in 1941 and was a starter playing at center on offense and linebacker on defense. Frank had two excellent seasons with the Thundering Herd before going on active military duty during World War II. After receiving his discharge from the service in 1945, Gatski enrolled at Auburn University to complete his college education and pursue his collegiate football career. He had a good outing for the single season playing center and linebacker. Frank was drafted by the Cleveland Browns in 1946 and became a starter at center and linebacker during the 1947 campaign. Cleveland dominated professional football in that era, and Gatski played a significant role in the game plans of the legendary head coach, Paul Brown. The Browns' Big-T formation relied on fancy plays, accurate passing, fast receivers and powerful centers. At 6-3, 240 pounds, Frank proved a fine blocker and, with his long legs, allowed the quarterback to receive the snap standing up and better able to read defenses quickly. He was ranked among the finest centers and linebackers in Cleveland Browns' football history. From 1946 through 1955, Gatski contributed greatly to the famous quarterback Otto Graham's success story. Even the opponents respected the rugged, strong, silent West Virginian. Frank was a serious competitor and hard worker who never missed a game or practice in his college or professional career. He made All-Pro four times, played in eleven championship games (helping the Browns win eight), and was named by the Cleveland Touchdown Club as the team's Most Valuable Player in 1955. In 1956, he played with the Detroit Lions and retired after the 1957 season. He scouted for the Boston Patriots until 1961, then became football coach at a West Virginia school. Gatski was named to the Pro Football Hall of Fame in 1985, was selected to the State of West Virginia Hall of Fame and made the All-Time Cleveland Browns team. In 1989, Frank was elected to the National Polish-American Sports Hall of Fame.

Doug Helkowski—Pennsylvania State—Punter—1991

Doug Helkowski came from Ruffsdale, Pennsylvania to Pennsylvania State University to become a four-year football letter winner and one of the Nittany Lions' most outstanding punters. He was red-shirted as a freshman in 1987 and became a starter during the 1988 season. Helkowski punted 68 times for 2,668 yards (average 39.2 yds. per punt) and his longest went for 54 yards. In 1989, Doug punted 57 times for a total of 2,175 yards and an average of 38.2 yards per kick. He continued to perform with excellent precision and punted 59 times in 1990 for a total of 2,327 yards (39.4 yds. average). In 1991, Doug became the all-time Penn State leader in number of punts and only the second player in school history to accumulate more than 9,000 punting yards (actually 9,391 yards). He had averaged 38.96 yards on 241 punts to rank him in a tie for the fifth position among Penn State's all-time specialists. He handled 57 punts in 1991 for 2,221 yards and averaged 39.0 yards. Helkowski had three punts of 50 yards against Georgia Tech, Miami and Pittsburgh. He had his busiest day of the year at Pitt when he punted nine times. His 44.2 yard average was the best of the season and among the best perform-ances of his career. With Pittsburgh threatening much of the second half, Doug performed brilliantly by punting under heavy pressure. However, Helkowski saved his best for the Fiesta Bowl when Penn State came from behind to beat Tennessee. He punted nine times for an excellent average of 48.0 yards, and was chosen to the 1991 All-Bowl team as a punter.

Henry Hynoski—Temple—Fullback—1974

An excellent running back at Mt. Carmel Area High School in Pennsylvania, Henry Hynoski earned all-state honors and was chosen to play in the Big 33 game. He enrolled at Temple University in 1971 to develop into a strong, fast and tough running back who ran over opposing tacklers. As a substitute during the 1972 campaign, Henry carried the ball 77 times for 331 yards and two touchdowns. He also had two pass receptions for 19 yards. He was a starter during the 1973 season and helped the Owls to a very successful 9-1-0 record. Hynoski carried the ball 156 times for 881 yards (5.6 yard average), and scored seven touchdowns. He also caught seven passes for 120 yards and three touchdowns. He was Temple's leading scorer with 60 points on 10 touchdowns. His best '73 games were against Akron when he rushed for 122 yards and Rhode Island with 108 yards. The 1974 campaign saw Hynoski finish as the Owls' leading rusher with 1,006 yards on 206 carries resulting in seven touchdowns. He was also the all-purpose running leader with 1,280 yards, 1,006 by rushing and 274 by pass reception. He scored two touchdowns on passes. His best game of the season was against Pitt when he rushed for 132 yards. The Owls finished 1974 with a good 8-2-0 mark. Hynoski rushed 439 times for 2,218 yards (5.1 yds. aver-age), and 16 touchdowns during his 1972 to 1974 career. He also caught 33 passes for 413 yards and five touchdowns. Henry was chosen first team All-Eastern College Athletic Conference full-back and Honorable Mention All-America. Hynoski was the Cleveland Browns' NFL draft choice in 1975.

Bruce Jankowski—Ohio State—End—1970

Bruce Jankowski came to Ohio State University in 1967 from Fairlawn, New Jersey to become a letter winner on the 1968, '69 and '70 teams under head coach Woody Hayes. Jankowski was a member of a strong freshman Buckeye squad in 1967 of which 19 players earned letters as sophomores, including Bruce. The 1968 Ohio State team was voted the "outstanding college football team of the sixties" and Jankowski contributed to their success. He caught at least one pass in each game including eight receptions against Michigan State to highlight the contest. He finished the year with 31 catches for 328 yards and one touchdown. The Buckeyes ended the '68 campaign with an undefeated, untied mark of 10-0-0. They were the Big Ten Conference and National Champions, and beat Southern California in the Rose Bowl. In 1969, Bruce was the Buckeyes' leading receiver with 23 catches good for 404 yards and five touchdowns. Ohio State had another awesome team, finished with an 8-1-0 mark and were Big Ten Co-Champs. Jankowski was the Buckeye leading receiver again during the 1970 season with 235 yards on 12 catches. He also rushed for 41 yards and returned kick-offs for 85 yards. Ohio State finished 9-1-0, were Big Ten and National Champs, but lost to Stanford in the Rose Bowl. Bruce was known for his excellent speed and a variety of good moves. He was one of the fastest players to be offensive end at Ohio State. Jankowski was drafted by the Kansas City Chiefs in 1971 and played two years of professional football. He was the National Accounts Manager of Cisco Systems in St. Louis, Missouri as of 1993.

Ron Jaworski—Youngstown State—Quarterback—1972

An outstanding athlete at Lackawanna High School in Lackawanna, N.Y., Ron Jaworski played football, baseball and basketball. He started as a running back and wide receiver, but was switched to quarterback because of his strong arm. Ron was a superstar at 6-2, 160 pounds as a senior and received the Kelly Award which is presented annually to the best all-round athlete in northern New York State. He was recruited by many colleges including Ohio State, Syracuse and Georgia Tech. He chose Youngstown State University because of his size and the opportunity to develop his talents as a quarterback playing at a smaller school. Youngstown State was coached by the innovating Dwight "Dike" Reede, who was the exponent of the Side Saddle T offense. In this formation, the quarterback never lined up directly over the center, and never took a direct snap from center. The objective of this offense was to confuse the opposing defense as to who had the ball and whom to pursue. As a freshman in 1969, Ron was a substitute quarterback and the Penguins finished with a 2-6-0 record. In 1970, Youngstown had a terrible season which ended with a 0-9-0 mark. Jaworski took over as starting quarterback mid-way in the season. With very little talent to support him, Ron improved Youngstown's record in 1971 to 2-6-0 while passing for 1,059 yards and seven touchdowns. He also punted

60 times for 2,135 yards for an average of 35.6 yards per punt. In 1972, Jaworski got his first opportunity to show what he had learned during the previous seasons, and performed well against Northern Michigan, Akron, Xavier, Central State and Central Michigan. The final 4-4-1 record was the best for the Penguins since 1966. Ron completed 139 of 259 passes to establish a new Youngstown State football record of 2,123 yards and 18 touchdowns. His performance in 1972 drew the attention of many professional scouts, and he was drafted in the second round by the Los Angeles Rams in 1973. He was used as a backup quarterback, and was traded to the Philadelphia Eagles in 1977. Jaworski and coach Dick Vermeil led the Eagles to some of their best years especially in 1980. The "Polish Rifle" enjoyed a brilliant 17-year NFL career. He played through 1989 and finished with career totals of 2,142 completions and 179 touchdowns. Ron was named the NFL Player of the Year, and given the Bert Bell Trophy from the Maxwell Club for leading the Philadelphia Eagles to the Super Bowl in 1980. He was a Pro Bowl selection in 1981. Jaworski is ranked in the top 20 in pro football history in three passing categories: attempts, completions and yards. Ron was inducted into the National Polish-American Sports Hall of Fame in 1991 primarily in recognition of his pro football achievements. In 1992, he was elected President of the Maxwell Club, which was founded in 1935 by former NFL Commissioner, Bert Bell. Jaworski was named to the Philadelphia Eagles Honor Roll in 1993. Ron is the owner of the Eagles' Nest Country Club in Sewell, New Jersey, a suburb of Philadelphia. He has expanded his golf club business by taking control of his fourth golf course in the greater Philadelphia—South New Jersey area in 1993.

Robert Kowalkowski—Virginia—Def. Tackle—1965

Robert Kowalkowski came to the University of Virginia in 1962 as an outstanding high school football player from New Kensington, Pennsylvania. Kowalkowski was a starter at right defensive tackle for the Cavaliers as a sophomore, and had an excellent 1963 season to earn his first of three varsity letters. He received second team All-Atlantic Coast Conference honors at the end of the season. At 6-3, 240 pounds, Bob was elected co-captain of the squad for the 1964 campaign, but unfortunately suffered a leg injury that plagued him for the remainder of the year. However, he had enough playing time to record a good performance and repeated as an All-Atlantic Coast Conference second team selection. He was elected co-captain again of the 1965 Cavalier squad and was mentioned on some pre-season All-America teams. Tom Harmon, in previewing the 1965 college football year, selected Kowalkowski as first team All-America along with Jim Grabowski of Illinois. Kowalkowski had a good season, but the leg injury the previous year prevented him from playing up to his standards and All-America honors escaped him. He graduated with a degree from the University of Virginia's School of Education in 1966. Bob was the second round NFL draft choice of the Detroit Lions in 1966 and went on to enjoy an outstanding professional football career with the Lions from 1966 through 1976. He retired from pro ball in 1977 after playing with the Green Bay Packers. His son, Scott, was an excellent linebacker for Notre Dame from 1988 through 1990, and was drafted by the Pittsburgh Steelers in 1991.

Glen Kozlowski—Brigham Young—Wide Receiver—1985

Born in Honolulu, Hawaii, Glen Kozlowski attended Carlsbad High School in California where he excelled in football, basketball, baseball and track. He was chosen first team All-CIF and team's Most Valuable football player for two years. Kozlowski enrolled at Brigham Young University in 1981 and had an outstanding freshman season. At 6-1, 193 pounds, he made several acrobatic catches and scored five touchdowns. Unfortunately, he missed the rest of the '81 and all of the '82 seasons due to injuries. In 1983, Glen was the Cougars' fifth leading receiver, caught 29 passes for 532 yards and five touchdowns. He was named Receiver-of-the-Week versus San Diego State, UCLA, and Utah State. Kozlowski was the team co-captain in 1984 and was the second leading receiver with 55 catches for 879 yards and 11 touchdowns. He caught three passes for 35 yards and scored a touchdown in the Holiday Bowl against Michigan. The Cougars went on to beat Michigan, 24-17, finished with a 13-0-0 record, and were ranked No. 1 in the nation. Glen was named first team All-WAC, Honorable Mention All-America, and the NCAA Scholarship Award Winner. In 1985, he was named Player-of-the-Game versus Boston College, led the nation in receiving, but injured his knee and missed the rest of the season. Prior to the injury, Glen was approaching the 44-game NCAA record, having caught a pass in 38 consecutive games. He was the Chicago Bears draft choice in 1986, and was the Bears' special teams stand-out in 1992. He finished his eighth year with Chicago in 1993. His brothers, Michael and David, also played college football.

Larry Krutko—West Virginia—Fullback—1957

Larry Krutko enrolled at West Virginia University in 1954 and became a starter at fullback in his sophomore year. His best game of the 1955 season was versus George Washington University when he gained 105 yards rushing in 21 carries. West Virginia finished with a 8-2-0 record under head coach Art Lewis, were the Southern Conference champions and were ranked 19th in the country. Krutko was a powerful runner who had an excellent 1956 campaign, especially against Penn State when he gained 120 yards in 20 rushes, and versus Virginia Military Institute when he repeated with 120 yards in 20 attempts. He was the Mountaineers' total offensive leader in 1956 with 124 plays for 584 yards (4.7 yards average) and four touchdowns. Krutko was also the rushing leader for the season. West Virginia finished with a 6-4-0 mark and repeated as Southern Conference champs. Larry continued as a strong, solid rusher, and was the rushing leader in 1957 with 100 carries for 403 yards for an average of 4.0 yards per carry. He was also the scoring leader with five touchdowns. West Virginia finished with a good 7-2-1 record. Krutko played in the Blue-Gray game in 1957 and the Senior Bowl in 1958. He was also selected for the College All-Star team in 1958 and played with Walt Kowalczyk, Lou Michaels and Jim Ninowski. Ninowski passed for two touchdowns and the All-Stars beat the Detroit Lions, 35-19. Krutko was the first round draft choice of the

Pittsburgh Steelers in 1958 and played pro ball for three years. Larry is a member of the West Virginia University 1950-1959 All-Time team.

Donald Majkowski—Virginia—Quarterback—1986

An outstanding athlete, Donald Majkowski lettered in football, basketball, baseball and track at Depew High School in Depew, New York. He played quarterback and defensive back in football and earned All-Western New York and Erie County All-Star honors. Don served as the team's captain in 1981, and was named Depew's Outstanding Athlete. He prepped for one year at Fork Union Military Academy and led Fork Union to its most successful season (8-0-1) in 10 years. He was named MVP of both the football and track teams, and also won Fork Union's "Best Athlete Award." Don made the Dean's List while lettering in three sports. Majkowski made his collegiate football debut at the University of Virginia by engineering an 11-play, 88 yard touchdown drive at Clemson in 1983 and capped the drive by running for the two point conversion. As a freshman in 1983, he played in two varsity games. Don played in all 11 regular season games in 1984 and came off the bench to lead the Cavaliers to victories over Virginia Tech and Duke. He took over as the starting quarterback in the sixth game and completed 83 of 168 passes for 1,235 yards and eight touchdowns. Don also rushed for 305 yards and five touchdowns in 83 carries for an average of 3.7 yards per carry.

At 6-2, 205 pounds, Majkowski ran Virginia's option attack extremely well. His best days were in the Cavaliers' last three regular season games, especially against Maryland and North Carolina. Don threw for one touchdown and ran for another in Virginia's 1984 Peach Bowl victory over Purdue. As a junior, he completed 95 of 199 passes for 1,233 yards and seven touchdowns. He was fourth on the Cavalier squad in rushing with 87 carries for 295 yards and six touchdowns. Don rushed for more yards than any other quarterback in the Atlantic Coast Conference. His best games of the 1985 season were against Clemson (threw two touchdown passes and rushed for 64 yards), and North Carolina (180 yards passing and 25 yards rushing for 205 yards total offense). During the 1986 campaign, Majkowski completed 104 of 199 passes for 1,375 yards and seven touchdowns. He also rushed for 102 yards and one touchdown. His collegiate football career statistics show that he had 286 completions of 579 pass attempts for 3,901 yards and 22 touchdowns. Don also rushed for 905 yards in 245 carries and scored 12 touchdowns in his career at Virginia. Majkowski was third in Cavalier career passing yards and third in total offensive yards. He was chosen by the Green Bay Packers in the NFL draft in 1987. He had his best professional football season with Green Bay in 1989 when he passed for a total of 4,381 yards and 27 touchdowns. Majkowski was selected to the Pro Bowl, and gave every indication of being one of the most promising young quarterbacks in professional football. Don's base salary for the 1990 season was 1.5 million dollars. Unfortunately, he suffered a severe right shoulder injury during the 1990 season. Since then, Majkowski has not been able to perform like "The Majik Man" of the outstanding 1989 campaign with the Packers. Don joined the Indianapolis Colts as a free agent in 1993 and played as a back-up quarterback hoping to regain the "magic form" that has left him.

Walter Michaels—Washington and Lee—Fullback—1950

One of seven sons of a Polish coal-miner, Walt Michaels was an outstanding football player in high school in Swoyersville, Pennsylvania who received an athletic scholarship to Washington and Lee University in 1947. (The original family name was Majka before it was changed to Michaels.) At 6-0, 230 pounds, Walt played fullback on offense and linebacker on defense at Washington and Lee, and performed extremely well at both positions. He had an outstanding season as a senior in 1950, and helped the Generals to a undefeated, untied conference record of 6-0-0 and the Southern Conference championship. Although his college credentials were very impressive, Walt did not receive sufficient media exposure to be named to any All-America teams. At the completion of his college football career, Walt went into professional football and was with the Green Bay Packers for one year in 1951. He then played with the Cleveland Browns under head coach Paul Brown from 1952 through 1961. Walt was an excellent linebacker for the Browns for ten years, and played on two NFL championship teams in 1954 and 1955. He was also selected for All-Pro honors as linebacker from 1957 through 1961. Michaels became the defensive coach for the Oakland Raiders in 1962 and played another year of pro ball with the New York Jets in 1963. He was also the defensive coach for the New York Jets from 1963 to 1972, and later coached the Philadelphia Eagles. Walt directed his younger brother, Lou, to play football at the University of Kentucky where the youth became an All-America and Hall of Fame member.

Eugene Modzelewski—New Mexico State—Def. Tackle—1965

Eugene Modzelewski was the youngest brother of Ed "Big Mo" and Dick "Little Mo" Modzelewski, both All-Americans at the University of Maryland and pros with the Cleveland Browns. Gene was appropriately nicknamed "No Mo." He was an outstanding high school football player in West Natrona, Pennsylvania who chose to enroll at New Mexico State University instead of Maryland. He started badly at New Mexico State by missing spring practice his freshman year due to a broken arm in a weight lifting accident. However, he was back in the fall and made his mark by lettering as a freshman in 1962. During the 1963 season, he was a substitute at defensive tackle. Gene improved his performance greatly from his sophomore year and became a starter in 1964. He had an excellent year and took over the leadership of the defensive line. Modzelewski was elected co-captain in his senior year and at 6-1, 225 pounds, headed the defensive unit for the Aggies. He was characterized as a very hard worker whose blocking ability had improved vastly over his junior season. He finished his college football career with good credentials and was eyed by various professional scouts. He was chosen by the Cleveland Browns in the NFL draft in 1966. In his spare time, Gene helped his brothers at their Cleveland, Ohio restaurant, Mo and Jr's.

Eugene's son, Dan, starred as a defensive end in football at Eastlake High School in the suburbs of Cleveland. He enrolled at New Mexico State University and played football as a junior defensive lineman in 1993.

John Niemiec—Notre Dame—Halfback—1928

John Niemiec was a 5-8, 170 pound halfback who lettered in football at the University of Notre Dame in 1926, 1927 and 1928. He was a versatile athlete who was an excellent runner, passer, and pass receiver, and kicked points after touchdowns. The Bellaire, Ohio native was a back-up halfback in 1926 but got a lot of playing time during the season. He caught the game winning touchdown passes in victories over Northwestern and U.S.C., and helped in wins over Beloit, Minnesota, Penn State and Georgia Tech by passing, scoring touchdowns and kicking PATS. In 1927, Niemiec led the team in passing by completing 14 of 33 attempts for 187 yards. He was a substitute halfback on the '27 national championship squad coached by Knute Rockne. As a starting halfback in 1928, John was again the leading Notre Dame passer who won the Navy game, 7-0, with a touchdown pass. The Army-Notre Dame classic was a hard fought battle played before a capacity crowd of 78,188 fans in Yankee Stadium. The first half ended in a scoreless tie. In the locker room at half time, Rockne told the squad about George Gipp's dying wish "tell the team to win one for me when the game isn't going right." Inspired by Rockne's moving pep talk, Notre Dame came from behind in the second half to tie Army, 6-6. Niemiec then threw a 45-yard touchdown pass to Johnny "One Play" O'Brien to lead the team to 12-6 major upset victory over Army in the famous "Win One for the Gipper" game. Notre Dame compiled an excellent winning record of 21-6-1 during Niemiec's three year college football career.

Steve Pisarkiewicz—Missouri—Quarterback—1976

A native of Florissant, Missouri, Steve Pisarkiewicz was an excellent baseball and football player in high school before enrolling at the University of Missouri in 1972. As a reserve quarterback during his freshman year, Steve completed 41 passes for 717 yards with the longest play being a 63 yarder. He was sidelined with injuries in 1973 and took over as Missouri's starting quarterback in the fourth game of his sophomore year in 1974. He finished the season with 70 pass completions for 829 yards and six touchdowns. His best season came as a junior in 1975 when he completed 113 passes for 1,792 yards and 11 touchdowns. Steve's best individual passing day was against Oklahoma State when he made 20 passes of 27 attempts, with no interceptions, for 371 yards. This performance set a Missouri record. He was named the Associated Press Offensive Player of the Week for the Oklahoma State game. Pisarkiewicz started the 1976 season by throwing three touchdown passes in the season opener against Southern California. Missouri beat the Rose Bowl champs for their only loss of the year in a major upset victory. He was chosen national Offensive Player of the Week for the U.S.C. game. Plagued with injury problems as a senior, Steve finished the campaign with 53 pass completions for 793 yards and six touchdowns. Pisarkiewicz had 236 career completions for 3,413 yards and 23 TDs. This gave him the most completions and most passing yards in Missouri's history. Steve played in three post-season games, and was the St. Louis first round NFL draft choice in 1977. He played four years of pro ball.

217

Joe Pliska—Notre Dame—Halfback—1914

A native of Chicago, Illinois, Joe Pliska was a four-year letter winner at the University of Notre Dame as a football halfback from 1911 through 1914. At 5-10, 170 pounds, Pliska was a speedy, deceptive runner and an excellent pass receiver who was a long distance threat on any offensive play. He was an outstanding member of the team that brought Notre Dame into the national collegiate football spotlight. As a back-up halfback in 1911, Joe helped Notre Dame to victories over Ohio Northern, St. Viator, Loyola of Chicago, and had a field day against St. Bonaventure by scoring three touchdowns, kicking three conversions and intercepting a pass. Pliska was the starting halfback on the 1912 squad and scored career-high four TDs in the victory over Adrian. He led the team with three TDs against St. Louis and had an excellent game in the win over Marquette. In 1913, Joe ran for three TDs against Ohio Northern and also scored three TDs versus Alma. He was instrumental in leading Notre Dame to a major upset victory over Army in their first ever meeting by scoring two TDs. He ran for the first score and caught a pass for another TD that put Notre Dame ahead for the rest of the game. (Knute Rockne was captain and left end on the '13 squad.) In 1914, Joe had a good season running 60 and 35 yards for TDs against Carlisle, and finishing with a TD victory over Syracuse. Notre Dame compiled an excellent winning record of 26-2-2 during Pliska's four-year college football career, and were undefeated, untied with 7-0-0 marks during the 1912 and 1913 campaigns.

Paul Romanowski—Butler—Quarterback—1991

Paul Romanowski was an All-State quarterback at Harrison High School in West Lafayette, Indiana. He was the leading passer in Indiana as a senior with 2,513 yards and finished his prep career with 3,700 passing yards and 27 touchdowns. Paul was named All-Conference, All-Area, team's MVP and honorable mention All-America in 1987. At 6-4, 194 pounds, Romanowski was used as a reserve quarterback at Butler University and saw very little action in 1988 and 1989. He got more playing time during the 1990 season and completed 18 of 30 passes for 184 yards and two touchdowns. Butler was one of the surprise teams in the NCAA Division II in 1991. Picked to finish seventh in the Midwest Intercollegiate Football Conference, the Bulldogs stunned the experts by posting a 9-1-0 regular season record, capturing the MIFC title and advancing to the first round of the Division II playoffs. Butler wound up fifth in the final NCAA Division II national rankings. The primary reason for Butler's success was Paul Romanowski. In the season opener against Northern Michigan, Paul completed 12 of 22 passes for 177 yards and three touchdowns to lead Butler to a 28-0 victory. His best individual performance of the season was against Hillsdale College when he completed 20 of 30 passes for career-high 384 yards and one touchdown to lead Butler to another victory. During his college football career, Romanowski attempted 296 passes, completed 173 (.580 average) for 2,402 yards and 19 touchdowns. Paul was selected Player of the Year by the Midwest Intercollegiate Football Conference and chosen first team All-MIFC quarterback.

Robert Skoronski—Indiana—Tackle—1955

The grandson of Polish immigrants, Bob Skoronski came from a close-knit, energetic family in Derby, Connecticut who learned early in life that success can only be achieved through honest hard work. Skoronski became an outstanding high school football player and was recruited by many colleges including Notre Dame. He could have gone to Notre Dame, but unselfishly chose Indiana University because the Hoosiers also offered his older brother a football scholarship. Bob earned his first football letter at Indiana University during the 1953 season by playing tackle, and followed with an excellent outing as a junior in 1954. He was an extremely intelligent, dedicated player who took over the leadership of the Hoosier line. He was elected captain of the 1955 squad, continued to perform brilliantly, and was selected the team's Most Valuable Player at the end of the season. Bob was chosen to play in the North-South All-Star game in 1955 and the College All-Star classic in 1956. He was drafted by the Green Bay Packers in 1956. As a rookie, Skoronski played tackle for the

Packers and then spent two years in the service. He returned to Green Bay and played ten years at left tackle under head coach, Vince Lombardi. He became one of Lombardi's devoted followers. Bob was a formidable 250-pound tackle who was a hard-working, dependable performer admired by his teammates. His best season came in 1967 when he was chosen to the Pro Bowl after an outstanding performance in Super Bowl I. In 1968, Skoronski started a school supply business which grossed 16 million dollars in 15 years. Bob was asked to become Indiana University's athletic director in 1970, but he chose to continue with his growing business venture. Skoronski graduated with a B.A. degree in marketing from Indiana in 1956, his two younger brothers were Harvard graduates, and his sister got a Doctorate degree. Of his four children, one was All-Ivy defensive tackle at Yale, another a basketball player at Indiana University, and the third boy went to Miami (Ohio) on a football scholarship. His only daughter graduated from Indiana. Skoronski was inducted into the Indiana University Athletic Hall of Fame as a charter member in 1982 with another outstanding Polish American grad, Ted Kluszewski.

Joseph Tereshinski—Georgia—End—1946

Joe Tereshinski came to the University of Georgia on a football scholarship in 1941 from Glen Lyon, Pennsylvania, a suburb of

Wilkes-Barre. Tereshinski was the fifth of eight children born to a coal miner from Jozefu, Poland. Joe feels that the Georgia football scholarship was the most significant event in his life because it enabled him to realize the American dream. He has never wavered in his fierce loyalty to the Bulldogs. He lettered at Georgia in 1942, 1945 and 1946, with his college football career interrupted by World War II. He played end under head coach Wally Butts, and during the 1942 season utilized his blocking skills to clear the path for All-America, Heisman Trophy winner, Frank Sinkwich. The Bulldogs finished the '42 campaign with a 10-1-0 record, were ranked number two nationally and beat UCLA in the Rose Bowl. They were also the Southeast Conference champions. The 1945 season ended with a winning 9-2-0 mark and a victory over Tulsa in the Oil Bowl. Tereshinski was outstanding during 1946 and was greatly responsible for Charlie Trippi's success as the Maxwell Award winning Georgia halfback. The Bulldogs finished the season undefeated and untied with a perfect 11-0-0 record. They beat North Carolina in the Sugar Bowl, shared the Southeast Conference crown with Tennessee, and were ranked number three in the nation. Joe was selected to the All-Southeast Conference team in 1946. Tereshinski played in the College All-Star game in 1947, and then reported to the Washington Redskins to begin his professional football career. He became a first stringer at the start and retained that position as a pro. Joe spent 13 years with the Redskins—eight playing and five coaching. Washington coach Joe Kuharich stated that Joe made himself an outstanding player, one of the most feared defensive ends in pro ranks, thru sheer determination, hard work and courage. As a long time member of the Washington Touchdown Club, Joe used his influence to have the Club honor his Georgia friend, coach Vince Dooley, with an award for "lifetime achievement in college coaching." Joe's ties to Georgia remained so close that he also named one of his sons Wally, for his old coach, Wally Butts, and both sons played football for the Bulldogs. Joseph. Jr. is currently the assistant strength and conditioning coach and also an administration assistant. He played center from 1974 to 1976 and was a member of the Georgia 1976 Southeastern Conference championship team. Wally Tereshinski was a linebacker in 1976 and 1977, and also a member of the Georgia 1976 SEC champ squad. The story goes that Joe Tereshinski's coach, Wally Butts, suggested that Joe change his name to Terry. Joe, proud of his Polish heritage, refused and informed Butts that he would make the coach proud of the name, Tereshinski. The University of Georgia acknowledged that Tereshinski is a name to be proud of in a tribute article that appeared in a 1991 Bulldog publication. As of 1994, Joe resided in Bethesda, Maryland and was a sales representative at American Service Center in Arlington, Virginia selling Mercedes, Rolls Royce and Ferrari automobiles.

Frank Tripucka—Notre Dame—Quarterback—1948

A native of Bloomfield, New Jersey, Frank Tripucka had the misfortune of enrolling at the University of Notre Dame when the Irish were loaded with brilliant quarterbacks. During the 1945 season, Tripucka and George Ratterman were used as substitutes for the team captain and All-America quarterback, Frank Dancewicz. Under head coach, Hugh Devore, Notre Dame finished the '45 campaign with a 7-2-1 mark and were ranked ninth nationally. The 1946 season saw Tripucka playing backup for the Notre Dame great, Johnny Lujack. In head coach Frank Leahy's debut, Notre Dame finished 8-0-1 and were number one in the country. Tripucka earned enough game time during the 1947 season to complete 25 of 44 pass attempts. He did a very commendable job in filling in for Lujack to lead Notre Dame to a 40-6 victory over Pittsburgh. In the second half of the Purdue game, he helped Lujack with an excellent passing attack to beat the Boilermakers, 22-7. He also helped Lujack to scuttle Navy, 27-0, with an outstanding passing offense. Notre Dame finished the year undefeated, untied with a 9-0-0 record and repeated as number one in the nation. Tripucka became the starting quarterback at the beginning of the 1948 season, and did an excellent job in leading Notre Dame to victories in their first nine games. He had a brilliant game against Purdue, and led in scoring for a 40-0 win over Pittsburgh. Frank threw a pass to Swistowicz who ran 15 yards for a touchdown against Michigan State, and followed with outstanding performances in wins over Navy, Indiana, Northwestern and Washington. During the last game of the '48

222

season against Southern California, Tripucka passed to Leon Hart to put Notre Dame ahead in the second quarter. Then disaster struck. On the last play before half-time, Frank was injured so badly that he was carried off the field and could not return in the second half. Sophomore quarterback, Bob Williams, replaced Tripucka but could only manage a tie with Southern California to end the year with a 9-0-1 record. At 6-2, 180 pouds, Frank was a four-year letter winning quarterback deserving greater honors. The talented quarterback was capable of being a four-year starter at any other Division I school except Notre Dame in those years. He finished with a total career offensive record of 1,060 yards and 21 touchdowns. However, he played an instrumental role in helping Notre Dame to win national championships during the 1946 and 1947 seasons as a super backup quarterback.

Harry Ulinski—Kentucky—Center—1949

A star athlete from Ambridge, Pennsylvania, Harry Ulinski enrolled at the University of Kentucky in 1946 to become a fouryear letter winner playing center on offense and linebacker on defense. After two excellent seasons in 1946 and 1947, Harry missed conference and national honors because of injuries in 1948. He did come back to help Kentucky in a late season drive especially against Tennessee. Ulinski was elected captain of the 1949 Wildcat squad which had Chet Lukowski, John Ignarski, and Ed Kozlowski as team members. Harry was rated one of the best linebackers in the South. His alert plays managed to stop the toughest Kentucky opponents, both on the ground and in the air. In the Mississippi game, Ulinski provided the crowd with a brilliant display of defensive tactics. On one play he brushed aside three Rebel blockers and dove over another to haul down their punt returner deep in 'Ole Miss territory. With his team-mates, Harry formed a tight front line defense that prevented scores by Wildcat opponents. The 1949 campaign ended with a 9-3-0 record under head coach Bear Bryant, an Orange Bowl loss to Santa Clara, and Kentucky was ranked 11th in the country. Ulinski was selected to the All-Southeastern Conference first team in 1949. He played on the College All-Stars team in 1950 and was Washington's NFL draft choice. Harry played center and linebacker for Washington for seven years and was a Pro Bowl selection in 1956. His older brother, Eddie, played football and graduated from Marshall University, and then played pro ball as guard with the Cleveland Browns for four years.

John Wojciechowski—Michigan State—Off. Guard—1985

John Wojciechowski won unanimous All-State football honors as defensive tackle at Warren Fitzgerald High School in Detroit, Michigan. He also starred as a wrestler, and won the heavyweight wrestling title in his senior year. John enrolled at Michigan State University in 1981 and had good seasons during the '81 and '82 campaigns. He played defensive tackle, nose guard and offensive guard. According to coach, Buck Nystrom, Wojciechowski became one of the best run-pull guards he had during his career in college football. John was headed for an all-star season in 1983, but an injury side lined him for the year. He came back strong to perform as an excellent offensive guard during the 1984 season. He was named Honorable Mention All-Big Ten Conference offensive lineman for the '84 campaign. Wojciechowski was a regular starter at his familiar right guard spot again in 1985. At 6-4, 246 pounds, John was intelligent, strong and displayed a wonderful attitude. He was instrumental in helping Lorenzo White to rush for a record 2,066 yards by opening gaping holes for the rushing back. Wojciechowski was a four-year letter winner and selected first team All-Big Ten at the end of the year. He was chosen for the Gerald R. Ford Up Front Award which is given to the Spartan offensive lineman who exemplifies the courage and integrity displayed by the nation's 38th President. John also received the Danziger Award as the outstanding player from the Detroit area. He played in the Senior Bowl and has been in professional football for seven years, currently with the Chicago Bears.

Bill Wolski—Notre Dame—Halfback—1965

A Muskegon, Michigan native, Bill Wolski was a three-year letter winner as an outstanding running back at the University of Notre Dame in 1963, '64 and '65. At 5-11, 195 pounds, Bill was a strong, durable, determined runner who was a backup halfback during the 1963 season. He carried the ball 10 times for 320 yards and two touchdowns, caught three passes for 11 yards, led the team in kick-off returns with 16 for 379 yards, and made six punt returns for 31 yards during the '63 campaign. Notre Dame finished with a poor 2-7-0 mark under head coach, Hugh Devore. During the 1964 season, Wolski began as a starter at left halfback under new head coach, Ara Parseghian. He led the Notre Dame runners with 136 carries for 657 yards and 11 touchdowns, caught eight passes for 130 yards, and returned two kick-offs for 49 yards. Notre Dame finished the year with an excellent 9-1-0 record under Parseghian and were ranked third in the country. In 1965, Wolski set the modern scoring record with five rushing touchdowns against Pittsburgh. He ran with the ball 103 times for 452 yards and eight touchdowns. Bill led the team in scoring with 52 points made by eight touchdowns and two two-point conversions. He caught one pass for eight yards, and led with six kick-off returns for 131 yards. Notre Dame finished 7-2-1 and were ranked ninth. Wolski was a candidate for the Heisman Trophy in 1965. His total career offense was 2,168 yards, made primarily on runs from scrimmage, and 21 touchdowns. He played in the East-West Shrine game in 1965 and was Atlanta's NFL draft choice in 1966.

CHAPTER VIII

FOOTBALL COACHES

Ed "Zeke" Bratkowski—Georgia—Quarterback—1953
Robert Bratkowski—Washington State—Wide Receiver—1977
Larry Czarnecki—Ithaca College—Def. Tackle—1975
Forest Evashevski—Michigan—Quarterback—1940
Ron Grzybowski—North Carolina—Offensive Line—1971
Jeff Jagodzinski—Wisconsin-Whitewater—Running Back—1984
Tom Kaczkowski—Illinois—Quarterback—1978
Robert Karmelowicz—Bridgeport—Def. Tackle—1972
Ted Kempski—Delaware—Quarterback—1962
Walt Kichefski—Miami (Fla.)—End—1939
Mike Kruczek—Boston College—Quarterback—1975
Gary Kubiak—Texas A&M—Quarterback—1982
Frank Kush—Michigan State—Guard—1952
Mickey Kwiatkowski—Delaware—Off. Guard—1969
Greg Landry—Massachusetts—Quarterback—1967
Ted Marchibroda—Detroit—Quarterback—1953
Fred Pagac—Ohio State—Tight End—1973
Tom Radulski—New Hampshire—Running Back—1978
Joseph Restic, Sr.—St. Francis & Villanova—End—1952
Jerry Sandusky—Pennsylvania State—Def. End—1965
Gregory Satanski—Central Michigan—Linebacker—1970
Jack Siedlecki—Union College—Running Back—1973
Gene Sobolewski—Pittsburgh—Def. End—1963
Henry "Hank" Stram—Purdue—Halfback—1947
Ron Tomczak—Wichita State—Tight End—1960

Edmund "Zeke" Bratkowski—Georgia— Quarterback—1953

Ed Bratkowski began playing football as a double-wing full-back at Schlarman High School in Danville, Illinois, and established the state high school punting record with a boot of 86 yards. Bratkowski went to the University of Georgia in 1950 on a football scholarship, and became one of the Bulldogs' most celebrated quarterbacks. He was a four-year letter winner at Georgia under head coach Wally Butts. Zeke was also an excellent baseball player for the Bulldogs. He was invited by the Brooklyn Dodgers for a tryout, but took his father's advice, stayed at Georgia, played football and got his college degree. Bratkowski established all sorts of University of Georgia and Southeastern Conference records, and earned numerous school, conference and national honors. He holds Bulldog records for most yards passing in a season (1,824 in 1952) and career (4,836), most attempts in season (262 in 1952) and career (734), most completions in season (131 in 1952) and career (360), and most yards total offense (4,824). Zeke ranks second in touchdown passes for one season (12) and career (24). Ed was also the SEC Passing Champion in 1952 (1,824 yards) and 1953 (1,461 yards), SEC Total Offense Champion in 1952 (1,774 net yards) and in 1953 (1,461 net yards), and the SEC Punting Champion in 1953. He was named SEC Back of the Year in 1952, and chosen the University of Georgia's Most Valuable Back in 1953. Zeke was also named a three-time All-SEC performer in 1951, 1952 and 1953, leading national Passer in 1952 and leading national Punter in 1953. He was selected to the Coaches' All-America, College All-Stars, North-South Shrine Bowl and North-South Senior Bowl teams. Ed was named an All-Time Specialist in Passing and Punting by the *New York Times*. Zeke was the Chicago Bears second round NFL draft choice in 1953 and went on to an outstanding 14-year professional football career with the Chicago Bears, Los Angeles Rams and Green Bay Packers. Bratkowski is best remembered as the "Super Sub" who replaced the injured Bart Starr in 1965, completed 22 of 39 passes for 248 yards to lead Green Bay to a 13-10 overtime play-off victory over the Baltimore Colts to clinch the Western Conference title. He played a major role in leading the Packers to 1965-66-67 world championships. In his NFL career, Zeke completed 762 of 1,484 passes (51.3 percent) for 10,345 yards and 65 touchdowns. Bratkowski began a second career in the NFL as an assistant coach with the Green Bay Packers in 1969 and 1970. He was reactivated for the 1971 season and played his final year of pro ball with the Packers. Zeke rejoined the team that drafted him, the Chicago Bears, and worked as an assistant coach for three years. When Bart Starr became head coach of the Packers in 1975, Zeke joined him to coach the quarterbacks. In 1982, Bratkowski became the offensive coordinator of the Baltimore Colts under new head coach, Frank Kush. When Kush retired in 1985, Ed became a coach with the New York Jets, and later joined the Philadelphia Eagles coaching the quarterbacks, and eventually became offensive coordinator. He rejoined the N.Y. Jets and was their offensive coordinator in 1995. Like his father, Bratkowski felt strongly about a college education for his children. One son, Steve, went to Arizona State University. His youngest, Kassie, is a University of Wisconsin graduate, and his oldest, Bob, attended Washington State. Ed was inducted into the University of Georgia Sports Hall of Fame in 1980, and the National Polish-American Sports Hall of Fame in 1995.

Robert Bratkowski—Washington State—Wide Receiver—1977

Robert Bratkowski is the son of the former University of Georgia and Green Bay Packers quarterback, "Zeke" Bratkowski. Robert was a three-year letter winner as wide receiver in football at Washington State University from 1975 through 1977. After completing his college football career at Washington State, Bratkowski devoted his time to coaching at the college level. He began as an assistant coach at the University of Missouri from 1978 through 1980. In 1981, Robert joined the football coaching staff of Weber State University and worked with the Wildcats for five years through the 1985 season. He earned his first offensive coordinator's job at Weber State in 1984, at the age of 28. He worked one year as offensive coordinator at the University of Wyoming in 1986 and had an excellent year. His offensive unit broke every school record for team and individual passing. Bratkowski joined head coach Dennis Erickson at Washington State University as his offensive coordinator in 1987, and the 1988 Cougar offense was ranked third nationally in total offense, 10th in scoring offense and 11th in passing offense. Robert followed Coach Erickson to the University of Miami (Fla) in 1989. In his first year at Miami as offensive coordinator, the Hurricanes finished the season ranked seventh nationally in passing offense, eighth in scoring offense and ninth in total offense. He spent three seasons at Miami under coach Erickson. Bratkowski is rated as one of the top young football coaches in the country, and was the architect of the one-back offense that helped the Hurricanes average 441 yards and 33 points a game during the 1991 campaign. In January 1992, Robert joined the Seattle Seahawks of the NFL, and was their offensive coordinator and wide receivers coach in 1995.

Larry Czarnecki—Ithaca College—Def. Tackle—1975

An outstanding lineman at Ithaca College, Larry Czarnecki was a four-year football letter winner from 1972 through 1975. He was a standout defensive tackle who earned honors for each year he played for the Bombers. Czarnecki was a four-time All-Independent College Athletic Conference selection, a three-time All-Upstate New York College choice, and a two-time All-Eastern College Athletic Conference first team pick. In 1975, he was named the ECAC Division III Player of the Year, and earned Kodak and Associated Press first team All-America honors. He was co-captain of the 1975 squad. Czarnecki received his B.S. degree in physical education in 1976, and his master's degree in 1977. In 1976, Larry was the defensive line coach at Ithaca, and in 1977, offensive line coach at Dartmouth College. From 1978 through 1986, Czarnecki worked at Cortland State University as defensive coordinator and then head coach. He returned to Ithaca in 1987 and was their offensive line coach in 1995.

Forest Evashevski—Michigan—Quarterback—1940

Forest Evashevski attended Northwestern High School in Detroit, Michigan where he played football as a tackle and center. He started his college football career at the University of Michigan in 1937 under Coach Fritz Crisler as a center, but was switched to quarterback after his freshman year. He became the trigger man in Crisler's intricate single-wing attack. Evy spent much of his time as a blocking back, and helped to make his friend, Tom Harmon, an All-American. Evashevski, calling the plays and throwing the blocks, and Harmon, carrying the ball, became one of the most famous backfield combinations in football history. Forest was one of the greatest blockers in Wolverine gridiron annals, but he was primarily an extremely intelligent quarterback. Unfortunately, he was also one of the most underrated players in college football. The press called his 1938 performance the "finest piece of quarterbacking by a sophomore in many years." He was chosen All-Big Ten Conference quarterback in 1938 although he had never previously played in the backfield. In 1939, Evy continued to perform as an outstanding quarterback, and was again chosen All-Big Ten. He was elected captain of the 1940 squad and helped Michigan to a good 7-1-0 record and the number three rank nationally. Once again Evy was selected All-Big Ten quarterback and was named All-America by several selectors. In addition to football, Forest was also a three-year letterman in baseball as varsity catcher. During his years at Michigan, Evashevski was a member of Sphynx, Michigamua, Phi Betta Kappa and President of the Senior Class. He was also the recipient of the Big Ten Medal of Honor, and the Big Ten Scholarship Award. After graduating with a degree in Sociology and Psychology, Evy became football coach at Hamilton College in New York, then an assistant coach at Pittsburgh. He was a Navy officer in World War II, and in 1942 played quarterback for the Navy Pre-Flight school team in Iowa City. After being discharged from the service in 1946, Forest became an assistant coach to Biggie Munn at Syracuse University. Two years later, he followed Munn to Michigan State, then stepped out on his own by taking the head coaching job in 1950 at Washington State University. Two years later, Evy became the University of Iowa's head coach. In his nine years as coach, Iowa teams won 52 games, lost 27 and tied four for a .651 percentage. Evashevski's 1956 and 1958 teams won the Big Ten title and the Rose Bowl games, and, in 1960, Iowa shared the Big Ten crown with Minnesota. He was honored by the New York and Washington Touchdown Clubs by being named Coach of the Year for 1953,'56,'57,'58 and '60. Evy retired as head coach in 1960, and became the Director of Athletics at Iowa from 1960 until 1970. He was chosen to the University of Iowa Sports Hall of Fame in 1989. Evy has become a successful businessman and lives in Petoskey, Michigan and Vero Beach, Florida with his wife Ruth, daughter of former U.S. Seator Prentiss Brown of Michigan. The Evashevski's have seven children, six of whom graduated from Michigan and one from Iowa. Evashevski and Tom Harmon remained close friends after college. Evy delivered the eulogy at Tom Harmon's funeral in 1991.

Ron Grzybowski—North Carolina—Offensive Line—1971

An outstanding football and basketball player at Our Lady of Lourdes High School in Shamokin, Pennsylvania, Grzybowski went to the University of North Carolina in 1968 on a football scholarship. He was three-year letter winner who contributed greatly to the Tarheels impressive conference play during the

1970 and 1971 seasons. In 1970, he helped North Carolina to finish with a good 8-4-0 record including a Peach Bowl game with Arizona State University. The Tarheels finished with a spotless 6-0-0 conference season in 1971, claimed their first Atlantic Coast Conference title since 1963, and played Georgia in the Gator Bowl. Grzybowski received the Cary C. Boshamer Award presented annually to North Carolina's Outstanding Offensive Lineman. Ron began his football coaching career with a two year stint at the University of Nevada Las Vegas and then at West Morris Mendham High School in New Jersey. He returned to Our Lady of Lourdes High School in 1975 as head football coach, and then became an assistant coach at Bloomsburg University from 1983 through 1985. Grzybowski began his Bucknell University football coaching career as a part-time coach working with the offensive line before moving to the defensive line in 1988. Ron joined the Bucknell staff full-time in 1989, and was the Bison's tight end coach for two years before returning to the offensive line assignment in 1991. Grzybowski completed his third season as Bucknell's offensive line coach during 1993. His primary recruiting areas include Philadelphia, Southeastern and South Central Pennsylvania and Western New York.

Jeff Jagodzinski—Wisconsin-Whitewater—Running Back—1984

Jeff Jagodzinski finished his fifth year at East Carolina University in 1993 as the youngest assistant coach on the staff at 29 years of age. Jagodzinski coached the offensive line after coaching the tight ends and assisting with the offensive line in his first three years at East Carolina. A native of Milwaukee, Wisconsin, Jeff attended West Allis Central High School where he was an excellent athlete. He was selected an all-conference back in football and participated on three conference championship teams in baseball. Jeff was the high school conference rushing and scoring leader as a senior with over 1,200 yards and 13 touchdowns. Jagodzinski enrolled at the University of Wisconsin-Whitewater in 1981 and developed into an outstanding small college football player. He starred at the university as a running back and was a

Wisconsin State University All-Conference selection as a back-field performer in 1983. Jeff began his college coaching career at his alma mater by teaching the running backs. He then served as a graduate assistant at Northern Illinois University for one year, working with the offensive line. In 1987, Jagodzinski helped with the offensive line at Louisiana State University as a graduate assistant. Jeff joined the East Carolina University coaching staff at the completion of the 1988 season. He completed his ninth year of coaching at the college level in 1993, and will be working with a talented but young group on the offensive line for the 1994 season. Jeff received his degree in Physical Education from Wisconsin-Whitewater in 1985.

Tom Kaczkowski—Illinois—Quarterback—1978

Tom Kaczkowski completed his eighth season as the head football coach at Ohio Northern University in 1993. Tom was also an assistant professor in the department of health, physical education and sport studies, as well as the quarterback coach. A native of Champaign, Illinois, Kaczkowski was an excellent football player at the University of Illinois, but an unfortunate knee injury ended his college football career as a promising quarterback. He graduated from the university in 1978 where he was able to participate in track and field for two years. Tom received his bachelors degree in health and physical education, and went on to earn a masters degree from DePauw University. From 1979 through 1983, Tom was an assistant football coach at West Chicago High School. He became an assistant football coach at Ohio Northern University in 1984, and was appointed head coach in 1986. He coached the offensive line and special teams as an assistant. As head coach, Kaczkowski and his staff have led the Ohio Northern football program back to respectability over the past eight years. The Polar Bears have shown a marked improvement and competitiveness in his tenure as head coach. Ohio Northern finished the 1993 campaign with a winning 5-4-1 record which put them in fifth position in the ten team Ohio Athletic Conference standings. Kaczkowski enters his ninth year at the helm of the promising Ohio Northern University football team that has 40 letter men and 13 starters returning for the 1994 season. Tom's goal is a better year and a higher rating in conference play.

Robert Karmelowicz—Bridgeport—Def. Tackle—1972

A graduate of Plainville High School in Plainville, Connecticut, Robert Karmelowicz enrolled at the University of Bridgeport in 1968. He was an outstanding three-year starter at nose tackle and a consensus Little All-American in his senior year at Bridgeport. Robert was also selected first team All-New England and All-Conference defensive tackle. He received his B.A. degree in Education at Bridgeport in 1972, and his M.A. in Education at Arizona State University in 1976. His college football coaching career began with a six year run (1974-1979) at Arizona State University. Short jobs followed from 1980 through 1982 at the University of Massachusetts and University of Texas. He was an assistant coach at the University of Illinois from 1983 through 1986, before joining Head Coach Dennis Erickson's Washington State staff in 1987. Robert came to the University of Miami with Erickson in 1989. As the defensive line coach, Karmelowicz guided one of the most talented and productive defensive lines in the history of college football. All four starters on the defensive line in 1989 received some sort of All-America recognition. The Miami interior established a new school record for sacks, while helping the Hurricane defense to a No. 1 national ranking in total defense. Miami also ranked No. 1 in fewest points surrendered and No. 2 in rushing defense. The Hurricanes finished the 1991 season with a 12-0-0 record and an Orange Bowl win over Nebraska. After a successful college coaching career, Karmelowicz was hired by the Cincinnati Bengals in 1992 as their defensive line coach.

Ted Kempski—Delaware—Quarterback—1962

Ted Kempski, the starting quarterback on the 1961 and 1962 University of Delaware football teams, returned to his alma mater in 1968 to coach the offensive backfield and entered his 25th season on the staff in 1993. Kempski helped to guide the 1962 team to the Middle Atlantic Conference Lambert Cup championship. He was named the Football Scholar-Athlete in his senior year. Ted received his B.S. degree from the University of Delaware in 1963 and his M.S. degree in 1965. He served as a graduate assistant at Delaware while working on his advanced degree. He went on to George Washington University as an assistant coach and then to Marshall University before coming back to Delaware. Since returning to Delaware, Kempski is credited with developing two All-Americans and 15 Blue Hen's leading all-time rushers. From 1968 until 1973, backfields coached by Ted led the nation's College Division teams in either rushing or total offense per game, and his 1979 backfield won both the total offense and scoring championships. In 1982, the Hens won both 1-AA scoring and rushing titles and were fourth in total offense. Kempski was a member of the American Football Coaches Association Assistant Coaches Committee (1981-1986). Ted is a native of Wilmington, Delaware and a graduate of Salesianum where he lettered in three sports, and in 1983, received their "Golden Helmet Award" for his performance in football. He was named MVP in the 1958 high school All-Star game. Kempski was given the Newark Touchdown Club's Special Achievement Award for his contributions to football in the State of Delaware.

Walt Kichefski—Miami (Fla)—End—1939

A native of Rhinelander, Wisconsin, Walt Kichefski was a long-time University of Miami football legend as an assistant coach. Walt was associated with Hurricane football for over 50 years. It began in 1936 when Kichefski earned his first football varsity letter playing as a two-way end. During the '36 season, Nat Glogowski and Henry Gostowski were on the squad with Walt. Kichefski lettered again in 1937, '38 and '39 with team-mates John Kurucza and Stanley Raski. He was the team's co-captain as a senior in 1939 and was named Honorable Mention All-America. Walt was tapped into the Iron Arrow Honor Society and the Kappa Sigma fraternity in 1940. He played professional football with the Pittsburgh Steelers from 1940 through 1942, and then returned to Miami to begin his college football coaching career. In 1970, Kichefski became the interim head coach and athletic director of the Hurricanes. Although the team's record under Walt that year was only 2-7, the highlight of that season was a 14-13 victory over the University of Florida, a team which Kichefski hated. He was a member of the football team that first played against the Gators in a 19-7 victory during the 1938 campaign. After 1970, Walt stayed at UM heading the newly created Athletic Federation. He retired from that job in 1978 but remained a consultant to the federation, as well as a loyal booster of UM and the world's No. 1 Gator Hater. Kichefski shares fifth place with Al Palewicz (class of 1972) in the individual career Miami football records with fumble recoveries. Walt was a member of the University of Miami Hall of Fame, the Hurricane Club and the Miami Kappa Sigma Alumni Association. While he was in intensive care with inoperable stomach cancer, UM coach Dennis Erickson dedicated the regular-season finale to Walt and awarded him a game ball. Kichefski died shortly thereafter in January 1992. The University of Miami has established the Walt Kichefski Football Scholarship Endowment Fund in honor of its former player and coach.

Mike Kruczek—Boston College—Quarterback—1975

Mike Kruczek began his varsity football career with the Boston College Eagles in 1973 when he was used primarily as a back-up quarterback. The Eagles finished the '73 season with a winning record of 7-4-0 under head coach Joe Yukica. Kruczek took over as the starting quarterback for the 1974 campaign, and not only led Boston College to another winning year, but also established national and Eagles' passing records. Boston College finished the '74 season with an 8-3-0 mark and were voted first in New England and third in the East. They hammered their opposition (37-0 over Navy, 70-8 over UMass, 38-0 over Holy Cross and 45-0 over Syracuse) to such an embarrassing extent that coach Yukica was accused of running up the scores. The Eagles had the scoring guns with Kruczek completing an awesome 68.9 percent of his passes in the season's last six games. Mike was being talked about as the best quarterback in Boston College football history. He was elected team captain for the 1975 squad, and the Eagles first test in the opening game was against Notre Dame. Kruczek was the best percentage passer in the country and everyone was counting on him to lead the Eagles to victory. Unfortunately, coach Yukica's game plan called for possession football and Kruczek was allowed to throw only 13 passes, completing nine. Notre Dame beat Boston College and Yukica was criticized widely for his play selection. The Eagles finished the year with a winning 7-4-0 record. Kruczek erased Roger Staubach's career college passing completion record of 63.1 percent, ending his college career with 225 completions on 337 attempts for a new NCAA record of 66.7 percent. He was awarded the Bulger Lowe Trophy as New England's Most Outstanding Player. In addition, Mike was selected to the All-East team and chosen All-America. Kruczek was the starting quarterback for the College All-Stars in the 1976 game against the Pittsburgh Steelers. He was Pittsburgh's second round NFL draft choice in 1976 and played five seasons with the Steelers and one year for the Washington Redskins. Mike played for two Super Bowl championships while a member of the Steelers in 1978 and 1979. Kruczek began his football coaching career when he joined the Florida State University staff in 1982. Mike followed with a one year stint in 1984 with the Jacksonville Bulls of the professional United States Football League, and then became a member of the University of Central Florida coaching staff in 1985. During 1993, Kruczek was in his ninth season as offensive coordinator and coach of the quarterbacks at Central Florida. Mike graduated from Boston College as a Marketing major and was inducted into the Boston College Hall of Fame in 1981 for his contribution to football.

Gary Kubiak—Texas A&M—Quarterback—1982

An outstanding athlete, Gary Kubiak came to Texas A&M University in 1979 after starring as a football quarterback at St. Pius High School in Houston, Texas. In his prep senior year, Kubiak was named All-District, All-State and All-America, and set the state passing record with 6,190 yards. He was also All-State in basketball for three years and All-State in track for two years. Gary was a reserve quarterback at Texas A&M during his freshman year in 1979. He was a back-up quarterback at the beginning of the 1980 season, became a starter early in the year, and held the starting position for the rest of his college career. In 1981, Kubiak had a fantastic season and in the process established three

Southwest Conference records consisting of the longest touchdown pass (92 yards against Louisiana Tech), the most touchdown passes in one game (six against Rice), and the best passing percentage in one game (90.5 against Arkansas). He also finished second in the Southwest Conference in passing with 1,808 yards and second in total offense with 1,986 yards. Gary was named the NCAA Scholarship Award Winner in 1981. He showed his ability to retain his poise under pressure and had the knack to determine enemy defenses and overcome them. He was an extremely intelligent football player. At 6-1, 195 pounds, Kubiak was elusive and fast. He continued to display his strong leadership qualities during the 1982 campaign, and finished as one of the top quarterbacks in the country. He was selected the Aggies' Most Valuable Player after the season, and was named first team All-Southwest Conference quarterback. Kubiak was the Denver Broncos NFL draft choice in 1983, and played with them for nine years. As a back-up Denver quarterback, Gary replaced injured starter John Elway in the fourth quarter of the 1991 AFC Championship game. He was outstanding in his relief role by completing 11 of 12 passes for 136 yards. He guided the Broncos to the three yard line and then carried the ball for Denver's only touchdown and score in the game. In January 1992, Kubiak retired from professional football at age 30, and began his football coaching career as an assistant coach at his alma mater, Texas A&M University. Stanford University was also interested in having Kubiak on their coaching staff.

Frank Kush—Michigan State—Guard—1952

One of 15 children, Frank Kush grew up in a small coal mining town of Windber, Pennsylvania where he was an excellent high school football player. He attended Washington and Lee University and earned a football scholarship to Michigan State University. Kush played guard for Michigan State and lettered in 1950, 1951 and 1952 when the Spartans had three exceptional winning seasons under head coach Clarence "Biggie" Munn. They were ranked eighth in the nation after finishing the 1950 season with a 8-1-0 mark. The Spartans went undefeated and untied (9-0-0) during the 1951 and 1952 campaigns, and were ranked No. 1 in the country. During Kush's three varsity football seasons, Michigan State compiled an outstanding 26-1-0 record. Michigan State had been admitted to the Big Ten Conference in 1950, but were ineligible to play in the Rose Bowl for three years. As a result, the Spartans could not compete in post-season bowl games despite their excellent records. Kush contributed greatly to the Spartans' success and was awesome in 1952 against Penn State. Frank's outstanding performances during the season were evident and he was chosen first team All-America guard. At 5-7, 175 pounds, Kush proved that hard work and determination were more important than lack of size when he was named All-America. He was selected to the North-South, Senior Bowl and College All-Star teams. Frank graduated from Michigan State with a B.S.

degree, and later received his M.S. degree from Arizona State University. Kush served in the U.S. Army and was the player-coach at Fort Benning in 1953 and 1954. In 1955, he joined head coach Dan Devine as an assistant coach at Arizona State University. In 1958, Devine was named head coach at the University of Missouri, and Kush was selected as his replacement at Arizona State. As head coach, Frank was one of the toughest, most successful football instructors in the country. He demanded excellent physical conditioning and drove his players to the limit. In 1970, the Sun Devils finished with an undefeated, untied record of 11-0-0, including a Peach Bowl victory over North Carolina, and were ranked number one nationally. They achieved a perfect 12-0-0 mark in 1975, beat Nebraska in the Fiesta Bowl, were ranked number two in the country, and Kush was selected Coach of the Year. Frank coached at Arizona State for 22 years and compiled an exceptional 176-54-1 record. Having won 76.4 percent of his games, Kush ranks among the elite coaches in college football. He also had an excellent 6-1-0 bowl games record. Frank coached in professional football from 1981 through 1986. In 1988, Kush received the Daugherty Award from Michigan State University, presented annually to an MSU football alumnus who has distinguished himself in endeavors on and off the field since his graduation. Retired from coaching, Frank ran a home for juvenille offenders in Arizona as of 1992. He once stated that most of the kids became delinquents because they had never been spanked. Kush was named to the National Football Foundation's College Hall of Fame both as a player and a coach in 1995. He has also been a nominee for election to the National Polish-American Sports Hall of Fame.

Mickey Kwiatkowski—Delaware—Off. Guard—1969

A native of Clifton Heights, Pennsylvania, Kwiatkowski starred as an offensive guard in the famous Wing-T at the University of Delaware in 1968 and 1969. Delaware won the Middle Atlantic Conference title and Lambert Cup both years. Mickey earned a B.A. degree from Delaware in 1970 and stayed on as offensive line coach for the freshman squad while completing work on his M.A. degree in Education. Kwiatkowski then served in the U.S. Army as a military intelligence officer for three years. In 1973, Mickey worked as an offensive line coach at Salisbury State College for two years before accepting a similar post at West Chester State College. He earned a second Masters, an M.S. degree, at West Chester. In 1977, he was named the offensive coordinator at Southwest Missouri State University and his Wing-T attack responded by setting numerous school and conference records. Kwiatkowski took over as head coach at Hofstra University in 1981, and compiled a 68-27-0 record in nine years. He turned Hofstra into a national football power, leading them into the NCAA Division III playoffs year after year. Mickey's '83 Hofstra team was ranked third in the country, compiled the greatest regular season record of 10-0-0, won the Lambert Bowl and qualified for the NCAA Division III quarterfinals. Kwiatkowksi was recognized as the Metropolitan Football Officials "Coach of the Year" in 1983 for his success and conduct on the field. In 1984, '86, '87 and '88, Mickey's teams finished with 9-1-0 regular season records and were ranked in the top ten nationally. Kwiatkowski became head football coach at Brown University in 1990. His variation of the Winged-T offense in his first year as coach of the Bears resulted in the setting of six Brown offensive records. His passing offense ranked first in the Ivy League in 1990 and 1991, and Brown ranked second in the League in total offense during those years. Mickey ranks in the top ten in winning percentage (.667) among active Division III coaches. During the 1993 season, Kwiatkowski's coaching and recruiting began to show results, as Brown went 4-6-0 and tied for fourth in the Ivy League, its best since 1987. However, Brown University announced that Kwiatkowski would not have his contract renewed after four seasons and replaced him as head football coach for the 1994 season. An eloquent speaker, Mickey is in constant demand and has been the featured speaker at many banquets and clinics, and was a guest lecturer in England in 1988.

Greg Landry—Massachusetts—Quarterback—1967

A native of Nashua, New Hampshire, Greg Landry was a three-year letterman as a quarterback at the University of Massachusetts. He played under head coach Vic Fusia during the 1965, '66 and '67 seasons when UMass compiled an excellent winning record of 20-7-0. Landry became the starting quarterback at the beginning of the 1965 campaign, and had a good season passing for 1,423 yards and eight touchdowns, and rushing for 614 yards and nine touchdowns. His longest touchdown runs were for 56, 48 and 33 yards. During the 1966 season, he passed and rushed for 1,007 yards and seven touchdowns. He was selected first team All-Yankee Conference quarterback at the end of the '66 campaign. Landry was chosen co-captain of the 1967 squad and again turned in an excellent performance. He passed and rushed for 1,719 yards and 14 touchdowns. His longest run was a 73 yarder for a touchdown against UConn. Landry was again chosen first team All-Yankee Conference quarterback and named first team All-America. He is the UMass leading performer in several categories. He is a leader in career scoring, most passing attempts in a career, most passes completed in a season and career, and most yards passing in a season and career. He also holds several UMass records with most yards gained passing in a play, and best passing percentage in a game, in a season and in a career. During his career at UMass, he passed for 3,131 yards and 16 touchdowns, and rushed for 1,632 yards and 22 touchdowns. Landry ranks number ten in Yankee Conference All-Time Top 10 with total offense career of 4,763 yards in passing and rushing. At 6-4, 207 pounds, Greg was drafted by the Detroit Lions in 1968 and played with them for 11 years through 1978. He was with Baltimore from 1979-1981, United States Football League from 1983-1984, and finished in 1984 with Chicago. Landry became the Chicago Bears offensive coordinator under Mike Ditka in 1992. In 1993, Greg was named offensive coordinator for the University of Illinois.

Ted Marchibroda—St. Bonaventure & Detroit—Quarterback—1953

A native of Franklin, Pennsylvania, Marchibroda enrolled at St. Bonaventure College in 1950 where he lettered in football as the starting quarterback during the '50 and '51 seasons. He performed so well as a freshman quarterback that the United Press named him an Honorable Mention All-East team member in 1950. Ted transferred to the University of Detroit in 1952 and became their starting quarterback. He established the national single game record with 390 yards gained passing while completing 27 of 54 passes against the University of Tulsa in 1952. This was a fantastic accomplishment considering Tulsa had an excellent team which finished the year with a 8-2-1 mark, was ranked 12th in the nation and played in the Gator Bowl. He was the Major College Annual Champion in 1952 when he led the nation in total offense with 1,813 yards by rushing for 176 yard and passing for 1,637 yards on 305 offensive plays. Marchibroda was named Detroit's Most Valuable Player in 1952 in addition to being an Associated Press Honorable Mention All-American selection. Ted established 12 new passing records in his two year varsity football career at the University of Detroit. At 5-10, 180 pounds, Marchibroda was the number one draft choice of the Pittsburgh Steelers in 1953, and had a good professional football career with the Steelers and Cardinals. He was the NFL's second leading passer in 1956. Ted began his football coaching career as an assistant coach with the Washington Redskins in 1961. In the following years, he was an assistant coach in Chicago, Detroit and Philadelphia. Marchibroda became a head coach for the Baltimore

Colts in 1975 when he was responsible for the best turnaround in NFL history when he took over the Colts. After finishing last in the AFC East with a 2-12 record in 1974, he led the Colts to a 10-4 season and the division title in 1975. He was voted the NFL Coach-of-the-Year as head coach of the Baltimore Colts in 1975. He guided the Colts to a 11-3 season in 1976 and 10-4 in 1977. Under Marchibroda, the Colts won three straight division titles. However, when the team had two losing years, Ted was fired. His next successful venture occurred in Buffalo where he was an offensive coordinator and quarterback coach with the Bills. He developed the No-Huddle Offense that was primarily responsible for two straight Super Bowls for Buffalo. In 1992 Marchibroda became head coach of the Indianapolis Colts and performed another miracle with them. He took over the team that had the worst record of 1-15 in the NFL in 1991, and led them to a winning 9-7 season in 1992. This tied the NFL record for a turnaround that Marchibroda's Baltimore Colts had established 17 years before in 1975. At age 64, Ted had devoted more than 30 years of his life to coaching in the NFL, and has enjoyed a fine pro football coaching career. He was inducted into the National Polish-American Sports Hall of Fame in 1976, and honored again in 1983 by being selected to the University of Detroit Hall of Fame.

Theodore J. Marchibroda, Jr. was a wide receiver at the University of Virginia during the 1977, 1978 and 1979 football seasons.

Fred Pagac—Ohio State—Tight End—1973

Fred Pagac was quite a versatile football player. In high school, he was a fullback and linebacker. He came to Ohio State University planning to be a running back, but played defensive end as a freshman, was switched to fullback, and finally settled in as tight end. Pagac, of Polish-Lithuanian ancestry, was a three-year starter at tight end for the Buckeyes from 1971 to 1973. He led Ohio State in receiving as a senior and was an excellent blocker. During his career, the Buckeyes posted a combined record of 25-6-2, won two Big Ten titles, and played in two Rose Bowls. Pagac played five years as a professional in the NFL. In 1974, as a rookie with the Chicago Bears, he received the Brian Piccolo Award, which is presented annually by the Bears to the player who best exemplifies Piccolo's inspirational qualities. Fred also played with Tampa Bay and retired from pro ball in 1978. He returned to Ohio State to begin his college coaching career as a graduate assistant under his old coach, Woody Hayes. Pagac was elevated to full-time status in 1982 by Earle Bruce, and then retained by John Cooper following the 1987 season. As the outside linebacker coach, Fred is the senior assistant on the Ohio State football staff in terms of longevity. During his coaching career with the Buckeyes, he has developed several outstanding players. Football experts consider Pagac to be one of the most underrated defensive assistant coaches in the country.

Tom Radulski—New Hampshire—Running Back—1978

A native of Salem, New Hampshire, Tom Radulski played both offensive and defensive back at Salem High School. He lettered two years as a running back at the University of New Hampshire before becoming a student assistant coach during his junior and senior years. Radulski graduated from UNH in 1979 with a B.A. degree. He continued at UNH through 1983 while earning his M.A. degree in public administration and working as an assistant coach. He was a defensive coordinator at Hamilton College for a season, and at Colby College the following year. Tom became the linebacker coach and defensive coordinator at Allegheny College in 1986 where he coached for three years. Radulski joined the football coaching staff of Columbia University in 1989 as coach of the inside linebackers and defensive coordinator. The great improvement in Columbia's defense in Ivy League competition was the result of Tom's work. He developed several defensive players including the outstanding tackle, Gary Kasprzak. Tom Radulski was named head football coach at the University of Massachusetts-Lowell in March 1993.

Joe Restic, Sr.—St. Francis & Villanova—End—1952

Joe Restic, one of ten children, grew up in Hastings, Pennsylvania where his Polish born father worked in the coal mines. After completing a fine high school football career, Restic volunteered for the Aviation Cadet Program in 1943. His knowledge of European languages qualified him to serve as a special agent in the U.S. Army Intelligence Corps. Upon discharge after 39 months of service, he enrolled at St. Francis College in Pennsylvania where he was an outstanding college football player for two seasons. Restic then transferred to Villanova University where he earned his undergraduate degree. He received a masters degree in Educational Administration and Supervision from Seton Hall. Joe played professional baseball with the Philadelphia Phillies and football with the Philadelphia Eagles as a wide receiver and defensive back. In 1955, he began his football coaching career at the high school level before joining Brown University to coach the defensive backs and ends. After three winning seasons with Brown, Restic served as offensive coordinator and chief recruiter at Colgate University through the 1961 season. In 1962, Joe became a professional football coach with the Hamilton Tiger Cats of the Canadian Football League. He was the top assistant and offensive coordinator until taking over as head coach in 1968. In his nine years at Hamilton, Joe coached in the Grey Cup six times, and was with four championship teams.

He was appointed head football coach at Harvard University in 1971. Considered to be an excellent, intelligent football teacher, Restic developed the Multiflex Offense which attempts to surprise and exploit the defense. He guided Harvard to five Ivy League titles starting in 1974 and the most recent in 1987. Joe was named Eastern Coach-of-the-Year by the Eastern Football Writers Association, and the New England Writers also chose him for their top coaching honor in 1974. Restic was again named New England Coach-of-the-Year in 1975 and 1987 when Harvard won their Ivy League titles. In 1990, he was honored by the Eastern Massachusetts Chapter of the National Football Foundation as its "Distinguished American," which is an award given to someone who "has carried the lessons learned on the football field into a lifetime of service for the community." Restic coached in several post-season college All-Star football games such as the Shrine, Blue-Grey, and Ivy League all-star contests. He is an active member of the New England Chapter, the National Chapter, and the National Football Foundation and Hall of Fame. He served as President of the American Football Coaches Association in 1988. Restic completed his 23rd year as Harvard University's head football coach and retired from coaching after the 1993 season. He had the longest coaching tenure in the 119-year history of Harvard University football and was also its most winning coach with an excellent 114-90-6 career record.

Joe Restic, Jr. was a Scholastic Academic Award Winner and an outstanding punter and defensive back at Notre Dame. He was named First Team punter and Third Team defensive back on the All-Time Notre Dame Football Team in 1983. He is a graduate of the UPenn School of Dental Medicine.

Jerry Sandusky—Pennsylvania State—Def. End—1965

An outstanding athlete at Washington High School in Washington, Pennsylvania, Jerry Sandusky starred in football, basketball and baseball. He enrolled at Pennsylvania State University in 1962, and became a three-year letterman as a starting defensive end in 1963, 1964 and 1965. Jerry earned his B.S. degree in health and physical education in 1966, and his M.S. degree in the same major at Penn State in 1970. He graduated first in his class and served as student marshall for his college at commencement in 1966. Sandusky began his college football coaching career as a graduate assistant at Penn State, and followed as an assistant football, basketball and track coach at Juniata College in the 1967-68 academic year. He then served one year as offensive line coach at Boston University. Jerry joined the Penn State coaching staff in 1969 and has been with Joe Paterno's Nittany Lions 24 years as of 1993. He started by coaching the linebackers and now serves as the defensive coordinator. Eight of Sandusky coached linebackers were named first team All-Americans, including Jack Ham and Charlie Zapiec. The success of his pupils in professional football has earned Penn State the title of "Linebacker U." Sandusky's defensive game plans have enabled Penn State to win two National Championships and make 22 post-season bowl appearances. He was named the nation's Assistant Coach-of-the-Year in 1986. Jerry is considered to be one of the best assistant coaches, as defensive coordinator, in the country. Sandusky and his father, Art, received the annual "Human Rights Award" presented by the Washington, Pennsylvania branch of the NAACP for their humanitarian work. Jerry is the author of *Developing Linebackers, The Penn State Way.* Proceeds from the book benefit *The Second Mile,* a charitable organization founded by Sandusky that is concerned with the welfare of young people.

E.J. Sandusky, one of Jerry's sons, was the starting center for the 1992 Nittany Lions, and began his college football coaching career as a graduate assistant at the University of North Carolina. E.J. received the Red Worrel Award from Penn State in 1992 which is presented annually to an offensive player for "examplary conduct, loyalty, interest, improvement and attitude."

Gregory Satanski—Central Michigan—Linebacker—1970

A native of Jackson, Michigan, Gregory Satanski graduated from St. John's High School after starring in football and earned All-State honors. He was a three-year football letter winner at Central Michigan University as a linebacker and defensive end. Satanski returned to his hometown after college and was an assistant football coach at Jackson Lumen Christi High School through 1972. He joined the Grand Valley State University football coaching staff as an assistant in 1973, and spent six of his ten years at Grand Valley as the defensive coordinator. In 1983, Gregory came to Eastern Michigan University, and as an assistant coach worked as defensive coordinator and tutor of inside linebackers. Satanski completed his tenth year as an assistant coach at Eastern Michigan University in 1993. Greg received his bachelors degree in Physical Education from Central Michigan University in 1970 and his masters in the same major from Central Michigan in 1973.

Jack Siedlecki—Union College—Running Back—1973

Jack Siedlecki was a 1973 graduate of Union College where he played football as a running back and linebacker. He went to Miami University (OH) for one year, but returned to Union College in 1972 to finish his football career. A back injury in his senior year at Union ended his playing days in 1973. Siedlecki began his college football coaching by joining the staff of the State University of New York in Albany. He helped the Great Danes of SUNY-Albany to the NCAA Division III National Playoffs in 1977. Jack then became a member of the Wagner College coaching staff, and helped the Seahawks to qualify for the Division III National Playoffs in 1980. Siedlecki became the head football coach at Worcester Polytechnic Institute in 1988 and had a very successful five year tenure. His WPI teams posted a winning 36-11-1 record, won the Northeast Division III ECAC championship in 1991, and qualified for the Division title in 1992. Following the outstanding 1992 campaign, Jack was honored by being selected District I Kodak "Coach-of-the-Year" by the American Football Coaches Association. He was also named "Coach-of-the-Year" by the Boston Gridiron Club in Massachusetts in 1992. At age 42, Siedlecki became the head football coach at Amherst College in Amherst, Massachusetts at the beginning of the 1993 season.

Gene Sobolewski—Pittsburgh—Def. End—1963

A native of Freeport, Pennsylvania, Gene Sobolewski earned three football and two basketball letters in high school and was co-captain of both teams his senior year. Gene received a scholarship to play football at the University of Pittsburgh in 1960. He was a three-year letter winner from 1961 through 1963, and a starting defensive end on the 1962 and '63 squads. The 1963 Pitt Team had four Polish Americans as starters with Sobolewski at end, Fred Mazurek at quarterback, Rick Leeson (Lezouski) at fullback and John Maczuzak at tackle. They finished with an excellent 9-1-0 record, and were ranked third in the nation. Gene distinguished himself during the Navy game by sacking the Middies All-America quarterback, Roger Staubach, seven times. Sobolewski graduated with a B.S. degree in Health and Physical Education from Pitt in 1964, and accepted a high school teaching and coaching position. He began his college football coaching career at Waynesburg College in 1966 where he was the defensive coordinator through 1970. In 1971, Gene became the offensive line coach at Clarion University. He was offensive coordinator from 1973 to 1982, and was named Clarion's head coach in 1983. During those ten years, Sobolewski has become an outstanding head coach in the Pennsylvania State Athletic Conference (PSAC) and in NCAA Division II. In his first season, Gene guided Clarion to the PSAC-West crown, the PSAC title, and third rank in Division II. He was voted PSAC-West and Kodak Region I "Coach-of-the-Year." In 1984, Clarion tied for first in the PSAC-West and in 1985 the Eagles were ranked 16th in the nation. Clarion won the PSAC-West title in 1992, and again, Gene was named PSAC-West "Coach-of-the-Year." A veteran coach in the Pennsylvania Conference, Sobolewski started his 22nd year coaching at Clarion University during the 1993 season. He was inducted into the Armstrong County Hall of Fame in 1980 for his athletic prowess at Freeport High School and the University of Pittsburgh. An extremely dedicated professor at Clarion, Gene was named co-winner of the Distinguished Faculty Award in 1977.

Henry "Hank" Stram—Purdue—Halfback—1947

Henry Stram (Wilczek) starred in baseball and as an All-State football halfback at Lew Wallace High School in Gary, Indiana, and was the All-City and All-Conference football scoring champion as a senior. Stram received a scholarship to play football at Purdue University in 1971. He played one year and then served in the U.S. Army from 1942 to 1945. He returned to Purdue in 1946 to finish his college education and play football and baseball for the Boilermakers. He won four letters in baseball, and three in football for 1941, '46 and '47. Hank was used as a fullback and halfback, and played in the backfield with halfback Harry Szulborski during the 1946 and '47 seasons. Hank received the Big Ten Conference "Medal of Honor" in 1948. This award is presented annually at Big Ten schools to student athletes demonstrating the greatest proficiency in scholarship and athletics. He was selected to play in the 1948 College All-Star game with Johnny Lujack and Ziggie Czarobski of Notre Dame. Stram graduated Purdue in 1948 with a B.S. degree in Physical Education. He remained at Purdue after graduation to serve as backfield football coach for eight years. In 1956, he became an assistant coach at Southern Methodist University for two years, and then spent two seasons at Notre Dame as an assistant backfield coach. He was an assistant coach at the University of Miami (Fla) for one year before becoming head coach of the Dallas Texans in the AFL. Under Stram, the Dallas Texans won the 1962 AFL championship, and the Dallas franchise moved to Kansas City in 1963. Three years later, Stram's Kansas City Chiefs captured the AFL flag but lost to Green Bay in Super Bowl I. In 1969, the Chiefs won the AFL crown again, and Hank experienced the highlight of his coaching career when his team upset the Minnesota Vikings in Super Bowl IV. Stram finished with one Super Bowl victory, three AFL championships and five Western Division titles in his fifteen years with the Dallas-Kansas City franchise and two years with the New Orleans Saints. He accumulated an excellent 136-100-10 record to finish among the leaders on the all-time list of professional coaching victories. Stram was named Pro Football Coach-of-the-Year four times. After retiring from coaching, Hank became an analyst commentator with CBS Television Sports and covered the NFL games for CBS Radio Sports. He received the Diamond Award as outstanding analyst in pro football. Stram's numerous speaking engagements keep him busy and constantly traveling. In 1985, Hank was inducted into the National Polish-American Sports Hall of Fame. He is a good candidate for the Pro Football Hall of Fame.

Ron Tomczak—Wichita State—Tight End—1960

A native of Chicago, Ron Tomczak attended Mendel Catholic High School where he competed in football, basketball, baseball and boxing. A gifted athlete, Ron was also an excellent student. Tomczak was a four-year letter winner in football at Wichita State University, and a three-year starter at tight end and defensive end positions during the 1958, '59 and '60 campaigns. He was also a two-year letter winner in basketball and baseball. Ron was selected to the All-Missouri Valley Conference team in 1960 in recognition of his achievements on the gridiron. Tomczak graduated with a Bachelor of Science degree from Wichita State and went on to play professional football with the Houston Oilers. He received his Masters degree in Education, and after retiring from professional football, became active in high school coaching in the greater Chicago area. Ron started as a football assistant and worked at several schools for eight years. He finally established himself as the head football coach at Thornton Fractional North High School, where he enjoyed a fine coaching career for twenty two years. He was named high school "Coach-of-the-Year" twice during that period. In 1986, Tomczak was inducted into the Illinois High School Football Coaches Hall of Fame in recognition of his thirty years of service as coach and teacher at the high school level. He joined the College of St. Francis (Illinois) football coaching staff as offensive line, special teams and strength coach in 1989. In addition to coaching and teaching his youngest son, Steve, Ron has worked with other players of Polish ancestry at St. Francis such as Paul Myszka (quarterback and punter), Brett Binkowski (offensive tackle), Robert Stanek (wide receiver) and Chris Stepanek (offensive guard).

His three sons followed in their father's footsteps and also competed in college football. Ron Tomczak, Jr. was a defensive back at Western Illinois University during the 1981 and '83 seasons. He runs a health club in Chicago and is a fitness instructor. Mike Tomczak was an outstanding quarterback at Ohio State University and was drafted by the NFL Chicago Bears in 1985. He still plays professional football and runs a furniture business. Steve Tomczak broke 14 high school passing records and established 13 records at the College of St. Francis before graduating with a business degree in 1993.

CHAPTER IX

NEXT CENTURY—CLASS OF 1994 PLUS

Doug Brzezinski—Boston College—Off. Tackle—1997
Ken Buczynski—Virginia—Off. Tackle—1996
Pete Chryplewicz—Notre Dame—Tight End—1995
Jim Hmielewski—Kansas State—Off. Tackle—1994
Dave Janoski—Washington—Wide Receiver—1996
Bryan Jurewicz—Wisconsin—Def. Tackle—1996
Mark Kacmarynski—Central College—Run. Back—1995
Rick Kaczenski—Notre Dame—Center—1996
Bob Kalkowski—Allegheny—Linebacker—1994
Eric Kasperowicz—Pittsburgh—Defensive Back—1997
Mark Kasperowicz—Carnegie Mellon—Linebacker—1995
Jim Kubiak—Navy—Quarterback—1994
Kevin Kwiatkowski—Eastern Michigan—Def. Line—1996
Ron Leshinski—Army—Tight End—1996
Tom Lukawski—Indiana—Offensive Guard—1995
Mike Mamula—Boston College—Linebacker—1994
Jason Maniecki—Wisconsin—Nose Guard—1995
Peter Marczyk—Pennsylvania State—Off. Guard—1996
Tony Mazurkiewicz—Yale—Defensive Back—1995
Scott Mutryn—Boston College—Quarterback—1997
Alan Pietkiewicz—Western Maryland—Wide Receiver—1994
Jerry Rudzinski—Ohio State—Linebacker—1997
Matt Szczypinski—Washington & Jefferson—Def. Tackle—1994
Rich Yurkiewicz—Kent State—Linebacker—1994
Trent Zenkewicz—Michigan—Defensive Tackle—1995

Doug Brzezinski—Boston College—Off. Tackle—1997

The recipient of numerous honors and awards for his outstanding football performances, Doug Brzezinski contributed greatly to the national ranking of the gridiron program at Detroit Catholic Central High School in 1992 and 1993. He was a dominating leader as an offensive and defensive lineman, and finished his senior season with 80 tackles and four quarterback sacks. Selected All-America prep football lineman by several publications, Doug also earned All-Midwest and All-State honors, was elected team captain as a senior, chosen to the *Detroit Free Press* Dream Team, and named All-Catholic. He was also picked to play in the Michigan East-West All-Star game. A versatile athlete, Brzezinski was an All-Area and All-Catholic shot putter on the track team, and won a Detroit-area power lifting competition. In addition, Doug was nominated by the Archdiocese of Detroit for the John Shada Award that recognizes civic and athletic excellence. As an exceptional scholar-athlete, he was highly recruited by many schools and enrolled at Boston College in 1994. Brzezinski was one of three freshmen to make the varsity squad as a back-up offensive tackle during the '94 season. At 6-4, 282 pounds, he is an extremely strong, agile and quick offensive lineman. The Eagles' football coaching staff was very impressed with his excellent spring showing, and he was placed in the line-up at offensive tackle starting the 1995 campaign. He enjoyed an outstanding season and is destined to become a prominent offensive lineman with his natural ability, superb work ethic, and intelligence.

Ken Buczynski—Virginia—Off. Guard—1996

An outstanding scholar-athlete at Wilson High School in Wyomissing, Pennsylvania, Ken Buczynski was named All-County and All-League football player, League's Offensive Lineman of the Year, and Outstanding Lineman of the Year as a senior. The two-year starter was chosen to the Pennsylvania Big 33 All-Star squad. Ken was a National Merit Scholarship Commended Student at Wilson High, member of the National Honor Society, and the Science Olympiad Team. He was also named to the All-County Scholastic Team, received the Good Citizenship Award, and was president of the Fellowship of Christian Athletes. Buczynski enrolled at the University of Virginia in 1992, and was redshirted in his freshman year. In 1993, Ken played in four games and in the post-season Carquest Bowl. At 6-3, 273 pounds, he played in all 11 regular season games and the Independence Bowl as a substitute for the Cavaliers during the '94 season. He was named to the Atlantic Coast Conference Honor Roll for the 1993-1994 academic year, and selected GTE Academic All-District III. Buczynski received the Michael Hakala Award in 1994 for excellence in academics and athletics while pursuing a medical education. He also received a special scholarship awarded by the Virginia Student Aid Foundation for outstanding academic achievement. Ken became a starting offensive guard for the 1995 campaign, and helped the Cavaliers to a great season including the fantastic victory over Florida State and a post-season bowl game. Buczynski is a member of the intervarsity Christian Fellowship and the Golden Key National Honor Society.

Pete Chryplewicz—Notre Dame—Tight End—1995

An excellent scholar-athlete, Pete Chryplewicz earned two letters in football playing offensive and defensive end at Stevenson High School in Sterling Heights, Michigan, and was team captain in his senior year. He also earned three letters in both basketball and track, and was two-time captain in both sports. His mother competed in shot put and discus for Poland's Olympic team, and one of his great athletic moments was breaking the high school shot put and discus records. Pete received the scholar-athlete award from the Michigan chapter of the National Football Foundation and Hall of Fame. He was chosen for numerous honors including prep football All-America, and Player of the Year in Michigan and all of Mid-West. Chryplewicz was rated as one of the top tight end prospects in the nation, and he enrolled at the University of Notre Dame in 1992. At 6-5, 233 pounds, Pete got his first letter as a freshman playing reserve tight end and member of the kicking teams. In 1993, he began the season as a back-up tight end, but took over the starting position in eight straight games contributing greatly on offense, primarily as a blocker. A broken bone in his right wrist in the third game of the 1994 campaign ended his contribution for the season. He earned a 3.067 grade point average during the 1994 academic year. Chryplewicz took over the starting tight end position at the beginning of the 1995 season and never relinquished it. He contributed greatly as an excellent blocker on running plays, and became one of the best Notre Dame tight ends as a sure-handed pass receiver.

Jim Hmielewski—Kansas State—Off. Tackle—1994

An outstanding scholar-athlete at East Leyden High School in Franklin Park, Illinois, Jim Hmielewski earned All-State football honors, was named to the *Chicago Sun Times* All-Area prep squad, and voted the top lineman in the West Suburban Conference his senior year. Jim also earned All-Academic honors and had a perfect 4.0 grade point average as a senior. He enrolled at Kansas State University in 1990, and was redshirted during his freshman year. In 1991, Hmielewski went down early with a leg injury and missed most of the season. He recovered sufficiently to practice during the last three weeks of the campaign, but did not play in any games. The 1992 season was his first one of full-time action. He participated in all games and was chosen to start in five, including four starts at offensive tackle and one at offensive guard. Jim started all 12 games at offensive tackle during the 1993 season, and helped Kansas State to lead the conference in passing offense with 245.3 yards per game. He had one of his best outings in the 10-9 victory over intrastate rival University of Kansas when he helped the Wildcats pile up a 1993 Big Eight Conference high 161 yards on the ground in a game that was controlled by the defenses. At 6-7, 310 pounds, Hmielewski had a fantastic outing during the 1994 season, and was honored for his performance by being chosen to the All-Big Eight Conference second team as an offensive tackle by Associated Press and the Big Eight Coaches. He was also named third team All-America, and chosen to play in the post-season Hula Bowl.

Dave Janoski—Washington—Wide Receiver—1996

A versatile athlete at Corona High School in California, Dave Janoski played football, baseball and ran track. He was named Riverside County Football Player of the Year, and league offensive MVP after starring as offensive end and defensive back. Janoski finished his prep football career with 1,239 yards in total offense and made 25 touchdowns. He averaged 8.5 yards every time he touched the ball. Dave enrolled at the University of Washington in 1992, and was red-shirted his freshman year. The Husky coaches were impressed with his good hands, quickness and toughness, and he fit right in to Washington's receiving corps during the 1993 season. Janoski played in all 11 games as a wide receiver, drew starting assignments in five, and finished with 14 receptions for 249 yards. His average of 17.8 yards per reception was second on the team. Dave was an Honorable Mention Pac-10 All-Academic team selection. At 5-10, 180 pounds, Janoski started every game during the 1994 season, and had 14 receptions including two TDs. He received the team 101 Scholarship Award, and was selected for Pac-10 All-Academic honors again. Janoski had an excellent outing in 1995 as a sure-handed split end and punt returner. He helped Washington to a share of the Pac-10 Conference championship with USC, and a Sun Bowl bid. He repeated with academic honors for 1995.

His father, Ed Janoski, was a three-year football letter winner as a line backer at Northern Illinois University. Ed was chosen first team All-Conferece linebacker in 1964, and inducted into the Northern Illinois Hall of Fame in 1986.

Bryan Jurewicz—Wisconsin—Defensive End—1996

An outstanding football star and scholar athlete at Deerfield High School in Deerfield, Illinois, Bryan Jurewicz was selected first team All-America by *Parade*, *The Sporting News* and *Prep Football Report*. He was chosen second team All-America by *USA Today*, named All-State Defensive Tackle, All-Area team member by *Sun Times*, and All-Midwest by *Super Prep*. Bryan made 103 tackles and 16 quarterback sacks in his last two prep years, and graduated as an honor student and a member of the National

Honor Society. Highly recruited by major schools, Jurewicz enrolled at the University of Wisconsin in 1992. He was redshirted
as a freshman. Bryan was the starting outside linebacker in the
last nine games of the 1993 season, and made 26 tackles including
five for losses. At 6-5, 261 pounds, he made season best five
tackles in the Northwestern game. At the end of the '93 campaign,
Jurewicz was selected third team Freshman All-America Linebacker by *Football News*. He switched from outside linebacker to
defensive tackle during spring drills, and was a defensive tackle
starter in the last eight games of the 1994 season. He finished with
26 tackles. Bryan was chosen Academic All-Big Ten, and named
Academic All-District by the College Sports Information Directors. Jurewicz was an outstanding starting defensive end for the
Badgers during the 1995 season, named the Most Valuable Defensive Player in the Wisconsin-Ohio State game, and chosen to
the Academic All-Big Ten team.

Bryan's father, Ron Jurewicz, was a three-year football letter
winner at Wake Forest University from 1967 through 1969.

Mark Kacmarynski—Central College—Tailback—1995

The youngest of nine Iowa farm children who were all highly educated, outstanding students, Mark Kacmarynski went to Central College in 1992. He followed his older brothers, Rich, a Central honor graduate and first team Academic All-America in 1991, and Phil, a football lineman and 1993 grad. Mark earned his first letter as a freshman reserve tail back during the 1992 season. He took over the starting tail back position in 1993, rushed for 1,103 yards, averaging 122.6 yards a game (5.7 yards per carry), and led the team in scoring with 96 points on 16 touchdowns. He was selected first team All-Iowa Conference and named the team's most valuable underclassman. He finished the 1994 campaign with 1,971 yards rushing for a fantastic 7.4 yards per carry, and led the team in scoring with 134 points and 22 TDs. Mark was named first team All-Iowa Conference again, chosen Conference football MVP, selected first team All-America Division III, and was the Gagliardi Award finalist for the NCAA Division III player of the year. He also received the Schilder Award as team's MVP. Kacmarynski was elected team co-captain for the 1995 season. He was named NCAA Division III pre-season player of the year, and featured in *Sports Illustrated* as top player in Division III. Mark performed brilliantly in the first two games, but broke his leg on the team's first play from scrimmage in the third game, and was lost for the season. He established eight new school scoring records, was named to the All-America Farm team, and given the Mentink Award for leadership and sportsmanship.

Rick Kaczenski—Notre Dame—Center—1996

A native of Erie, Pennsylvania, Rick Kaczenski was a threeyear starter and letter winner as a football offensive and defensive end at Cathedral Prep High School. Rick caught 21 passes for 310 yards and three touchdowns as a senior tight end, led his team in receiving, and was an excellent blocker. He made 60 tackles and nine quarterback sacks as a junior defensive end, and followed with 79 stops, four sacks, 11 tackles for loss and one interception in his senior year. He was first team All-City for two years, and chosen first team All-State by Associated Press as a senior. Kaczenski was rated among the best prep prospects in the nation, and one of four top tight ends. Rick was prep All-America selection by *Prep Football Report, Blue Chip Illustrated* and *Super Prep. USA Today* named him an Honorable Mention All-America. He was also selected for the Pennsylvania-Ohio Big 33 All-Star game. Highly recruited by major colleges, Kaczenski followed the suggestion of a fellow Erie native, Mark Stepnoski, and enrolled at the University of Notre Dame in 1993. Rick did not play in a game as a freshman in 1993, but was switched to center after coming in as a tight end prospect. At 6-4, 263 pounds, Kaczenski played in five games as a reserve center during the 1994 season. He took over the starting center position in the 1995 campaign and performed with distinction. Rick helped Notre Dame to a winning 9-2-0 season and an Orange Bowl bid.

Rick's older brother, Robert, played for Pennsylvania State University's 1986 national football championship team.

Bob Kalkowski—Allegheny—Linebacker—1994

Bob Kalkowski was an outstanding scholar-athlete at Mars High School in Valencia, Pennsylvania where he played football as a linebacker, tail back and punter. He received the prestigous Scholar-Athlete Award in his junior and senior years at Mars High School. Kalkowski enrolled at Allegheny College in 1991, and won his first letter in football as a freshman reserve linebacker finishing with 13 total tackles for the year. In 1992, Bob was Allegheny's fifth-leading tackler with 47 stops (20 unassisted) despite the fact that he did not start in a game, but played in all 10 during the season. He took over the starting linebacker position at the beginning of the 1993 campaign, and turned in an excellent performance. He finished as the team leader with 84 tackles of which 31 were solos, and was fourth on the squad with six tackles for losses. Bob added seven tackles to his total against Mt. Union in the NCAA Division III Playoffs. He helped Allegheny to a winning regular season record of 9-1-0 in which the Gators outscored the opposition 432 to 91, and won the North Coast Athletic Conference championship. Bob had career high 17 tackles against Westminster, and was outstanding in the Wooster and Carnegie Mellon games. At 5-11, 194 pounds, Kalkowski was selected first team All-NCAC linebacker for his performance in 1993. He was also named an Honorable Mention All-America by *Football Gazette*. A math major, Bob was tri-captain of the 1994 Allegheny squad, chosen All-NCAC linebacker again, and received All-America linebacker honors on a 10-0, NCAA-playoff team.

Eric Kasperowicz—Pittsburgh—Defensive Back—1997

An outstanding quarterback and Honor Roll student from North Hills High School in Pittsburgh, Pennsylvania, Eric Kasperowicz enrolled at the University of Pittsburgh as one of the most highly regarded prospects in the nation. He was a four-year starter at North Hills High, and named team Most Valuable Player in his junior and senior years. Eric also played safety and was chosen the team's Most Valuable Defensive Back as a senior. Kasperowicz passed for 2,781 yards and 21 touchdowns in 1993, and led North Hills to the number three ranking in *USA Today's* national high school football poll. His team finished with a 15-0 season and the PIAA Quad A state championship. He accumulated 6,865 passing and rushing yards, and scored 83 touchdowns during his prep career. Eric was named the Associated Press Pennsylvania High School Player of the Year, selected to play in the prestigious Big 33 Football Classic, named *USA Today's* Pennsylvania Football Player of the Year, and chosen the *Pittsburgh Post-Gazette's* Quad A Player of the Year. Kasperowicz was also selected All-America by *Parade* and *Blue Chip Illustrated.* He was listed in the *Who's Who in American High School Sports* as a junior and senior.

At 6-0, 205 pounds, he was switched to a defensive back in 1994, played in 10 games during the season, and was named a YMCA Scholar-Athlete. He performed well as a defensive back in Pittsburgh's losing cause in the 1995 campaign.

His older brother, Mark, was a scholar-athlete and an outstanding linebacker on the Carnegie Mellon University football team.

**Mark Kasperowicz—Carnegie Mellon—
Linebacker—1995**

A scholar-athlete at North Hills High School in Pittsburgh,

Pennsylvania, Mark Kasperowicz enrolled at Carnegie Mellon University in 1992, and played varsity football as a back-up linebacker during his freshman year. At 6-2, 231 pounds, Mark became the starting interior linebacker in the beginning of the 1993 campaign, and performed with distinction during the year. As a two-year letter winner, Kasperowicz finished the season as the Tartans' third leading tackler with 43 stops of which 31 were unassisted. He also had four tackles for losses, two sacks and one interception for a touchdown. Mark helped Carnegie Mellon to its 19th consecutive winning season, and third University Athletic Association title in the past four years with a 8-2-0 overall record. Kasperowicz was selected first team All-UAA linebacker by the association coaches, and named the UAA Defensive Player of the Week for his performance against Catholic University. Mark was an outstanding defensive linebacker during the 1994 campaign finishing with 89 tackles. Once again he was selected first team All-UAA linebacker by the coaches. Kasperowicz completed his college football career in grand style playing as an outside linebacker. He finished fourth on the team with 56 tackles of which 32 were solos. He also caused one fumble, broke up one pass, made six tackles for loss of 24 yards, had three quarterback sacks for 15 yards, and one interception. Mark was named to the All-UAA team again.

His younger brother, Eric, enrolled at the University of Pittsburgh in 1994 and was playing as a defensive back.

Jim Kubiak—Navy—Quarterback—1994

Jim Kubiak earned All-States All-Western New York and All-Catholic honors as a football quarterback at St. Francis High School in Athol Springs, New York, and was elected team captain and MVP in his senior year. He played a year at the Naval Academy Prep School before entering the U.S. Naval Academy in 1991. As a plebe, Kubiak started in five games, set a pair of Navy passing records vs. Wake Forest, and was named ECAC Rookie of the Week for the Tulane game. He completed 13 of 16 passes for 157 yards to lead the winless Middies to a surprising 24-3 win over Army. His 1991 totals showed 93 completions in 154 attempts for 957 yards and two TDs. Jim suffered a dislocated shoulder in the 1992 season opener against Virginia, underwent surgery and missed the remainder of the year. In 1993, Kubiak was chosen for ECAC honors five times, named MVP in the Army-Navy game by completing 16 of 26 passes for 208 yards and a TD, and earned praises for his excellent performance in the first half of the Notre Dame game. He finished with 248 completions of 401 attempts for 2,628 yards and 11 TDs. Jim set twelve Naval Academy records in 1993, and was named "Almost All-America" quarterback by *Football News*. Kubiak was elected co-captain of the 1994 Navy squad, and during the season passed for 2,388 yards and 10 touchdowns. He finished his Naval Academy football years with brilliant performances, and established eighteen Academy records including career passing for a total of 6,008 yards.

Kubiak's cousin, Ron Jaworski, was an outstanding college and professional football quarterback.

Kevin Kwiatkowski—Eastern Michigan—Defensive Line—1996

A two-time letter winner in football and basketball at Holy Name High School, Parma, Ohio, Kwiatkowski received the "Distinguished Athlete Award" from the U.S. Marine Corps. He was selected first team All-North Coast League in football as a senior, and chosen "Lineman of the Week" four times by the coaches. Kevin was also a second team pick in basketball as the leading rebounder. He enrolled at Eastern Michigan University in 1992, and was redshirted as a freshman. At 6-4, 250 pounds, Kwiatkowski played in all 11 games and started in the last three during the 1993 season. He made 39 tackles, including six for loss of 26 yards. He received the Sponberg Award as the team's top lineman scholar athlete. Kevin started all 11 games in 1994, and finished with 66 tackles of which 35 were solos. He was fourth in the Conference in tackles for loss with 13 for 59 yards. He was named "Defensive Eagle of the Week" for the Central Michigan game after making nine tackles. His season high came against Kent State where he had 12 tackles. Kwiatkowski received the Sponberg Award again as a scholar athlete with a 3.0 GPA. He was a second team All-Mid America Conference defensive lineman selection at the end of the year. Kwiatkowski was elected co-captain of the 1995 Eastern Michigan football squad. He played in all 11 games, but did not perform as well as he had the previous year. He finished the 1995 campaign with 26 tackles of which 13 were solos, four were for loss of 13 yards and four quarterback sacks for 15 yards. Kevin has another year of football eligibility at Eastern Michigan.

Ron Leshinski—Army—Tight End—1996

An all-star scholar athlete, Ron Leshinski earned three letters in football at Vermillion High School in Vermillion, Ohio where he was used as both tight end and defensive back. He won two more letters in basketball, and was team captain in both sports as a senior. Leshinski established eleven school records in football which included offensive pass receiving and defensive pass interception marks. Ron was selected County Most Valuable Player in football, and was given the Golden Helmet Award. He attended the U.S. Military Academy Prep School after graduating from high school, and played both split end and tight end on the prep football team. Leshinski entered the U.S. Military Academy in 1993, and was a member of the Army football team as a freshman. He was the starting tight end in the opening game of the '93 season with Colgate, and remained the starter for the rest of the games. In starting against Colgate, Ron became the first plebe other than a punter or kicker to start in a season opener for Army since 1980. He was used primarily as a blocker in Army's run-dominated wishbone offense during 1993. At 6-3, 240 pounds, Leshinski started in all eleven games of the 1994 campaign, and finished with 14 pass receptions for 132 yards including three touchdowns. He was also an excellent blocker for Army's running backs. He started every game (22) in his two-year Army football career. Ron finished with an outstanding 1995 season as Army's most consistent and reliable blocker and receiver. He was instrumental in almost beating Notre Dame by making a key touchdown pass reception.

Tom Lukawski—Indiana—Offensive Guard—1996

An excellent scholar athlete, Tom Lukawski was a three year football letter winner playing as a guard on offense and nose guard on defense at Central High School in East Chicago, Indiana. He ranked No. 2 scholastically in a high school class of 460, and was selected to the All-Conference, All-Area, All-State and Academic All-State football teams after his senior year. Tom graded very highly as a blocking guard on offense, and finished with 62 tackles (nine for loss of yards) on defense. Lukawski also won four letters in track, and holds the high school record in shot put. Highly recruited, Tom enrolled at Indiana University in 1992, and was red shirted as a freshman. He played center on the scout team, but was switched to the offensive guard position in 1993. He was used in a three guard rotation system for most of the season, and received high praise from the coaches for his excellent performance as a starting offensive guard against Penn State. Tom was chosen an All-Big Ten Conference Academic team member at the end of the year. At 6-2, 282 pounds, Lukawski started in all eleven games as an offensive guard during the 1994 season. He enjoyed an excellent year, and was chosen again to the Academic All-Big Ten squad. His performance as an offensive line starter was outstanding during the 1995 campaign, and he was selected to the Academic All-Big Ten team for the third straight year.

Tom's father, Chet Lukawski, was a two-year football letter winner for the University of Kentucky in 1950 and 1951. He coached football for eleven years at East Chicago Roosevelt High School.

Mike Mamula—Boston College—Defensive End—1994

Mike Mamula was captain of the football, basketball and track teams at Lackawanna Secondary School in Lackawanna, N.Y. He was selected All-Western New York and All-State for his prep football achievements, and named MVP in basketball and track. Mamula enrolled as a sociology major in the College of Arts and Sciences at Boston College in 1991, and did not play varsity football as a freshman. He injured his shoulder on the first play from scrimmage as a varsity player, and missed the next three games during the 1992 season. Mike was used sparingly for the rest of the year. He became an outstanding starter on the weak side of the defensive line in the 1993 campaign, and was named NBC's "Player of the Game" after his excellent performance against Notre Dame. He was fantastic with 14 tackles to lead and inspire the Eagles to a surprising defensive showing against the top-ranked Fighting Irish. Mike also starred in games against Syracuse, West Virginia and Rutgers. He made 84 tackles in 1993 of which 53 were solos, and had six tackles for loss of 28 yards. Mamula finished his college football career in 1994 making 73 tackles with nine for loss of 25 yards, and 13 quarterback sacks for 97 yards loss. He led the Big East Conference with 11 quarterback sacks for 73 yards loss, and developed into the best pass-rusher in the Big East. Mike was selected as the 1994 Eastern College Athletic Conference Division 1-A Defensive All-Star. He was the Philadelphia Eagles' first round draft choice in 1995, and is performing superbly as a professional defensive end sack artist.

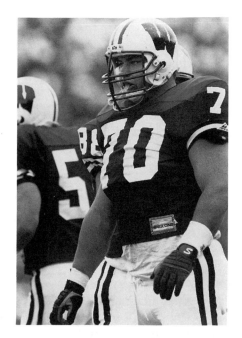

Jason Maniecki—Wisconsin—Nose Guard—1995

Jason Maniecki overcame many obstacles and made numerous adjustments to become an outstanding college scholar athlete playing football at a Big Ten Conference school. He emigrated from Poland at age 10, and experienced some major changes in his new, young life. He succeeded admirably and earned honors for four years at Wisconsin Dells High School. Jason won the state wrestling title twice, and was named the football team's MVP in his senior year. He was selected first team All-State, and named an Honorable Mention All-America by *USA Today*. He enrolled at the University of Wisconsin in 1991, and earned his first letter in football by playing in seven games as a freshman. He was redshirted in 1992, and returned to action during the 1993 campaign playing as a reserve defensive lineman. An excellent student, Maniecki carried a 3.70 grade point average, and was selected a member of the Big Ten Conference All-Academic team after the '93 season. At 6-5, 290 pounds, Jason was moved to nose guard for the 1994 campaign. He started in all 11 games, and made 76 tackles including 13 for losses. Maniecki was selected second team All-Big Ten by the media, and chosen Academic All-Big Ten again. He was also named Academic All-District IV after the '94 season. Jason was elected team co-captain for the 1995 campaign, and turned in some outstanding defensive performances especially in the Wisconsin-Ohio State game. He was named All-Big Ten by the coaches and media, chosen Academic All-Big Ten for the third year, and nominated for the National Football Foundation Postgraduate Scholarship Award.

Peter Marczyk—Pennsylvania State—Off. Guard—1996

An outstanding football player at Holy Spirit High School in Abescon, New Jersey, Peter Marczyk became only the second player in 30 years to be named to the *Philadelphia Inquirer* All-South New Jersey team for three consecutive years. He was selected first team All-America by *Parade*, and named as a second team All-America by *USA Today*. Peter was the All-State center on Holy Spirit's Jersey Parochial League championship team. He was also a member of the track team in shot put and discus throw. Marczyk was highly recruited as an excellent scholar athlete by many major colleges and universities, and enrolled at Pennsylvania State University in 1992. He was red-shirted during the '92 season. Although he came to Penn State as a center candidate, Peter was switched to offensive guard at the start of the 1993 campaign. At 6-3, 280 pounds, Marczyk saw action in six games getting the most playing time against Maryland, Minnesota and Rutgers. An excellent student, he had a 3.1 grade point average as a labor and industrial relations major, and was chosen a member of the Big Ten Conference All-Academic team after the '93 season. Peter helped the offensive line as a strong reserve and saw considerable action in 1994. He was on the field for the longest times in games with Minnesota, Ohio State, Southern Cal, Temple, Iowa, and Rutgers. Once again, Marczyk was chosen to the Academic All-Big Ten Conference team. Peter was a solid contributor to the strong offensive line, and helped Penn State to a winning season and an Outback Bowl bid in 1995. For the third straight year he was chosen Academic All-Big Ten.

Tony Mazurkiewicz—Yale—Defensive Back—1995

A native of Glenwood, Illinois, Tony Mazurkiewicz played football and baseball at Mt. Carmel High School, and was captain of both teams as a senior. The football team was state champion, and the baseball team won the Catholic League championship. Tony was chosen all-league and all-area defensive back in football, and was named Most Valuable Defensive Player as an outfielder in baseball. Mazurkiewicz enrolled at Yale University where he became a hard-hitting strong safety on the football team as a sophomore. He played in nine games and started in three to end the 1993 season with 33 tackles, including two for loss of yards. At 5-10, 200 pounds, Tony turned in an excellent performance in 1994, becoming a leader as an Eli defensive back. He finished second on the squad with 75 tackles, of which 43 were solos, and four intercepted passes. He was selected defensive MVP after the Princeton game in which he had a season high 13 tackles. Tony was also named defensive MVP after the Lehigh game. Mazurkiewicz was elected captain of Yale football for the 1995 season, and finished the campaign as an outstanding defensive performer. He led the Bulldogs with 97 tackles of which 41 were solos, made four tackles for loss of 11 yards, recovered one fumble, intercepted three passes for 17 yards, and broke up five passes. Tony was named Honorable Mention All-Ivy League, chosen GTE/CoSida Regional Academic All-America, and invited to play in the Epson Ivy Bowl. This bowl game is played in Japan and pits outstanding Ivy League seniors against a team of Japanese college and university stars.

Scott Mutryn—Boston College—Quarterback—1997

An outstanding football quarterback at St. Ignatius High School in Cleveland, Ohio, Scott Mutryn was one of the most sought after college prospects in the country. He was ranked among the top four quarterbacks in the nation. Scott led his St. Ignatius team to a 28-0 record, and back to back state titles in 1992 and 1993. St. Ignatius was ranked No. 1 nationally in 1993 following their 38-20 win over Cincinnati's Moeller High School when Mutryn threw for three TDs and ran for another. He also starred in the Big 33 High School All-Star game by leading Ohio to a 35-20 victory over Pennsylvania. Scott completed 53 percent of his passes for 2,019 yards and 22 TDs, and also ran for six TDs as a senior. He finished his prep career with nearly 4,000 passing yards and 42 TD passes. Mutryn earned All-America honors from *Super Prep* and *Parade* magazines, was chosen to *Blue Chip Illustrated's* All-America Dream Team, named Associated Press All-State and All-District as a junior and senior, chosen two-time *Cleveland Plain-Dealer* All-Scholastic, and won All-Independent League honors in 1993. Highly recruited, Mutryn enrolled at Boston College in 1994. At 6-4, 205 pounds, Scott started in the third game of his freshman year versus Pitt and completed 18 passes for 186 yards including two TDs. He finished the '94 season as a reserve quarterback. Mutryn was recovering from a broken bone in his right wrist, and so he contributed little during the 1995 season, but his future is promising.

Scott's late great-uncle, Chet Mutryn, had an outstanding college and pro football career as an excellent running back. He began playing football at Cathedral Latin High School in Cleveland, Ohio. At 5-9, 170 pounds, Mutryn was a versatile athlete who excelled as a runner, passer, receiver, place kicker and punter. As a star footballl player at Xavier University, Cincinnati, Ohio, he received Little All-America honors twice and was chosen to the Legion of Honor. Chet established two season scoring records at Xavier in 1941, and was named the outstanding college player in Ohio. After service in the U. S. Navy during World War II, Mutryn joined the Cleveland Browns and was traded to the Buffalo Bills. He became a starting running back at Buffalo and earned three consecutive All-Pro honors while helping the Bills to become a top pro team. Chet retired in 1950 after five years of pro ball and entered the real estate business. After a successful real estate career, Mutryn died in April 1995 in Cleveland at age 76.

Alan Pietkiewicz—Western Maryland—Wide Receiver—1994

What Alan Pietkiewicz lacked in size, he more than made up for in determination and hard work by becoming an excellent football player at Shenandoah Valley High School in Pennsylvania. He enrolled at Western Maryland College in 1991, and played in a reserve role as a freshman receiver. At 5-9, 160 pounds,

Pietkiewicz took over as starting wide receiver at the beginning of the 1992 campaign. He was the leading pass catcher for the Green Terrors with 16 receptions for 292 yards and two TDs. Alan also returned nine punts for 25 yards, and one kickoff for 17 yards. In 1993, he led the team again with 59 receptions for 758 yards (12.9 yds. average) and seven TDs. He was also first with 21 punt returns for 152 yards, and second with seven kickoff returns for 110 yards. In addition, Pietkiewicz finished second in team scoring with 42 points, and rushed two times for seven yards. He made a strong showing in Centennial Conference games finishing second in receiving, fifth in punt returns, seventh in all-purpose running, and tied for eighth in scoring. Alan received second team All-Centennial Conference honors after the '93 season. His career totals of 76 receptions and 1,076 receiving yards place him fifth in both categories in the Western Maryland record book. Alan was elected co-captain of the football team for the 1994 campaign, and named a Pre-Season NCAA Division III All-America wide receiver by the College Football Preview. Pietkiewicz finished his college football career as one of the best receivers in the Conference, and repeated with All-Centennial Conference honors.

Jerry Rudzinski—Ohio State—Linebacker—1997

A versatile football player and an excellent scholar athlete, Jerry Rudzinski was an outstanding offensive and defensive star at Kettering Alter High School, Centerville, Ohio. He was the Ohio Division III Defensive Player of the Year, and a two time first team All-State selection. Rudzinski made 144 tackles as a senior defensive back with six quarterback sacks and 14 tackles for loss. As a senior quarterback, Jerry passed for over 1,300 yards and nine touchdowns, and rushed for 143 yards and four TD's. During his high school career, he made 303 tackles, passed for 2,594 yards and 20 TD's, and rushed for 480 yards and 12 TD's. He served as a two-year football team captain, and helped the basketball team reach the state semi-finals in 1993. Jerry was an excellent student who made the honor roll every year. Rudzinski earned Honorable Mention All-America honors from *USA Today*.

He enrolled at Ohio State University in 1995 and quickly impressed the coaching staff. At 6-1, 220 pounds, Jerry was the Buckeye starting linebacker as a freshman during the 1995 season, and performed like a veteran. He helped Ohio State to finish with a winning 11-1-0 record and a bid to the Citrus Bowl.

Jerry's father lettered in football at the University of Dayton. Uncle Joe Rudzinski was a four-year letter winner as a linebacker at the University of Notre Dame from 1979 to 1982. Uncle Paul Rudzinski was a four-year letter winner as a linebacker at Michigan State University from 1974 to 1977. He won many college honors, and played pro football with Green Bay.

Matt Szczypinski—Washington & Jefferson—Def. Tackle—1994

An outstanding scholar athlete at Canevin Catholic High School in Pittsburgh, Matt Szczypinski enrolled at Washington and Jefferson College in 1991, and became a starting defensive tackle on the varsity football squad in his freshman year. At 6-0, 228 pounds, Szczypinski was sixth on the team during the '91 season with 47 tackles (24 solos, 15 assists, three for losses, and five sacks), and returned one interception for 23 yards. He helped Washington and Jefferson to a winning 8-2-0 record and the NCAA Division III Playoffs. In 1992, Matt made 49 tackles (33 solos, seven assists, four for losses, and five sacks), and recovered two fumbles. The Presidents finished with an 11-2-0 record, and reached the NCAA Division III Championship game for the first time in school history. Szczypinski had an excellent outing in 1993, and finished third on the team with 83 tackles (41 solos, 26 assists, seven for losses, and nine sacks). He also intercepted two passes, and recovered one fumble. He was named the President's Athletic Conference Defensive Player of the Week, and *Football Gazette* Regional Player of the Week. Matt was also chosen first team All-PAC defensive tackle. Washington and Jefferson finished with an 11-1-0 overall record, losing to Rowan in the Division III Playoffs. Szczypinski, leader of the Presidents' defensive line and team co-captain, was selected NCAA Division III Defensive Tackle, named NCAA Division III National Scholar

Athlete, and chosen to the Eastern College Athletic Conference Division III Southern All-Star Defensive Line following the 1994 season.

Rich Yurkiewicz—Kent State—Linebacker—1994

Rich Yurkiewicz was chosen All-Ohio wide receiver by Associated Press as a senior at Valley Forge High School. He was also an All-Lake Erie League and All-Northeast Ohio selection, and a member of the Cleveland Plain Dealer All-Scholastic Team. Yurkiewicz enrolled at Kent State University in 1991 as a wide receiver, but became an outside linebacker in the fall. He played in six games and saw action on special teams. Rich took over the starting linebacker spot in the second game of the 1992 season, and finished as the team's fifth leading tackler with 74 of which 55 were solos. He had a team high five sacks, caused two fumbles, recovered two others, and returned one recovery for a 32-yard touchdown against Akron. He was named MAC Defensive Player of the Week for the Akron game. His season performance earned him Honorable Mention on the All-Mid America Conference Team. Rich was elected team captain for the 1993 campaign and had an excellent outing. He finished the year as Kent State's leading tackler with a total of 129 stops of which 58 were unassisted and 71 assisted. He also had team highs of 10 tackles for loss (minus 51 yards), six sacks (loss of 43 yards), four fumble recoveries, and six passes broken up. He was selected Mid-America Conference Player of the Week once, and team's Defensive Player of the Week six times. Rich was named first team All-Mid America Conference at the end of the season. One of the best linebackers in MAC, Yurkiewicz was elected captain of the 1994 team. At 6-3, 220 pounds, the three year letterman earned All-MAC honors again in 1994.

Trent Zenkewicz—Michigan—Defensive Tackle—1995

An outstanding football player at St. Ignatius High School in Cleveland, Ohio, Trent Zenkewicz was the most sought after prep lineman in the nation in 1990. During his three year career, St. Ignatius compiled a 37-1 record and won two state titles. As a senior, Trent made 102 tackles, 29 for losses and 20 sacks. He earned All-State honors as a junior, and received many awards in his senior year. He was named first team All-America by every major selector, chosen Ohio Player of the Year, picked Ohio Lineman of the Year, selected All-State by AP and UPI, and received All-Scholastic Team honors. Zenkewicz was highly recruited, and enrolled at the University of Michigan in 1991. He was red-shirted as a freshman and earned his first letter playing reserve tackle in 1992. He had his best day against Northwestern by making five tackles including three for loss of 19 yards, and two sacks for loss of 18 yards. Trent suffered a knee injury in the second game of the 1993 season against Notre Dame and required arthroscopic surgery. He saw action in only four games during that year, but recorded a tackle for loss in three games including a key sack in the Hall of Fame Bowl. At 6-6, 270 pounds, Zenkewicz started at defensive tackle in 1994 and had an outstanding year. He earned awards for his defensive performances in the Boston College and Wisconsin games, was named the top Michigan defensive lineman, and chosen second team All-Big

Ten. In 1995, Zenkewicz was a starting defensive tackle, helping Michigan to an 8-3-0 season, an Alamo Bowl bid, and All-Big Ten honors again.

The roster of Polish Americans in college football continues into the next century with:

Todd Baczek—Northwestern—Offensive Tackle—1994

At 6-3, 287 pounds, Baczek became a starter in 1992, and was the strongest player on the Wildcat team. A native of Grayslake, Illinois, Todd graduated from Mundelein Carmel High School where he was chosen All-Conference, All-State and All-Area playing as an offensive and defensive lineman.

Brent Banasiewicz—Clemson—Offensive Line—1997

A native of Monticello, Florida, Banasiewicz graduated from Aucilla Christian Academy as a high honors student and member of *Who's Who in American High Schools.* At 6-3, 290 pounds, Brent was ranked as the fourth best offensive guard and 12th best offensive lineman in the nation.

Brian Gabrieszewski—Akron—Offensive Tackle—1996

At 6-5, 295 pounds, Gabrieszewski took over the starting right tackle for the University of Akron as a freshman in 1993, and was an outstanding offensive lineman in 1995. A graduate of Hanover High School in Wilkes-Barre, Pennsylvania, Brian was named an All-State and All-Conference tackle in 1992.

Gary Glowacki—Central Michigan—Offensive Tackle—1997

At 6-4, 290 pounds, Glowacki was a starter at offensive tackle for the Chippewas for the last nine games of the 1994 season. He is majoring in industrial technology and carries a 3.30 GPA. Gary played football, basketball, and ran track at Sault Area High School, Sault Ste. Marie, Michigan.

Jay Janicki—Yale—Tight End—1994

A big, fast offensive end at 6-3, 235 pounds, Janicki was a key ingredient as a blocker in the Eli running game. Jay graduated from St. John's High School in Maumee, Ohio, where he was chosen All-Area, All-City defensive end (he also played offensive eight end).

Doug Karczewski—Virginia—Offensive Tackle—1997

Karczewski graduated from DeMatha High School, Gaithersburg, Maryland where he was football team captain as a senior. At 6-5, 252 pounds, Doug was selected All-America, All-Region, All-State and named Most Valuable Lineman. He helped the Cavaliers to a very successful 1995 season as a starter.

Andy Korytkowski—Central Michigan—Swing Back—1994

A six letterman in football, basketball and track at Grand Rapids Northview High, Korytkowski was also a member of the National Honor Society. Andy earned a starting job and scholarship at CMU as a walk-on. He finished with a 3.24 cumulative GPA with a major in finance, and was named to the Academic All-MAC Team.

Mike Kowalski—Montana—Linebacker—1995

At 5-10, 181 pounds, Kowalski was one of UM's leading tacklers and has been chosen to the All-Big Sky Conference Academic Team the last three years. Mike graduated from Cut Bank High School, Montana where he was chosen first team All-State running back and linebacker in his junior and senior years.

Bill Koziel—Northwestern—Nose Guard—1994

An outstanding nose guard starter at 6-1, 261 pounds, Koziel earned his first varsity letter as a freshman at Northwestern. A native of Chicago, Bill graduated from Gordon Tech as a member of the National Honor Society, earned All-League honors, and was team captain and team MVP in his senior year.

Kevin Krusenoski—Holy Cross—Nose Guard—1996

At 6-0, 250 pounds, Krusenoski earned a starting role at Holy Cross in 1994. The graduate of Lockport High School in Orland Park, Illinois was a National Football Foundation and Hall of Fame Scholar-Athlete, and member of the National Honor Society. Kevin was named two-time All-League and All-Academic.

Chris Kurpeikis—Michigan—Offensive Tackle—1997

Kurpeikis, of Polish Lithuanian heritage, transferred from Notre Dame in 1994. At 6-6, 281 pounds, Chris was a prep All-American selection after starring as an offensive and defensive tackle at Central Catholic High School, Pittsburgh, Pennsylvania. He is a National Honor Roll student.

Keith Lozowski—Northwestern—Linebacker—1996

An outstanding athlete, Lozowski earned 10 letters (football, basketball and track) at Fremd High School, Palatine, Illinois. He played in nine games at Northwestern during the 1994 season and became a starting linebacker in 1995. Keith helped the Wildcats to a share of their first Big Ten Conference title since 1936 and a post season bowl game.

Jason Malecki—Boston College—Punter—1998

Malecki earned All-America honors as an outstanding punter

at West Springfield High School, Springfield, Virginia. He enrolled at Boston College in 1995 and became their starting punter as a freshman. He is an excellent student who was a member of the National Honor Society and the Latin Honor Society in high school.

Dan Markowski—Massachusetts—Offensive Tackle—1996

At 6-6, 284 pounds, Markowski was an integral part of the UMass offensive line as a freshman and a very good pass blocker during the 1995 season. A graduate of Liverpool High School in Liverpool, New York, Dan was first team All-New York State selection, and chosen starting tackle in the state All-Star game.

Chris Merski—Allegheny—Placekicker—1994

The All-American, Merski, finished his fourth year as a starter at 5-11, 180 pounds, and was Allegheny's all-time kick points leader and second in conference career kick points. A native of Erie, Pennsylvania, Chris lettered at Cathedral High School, and was named Athlete of the Year in 1991.

Dave Miloszewski—William & Mary—Offensive Guard—1995

At 6-4, 270 pounds, Miloszewski was a starting offensive guard in 1994 and 1995. A native of Emlenton, Pennsylvania, Dave lettered at Allegheny Clarion High School, and was named All-Conference first team tight end and second team defensive end. His father, John, played college football at Maryland.

Dan Modzelewski—New Mexico State—Defensive End—1994

At 6-1, 252 pounds, Modzelewski played at defensive end

during the 1994 season. A graduate of Eastlake (OH) North High, Dan is the son of Gene Modzelewski who played for the Aggies and in the NFL. His uncles, Ed and Dick, were All-Americans at the University of Maryland and also played professional football.

Jason Sepkowski—Pittsburgh—Offensive Guard—1997

At 6-2, 275 pounds, Sepkowski was one of Pittsburgh's top recruits and is an Athletic Director's Honor Roll student. He was named to the Pennsylvania Scholar-Athlete team, and to the 1995 Big East Football All-Academic team. Jason was an All-Region, All-Conference and All-State player at North Pocono High School in Moscow, Pennsylvania, and a member of the National Honor Society.

Ron Stopkoski—Sacred Heart—Halfback—1994

One of the region's premier running backs at 6-0, 200 pounds, Stopkoski was named All-New England by Associated Press. A native of Clinton, Connecticut, Ron played at the Morgan School where he rushed for a record 4,300 yards and was named All-Conference and All-State. His twin brother, Rob, was an outstanding linebacker at Sacred Heart.

Steve Szymanowski—Kent State—Defensive End—1995

Defensive end starter at 6-2, 228 pounds, Szymanowski received the Matt Ramser Award for excellence in spring drills. Steve led his St. Joseph High School team to three Midland Athletic Conference titles, and was named All-Ohio by AP and UPI, MAL Player of the Year, and *USA Today* All-America.

Jeff Tamulski—New Hampshire—Tight End—1996

A native of West Seneca, New York, Tamulski played in three sports at The Nichols School lettering in football, baseball and basketball. At 6-2, 245 pounds, Jeff led UNH to the Yankee Conference Division Title in 1994 and finished as a top offensive contributor during the 1995 season.

John Wojciechowski—Duquesne—Defensive End—1995

A graduate of Plum High School, Pittsburgh, Pennsylvania, Wojciechowski was a four-year starter for Duquesne at defensive end. He was named second team All-Metro Atlantic Athletic Conference in 1994, elected team captain for the 1995 season, and finished with All-MAAC honors in 1995. John was a member of the Athletic Director's Honor Roll.

Kyle Wojciechowski—Hillsdale—Offensive Tackle—1996

A native of Toledo, Ohio, Wojciechowski is an outstanding student athlete at Hillsdale College with a 3.86 cumulative GPA who plans to attend medical school. At 6-2, 277 pounds, Kyle has been an offensive line starter since the middle of his freshman year. He was a CFP National Scholar Athlete selection for 1995.

Joe Zabielski—Bucknell—Tight End—1994

A fine blocker and receiver at 6-3, 230 pounds, Zabielski graduated from Old Forge High School in Pennsylvania as the school's first four-year, four-sports Honors Student. Joe was a prep quarterback who threw for a school record 3,108 yards, and was named one of the top football players in Pennsylvania.

Mike Zimirowski—Holy Cross—Offensive Tackle—1996

A native of Lynn, Massachusetts, Zimirowski earned numerous athletic and scholastic honors at Lynn English High School before enrolling at Holy Cross. He became a starting offensive lineman during the early part of the 1993 season, and received All-Patriot

League honors in 1994 and 1995. Mike is majoring in biology and plans to study medicine.

REFERENCES

Benagh, Jim. *Incredible Football Feats.* Grosset and Dunlap Publishers, 1974.

Bradley, Bob. *Death Valley Days, The Glory of Clemson Football.* Longstreet Press, 1991.

Brady, John T. *The Heisman: A Symbol of Excellence.* New York, 1984.

Brondfield, Jerry. *100 Plus Years of Football, The All-America Teams.* Scholastic Book Services, 1975.

Bukowczyk, John J. *And My Children Did Not Know Me, A History of Polish Americans.* Indiana University Press, 1987.

Connor, Jack. *Leahy's Lads, The Story of the Famous Notre Dame Teams of the 1940s.* Diamond Communications, Inc., 1994.

Falla, Jack. *Till the Echos Ring Again, A History of Boston College Sports.* The Stephen Greene Press, 1982.

Football Media Guides from colleges and universities on file at the College Football Hall of Fame. The 1995 editions were filed at Pat Harmon's home in Wyoming, Ohio.

Football Media Guides from the following college football conferences: Atlantic Coast, Big East, Big Eight, Big Sky, Big Ten, Big West, Eastern College Athletic, Ivy League, Mid American, National Association of Intercollegiate Athletics, (NAIA), Pacific-10, Southeastern, Southern, Southwestern, and Western Athletic (1994 and 1995 editions).

Gutman, Bill. *The Signal Callers, Sipe, Jaworski, Ferguson, Bartkowski.* Grosset and Dunlap Publishers, 1981.

Harmon, Tom and Jim Benagh. *Sports Information Book.* J. Lowell Pratt and Co., 1965.

Jarrett, William S. *Timetables of Sports History, Football.* Facts on File, New York and Oxford, 1980.

Kramer, Jerry and Dick Schaap. *Distant Replay.* New York: G.P. Putnam's Sons, 1985.

Larson, Melissa. *The Pictorial History of College Football.* W.H. Smith Publishers, Inc., 1989.

Matuszak, John and Steve Delsohn. *Cruisin With the Tooz.* New York: Charter Books, 1987.

McCarty, Bernie. *All-America, The Complete Roster of Football Heroes, Volume I (1989-1945).* Published by Bernie McCarty, 1991.

Michener, James. *Sports in America.* Fawcett Publications,Inc., 1976.

National Football Foundation's College Football Hall of Fame—Inductees Booklets (1990 through 1995 editions).

Newcombe, Jack, ed. *The Fireside Book of Football.* New York: Simon & Schuster, 1964.

Newhouse, Dave. *Heismen, After the Glory.* Sporting News Publications, 1985.

O'Brien, Jim, ed. *Hail to Pitt: A Sports History of the University of Pittsburgh.* Wolfson Publishing Co., 1982.

O'Brien, Michael. *Vince, A Personal Biography of Vince Lombardi.* William Morrow and Co., Inc., 1987.

Perrin, John. *Football, A College History.* McFarland and Co., Inc., 1987.

Porter, David L., ed. *Biographical Dictionary of American Sports Football,* Greenwood Press, 1987.

Rappaport, Ken. *The Nittany Lions, Penn State Football 100th Anniversary Edition,* 1987.

Sammis, Fred R. *The College Game.* A Rutledge Book, Bobbs-Merrill, 1974.

Schoor, Gene. *100 Years of Notre Dame Football.* New York: Avon Books, 1987.

Snypp, Wilbur and Bob Hunter. *The Buckeyes, A Story of Ohio State Football.* The Strode Publishers, 1988.

Stabley, Fred W. *The Spartans, Michigan State Football.* The Strode Publishers, Inc., 1982.

Summers, Gregory J., ed. *National Collegiate Athletic Association—Official 1993 NCAA Football.* Kansas: National Collegiate Athletic Association, 1993.

Tarapacki, Thomas, ed. *Polish-American Journal.* Panagraphics, Inc. (1991, 1992, 1993, 1994 and 1995 monthly editions).

REFERENCES

Van Vlakenburg, James M., ed. *National Collegiate Athletic Association—NCAA Football's Finest*. Kansas: National Collegiate Athletic Association, 1990.

Whittingham, Richard. *Saturday Afternoon College Football And The Men Who Made The Day*. New York: Workman Publishing, 1985.

Whittingham, Richard. *What A Game They Played*. Simon & Schuster, Inc., 1984.

INDEX

Also from Hippocrene Books . . .

Polish Customs, Traditions & Folklore, Revised Edition
by Sophie Hodorowicz Knab
with an Introduction by Rev. Czeslaw Krysa

Best selling author Sophie Hodorowicz Knab has updated her first book to include a new chapter on "Customs for Kids!"

A richly detailed and well-informed month-by-month accounting of all the major Polish customs and traditions practiced over the centuries. Ms. Knab stirs and reawakens our ancestral memory." —*The Kosciuszko Foundation Newsletter*

ISBN 0-7818-0515-5   (500)
340 pages   illustrations $19.95 hardcover
Now in its fourth printing!

Polish Herbs, Flowers & Folk Medicine
by Sophie Hodorowicz Knab

Besides taking the reader on a guided tour through monastery, castle and cottage gardens, this book provides details on over one hundred herbs and flowers and how they were used in folk medicine as well as everyday life.

ISBN 0-7818-0319-5   (573)
207 pages   illustrations $19.95 hardcover

STEEL WILL: The Life of Tad Sendzimir
by Vanda Sendzimir

One of the world's greatest inventors and entrepreneurs, Tad Sendzimir introduced innovations in steel-making that lie behind many of the great technological developments of the last sixty years, from war-time radar to the space program. An American by choice, Sendzimir remained passionately Polish as well. Meticulously researched and beautifully written by his daughter, this biography brings a deeper understanding of the genius of Tad Sendzimir.

ISBN 0-7818-0169-9 (263)
520 pages   photos $24.95 hardcover

CASIMIR PULASKI: A Hero of the American Revolution
by Leszek Szymanski, Ph.D.
Foreword by Brig. Gen. Thaddeus Maliszewski

Until now there has been no readily available, authoritative, and documented biography of Pulaski's American years. The man who was willing to "hazard all for the freedom of America" did not live to tell his own story. This thoroughly researched and objective book will set the record straight.

ISBN 0-7818-0157-5 (30)
300 pages   maps $24.95 hardcover

THE POLISH WAY:
A Thousand-Year History of the Poles and Their Culture
by Adam Zamoyski

"Zamoyski strives to place Polish history more squarely in its European context, and he pays special attention to developments that had repercussions beyond the boundaries of the country. For example, he emphasizes the phenomenon of the Polish parliamentary state in Central Europe, its spectacular 16th century success and its equally spectacular disintegration two centuries later.... This is popular history at its best, neither shallow nor simplistic ... lavish illustrations, good maps and intriguing charts and genealogical tables make this book particularly attractive." —*New York Times Book Review*

ISBN 7818-0200-8   (176)
422 pages   170 illustrations $19.95 paperback

Forgotten Few
The Polish Air Force in the Second World War
by Adam Zamoyski

Winston Churchill, speaking about the Battle of Britain in 1940, said: "Never was so much owed by so many to so few." This is the story of some of the few who are rarely remembered by our Allies today. Some 17,000 men and women passed through the ranks of the Polish Air Force while it was stationed on British soil in Wold War II. They not only played a crucial role in the Battle of Britain in 1940, they also contributed significantly to the Allied war effort in the air. This is the story of who they were, where they came from, and what they did. Adam Zamoyski is the author of many books on Poland, including the much acclaimed *The Polish Way*.

ISBN 0-0421-3   (493)
172 pages   illustrations & maps $24.95 hardcover

Old Polish Legends
retold by F.C. Anstruther

A fine collection of eleven classic fairy tales, illustrated with handsome engravings by J. Sekalski.

ISBN 0-7818-0033-1 (98)
66 pages   woodcut engravings $10.00 hardcover

Old Polish Traditions in the Kitchen and at the Table

A cookbook and a history of Polish culinary customs. Covers Polish hospitality, holiday traditons, and the exalted status of mushrooms. Recipes are traditional family fare.

ISBN 0-7818-0488-4 (546)
304 pages   illustrations $11.95 paperback

The Polish Heritage Songbook
compiled by Marek Sart, illustrated by Szymon Kobylinski
annotations by Stanislaw Werner

A unique collection of 80 songs that echo the struggle for freedom carried out by generations of Polish men and women. With annotations in English, the songs are in Polish.

ISBN 0-7818-0425-6 (496)
166 pages   65 illustrations $14.95 paperback

All prices subject to change.
TO PURCHASE HIPPOCRENE BOOKS contact your local bookstore, call (718) 454-2366, or write to: HIPPOCRENE BOOKS, 171 Madison Avenue, New York, NY 10016. Please enclose check or money order, adding $5.00 shipping (UPS) for the first book and $.50 for each additional book.